Clauueue Walker

TO LOVE THE ROSE

(Is Washington Stoned?)

ABACUS BOOKS, INC.
USA

Abacus Books, Inc.
Abacus Books, Inc., P.O. Box 55302
St. Petersburg, Florida 33732-5302, U.S.A.
www.abacusbooks.com

Library of Congress Cataloging in Publication Data
Walker, Claudette
To Love The Rose (Is Washington Stoned?).
I. Title

ISBN 0-9716292-1-8

Released September 2004

Printed in the United States of America
Set in Times New Roman

This is a work of fiction. Names, characters, places, and
incidents are either the product of the author's invention and
imagination or are used fictitiously, and any resemblance to
actual persons either living or dead, events, or locales is
entirely coincidental.

FROM THE AUTHOR

This is a work of fiction. Fiction contains chimes of truth within the background murmur of a fib. The story you are about to read is based in part on some events of the times. The individual characters are not real; any similarity to any person is purely coincidental. May you enjoy the reading of this book as much as I have enjoyed the writing of it. Remember, this is just a novel of fiction, for your pleasure!

This book is dedicated to the angel in heaven who watches over me - my father, and to the love of my life, my daughter NeCole.

OVERVIEW

Jacqueline is thrust into adulthood during the 1970's drug culture and the sexual revolution that follows. The path she takes will lead her from the Midwest to The Hospital of Mercy in San Francisco, California. During her lonely nights, she finds young interns and cocaine in the teaching hospitals, and she discovers the opium dens high in the canyons of California. From her beginnings as a child-bride, she experiences the sexual revolution, and blossoms from a shy girl to a sensual woman.

After her mind-opening experiences, Jacqueline begins a quest for knowledge. She finds her way to the political inner circles of Washington D.C. She is exposed to its dark side, as she views the monumental drug abuse prevalent in the inner circles of the rich and powerful, while she falls in love with the power elite of the United States Government. She lives and loves. Eventually, she flees to protect her daughter and herself from the government secrets she has learned. She survives those secrets, while nearly dying at the government's hands. This is one woman's journey, the first forty years. This is the story… a novel.

PROLOGUE

Florida April 1, 1989

Rose begins to dictate into his microcassette recorder. Jacqueline goes into the living room and asks him one more time if he would like to eat dinner. He abruptly tells her, "No I told you, I am not hungry." He begins his dictation again. Rose appears to be making a list of people; some of the names she recognizes. They are people he does not like. She hears Rose again; this time it is the explosive Astrolite A-W-1 that he is talking about on the recorder. She continues quietly cleaning up the dinner dishes. Rose calls to her in the kitchen, "Jacqueline will you copy the libretto to the 'Three Penny Opera?' " That was a fast change - from explosives to opera! Jacqueline just had no idea what Rose was thinking these days.

She calls back to him, "As soon as I finish washing the dishes, honey." She can still hear him dictating into the machine and he is *snickering* while he is doing it! A couple of minutes later the same request, "Will you copy the libretto, Jacqueline?" She responds, "Honey, I am almost finished with the dishes, and I will copy it in just a minute." The next voice she heard was angry. "Can't you do anything I ask?" Marie was doing her homework at the kitchen table. Jacqueline and Marie just look into each other eyes as Jacqueline goes immediately to copy the libretto, so Rose will not upset Marie. While upstairs in the office, she hears an argument brewing downstairs. Rose is yelling at Marie about something. Quickly, she returns to the living room, and sends Marie upstairs to do her homework.

When Jacqueline inquires about what was going on, Rose angrily says, "Marie left the light on in the kitchen!" Jacqueline explains, "Marie must have thought I was coming right back." Knowing that his anger will continue to flare, she tells him, "I am going upstairs to read a book and let you just relax for awhile." His outbursts have been a daily occurrence since New York; the only questions each day are when something will trigger him, and what it will be. With a gentle kiss to his head, she leaves the room. Stopping by Marie's room, Jacqueline tells her, "Take it easy. He is just upset again."

Jacqueline enters the bedroom she and Rose share, at the top of the hallway stairs. Laying herself on the bed, she begins to read a novel. She had been looking forward to starting the book, and finally, she is able to start reading it. Despite her anticipation of the novel, she can't help but think about life with Rose.

By now she is completely exhausted; the day-to-day care of Rose has not been easy. Dealing with his bipolar mania, anger, and depression is wearing her out. His mood swings are now only intensified by his extreme drug use. She spends every hour of every day worrying about his pill popping. She has looked at the many drug reference books Rose keeps at the house. She knows that some of the doses he is taking exceed a lethal dose. She cannot stop him! He cannot die of an overdose after all the work that was done to save his life in New York.

Dr. Green is of absolutely no help to her. Green is encouraging Rose to use the medication. He writes Rose prescriptions just as fast as Rose asks, and Jacqueline knows that Green doesn't care that Rose is addicted. After they returned from the hospital in New York, Dr. Green told Rose and Jacqueline that he would give Rose the drugs for a while. If he saw that Rose was going to live, he would put him in St. Adele Hospital and quietly withdraw him. Jacqueline had made a calendar to follow Rose's medications. Dr. Green had been at their home recently, and she showed him the calendar and how long this over-medicating had gone on.

Dr. Green told her that he cannot put Rose in St. Adele Hospital because, *"they do not do drug withdrawal!"* "But you said you would!" she told him. He told her, "Mind your own business, I will deal with Rose." She asked if he was going to cut down on the prescriptions. Green said "No," and left. This most recent clash over his prescribing drugs to Rose was just two days earlier, when Green increased the dosage of Prozac that Rose was taking. Jacqueline knows that the Prozac dosage increase, combined with all the other pain and sleeping medications Rose is taking, is going to result in disaster.

Jacqueline gives up trying to read. She decides to rest on the bed; at least it is a retreat from the turmoil in her life. But her mind won't let her rest. She thinks again about the conversation with Dr. Green a few days ago. Questions racing through her mind will not let her relax. "Why is Dr. Green doing this? Why is he prescribing for Rose like this? Does Rose have something on him? Does Green really believe he is doing the right thing? Is he afraid to attempt to take Rose off these drugs? Does Green truly believe Rose is a walking dead man? Is Green afraid that without the drugs Rose will die in pain?" Finally, her thoughts drift off this terrible mess, as she begins to relax. It is so rare for her mind to allow her to rest since Rose's *cancer blew in with the wind.*

After only a few minutes of resting on the bed, Jacqueline hears Rose coming up the stairs. She knows that he is sorry. Rose is always sorry; after all, he does love them. Rose enters the room, smiling at Jacqueline as he walks toward the end of their bed and places his hand gently on her ankle. She smiles, as his fingers touch her skin. She is ready to accept his apology. His touch has become so rare since the cancer that even the smallest touch to her ankle pleases her.

Suddenly his soft touch is hard and violent, as though at that moment he has forgotten what he is doing. Rose's hand latches in full grip, his hand to her ankle. She can see his fingers, as they go from a soft touch to a cruel, vise-like clamp. Then she feels the sudden tug as he pulls on her ankle. Jacqueline's body is being violently pulled from the bed! The door is getting closer; he is dragging her toward the hallway! She falls to the floor with a *thump!* In complete shock, Jacqueline is struggling with him every inch of the way. As her adrenaline begins to pump, she is fighting her way back toward the bed, reaching for anything to hold onto!

But she cannot overcome his strength. He has pulled her the ten feet from the bed to the door. He is now dragging her by the ankle out of the room. Now, she is entirely in the hall. Suddenly, he releases Jacqueline's ankle in the h~¹¹ For a split second, she breathes a sigh) feel pain as her head is bein~ y wall. She can hear Mari pain each time her head c suddenly as he pulled her ¹ r head and he flees down t feet connect on every thir ts the lower level.

Gathering feet and heads to Marie's ...u of the hall. Marie has it bloc ...ie quietly calls her name. "Marie can ..car me?" Jacqueline hears Marie tearfully say, "Yes Mom." "Marie, listen to me! When you hear me downstairs in the kitchen, take flight down the staircase and out the front door." Jacqueline whispers, "Don't stop for me or anything else. *Rose has lost it.* Do not open this door until you hear me down in the kitchen. Do you hear me?" Marie's voice is shaking, "Yes Mom, but I am scared!" Jacqueline replies in a firm voice, "Just listen for me to get to the kitchen. Get ready!"

As Jacqueline turns to walk toward the top of the stairs, she sees Rose out of the corner of her eye. "My God! He is coming back up the staircase, with a 10-inch knife held high over his head! He looks like a madman!" Jacqueline swings into their bedroom, barricading the door closed with her small body. Rose is pushing on the door and it opens about six inches.

Suddenly, his arm and the knife come through the six-inch space in the door. Rose is stabbing wildly at her from the other side with the knife!

She is pushing with all her strength. Five, six times the knife misses her by an inch. She is looking directly at the blade. That is the only way she can avoid his wild swings, while still keeping her weight on the door. The door opens wider, as the knife abruptly retreats from the open space. Then just as suddenly, the door slams closed with a bang!   She hears Rose heading down the stairs again. Quickly, without a thought, she goes to Marie's door again and tells her "Get ready!" Then she heads down the staircase, not knowing where he and the knife are. Jacqueline is simply thinking, "I have to get Marie out of this house!" Jacqueline knows she must flee or fight, and when it comes to getting Marie out, she will fight!

Entering the kitchen from the hall stairs, she can see Rose is at the west side of the oblong dining table. His eyes are wild, but he is not holding the knife! Jacqueline heads toward the east side of the table, to draw him away from the front door, Marie's only exit. Suddenly, he grabs her; the buttons pop from her blouse as he swings her into a chokehold and begins to squeeze. She cannot breathe! Her lungs are on fire, and her heart is pounding! She knows she is losing consciousness. Rose is screaming, **"I will not die and leave you,"** then over and over again, **"You are going with me, Jacqueline! I cannot leave you behind!"**

WHEN YOUR LIFE IS IN BLACK, IT IS DOOM
WHEN YOUR LIFE IS IN BLUE, IT IS SAD
WHEN YOUR LIFE IS IN PINK, IT IS HAPPY

FROM "LA VIE EN ROSE"
BY EDITH PIAF

Life in Pink

"I thought that love was just a word they sang about in
songs that I heard,
It took your kisses to reveal that I was wrong and love
was real."

CHAPTER ONE

JUST THE BEGINNING

The smell of lilacs was an opiate to Jacqueline's thoughts, as the "N Judith" cable car began its ascent from Market Street. Lilac-scented air flowed through the open cable car windows. The intoxicating fragrance was only intensified as the cable car climbed. The last stop on the line was the Hospital of Mercy at San Francisco, overlooking the beautiful city filled with magnificent architecture and cascading hills. This would be Jacqueline's home for many years, and the battlefield for her infant daughter Marie's life.

It was the summer of 1973 and the sounds of the city were all new to Jacqueline. The clanging metal-to-metal noise of the wheels on the track seemed to play a melody as the cable car climbed higher. The squeaks and rattles of the old cable car provided lyrics in her mind. The voices of the people produced a continuous stream of harmony. This was life's new tune. There was no fear, just newness all around her.

The San Francisco Hospital of Mercy sat at the top of the hill; its buildings' roofs seemed to be just short of touching the clouds in the mosaic California sky. It was building after building, the old brick architecture connecting to its modern glass additions. Rolling hills of forest green paved the way to the hospital, and behind it was an unending backdrop of blue sky. The Hospital of Mercy at the top of the hill seemed almost to be waiting for their arrival. Today was her birthday. Jacqueline was seventeen years old on this warm California day.

Holding Marie tightly in her arms, Jacqueline began the climb, going up the sidewalk that curved up the grass-covered hill. She was looking for the sign that read "Admissions." Marie was laughing, filled with baby chatter. As Jacqueline's arms began to tire, they sat together on the hill. Marie, full of life, lay on the warm, plush, green lawn. The breeze was carrying the warmth of the San Francisco sun.

"Just a little farther to go," Jacqueline thought, as she lifted Marie back into her arms and continued the climb. Nothing in San Francisco is flat, not even a sidewalk.

Jacqueline could not see the future. She felt relief that she had found help for Marie. The years of pain and struggle, dueling with the system and the devil himself for Marie's life, had only just begun. Had the young mother known what lay ahead, would she have felt so calm? Marie had been born with a rare birth defect called Hirschsprungs. Before these California days would close, there would be a sum total of ten surgeries, and five years of life in hospitals. Marie would not just survive; she would thrive. God was on her side, and Marie's. How else could a *seventeen-year-old* mother manage such a miracle?

As she left the Midwest, she could feel the silent disapproval among many of the people in the town. The doctors there gave Marie no hope of a normal life. The three surgical procedures they had performed on Marie could not make Marie's body whole. So Jacqueline left with Marie, seeking the best treatment she could find for her daughter. She sought a cure for Marie's condition, and her search brought her here. Jacqueline left her birthplace expecting that her daughter would be cured. To some in her hometown, Jacqueline would return as a hero, to others, she would be a villain. The views of other people would depend on the success or failure of the medical treatment she sought for Marie.

But Jacqueline knew what no one in her hometown would have considered. First, Jacqueline never planned to return to her Midwest hometown. For Marie and for herself, she wanted to see the world. Jacqueline knew that there was much more to experience beyond the boundaries of her birthplace. Second, Marie would survive; of this outcome she had no doubt, whether because Jacqueline was young and foolish, or because she could see the full life that was Marie's destiny. Jacqueline had taken the first plane to anywhere, and she had no regrets.

There was a doctor at The Hospital of Mercy who had agreed to take a look at Marie's case. Dr. Delmar was a surgeon who specialized in Hirschsprungs. Jacqueline and Marie waited for hours to see him. He stood about six feet five and was a ruggedly handsome man in his fifties. His nature was extremely gentle for his massive size; compassion was the sound in his deep voice. After only a few minutes with Marie, he too was in love with her.

He told Jacqueline that he would attempt to close the surgical device placed on her in Ann Arbor and that it would probably take more than one surgery. Marie would be hospitalized a great deal and there were no guarantees. "We are checking her in; I just want to observe her for a few days. Do you have a place to stay?" asked Dr. Delmar. Jacqueline told him that she did.

Dr. Delmar inquired, "Did you just get off a plane?" Jacqueline replied, "Yes," lowering her eyes. "Where is your luggage?" he asked. "It is being held for me at the airport," she replied. "You can stay with Marie, there are couches in the rooms. After you get her settled, my wife will take you to get your luggage" stated Delmar in a deep, yet gentle voice. "Can we wait?" Jacqueline asked. "I don't want to leave Marie until she has adjusted." "Of course," he said with a smile.

Ann Arbor University was a wonderful hospital, filled with brilliant doctors, but they seemed resigned; they had done all they could do. Marie's condition was outside their areas of expertise. Besides, they knew Delmar was the leading expert in this field, and he was in California. That was when Jacqueline knew her search for Marie's medical care would take her away from home. She knew that some day Marie would be free of the surgical device they had placed on her at only five days old. In her mind's eye, Jacqueline could see Marie playing without it. She just needed to find the surgeon who was going to take it away. Dr. Delmar was that man, so here the series of surgeries toward one goal would continue. For more than three years, Dr. Delmar's team worked on Marie.

Dr. Delmar's wife, Elizabeth, helped Jacqueline to find a job. Mrs. Delmar was a lovely woman in her forties, with all the elegance of a fine lady. It showed from her freshly cut hair, to her perfectly straight skirts with silk blouses and high heels. Elizabeth Delmar seemed born to a life of luxury and grace. She spoke using the most beautiful English, in a warm gentle tone. Her face was always graced with a smile, and her eyes were as blue as the California sky. So much kindness rested inside them. They revealed the goodness in her heart.

She assumed Jacqueline was of legal age, or chose not to ask. Mrs. Delmar told Jacqueline that she knew where Jacqueline could get a job. They went together on the cable car that Monday morning. While they walked from the hospital toward the cable car tracks, Elizabeth said, "We will take the cable car route, so you will know how to get back and forth." Stepping aboard the "N Judith" that had brought Jacqueline and Marie to The Hospital of Mercy, they began their journey.

The streets were filled with long-haired young men and women, their locks blowing in the San Francisco breeze. The men wore jeans and tattered t-shirts emblazoned with peace signs on their backs. The girls wore brightly colored dresses with flowers in their hair. All were walking peacefully together, and some were carrying signs. The first one Jacqueline saw read, "Make Love Not War." The next one said, "Bring our Boy's Home," then another that demanded, "Stop The Bombing." You could hear the crowd of 500 or more shouting, "NO MORE WAR! HELL NO, WE WON'T GO!"

As the N. Judith cable car approached the Market Street stop, Mrs. Delmar pointed out the open cable car window toward a building. Jacqueline saw before her a beautiful lobby inside a glass building, filled with San Francisco's elegant society moving in a slow peaceful motion. It was as though by simply turning her head, Jacqueline had stepped into another world. "This is the Caucus Regency Hotel. This is where you will work," Mrs. Delmar said with pride.

The doorman, in his red coat and hat, opened the large glass door. The gold trim of his uniform flickered and glinted in the California sun. Jacqueline followed behind as Mrs. Delmar spoke to a lady seated behind a large counter of marble. "Mr. Mason, please." The young woman immediately responded, "Yes, Mrs. Delmar, he is expecting you." A tall, darkly tanned man, maybe in his forties, dressed in a striking blue suit, came out immediately. He was smiling as he approached the women.

"Mrs. Delmar, how are you?" the gentlemen said. Jacqueline thought that he acted as though Mrs. Delmar signed his paycheck. "It is so nice to see you; what can I do for you?" he continued, in an attentive voice. "I would like you to meet Jacqueline," Elizabeth Delmar replied. "The doctor and I would appreciate it if you would find a position for her on your staff." Basically, she was insisting that the Caucus Regency of San Francisco hire Jacqueline.

Jacqueline saw that this woman did not take no for an answer, not that Mr. Mason had a chance to speak. In the next breath, Mrs. Delmar reminded him of the upcoming hospital functions to be held at their hotel and told him that she was sure that Jacqueline could be of assistance in hosting. She was one powerful woman! She also explained that if Jacqueline's daughter became seriously ill, the hotel would need to work around her absences!

It was obvious that Mr. Mason clearly understood his role. The gentleman asked Jacqueline, "Would you like to be our hostess?" She quickly said, "Yes," and thanked him for being so kind. Mrs. Delmar told him that she would be sure to tell Dr. Delmar and everyone else at the hospital of his kindness and support. She hinted that his continued cooperation could very well mean that the Caucus Regency would be the site of even more hospital events in the future.

Mrs. Delmar was clearly pleased that she had accomplished what she had set out to do. Glowing from her achievement, she insisted Jacqueline come to her home. "My daughters and I have lots of clothing! There is no point for you to buy work clothes," she said. Together, they stepped aboard the cable car returning to the hospital. Jacqueline was thrilled with her new employment, but her head turned as she heard the chanting of the crowd. Mrs. Delmar said, "This is a very bad time in America. I do not agree with this war either. At first, I thought that we were doing the right thing, but not anymore." They continued back up the hill in silence, as Jacqueline pondered all that she had just seen and heard.

Jacqueline lived in Marie's room at the hospital for the next three months, while working nights as a hostess for the Caucus, wearing the clothes of a doctor's family. It was Mrs. Delmar who shaped Jacqueline's style of dress, and enforced her determination and strength of character. It was the movements of the time in San Francisco that shaped her thoughts and feelings.

Dr. Delmar decided that Marie was healthy enough to begin surgery right away. Jacqueline would not even begin to look for an apartment until she knew Marie would be home for a while. This gave her time to save. She had arrived in San Francisco with two thousand dollars that her father had given her. Her life was lived in the hospital, at work, and traveling on the "N Judith" cable car for the first few months. No one, not even Dr. Delmar, knew that she was barely seventeen years old.

Even the first months of hardship provided many new experiences for Jacqueline. She began her quest for learning by drawing from everyone and everything around her. She discovered her thirst for knowledge while looking up at The Statues of the Angels guarding the Museum of Fine Arts, and wondering who had created this magnificent work. She walked the peace marches of the Haight Ashbury District, gave her support to the Gay Rights Movement, and watched the cults prevalent in the San Francisco streets. Viewing the massive drug abuse of the time, Jacqueline was learning, quietly absorbing everything from everyone around her, and storing all the new information as though she was the Library of Congress. She carefully made decisions on the basis of the information she had obtained. Jacqueline already knew that all information had value; she recognized that certain knowledge had much greater value.

She had seen the beauty of the sun breaking over San Francisco Bay. In the first years, between hospitalizations, she taught Marie to roller skate at the Fisherman's Wharf. Once, she found herself removing fishing line that had entangled the wheels of Marie's roller skates. When Jacqueline had fixed her skates and Marie was again skating, the ocean breeze was blowing Marie's curls as she tried to get further ahead of her mother. Jacqueline was in close pursuit, knowing that in case of a fall, she could easily catch her daughter. Marie was sick, but Jacqueline kept her life as normal as possible.

Jacqueline was in San Francisco for the September, 1975 capture of Patty Hearst. While the news media were breaking the story, police were combing areas of San Francisco neighborhoods block by block. FBI agents scared the occupants of every drug-filled home in town. In her neighborhood, Jacqueline saw bamboo pipes and bags tossed out apartment windows and heard a symphony of swirling water as marijuana was being flushed down the toilets. She felt the change – there was a sudden sense of peace when the neighbors realized all they wanted was Patty Hearst, and not to bust all of them for drugs. Everything was new, and the experiences were quickly absorbed by Jacqueline's young, searching mind. What she learned from her keen observations of people, places, and things added polishing touches to her teenage years, changing her from a girl to a woman. San Francisco was her finishing school.

From the reluctant, inexperienced girl, who had married at fifteen and found herself a mother at 16, she had come a long way. Marie was a Vietnam baby. When she was a young teenager in the Midwest, it was a time of peace, love, and keeping more boys from going to war. Jacqueline's husband knew when they married that his draft status would change from I-A to IV-A if Jacqueline became pregnant, as she did. They were infatuated with each other, or possibly in love. But could they even know the meaning of true love so young? He must have thought that the change in draft status was a very convenient benefit, since he could not wait to marry her until she was of legal age. It would be logical to assume that this was more than just a coincidence, and less than malice.

How she became pregnant seems to still be an amazing question. Jacqueline was a virgin who did not even understand sex. She went from her tomboy ways to his bed, and found nothing but fear. Somehow, she managed to get pregnant right away. It might have been because her husband *tossed* her birth control pills out the window – the pills that she had gotten for the very first time only two days after the marriage!

Within months of Marie's birth, their life together would end. Jacqueline still had no real understanding about sex. The divorce was the result of marrying too young, and nothing more. He was neither mean nor bad; they were just too young. The tragedy of Marie's illness needed only one master; Jacqueline decided it must be her. Medical decisions could not be questioned, and everyone was questioning every decision anyone made. Family fights in the waiting rooms of Ann Arbor became daily events. All had good intentions, but they were not always helping. Jacqueline put a stop to that! She took control of Marie's destiny.

Now she was light-years away from that life. She had traded her reluctant fear of sex for chemistry laboratories and young interns, either because she was lonely, or because she needed a little help navigating the medical system. One reason became as good as another. Life had given her real fears. She was no longer scared of a little thing called sex; Jacqueline was finally curious about the true feeling of sexual emotion.

San Francisco was where she would experience her first lines of cocaine. "Ninety-nine percent pure," the intern said. The nights in a teaching hospital are long and lonely; and the children are usually asleep from strong medications such as Phenobarbital and morphine. Young interns were available by the dozens;

they too were lonely, and usually away from home doing their internship. Dark rooms and labs became their havens for the free sex movement. Jacqueline was there to participate in full.

Alex was a young intern who looked more like a bodybuilder. With his fifty-four inch chest, he was not the usual intern. Blessed with coal black hair, his beautiful face was crisp with fine features and green eyes that seemed to be outlined by his black full lashes. He attracted Jacqueline. Alex gave Jacqueline cocaine on a few occasions in the hospital library, where they had met a few weeks before. He told her that it would make her feel better. "After all, I am the doctor," he said, and she agreed.

The first time she tried it, she blew most of it away, but Alex didn't seem to mind. In later years she would realize just how expensive the drug she blew away was, and yet he had never complained. Although Alex loved cocaine, Jacqueline did not care much for it. After a few tries in the library she told him she did not think she liked it. He told her, "I will show you something that you might enjoy."

Alex told her to meet him in the chemistry lab of the old hospital about nine o'clock, after he had finished his rounds. The university's old brick buildings were filled with dark, petrifying corridors straight out of Edgar Allen Poe's "The Cask of Amontillado." But Jacqueline needed a friend, and he seemed so nice, much older, maybe ten years older, and she was attracted to him. She met him at the room, and he kissed her. She felt so lonely and scared as he placed her on the sofa and had sex with her. Yes, it was just as drab as that statement seems. The fear that she felt on that sofa was less than what she had felt as a new wife two years earlier. But she still did not enjoy the experience. "There must be more," Jacqueline thought.

The next day, he told her to come to a lab on the fifth floor of the old hospital. She was not sure she wanted to have sex again, but she went. After midnight, the corridors of the hospital were always empty. Following the directional lines on the floor, she took, "the yellow line to the blue line, then turn left at the green," as she was instructed by Alex. By the time she had maneuvered the halls, she was glad to find Alex in the lab. He gave her more cocaine, and then he began placing it on her body and having sex with her. When they met for the third night in a row, she told him that she didn't like the racing-heart feeling she experienced from the cocaine. Alex asked, "Did you like the sex?" "Yes," she lied. "Then you don't have to snort it." What she needed was companionship, and she was willing to settle for Alex.

Alex wore heavy musk cologne that she could smell from down the hallway. He would be all coked up when she arrived; the metal tables showed traces of the lines he had been snorting. Jacqueline was young, with a newly found curiosity of sex. She realized that she was just beginning to enjoy it. Alex would lift her up and lay her on the cold metal table, kissing her as he undressed her shivering young body. The sterile smell that normally occupied these rooms was overcome by the strong sent of his musk cologne. No longer could she smell the lilacs. Her heart would race from fear or excitement; which one she did not know.

Alex would begin to rub the cocaine on her body. First she could feel the tingle of her nipples. Next he would place it on the lips of her body, and then the cold of the room would suddenly disappear. Just as her whole body was feeling electricity, he would begin licking it off. The cocaine he had ingested fueled a rush of adrenaline in him, which he applied to satisfying Jacqueline. The physical sensation of cocaine on her body was far more pleasant than ingesting the stuff.

It was not the best sex she would ever have, but it was interesting. With Alex, Jacqueline began building the foundation of experience that would shape the rest of her life. They met in the cold lab on a few more occasions, until Jacqueline became bored. Alex was a troubled man, and Jacqueline knew it. She decided to go back to reading her books at night, as they seemed to have more to offer.

Next would be the San Francisco opium dens and a feeling Jacqueline knew she liked...*too much*. One day, Jacqueline needed a break from her days at the hospital and her evenings of work at the Caucus Regency. She decided to go to San Francisco's Golden Gate Park for the afternoon. She took a book, and planned to read some of it, and enjoy the sound of the waterfall. She thought that she would stroll over the brick bridges, sit on the grass under the trees at the Portals of the Past, and relax. Instead, she met a young lawyer.

She first saw him walking his dog. The small spaniel managed to slip its collar, and flew straight for her, as she was sitting on the grass. There was the man, holding an empty collar on the end of a leash! She laughed aloud. The dog nearly licked her to death – it was so friendly! The young man came rushing over to capture his pet. Jacqueline tried to help, but the dog was quite squirmy, and it nearly got away from her, too. With her help, the man got the collar back on the dog. They were both laughing, and the dog was still wagging its tail and licking her. The young man introduced himself as Mark, and his dog as Charlie. "Charlie is quite a good judge of character," he chuckled. The three of them sat, and Jacqueline and Mark talked as they played with Charlie. Mark was a judicial clerk in the Federal Ninth Circuit Court of Appeals. When they parted company, he told her, "Charlie will be heartbroken if he never sees you again." Jacqueline said, "We can't have that," as she gave Mark her telephone number. She was attracted to him, and she hoped that he would call. He did.

He would pick Jacqueline up at the hospital on her nights off and take her to dinner, then while walking slowly in the evening sunset, he would show her all the things San Francisco had to offer. A simple call to the nurse's station would confirm Marie's peaceful rest.

Night after night they sat in Ghirardelli Square, watching the street artists playing their music and performing their plays. They talked of her stay in San Francisco, and the work he did as a clerk. They would walk the pier of the Grotto 9 and speak of their dreams to one another. Then during the early morning hours he would return her to the hospital, while Marie was still fast asleep on the medications. Mark seemed very nice and he was quite handsome. He was a small man of about five feet eight inches, possibly of Russian decent, with dark curly hair and brown eyes. Jacqueline so enjoyed his company. One night, he asked her if she had ever done drugs. She said "Just a little." "I want to take you somewhere," Mark said.

She agreed, and he drove north on the scenic coast highway, Highway 101, heading up into the canyons, deep in the hills of San Francisco. Jacqueline was beginning to get a little nervous, as she had never been to the canyons before. Mark stopped the car at the side of the road. He kissed her deeply and told her he wanted to make love to her. Part of her was afraid to agree, the other part wanted his body inside of hers. She said, "Yes" as she began to unbutton her blouse. "Not here," he said. She stopped unbuttoning her blouse. A part of Jacqueline was relieved, but another part of her was a bit disappointed. He drove for another fifteen minutes or so. Then they walked up the canyon, and to a cave almost completely hidden among the trees and plants. She followed Mark inside.

A wild, peacefully overpowering, wonderful flower scent filled the cave, as Mark stopped to light a pipe he was carrying. As soon as Jacqueline tasted the smoke, a feeling of euphoria came over her. Mark took her arm and guided her into the cavern. Barely able to walk because of her spinning head, she suddenly heard the faint sound of Jim Morison's' music. Before Jacqueline's eyes appeared candles, rugs and pillows through a thick haze of the wildly pleasant smoke. Jacqueline was overcome by an uncontrollable ecstasy. People seemed to be everywhere, with long hoses attached to a pipe in the center of the room. Then through the candlelit haze of smoke and her distorted vision, she suddenly realized they were all naked, and some were even having sex!

Mark handed her a pipe hose and she smoked it. The opium sent her mind into a realm of passion never before known to Jacqueline. Mark removed his clothes and then Jacqueline's, as he laid her on the rug and placed a pillow under her head. She was still smoking one of the long hoses of the pipe. The taste of opium was sweet on her lips and the fragrance was that of a flower that she longed to smell. When Mark began touching her body with his lips, it sent Jacqueline's senses soaring. He kissed her nipples, and asked if she would like a man or a woman. In the faint bit of reality Jacqueline had left, she did not answer.

Then she felt another touch as Mark was kissing her lips. It was another man making the sensations on her breast! Mark handed her the pipe again. Over and over she smoked, as her body was reeling with unknown sensations. Suddenly, she felt something between her legs, a wet wonderful feeling. She tried to raise her head, but she could not lift it from the pillow. The sensations increased upon her lips, breasts and body as she began seeping onto a moist wet tongue. Mark's hands were rubbing oil all over her body; his voice was asking if she wanted more. The music was playing softly, and the voices of the people slowly began fading into the music.

Mark's voice was barely audible to her. She was unable to lift any part of her body; but her mind was soaring with her passion. Mark kissed her face as he stoked her head; people were touching all of her body, causing her unlimited satisfaction to every area at once. Then, Mark placed her on her side with her head still on the pillow. As he stroked her hair, Mark put the pipe in Jacqueline's mouth again. Then she was spinning, as if her body was rolling over and over, while being given pleasure in all places, from all directions at once.

In every possible way, her body went wild with euphoric sensations. Lips were on her lips, while lips touched her breasts, and lips caressed both sides of her body. Oil dripped from her body as it was heated from the friction of hands rubbing her. Her body was paralyzed with pleasure and massive orgasms. The fragrant smell of the opium flower made sex reach an even higher level. The taste on her lips alone could make a young woman seep. Jacqueline was becoming a woman! Mark was there to comfort her and to keep the pipe going. Then came the sudden fulfillment inside Jacqueline. Jacqueline's orgasms continued in unending waves, her body spinning and her mind whirling, until she was completely overcome.

When she awoke, she was dressed and Mark was holding her head. No one else was around. She asked Mark, "What happened?" He said, "Just what you think." They began the drive back down the winding canyon road. The car was quiet. Jacqueline asked, "Did a lot of people have sex with me?" He said, "You were a delicious delight and *we all enjoyed pleasing you*." Jacqueline had to ask, "Were they men or women?" She was almost afraid to hear the answer. He replied, "Jacqueline, I watched as two women and two men brought you into full sexual awareness." "*I thought you wanted to make love to me!*" she snapped.

"After I watched as they brought your body to the maxim height of sexual arousal, it was me inside you that made you pass out, only my body was ever inside you. It was their lips together on your body; only lips and hands could touch you, and tongues could enter you until I was ready. You went wild as both the men and the women feasted together on you. I watched as their lips were on your breasts, and their hands rubbed your oil-soaked body. Then I watched as they feasted between your legs, taking turns drinking your dripping juices. They were in paradise, enjoying your taste."

"I watched as they all gently restrained your body, leaving one woman to dine on you, as only a woman could know how. Then another joined her in harmony, causing the wet seeping, while they relished your dripping juices. I only allowed their tongues to provide pleasure. I watched as the men entered the women who were providing your pleasure, rewarding them by the amount of pleasure they provided you."

"Finally your body so naturally rolled to find mine and prepared me to please you. I have never felt a more gentle, beautiful touch than your lips instinctively seeking my body in your stoned haze. Then they all watched as I entered you. I was listening with excitement to your screams of passion. As I filled you, you passed out." Jacqueline knew that this evening opened new avenues for her sexually, and that was not all bad! She had been afraid, but she was no longer.

However, this was not what she was looking for. Jacqueline made the decision to seek this kind of sexual high without the use of drugs and with one man. If she did not find this kind of sexual satisfaction without drugs, she would return to the opium dens to die naked in orgasm when she was old. But for now, she would leave that drug and Mark alone.

The decisions she made on the way back from the canyon would set the tone for Jacqueline's life. With all the possibilities that San Francisco had to offer for Marie and Jacqueline, these toys could not be a part of it. Neither Mark nor the opium could be in their lives. It was those choices that made the road safe for them. It was also those decisions that would make Jacqueline the woman she would become.

Since her flight from the Midwest at seventeen with Marie, to the close of Marie's hospital days, Jacqueline had ended her teenage years. She was now twenty-one years old. At first, she had survived by altering her birth certificate so she could work. She drew welfare checks, and lived hand-to-mouth. She walked the hills of San Francisco when the twenty-five cent cable car fare was more than she could afford, and she bought and sold at art and antique festivals to make money. After her experiences with Alex and Mark, she chose the stability of living with older men, for Marie's sake and for her own.

It was the early spring of 1977. Jacqueline was asleep in the waiting room at Hospital of Mercy when Dr. Delmar came in. Gently stroking her hair to wake Jacqueline, this brute of a man was smiling. Marie's colostomy was closed. He looked exhausted, but Jacqueline could see peace in his eyes. The surgery had lasted for over nine hours. He had succeeded! Marie would be released for good in three weeks. Now she would grow stronger and stronger.

Marie was a small child from all of the surgeries. She never weighed more than twenty pounds until her fourth year of life. Her hair was a mass of golden curls, and her eyes were an ever-changing green. Marie had the constant fragrance of flowers, which was her natural scent. Her rebounding spirit and love of life only intensified the beauty of this child. She had begun to talk very clearly during her first year of life. She became Jacqueline's most enjoyable companion.

To Jacqueline, she was like having a playmate at all times. After a long surgery, even before the haze of the anesthesia had worn off, Marie would cast a smile that would light the room. She was always a happy child. Jacqueline knew that despite the years of struggle, Marie had been a blessing to her. From Marie, Jacqueline drew her strength.

Now that Marie was well, Jacqueline's first step would be to correct her falsified age. She had changed her birth date in so many ways that she had to question how old she really was. Jacqueline decided that it was time to straighten out the mess, and to reclaim her true birth date. She hired a lawyer to help her. She wanted to assure that her earlier age falsification to get work could never harm her family's future. She wanted everything in her life to be legal again, except for the occasional wisp of smoke.

But Jacqueline found herself drawn to the causes of the times, despite the risks. Maybe it was all of the twists and turns that her life had taken ever since Marie was born. Maybe it was that Jacqueline had been exposed to a much larger world than the one that existed where she was raised. Or maybe it was that she

37

wanted a better future for Marie, and she was willing to assume some risk to achieve that future. Jacqueline saw that more social change was needed, and she decided that she had to be part of that change.

All of the surgeries had been completed on Marie. She was stable, out of the hospital, and doing well. Because of that, Jacqueline had more time to pursue her own interests than she had since Marie was born. Of course, Jacqueline still had to work, and she spent a lot of time with Marie. But still, she found some time for herself. Even while Marie was still sick, Jacqueline had walked the streets of San Francisco with thousands of other young Americans to see an end to her peers dying on foreign soil.

The war in Vietnam had ended. According to the official government statistics, America had lost 58,168 young men and women, and 153,303 others were wounded in the war in Southeast Asia. And then there were those who were missing in action. They were in the never-land of the statistics; they did not come home, but they were not listed among the death toll, either. America had paid its price.

The gay rights movement and activism toward the liberation of women were in full swing. The 1973 United States Supreme Court decision in Roe v. Wade had broken the barrier, but there was still much farther to go. The people of San Francisco seemed to live and let live in a very non-judgmental society. Sadly, it was not the same in the rest of the country. Even in San Francisco, there were those who were not in favor of equal rights for all Americans. Even worse, many of those people were those in power.

Jacqueline's opinions and attitudes in favor of freedom of choice and all civil rights were well formed by then. She threw all of her effort into the Human Rights and Women's Rights movements. In her small San Francisco apartment small groups of women met. She organized her seventy-five volunteers daily. This was her territory. The movement had cleverly divided the country into small groups. Jacqueline's section was the University of California at San Francisco area. That was great, since her volunteer workers were educated and ambitious. They would spend the late nights at her apartment, creating flyers and duplicating them with carbon paper, and preparing for the next days activities.

Jacqueline found it very hard to believe that anyone could really think that she should have lesser rights because she was female. This thought alone drove her to excel as she raised Marie. Jacqueline knew that no one would every make her less that she chose to become. Whatever the choices a woman wanted, she should be able to make those choices. Jacqueline's opportunities would be the same as those of anyone else. She would see to that. She was convinced that the opportunity of every man and women regardless of race, religion or sexual orientation should be equal.

As the young people sat around the third floor apartment creating the flyers they planned to change the world with, they smoked great pot! The times were as casual as anyone could have imagined. The girl who lived next door had just bought a new car. Such things did not impress Jacqueline and her friends. This was a time of mind-opening experiences, and throwing open the doors to freedom for everyone, and Jacqueline was there for it all.

She knew that much of the establishment was against all of their most important ideas of freedom. Just how much, she would soon find out. As her group finished the flyers for the next day's march, they decided to go to the Market Street district to see how the night shift of marchers was holding up. By late night, things usually tended to heat up a bit with the police. Even so, the marches or sit-ins on the city were peaceful. At night the pigs would start trouble, so they could arrest a few protesters for the next day's edition of the San Francisco Chronicle newspaper.

The mayor liked to find a reason to create publicly for himself. He would give press conferences the following day, so he could hear himself talk. Usually the police officers would walk up and kick a girl that was in the sit-in, and then the trouble would start. Usually, two or three protesters would be arrested. The police would hold the arrestees for about twenty-four hours, get the publicity for the arrest, and then very quietly release the protesters.

As the group arrived at the market street entrance, Jacqueline could see the trouble had begun. Before her eyes was an officer holding a women by the hair and striking her with a billy club. This was the worse violence Jacqueline had personally viewed. Within seconds, the officers had the hapless victim of the brutality in a police vehicle, and the cruiser pulled away.

The next day, the headlines were there, and the mayor was listening to himself talk on the television again. Supposedly, the young woman had spit on the officer. Jacqueline never believed that story, as she had heard that excuse for a beating or an arrest too many times. Besides, even if the woman had spit on the policeman, he had no right to beat the woman. Jacqueline saw what he did, so there was no question in her mind that at best, the officer had lost control of himself, and at worst, he was downright malicious.

The following day the other women were released unharmed. The victim of the brutality was also released, but she was not unharmed. The officer had fractured several of her ribs when he beat her. That story did not make the newspaper or the television news. Jacqueline considered trying to get a reporter to hear the protestor's side of the story, but the woman was too afraid of police retribution to go public with the truth.

It was hard for Jacqueline to comprehend why the simple demand for equal rights for all Americans was so challenged. She refused to stop her work. However, she knew she had to be careful. For Marie's sake, Jacqueline could not afford to be arrested. But, she knew that she could not let a world continue unchanged, if an unchanged world meant that Marie would grow up to be a second-class citizen. It was a thin line, but Jacqueline planned to walk it.

Besides, Jacqueline best served the movement as an organizer. She had developed skills that would allow her to create the propaganda material for the movement. She took the challenge of this movement

41

and honed her organizational skills. Late at night, she would create plans weeks in advance for marches. Then she would go to her list of volunteers, and decide who would be at what location. She divided the time in eight-hour shifts, to keep the marches and sit-ins going around the clock.

Jacqueline had divided her volunteers into three groups based upon job description. The first were women without husbands or children. They were the active protesters. They were the most visible face of the movement in the press and on television. That group staged the demonstrations and sit-ins, and they were the most at risk of arrest. These women knew that they could be jailed or beaten, and they were willing to assume the risk.

A second group would stay on the move passing out flyers. These women were runners and athletic types. Because they were constantly on the move, they were less likely to be jailed. Jacqueline called them her "town criers," and their other job was to pass along critical information to all volunteers with whom they came into contact. They were less apt to be on the news or in the papers, but they came into contact with thousands of people every day, and were perhaps the most likely to sway public opinion. They were the women who put a face on the issues, and the women the public would remember when photographs of arrests were on the television or in the newspapers.

The third group created the flyers with typewriters and carbon paper. That group of women also planned where to best distribute the material. Without them, the first group would not have the support of the public, and the second group would not have the material to distribute. These women were least at risk of arrest, since they were working behind the scenes. Almost all of them had children. None of them could accept a high risk of going to jail, for one reason or another. Yet, each of them was committed to the success of the movement, and each gave selflessly of her time and talent.

Each group was critical to the success of the movement. Every group was interdependent on the other groups. Jacqueline planned and coordinated the actions of all three groups. When problems occurred, Jacqueline was the one that everyone turned to for solutions. She was also actively involved with the daily activities of the creative group.

There were those who supported the movement, such as professionals who owned their offices in the area, who could donate office materials and the use of their offices and equipment, but who could not give significant amounts of their time. Members of the third group could go into offices and use the copy machines and materials for free. Many men also supported their cause. Some of them were the people who would allow Jacqueline's volunteers to use their offices and materials to make flyers and signs. Others, both men and women, who did not have much available time or the freedom to actively participate, would provide funds for materials and food for the marchers.

Elizabeth Delmar was one of the people who provided funds. She would come by Jacqueline's apartment every couple of weeks with supplies and money to help the cause. She would only stay for a few

minutes, and she asked that Jacqueline not tell people
that she was helping the cause.   Mrs. Delmar needed
the cooperation of the city for many hospital projects
for the children, and she had to mingle with many
conservatives of San Francisco society. "As a result,"
she told Jacqueline, "I cannot afford to be publicly
connected with the movement."   But she gave
Jacqueline her home telephone number and told her, "If
you every get arrested, call me. I will come bail you
out, and I will get you safely home." Mrs. Delmar
believed in the movement, and helped Jacqueline in the
only way she could without compromising her value to
the hospital and all of the children that it helped.

She warned Jacqueline that if the city
government officials realized that Jacqueline was
helping to organize the movement, that they would
come for her. Mrs. Delmar made her promise to keep
her number on Jacqueline at all times. "Jacqueline,"
she said, "the police will come if they find out. They
are trying to stop this movement. I will keep my ear to
the ground, and if I hear anything from our friends in
power, I will let you know. Please be careful. The
movement is beginning to work, and many people are
angry. Dr. Delmar worries about you all the time. But
he understands what you must do. Our friends in
powerful positions who believe in the cause are trying
to change it from the inside."

Jacqueline appreciated everything that Mrs.
Delmar did and was grateful for her concern. But
Jacqueline really did not believe that the government
would come for her. Jacqueline saw herself as a very
small piece of an enormous movement. Jacqueline did
not think that she was important enough for the

government to even notice her. But even if she had come to the attention of the authorities, she knew that she could not be guilty of the crime of silence. Marie's future depended on Jacqueline. So, with the knowledge of Mrs. Delmar's warning, she continued organizing and supporting the movement.

Jacqueline had become involved in the movement while Marie was still being treated, but it was not until after Marie's surgeries were over that Jacqueline had the time to become truly active in the cause. After Marie was released from the hospital for the last time, Jacqueline spent months burning the midnight oil late into the nights working for women's rights. She continued to work at the Caucus Regency, and on her days off, she spent long hours on her projects. Marie practiced her printing on equal rights fliers. She perfected her childish art skills on the protesters' signs. Marie was growing up in the movements of the times. Late at night, after Marie fell asleep, Jacqueline and her friends would continue to work, after pausing only long enough to get high on pot.

One morning in late July, Jacqueline saw a volunteer named Katie fast asleep on the steps to Jacqueline apartment building. Waking Katie, Jacqueline asked, "What are you doing here?" Katie said, "Last night someone came through the sit-in passing out a drug called Quaaludes and I took one. I barely made it to the safety of your steps before I passed out." Jacqueline brought Katie in and put her to bed. Then she called Mrs. Delmar and asked her what this Quaalude drug was.

Mrs. Delmar checked and called her right back, explaining, "What you are calling Quaalude is actually a brand name for a drug called Methaqualone. Another brand name is Sopor. In general, Quaaludes are very similar to alcohol and other depressants. Methaqualone combines both sedative and hypnotic properties. The drug produces depression of the central nervous system. The onset of its effects usually occurs within 10 to 20 minutes of ingestion and may last 6 to 10 hours. Small doses create a feeling of euphoria, relaxation, horniness, and/or sleepiness. Larger doses can bring about depression, irrational behavior, poor reflexes and slurred speech."

Jacqueline called other members of the movement who had been present for the sit-in. Each one she could contact told her pieces of the same story. Jacqueline heard from some that there had been a number of arrests of sleeping activists. Others told her that the drugs had been handed out to activists. Others told her that activists who had taken the drug fell asleep. Jacqueline was the first to put it all together. All of the activists who had been arrested had all taken the Quaaludes that had been handed out to them, and others had passed out from the drugs, but had avoided arrest.

Jacqueline realized this had been done intentionally. She immediately called her runners on the town crier team. Jacqueline told them to get the word out not to take a drug called Quaalude at the marches or sit-ins. Someone is trying to set us up. She told the criers, "You need to tell everyone that if people are doing any drugs, to make sure that they know their source. This could wipe out the movement." That afternoon, the flyers went out with warnings about Quaaludes and other drugs.

There seemed to always be so much to do and so many people to look out for. Less then a month later, someone was passing out the hallucinogenic drug LSD, in small pill form. Jacqueline had to care for more than five persons in one night. They had become so high from the little orange pill that they were simply seeing an array of colors and walking out into traffic.

The newspapers were covering the movement as if it were just an excuse for a drug party in the streets. The authorities were spinning it that way, and the media were following the government's lead. The movement was losing credibility and its members were being portrayed as stoners by the media. The government was sending undercover agents into the protests, and had the spies handing out drugs, in order to destroy the movement. Those in power had been unable to stop the movement any other way.

Jacqueline was not about to be ensnared in their clever trap herself. Jacqueline chose not to play with most of the dangerous drugs of the times. She wanted nothing to do with this drug, Quaalude. After saving several of the volunteers from their own stupidity, she felt even stronger about LSD and other hallucinogens. She was seeing the results of drug use and abuse all around her. Finally, Jacqueline did the only thing she could do to keep from losing more ground in the public opinion polls. She called a meeting of all of her volunteers.

At the meeting Jacqueline explained that the way their progress was being destroyed was that they were losing credibility with the public. The media had blown the drug thing all out of proportion, and there was no way that the government would ever be implicated as causing the incidents that led to the bad press. The government had found their weakness, and was exploiting it. That weakness was also their strength – it was their freedom of spirit. The same reasons that brought them to fight against oppression made them recognize that recreational drug use was okay. But there were members of the public who were not as open-minded as they all were. Each of them could individually handle public embarrassment. But if the public saw them as buffoons, then their causes, no matter how important or how noble, lost too.

Jacqueline asked for the cooperation of her volunteers. She would not order them to do anything. At that meeting, Jacqueline asked her volunteers to agree not to use any drugs at any time when they expected to be in contact with the public. She asked them not to use anything during any demonstrations, not even alcohol. And if they were going to smoke pot do it before they get to the demonstrations. Once she had explained the big picture to everyone, there was not one person who hesitated. Everyone gladly agreed to forgo use of any sort of mind-altering hallucinogen substance before and during any contact with the public for good of the movement. It hurt Jacqueline to do that – her personal philosophy was that people should be able to do whatever they wanted to do, as long as it did not harm others. But she also knew that personal sacrifices by individuals had to be made for the greater good.

On March 1, 1977, Mrs. Delmar had made plans to take Marie to the zoo. They had both been looking forward to a fun day. Jacqueline planned to relax for the day, so she told all the workers not to call or come by the apartment that day. Mrs. Delmar picked Marie up about nine o'clock a.m., and Jacqueline fell back to sleep.

About one o'clock p.m., Jacqueline awoke to a noise outside the apartment. Looking out her kitchen window, she saw a couple of men in suits and sunglasses. Believing it was just some businessmen shopping to buy property in area, she walked to the refrigerator for a glass of milk. A few seconds later she heard someone rushing up the stairs and then a deep voice said, "FBI! Open the door!" Jacqueline was in a panic. She peered out the peephole, and saw a man holding a badge up. Again she heard "FBI! Open the door!"

Jacqueline opened the door, and three men walked right past her into her apartment. Two men began looking around and knocking over stacks of flyers, while the third man spoke to Jacqueline. He said, "You have been causing disruption in this city!" Jacqueline asked, "Do you have a search warrant?" The man did not answer her question. Instead he said, "We are looking for drugs." Jacqueline replied, "Get out! I have no drugs in this house!" They continued messing up the place as the third man said, "We are going now. This is just a warning of what can come." With that, they all left the apartment.

As Jacqueline looked around her living room, which had been serving as an office for the various human rights movements, she saw complete disarray. Papers that had been neatly organized were scattered about. She fell to her knees, and she began to cry. Jacqueline did not cry long. She told herself that she was too angry to collapse into a heap on the floor; that would accomplish nothing. There was too much to do. She looked at the shambles around her, and shaking her head, started the huge task of reorganizing the disaster.

After only a few minutes, two of her neighbors came into the apartment, and began to help Jacqueline sort the mess the men had left. Jacqueline said, "Well, at least they did not find my pot stash!" Jacqueline rolled a joint, and she and her neighbors smoked it, while they cleaned and reorganized all the documents. It took hours to fix what the FBI agents had destroyed in only a few moments. When the work was finally done, the material was arranged even better than it had been originally. Jacqueline had recovered completely from the traumatic experience, and joked, "Those clowns did me a favor! This place is in better shape now than it has been in months!

But after everyone finished and had gone, Jacqueline began to think. What if Marie had been here? It would have scared Marie to death if she had seen her mother being accused that like. Jacqueline knew that she could take the heat, but she could not subject Marie to that. Jacqueline began to realize that it was time for her to leave San Francisco, her home of several years. She never had wanted to leave her new hometown.

She stayed to see the April 5, 1977 sit-in for disabled Americans. She created and distributed her last fliers for that sit-in. It was little-known civil rights movement. But with Marie being disabled for so many years, it was an important issue to Jacqueline. It was as important to her as Selma or Stonewall were to the participants in those acts of civil disobedience. The plan was for a band of disabled people to stage a sit-in at a federal office building in San Francisco and stay until the law was enforced.

The demonstrators were calling for enforcement of the first major law to ban discrimination against the disabled. Despite being on the books, no federal agency was enforcing the law, and the disabled were suffering. Jacqueline believed that enforcement of the law would bring one of the nations most isolated and powerless groups into the mainstream.

The late 1970s had been filled with protest, but Americans had become used to seeing civil-rights marches. This would open their eyes again! There would be people in wheelchairs, people on portable respirators, deaf people, people with mental retardation, and people with IV poles, all in the streets to protest. Most of them were fighting mad at the lack of consideration they received in access to facilities and buildings and they were out for change.

What they demanded was the signing of regulations to enact a law known as Section 504, an administrative enforcement provision for the 1973 Rehabilitation Act. The Rehabilitation Act statute had been in the United States Code for several years, but Congress had not seen fit to enact enforcement provisions, and the Department of Health, Education, and Welfare had stonewalled implementation of enforcement regulations in the Code of Federal Regulations. The 1973 act purported to force hospitals, universities - any place that got federal money - to remove obstacles to services for the disabled and to provide access to public transportation and public places for the disabled. But complying with the law was often considered too expensive, so for nearly four years, the government failed to enforce the law.

In April 1977, sit-ins were organized across the country. Demonstrators in New York, Washington, D.C., Chicago, and throughout the country were ready to fight with what power they had. Not all of them had the power to fight, but all of them had the power to remain stationary. Jacqueline was asked by the other organizers in the area to help. She knew this would be her last, for a while. She pulled her people together for one last fight, and began making the fliers and posters for the upcoming event.

On April 5, the protesters started rolling their wheel chairs into the U.S. Department of Health, Education and Welfare building. At the front of the group were disabled veterans of Vietnam, stoned as they could be, and not afraid of anything. The protesters in San Francisco would not surrender – they were in for the long haul. In some other cities, protesters gave up and left the protest locations after only a few days. In San Francisco, more than 100 disabled demonstrators stayed in the building for weeks, refusing to leave until the regulations were signed.

Jacqueline watched from a distance, and she followed every television and radio news broadcast with more pride than she had ever known. She knew that this group of disabled Americans would be an impossible force to stop. Public opinion supported the demonstrators. If the government had attempted to do anything to those disabled people, the public outcry would have dethroned a king! On April 28, 1977, nearly four weeks after the sit-in had begun, Secretary Joseph Califano endorsed the regulations of Section 504, and the sit-in ended. The protesters had won.

After it was over, Jacqueline sat quietly in Golden Gate Park by herself, and smoked a joint while she looked over the city she loved so much. But she knew it was time for her and Marie to leave the bay area. She had already been planning a move to Southern California when this last protest came about.

Jacqueline left San Francisco. She knew when the FBI entered her home that it was time to move on. A few days after the victory by the disabled, Jacqueline and Marie loaded Jacqueline's 1966 Mustang. They attached a trailer to the car, and began the ride to their new home. Jacqueline had leased a house in Venice Beach, near Los Angeles. Jacqueline drove down the Scenic Coast Highway 101 to Venice Beach, the new home for her daughter and her.

Venice Beach is a small community south of Santa Monica. It was built in the 1920s by a man who fell in love with the canals of Venice, Italy and set out to reproduce them. Venice Beach was row after row of small, bungalow houses, divided by water-filled canals. This area had been taken over by the beatniks in the sixties. They were peacefully sharing the community with the hippies and the Hare Krishnas in the seventies.

When they arrived, the house was just as it had been described to her. It was a small half-bungalow just off the intersection of Pacific Avenue and Venice Boulevard. The term half-bungalow was a bit misleading; it was actually two attached residences. The entrance to one side was set back from the entrance to the other side by a few feet. Each side had access to the large back yard and the canal behind. As Jacqueline pulled up, her landlord, Mabel Carmen, came out of the front half where she lived. With open arms, this new friend welcomed them in for dinner.

Mabel had seemed to be quite a character on the telephone, and she was even more colorful in person. This thin woman in her early seventies had been part of the civil-rights movement in Southern California since it began. She wore her gray hair long and straight. Over the years, she had been an organizer who maintained contact with Jacqueline in San Francisco. When Jacqueline had told her of the FBI invasion of Jacqueline's home, Mabel immediately offered to rent one of her homes to Jacqueline and Marie.

As they settled into the back yard and began to eat a spaghetti dinner, Jacqueline's new neighbors and local friends of the movement began showing up. Jacqueline and Marie felt right at home. Jacqueline was already making new friends. Marie already had several new best friends among the children who were there.

Mabel seemed to be everybody's mother, and it was really no surprise to Jacqueline that Mabel was the first to pull out a joint that evening. The backyard had filled. About twenty people ended up eating spaghetti. After everyone had eaten, Mabel said "All right everybody, I filled your stomachs and got you high. Now it is time to get Jacqueline and Marie moved in." A guy named Gary was the first to be ready to lend a hand.

Jacqueline opened up the trailer, and gave Gary the key to her car. Mabel told her, "You have had a long drive. Just sit down in the kitchen and tell everyone where you want the things to go in the house." Then Mabel poured Jacqueline a glass of Napa Valley Napa Rosé, and sat her in a chair. Jacqueline watched and directed, and people passed with all of Jacqueline and Marie's belongings. After a while, things started coming in that did not belong to Jacqueline. Mabel said, "I thought you might be able to use these things, if you want them."

Most of what Jacqueline had brought was for Marie. The San Francisco apartment has been rented furnished, and except for Marie's bed, toys, and the barest of essentials, Jacqueline did not own much. She had thought that she would sleep on the floor until she could find furniture. So she readily accepted Mabel's offer, and by one o'clock a.m., her house was set up and Jacqueline was asleep in her new bed.

Neither Marie nor Jacqueline woke until late the following morning. Jacqueline sat on the porch, as Marie played in the yard. A gentleman from the night before, the man named Gary, came up and asked if he could join her. "I live three houses down," he said. "I am an architect for the City of Venice. What do you do?" Jacqueline replied, "I was a hostess in San Francisco, but now I am unemployed, and I need to find a job fast." Gary said, "Well, maybe I can help you."

Just then, Mabel walked up and said, "Oh, no Gary. You can't have her. I have plans for her." Jacqueline replied "Really, Mabel?" Mabel said, "Yes. Both of you come with me." They walked through the side gate of the yard. There they were standing in a huge paved lot that faced Ocean Blvd. It was fenced with a twelve-foot high fence that contained two large gates that a car could drive through. The paved area was large enough to park ten cars.

Mabel said, "Jacqueline, I have had an idea for this land for many years. But I am too old to do it myself. I own this, and I have three storage units filled with antiques. I would like to have some of them brought to this property and sold on the weekends. They should bring a pretty penny, and this location has some of the best traffic in the area. I think you could make a good living even if you only set up four days a week. I will split 50/50 with you whatever you sell. My nephew Mike is a college student, and he will help you move the items out and in. What do you think?" Jacqueline relied, "It sounds great to me, until I can find some full time work." Mabel told her, "Well, take your time. I know how much money you will make."

For the next several months Jacqueline sold antiques, while lying in the sun stoned, watching Marie play. Over that time, Gary and Jacqueline had developed a friendship. He was 40 years old, a good-looking man of 5 feet 10 inches. He was always well tanned for a fair-haired man. Gary was very nice to her, and he liked to get her high. He was always trying to have sex with her, but she was never attracted to him for some unknown reason.

He seemed to find Jacqueline's youthful spirit interesting. But as their friendship developed, he also seemed to try to tell her what she should do and what she should wear. Jacqueline found this very upsetting, and decided that she did not want to date him. Mabel was not surprised at Jacqueline's distaste for his behavior, and advised Jacqueline to get rid of him. Mabel told her, "He is trying to control you." Jacqueline told Gary she did not want to see him any more, but he kept coming around.

Jacqueline just refused to go out with him at all or have any further relationship with him. She continued with her new business, and began buying books to learn about antiques and annuities. Within a few months, she had found a position a local antique and art gallery. She was meeting a new set of friends and learning a great deal about the business. An artist from Chile by the name of Carlos had taken an interest in Jacqueline. He was a small man of maybe five feet six. He had long black hair and a pleasant face. Carlos was extremely funny and filled with ideas, and Jacqueline was interested in him.

After a few months, they began sleeping together and she found him pleasing. He was always very busy, and did not seen to be possessive of Jacqueline at all. One evening after an art showing, Carlos and Jacqueline were smoking hash while lying in bed. Carlos said, Jacqueline, I would like to paint you." She replied, "Oh, that would be lovely!" He asked, "Can we start tonight?" Jacqueline replied, "Well, I am not dressed for that." Carlos told her, "Oh, yes you are! I want to paint your body, then photograph you and paint you in oil from the photograph."

Jacqueline thought for a few minutes and said, "Why not?" He laid her on a canvas on the floor, and took out some paint. Jacqueline asked, "Does this come off?" He replied, "Yes. It is just body paint, and it showers right off." She said, "Great! I love your work, and I'm sure this will be wonderful, but I don't think that I would want to wear it forever." Carlos laughed. "Jacqueline," Carlos said, "Get good and stoned on the hash. This will be fun!"

Jacqueline lay naked on the large canvas, smoking the hash pipe, as Carlos prepared the paints. He began by painting her arm, and he asked her how it felt. She told him, "It is really a wild feeling, and I like it." He continued to paint her body with an abstract pattern of purple, pink, blue, green and yellow. As the brush moved to her breast, she felt her body start to heat up. The bristles of his paintbrush were arousing her.

"Carlos, I am getting excited from the brush touching my body!" Carlos told her, "Wonderful! By the time I get you completely painted, you should have a great expression on your face when the Polaroid is taken for the oil painting." Jacqueline was getting more and more excited as he painted her body. When her body was completely painted and dried, Carlos sat her up in a wicker one-armed fainting sofa with a lilac cushion. Then he got out the Polaroid camera and sat it on the table. Jacqueline said, "Hurry up and take the pictures. I am really hot and I want to fool around, dear."

Instead of snapping the photographs, he walked over to the antique wicker fainting sofa she had sold him. She was still reclining for the photographs. He separated her legs with his hands, as he slowly began making her come with his lips. Jacqueline was wild with desire and dripping in orgasm, as he got up and reached for the camera. He pushed her legs closed as she rested her head back in complete satisfaction. Then he began shooting the pictures. She was amazed at the quality of the pictures. The expression on her face in each was one of complete satisfaction.

Carlos had agreed that he would give her the pictures when the painting was complete. He told her that the oil painting would be a gift to her when he had painted it. She could not wait to see the portrait. She had never imagined that he planned on that method of putting a smile on her face for the camera, but she was thrilled at both the method and the photographic result.

About two weeks later, he brought her over to see the results of his hard work. It was a beautiful portrait of a young, sexually charged woman in body paint. A thin veil of lavender covered her face. You could still see her face below the painted veil, almost in shadow form. She could hardly believe that this beautiful woman was she. The finished portrait was truly a work of art. He gave it to her, and as he had promised, he also gave her the pictures he had used to create it.

Later that evening, he also told her he was returning to Chili for a year or so. Jacqueline thought that she might be falling in love with Carlos, and she was hurt that he would leave her. Even more, she was confused that he would leave her after giving her such a beautiful gift. She asked him why he would go alone to Chili, and leave her behind. His reply stunned her. "I am married, but I am in love with you. If I do not return to my wife now, I will never be able to go back – I will want to spend the rest of my life in your arms. That would not be fair to my wife, and it would not be fair to you." Jacqueline was devastated and asked, "Why did you not tell me? I would never have slept with another woman's husband." Carlos replied, "I know I should have told you in the beginning, but I wanted you so much." Jacqueline picked up the oil painting, and the pictures. The only other words she uttered were, "Goodbye, Carlos," as she walked out the door.

      With this sad experience, she decided that maybe it was time to leave California and return to the Midwest, as her family had wanted for so long. So with Marie and her belongings in the car, she traveled across the country toward home. Marie loved to travel with Jacqueline. They had so much fun on their journey, sightseeing throughout the trip. Jacqueline was in no rush to return to her hometown. She had plans for the future, but she and Marie needed to enjoy the present, too. Her next step would be more employment and maybe college. Now that Marie was well, Jacqueline could work two or three jobs. This would be the theme of the next few years. Although she never obtained a degree, Jacqueline took classes in everything. She attended the local community college and a university. Slipping in on hospital seminars and reading every book she could find while Marie was ill had helped her prepare for her college years.

The sun shone brightest on Jacqueline in her early twenties, after she had a little college under her belt. This woman of clove-colored hair, green eyes and cinnamon skin was on her way to a new life for herself and Marie. If the devil could not defeat her, look out world! Things were right. Marie was school-aged and the battle was over; deeply buried were the memories of the struggle. The joy of her daughter's laughter and the knowledge acquired in her travels created the finished woman. No longer was she that small-town girl of so long ago.

Jacqueline had spent a few years recovering from the sheer physical and mental strain of Marie's illness, but she was still working one or two jobs, while trying to change the world and also going to college. It was a time of change for Jacqueline and Marie. Marie would meet her father for the first time in her memory. Jacqueline and Marie had talked, and Marie was looking forward to the reunion.

Marie and her father spent a year or so learning to know and love each other. Jacqueline attempted to keep this experience for Marie as positive as possible. After all, she always found her former husband a fun guy. Seeing old friends and having freedom was a nice change. But Jacqueline regretted moving back to the north the very day she arrived. Although she loved her family and friends, she hated having Marie in cold weather. After the years in California, Jacqueline did not like it much either. She felt that she no longer belonged there. Her mind and beliefs had outgrown her hometown. The townspeople could not see the bigger picture. When she talked about important things like women's rights with her old friends, they seemed disinterested. The subjects of critical importance to her were not at all important to her old friends. And how could she ever explain who she was and how she had obtained her values. The older men and women seem to accept the changes in Jacqueline, but Jacqueline was still unhappy living there. She began to think that it was time to move on again, maybe to Florida.

Her first step in leaving Michigan again was finding a job elsewhere. The spotty bits of college had helped her get her insurance license. The company she was working for in her hometown knew of her desire to move. They offered her thirty days of paid leave to go to Florida, and they hoped that she would change her mind. She knew that she would not. She wanted to return to somewhere with beaches and sunshine.

Her parents had decided to retire to Florida. They wanted Jacqueline and Marie to come there instead of returning to California. Jacqueline knew it would be easier to work long hours with her parent's help. Besides they had missed her and Marie so much while they were living in California and Marie was crazy about her grandparents. So Florida became their next home.

Once she had seen the swaying palm trees and rich beaches again, she knew she would have no desire to leave. She had missed the sunshine and warmth of California since the day she arrived back in Michigan. She had thirteen job interviews in Florida, and thirteen job offers. The years of fighting the medical system had given her the ability to achieve.

After settling into her new office, Jacqueline immediately began to look for a niche. Something special, so she could quickly make a name and money. It seemed there was a need for professional malpractice insurance. It was not a bad idea; besides, she liked the clientele. They would be doctors, lawyers, architects, and engineers. That sounded like it could be fun, and so away she went.

Her years of dealing with Marie's illness prepared her to deal with educated people. To say the least, she was not intimidated, but then did anything intimidate her? It was time for the world to look out - money was the name of the game for her. Jacqueline had learned money's true value. It was peace of mind. In no time, she was selling to the power elite. She knew she would never go to the cabinet and find it empty again. Her years of struggle were over. Marie would not want for anything. That was her goal.

She worked her schedule so that Marie would never be a latch key kid or a constant burden on Jacqueline's retired parents. Prior to accepting her new position, she negotiated with the company for Marie to be dropped off at her office by the school bus. There, she could play and wait for her mother if necessary. This part of Jacqueline's contract was more important than her salary or an office. But Jacqueline was smart; she negotiated it last, as though it was the little term holding up the signing of the contract. Such a little request would never stop a good businessman. Besides, Mr. Strong was a good family man, and he owned the company.

Dating would only be in her spare time. She had met a few nice men in Florida and they seemed to enjoy her company. Some, the "special" ones, could even spend time with her daughter. She didn't let many people around Marie. Only friends with interesting qualities would be given the opportunity to meet Marie. Marie would be protected at all costs. Jacqueline had taken to her early motherhood like a bird to the sky. Although she was not a perfect mother, she truly did her absolute best. She also knew that she must find some time to develop a personal life.

Jacqueline had not found a lover yet. This was important, because the years had created a complete woman. With a remarkable ability for the enjoyment of sex, no longer was she the scared little girl from the Midwest. Jacqueline had come beautifully into full sexual awareness. She needed someone who could fill her womanly needs in a monogamous way, not some man who would try to cling to her while she was still growing. Jacqueline had already come to understand that the flower blooms, and she knew that she had not reached her full potential. She felt that a younger man would hold her back, but she had left a trail of older men in California.

Yes, even Jacqueline believed that there was someone out there who could love Marie and herself completely. She knew she would need a steady lover until she found Mr. Right. Those two things would be separate; a steady lover would satisfy her physical needs and afford her the luxury of time to search for the man of her dreams. Jacqueline did not expect to easily find someone she wanted for the rest of her life. The years had made her a complex woman. She was prepared to wait, but a monogamous lover would make the wait more bearable. It was the spring of 1983.

CHAPTER TWO

ODE TO MAXWELL

There was a man soon to enter Jacqueline's life, a lover just as busy as she was. They would fill each other's needs, and enjoy the time when they could be together. He lived in Washington, DC. This was perfect for Jacqueline; she did not want anyone to interfere with her business and her "life," her daughter Marie.

Maxwell wrote the ninety-nine steps to HUD financing. That means he had mastered the many steps required to get a multi-million dollar project financed by using government funding. This was a very lucrative business for Max. He lived in the glitzy world of politics and power that she enjoyed. She would fly to Washington or he would arrive in Florida. Their theme was to keep it simple, and to enjoy each other. Their only commitment was to sleep with only each other. If the time came when they wanted someone else, the other one would walk away. In their very busy worlds, this was perfect. It was more than just sex, and maybe it was love, but only time would tell.

Maxwell had been passing through Tampa regularly over the last few years. While staying at the Hyatt, he had befriended Betty Jean, a local barmaid. Jacqueline never knew whether he just happened to be in town for business that day, or came for Betty Jean's wedding. Jacqueline saw him across the room, speaking with Betty Jean and her new husband. As she walked toward them, Betty Jean's eyes lit completely up.

Then came the legendary introduction at the wedding reception, from Jacqueline's best friend of thirty years or so, Betty Jean. Books could be written about these true friends. This day was the day of Betty Jean's ceremony, and Jacqueline was her maid of honor. When Betty Jean was married the first time, they had not lived close enough for Jacqueline to be her maid of honor. The wedding reception was held at the Hyatt where she worked. As she stood next to a strikingly handsome man, Betty Jean's introduction went like this: "Max I would like you to meet the smartest woman I know, Jacqueline. Jacqueline, I would like you to meet the richest man I know, Maxwell."

Well, after that introduction, what could Jacqueline say? Thinking fast, she responded, "Max if we can live through that introduction, we can live through anything!" From that day they played for a time.

It was early afternoon when she was introduced to Max. The reception for Betty Jean had just begun. Max and Jacqueline spent the afternoon talking, laughing and dancing. The Hyatt in Tampa was always filled with excitement. It was a tall building of glass with limitless views of the Gulf of Mexico and Tampa Bay. This edifice in the beautiful sunshine state was the backdrop for evenings filled with fun and romance. People traveled in and out on business. This is what had brought Max to her.

Max told her of his busy world, and his office on Pennsylvania Avenue in Washington, DC. She listened as he explained the fine art of big-business finance. He talked of places she had never been, as they danced and laughed the evening away. The first time they danced, Jacqueline knew his touch pleased her. She could feel the heat stirring inside of her body as his arms wrapped around her. Some men can hold you in their arms and dance as though the magic of the night will never end. Max's touch gave Jacqueline that feeling.

Everyone at the Hyatt seemed to know and like Max. Hours passed, as the evening became night.

Jacqueline explained to Max that she had to leave; it was a thirty-mile drive across the Crystal Cove Bridge. "But Max," she said, "I need to eat a little something first." Max asked, "What would you like Jacqueline?" She responded, "A lobster tail, but it is 12:30 a.m., and the kitchen is closed here at the Hyatt." Max said, "It is not closed to you. Wait here, and I'll be right back."

Jacqueline knew better, and taking his words lightly, Jacqueline began saying her good-byes to Betty Jean and her new husband. Today was their day! Jacqueline had spent most of the reception talking and dancing with Max. Throughout the evening, she had been slipping looks at her old friend, to see Betty Jean enjoying her day. Betty Jean's eyes met Jacqueline's off and on during the evening. Jacqueline recognized her old friend's look of approval. Every now and then they would catch one another's glance. Without a word, their eyes did the communication between them. Then they would meet in the ladies room. Betty Jean told Jacqueline, "Max is a wonderful man. Jacqueline, I have never seen him so taken with a woman. But that really does not surprise me. I had hoped he would be here to meet you!" Some friends are for life; Betty Jean was Jacqueline's life-long friend. As children, both knew that their friendship would be theirs forever, and it was.

To Jacqueline's amazement, Max returned and stated, "Dinner awaits you." Betty Jean smiled as they walked away. Max took Jacqueline's arm and led her to a table in the closed Hyatt restaurant! He told her that he had already ordered for them, as the waiter brought the champagne. Then Max excused himself for a moment, and left Jacqueline to her thoughts. It was

Friday night, and she was totally enchanted with this man. She sat, sipping champagne and laughing to herself about their introduction. She knew that she was far from the smartest woman in the world, but Betty Jean's dear friendship and her words of praise did make her smile.

The view from the windows of the restaurant overlooked the lights of the city and a horizon of water. The twinkling of the lights reflecting on the water placed Jacqueline in a trance. As she thought about this new place, she felt pleased that she had chosen it as a new home for Marie and herself. She realized how good business was becoming. Her days of scrambling to make ends meet were over. Their lives in Florida were just beginning, and the path they had taken looked to be leading to a glorious future.

And how much fun she was having with Max! Gentle thoughts of the day flowed through her mind. She recalled the crazy white limousine that had carried her and Betty Jean to the high noon wedding, and the silly stop for the white cowboy hat Betty Jean had insisted on wearing in the marriage ceremony. She laughed out loud, remembering having to hold her best friend up at the altar, after Betty Jean had drunk way too much champagne in the limousine. The day had been so beautiful and fun, and Maxell was a surprise bonus. Jacqueline loved how intelligent and interesting he was. She was beginning to feel desire for that method of expression that few men could inspire in her. She knew that she would sleep alone tonight. She had already decided that much earlier. Besides, she had too much to drink that evening, and she wanted to have Max sober, so she did not miss a thing! She knew how good it would be. Jacqueline knew they would see each other again.

As she continued to wait for Max's return, her thoughts drifted. Most of all, she thought about how good God's life was becoming for Marie and her. Jacqueline always knew he had a special plan for them. When things start out as hard as they had been for the mother and daughter, improvement was all that could have been on the horizon. Now, as she gazed out over the water, she could feel the glow of the good life. Maxwell returned a few minutes later, and they began to enjoy their lobster tails.

They talked of business and their inability to have a relationship while living in the world of business. They spoke of Betty Jean, and the long history the women had together. Max had known Betty Jean as the barmaid at the Hyatt for the last two years. He had always liked her, and he recognized the life-long friendship between Jacqueline and Betty Jean. Max said, "Every time Betty Jean mentioned you, I could not believe how she raved about you. Now I understand why she said I would have to meet you. We talked about you every time I saw her in the two years I have known her. I made it a point to see her every time I traveled in and out of Florida on business. She was so excited when you decided to move to Florida, but I never expected that you would be so real, and so beautiful."

Jacqueline had to ask how he was able to open the Hyatt restaurant for only them. Max did not hesitate to tell her. *"Money and power are one and the same."* He continued, "Be my friend Jacqueline, and I will show you." From the sound of his voice, she knew he was not bragging. He was extremely serious, and he had offered her a chance to learn. He did not know that the first requirement for a man to hold Jacqueline's interest was an ability to teach her. He definitely had captured her interest! Max and the evening seemed perfect.

His hand reached across the white linen tablecloth toward her. The flickering candlelight was reflecting off the windows. Slowly, Maxell opened his hand to expose the shiny golden key he was holding. Jacqueline quickly explained that she would not be spending the night in his room. He laughed a most wonderful laugh! Then he informed her that this was her key, and that it also allowed the elevator to access her room on the top floor. His key did not fit the special lock in the elevator for her floor. This was the beginning of two years of fun and friendship. Play they did, without any other commitment. When their paths could cross they would enjoy. Jacqueline was just barely twenty-six.

Max was a bachelor of 43 years, standing six feet, two inches tall. He was of slender build, weighing maybe 185 pounds. He ran six miles every day in Washington, and had that thin but muscular body of a runner. His hair was black, curly, and thick. There was no gray, and no chance that he would ever lose his full, rich hair. His eyes were deep brown, and he wore black-framed glasses, almost as if he wanted to conceal his good looks. Max was a quiet man, but always happy, the life of the party in his own quiet way. Like Jacqueline, he seemed to work a lot and enjoy his work.

There was something deep in Max 's eyes; something his outgoing appearance did not show. It was a deep loneliness, perhaps. He was Harvard educated and obviously very successful in business, although the only things she would really learn from Max would be how to finance a very big construction project and a deeper joy of sex. She would later think, "That was enough for any one man to teach."

They laughed and talked as they feasted on lobster and champagne. His smile was captivating as he fed her fresh berries for dessert. They walked slowly arm in arm to the elevator of the Hyatt. He was telling the truth; he asked for her key to start the elevator as he escorted her to her suite. As they reached the door, Max handed her the key, then he kissed her softly and told her to sleep well. She turned the key in the lock as Max re-entered the elevator. The suite was exquisite. After she retired, Jacqueline gazed out the glass doors of the balcony from the king size bed, housed in its beautiful room of gold and ivory. The entire evening played back in her mind, as she began to fall peacefully asleep.

Waking before sunrise, she found the beautiful white terry robe that the Hyatt had supplied. She bathed, while a pot of coffee was brewing on the bathroom counter. As she bathed, she thought about Max and their evening the night before. Then she slipped her wet body into the soft terry robe and poured the coffee. Walking out onto the balcony, she laid her body on the chaise lounge as she began to enjoy the dawn. Jacqueline had always thought that the early morning was the best part of the day – she enjoyed the quiet before the world awoke.

Enjoying the beautiful view of the city as the sun was beginning to rise, Jacqueline was thinking of Max, who had told her that he had to leave on the red eye for Washington that morning. The evening was playing over and over in her mind. He was so handsome and smart. She could not remember having a better time! Just then the telephone rang in her room. Max said, "Good morning beautiful, I just wanted to tell you what a wonderful time I had last night! I am leaving for Washington this morning. Can you come down to the lobby, to say good-bye?" She told him "I am still in my robe, but I am having coffee on the balcony, if you would like to come up." Max said, "I will be right up." A few minutes later, he arrived at her room. Dressed in his Ivy League attire, white shirt, khaki pants, blue blazer, loafers and that Harvard stripe tie, he joined Jacqueline on the balcony.

As she poured his coffee, they spoke of their wonderful evening together. She asked him, "If your key did not fit the elevator to this floor, how did you get up here this morning?" He chuckled and said, "I am not above bribing a bellman." They laughed. "Just curious," she said. "Good question," he replied. "I like smart women." Max had a very infectious laugh. Jacqueline knew her desire for him was increasing with each word he spoke.

Max told her of his plans to return to Washington and asked, " Will you come to visit?" He told her that she was the most interesting woman he had met in years. Then he asked, "May I kiss you goodbye?" Last night he had given her a gentle kiss at the door of her room, so why was he asking now? She said, "Yes."

He slowly lifted her from the chaise to her feet. Then his lips caressed hers far more deeply this time. Gently, he locked her in the deepest of passionate kisses that seemed to last forever, unlike the gentle goodnight kiss. It was joyful. His fragrance became intoxicating. His soft lips tasted of honey. His lips slowly drew away as he sat her back down and then returned to his seat.

Max told Jacqueline he was looking for one solid lover, a woman as busy as he was. One woman who could wait to make love till they could be together, but spend all of the time they could find loving. He asked her to think about it, and if she would like, to come to Washington. They had talked about how busy their worlds were. He knew she was not looking for a man who required a lot of day-to-day attention, and he was not looking for a clinging woman.

Jacqueline thought her answer: "Oh, yes!" She was attracted to him, and he was smart enough to hold her interest. She wanted a monogamous lover without the emotional baggage. Max said, "I have to go, my plane leaves in an hour." Jacqueline asked, "You have a meeting in Washington on a Saturday?" He told her, "I was just planning on getting some rest for Monday. I would not have booked this flight, had I known I would meet you last night, Jacqueline." It had been a long time since Jacqueline had felt a man's touch. Her body was ready for Max. She was filled with longing and desire, desperate in her anticipation of his touch. She had waited for Max to come along. Calmly, she told him that if he would like to miss that plane, she could give him her answer now.

Max's eyes met Jacqueline's. His rose colored, soft lips smiled as he removed his glasses for the first time. His eyes were even more beautiful than she had imagined. He was also more handsome than she had realized. Max rose from his chair, lowering himself to his knees beside her chaise. His lips became more deeply locked onto hers than before. His hands slowly separated the white terry cloth robe she was wearing, revealing her dark, naked skin below.

His fingers slid gently across her nipples, as the robe fell from her shoulders. Max 's eyes looked up tenderly into hers then slowly lowered to view her naked body. Jacqueline's silver dollar nipples began to grow from the swell of her breast. Harder and harder, bigger than she thought possible. His kisses were delicious, warm and wet. Her body was ready for the delight of Max. She felt more desire than she had ever known.

Beneath the Hyatt's terry robe lay only her brown skin for his viewing, as she was feeling the Florida sun from the high balcony baking down on her. Still dressed in his blazer, his lips began to slide down her neck, planting soft kisses as he approached her breast. He replaced his warm hand on Jacqueline's breast with his lips. Max's soft tongue felt like fire on her skin. Her nipples grew even more erect for him, as his eyes looked gently up at the smile on her face. Jacqueline's hands were stroking his curly black hair.

The sun began to beat hotter, as his lips slid down her stomach, covering it with passionate reams of small kisses. She could smell gardenias in the fresh balcony air. Then he softly separated her legs, pulling them slowly apart. He was looking up at her face, as though he knew she was about to feel something she had never truly felt before. His tongue began small soft licks. Then she began feeling the heat, as Max began to draw the juice from her body so very gently. Now she could feel his tongue inside her, deeper than she knew possible, while his hands were rubbing the tightly drawn skin of her breasts.

Jacqueline could feel the full strength of the sun and the fresh morning air, as she came from the slow movements of his warm, wet tongue. She wanted to cry out, but tried to hold the sound in. It was of no use. The deeper his tongue went inside her, the harder it was to keep silent. The sun beating down on her only intensified the effect. Sweat began to drip down across her breast. Then came the sudden snap she had never felt before. Her body was gushing and snapping in orgasm after orgasm. Max somehow knew this was the first time she had snapped in multiple orgasms. He was enjoying making it happen.

There was no longer silence on the balcony. Max looked up at her and said, "My beautiful little girl, this is only the beginning." As he continued to slide his tongue deeper and deeper inside her, Jacqueline's silence had turned to screams of passion. There was something exciting about seeing a man in a blazer and Ivy League tie with his lips between her naked legs – *it was her feeling of absolute power*. They continued to make love until his Monday morning flight. Thankfully, the Hyatt had room service.

A few weeks later, Jacqueline made her first trip to Washington, D.C. Max met her at the plane with fresh flowers and candy. He blushed as he gave her the gifts. They had lunch in the city; Max was excited to see her, and she was ecstatic about seeing him. He told her he had some meetings that day that he hadn't been able to reschedule, and gave Jacqueline his business card. "The address of my office is on there. Enjoy the city and meet me there at about five o'clock." Max said. The card read "Project Development Finance, Inc., President, Maxwell O. Lanna, 1100 Pennsylvania Avenue NW, Suite 1200, Washington, D.C. 20004"

Jacqueline did the standard tour of Washington. She went to the Washington Monument, the Lincoln Memorial, and the Library of Congress. The last building she viewed was the White House. Looking across its front lawn, to its beautiful white pillars and window after window, Jacqueline thought, "All of America's history is before me." But her period of reflection was brief; all she really wanted to think about was Max. Which building was Max's office? At about fifteen minutes to five o'clock, she hailed a taxi to take her to the address he had given her. The taxi driver told her it was just a few blocks away, but he did not seem to mind the short trip. She knew it had to be in the immediate area; after all she was at 1600 Pennsylvania Avenue. But she had been walking all day, and she wanted to be sure she arrived at the right building, and on time. Besides, she hoped that she needed to rest up.

Max was walking slowly out of the tall glass building as the taxi pulled up. He got into the taxi with her, kissed her, and then told the driver the name of an oyster bar in Georgetown. As they arrived, she could see a place filled with educated men in suits and polished woman in their best Vogue attire, each one looking to find another, and all looking to climb the ladder of success. From the doorway, the sounds of business chatter, the constant pouring and ringing of glasses from behind the bar, and the sound of money changing hands were the background noises, and signified the power within.

As Max and Jacqueline entered, the introductions and handshakes began immediately. Everyone was buying them drinks. Max was obviously well known. A gentleman immediately gave Jacqueline his seat at the bar, as Max stood next to her. People were asking Max if he had heard anything on this or that project. Others were telling Jacqueline how much Max could get done in Washington. One gentleman said, "We have considered renaming Washington. It ought to be called Maxwell's town!" Everyone within earshot howled, and Jacqueline and Maxwell joined in.

Jacqueline still was laughing as she excused herself to go to the ladies room. As she entered, she noticed a woman at the vanity dressed in beautiful business attire. She looked up, and Jacqueline realized she was snorting lines of powder from a vial she had on the counter. The woman asked, "Would you like some?" Jacqueline replied, "No thanks, I just did some." When she came back from the ladies room, she immediately told Max about it. He said, "This is the cocaine capital, Jacqueline." She asked if he did cocaine, and Max replied, "No, I won't waste my money on something as addictive as cocaine. But many of them think I do," as he gestured at the room.

Jacqueline could see the people walking in Georgetown through the plate glass window over the oyster bar. This was a great place to people watch! In a few moments, Max was back to presenting her to more people. A lady stopped at the bar, and Max touched Jacqueline on the shoulder to introduce her. As Jacqueline turned around, Max said, "Jacqueline, I would like you to meet Judge Linda Cherry." "How do you do?" Jacqueline said. She tried not to sound stunned. The woman said to Maxwell, "Oh we just met in the ladies room. How did you get so lucky, Maxwell?" After she left, Jacqueline looked at Max and said, "She was the lady with the cocaine in the bathroom!" Max winked and told Jacqueline, "Never be surprised by what you see in Washington. By the way, thank you. If I ever need a little help from her, she now knows I am aware of her cocaine habit. You may turn out to be very lucky for me, Jacqueline."

As Max and Jacqueline enjoyed dinner, Maxwell made another introduction. It was something new to her, a drink called Grand Marnier. Throughout their meal, dozens of Max's friends came up to greet Jacqueline. Everyone seemed to know and like Maxwell. It seemed as if all of his friends had been waiting to meet her. One gentleman, Max's tennis partner, told her, "I almost sat in your chair." She really did not understand what he was talking about, and she told him that his remark puzzled her. He and Max laughed, and Max told her that he would explain later. She was glad to know Max had told them of her. Most of Max's friends were lawyers, businessmen or politicians. The couple had a glorious evening, filled with fine food, spirits, friends and fun.

As the night set in, Jacqueline mentioned that she had not seen Max's office. Very intoxicated, they took a cab back to his Pennsylvania Avenue office about one a.m. As Max placed his key in the street door, the guard greeted Max and Jacqueline. The security guard said, "Mr. Lanna, I am surprised to see you here so late." Max replied, "Tony, this is Jacqueline and we will be here for a little while." The guard said, "Everything is secure and your floor will not be disturbed, Mr. Lanna. Have a good evening."

They took the elevator to the twelfth floor. Max kissed her passionately as the elevator climbed. His arms held her tightly, feeling her body through her thin, silk dress. Then he asked, "Did you enjoy the sights of Washington today?" She told him of all the places she had seen. As the elevator doors opened on the twelfth floor, her vision was filled with plush, green carpet, the green of money. There was fine art along long corridors, each with office doors every twenty-five feet. She asked, "Which is your office?" Max replied "All of them, but this one is where I work." They walked to a set of double cherry wood arched doors. His office was huge, with an entire wall of floor-to-ceiling windows. The ceiling was tall, twenty feet high or more, and the windows overlooked the White House lawn where Jacqueline had been earlier. The city was filled with glittering lights.

There, filled with liquor, Max kissed her as he sat her on his large cherry wood desk in front of the window. He placed a pillow from the tapestry sofa behind her. Kissing her deeply, his hands warming her breasts, he slowly laid her back, making sure she could see the view from the window. He pulled his chair up close to her. "Bring my beautiful little snapper here," Max requested softly. Max lifted her dress slowly, and realized to his surprise that she had nothing on under the silk dress. She told him "I have been waiting for you." He smiled, as he told her that she was a woman of infinite delight. Then he looked deeply into her eyes and said, "Baby, look out and enjoy our city."

Slowly, he gently raised her up to pull her only clothing, that black silk dress with its tiny, red, hand-painted hearts, over her head and off of her. Then, as she lay back across his six-foot desk with only her black high heels on, he began kissing her body as she viewed the city. Lights flickering out the one-way window seemed to be there for only her viewing. He kissed her body for a very long time at a slow pace, and she came to orgasm. Then, suddenly, the snapping began again. Jacqueline knew it was from the power of the city and Max. They made love on the rich green carpet, overlooking the White House lights, for hours. While the stars were still full in the sky, Maxwell took Jacqueline to the big window and turned her directly to face the view of Washington at night. As she stood naked in front of the one-way window, slowly he slipped his body into hers without blocking her view. There, for a very long time, she came from the power of Maxwell. Power really is a beautiful thing.

Sometime near sunrise they left in a taxi. Max held her in his arms. He instructed the driver to tour the city. Max told her that this was his favorite time of day, just as the sun breaks on Washington. He said, "This is when all the power is just beginning to stir. Kind of like the quiet before a storm." The taxi drove them, while Max offered a tour of the real Washington. He knew this town inside out, and he loved it. Then he directed the taxi to take them to the Dark Horse Inn, which was Max's home.

Max suggested that Jacqueline might enjoy a hot bath while he checked his messages. As she came out of the bathroom, she noticed a degree hanging behind one of the doors of his co-op. When she asked him about it he replied, "It was another time in my life. I graduated Harvard and Yale." Maxwell had a Law Degree from Harvard and a Masters in Business from Yale! She said, "Max you told me you graduated from Harvard. You forgot to mention Yale!" "Jacqueline I did not want to intimate you," was his reply. "I wanted to get to know you before I told you any more. Jacqueline, I speak nine languages, not including two Chinese dialects. They are unimportant, just earlier achievements in my life. I do not live on those achievements. I live for the new things I achieve daily. Besides the only thing that is important is making my beautiful lady snap."

He asked her, "Was the balcony the first time that you had ever snapped in multiple orgasms?" She responded, "Like that, yes!" Max said that it pleased him so to be the one to take her that high. "Jacqueline, few women have the capacity or ability for that level of enjoyment." Jacqueline thought, "Now I know what they teach at those Ivy League schools! It is smooth talking – and he must have a master's in that too." She liked the hell out of her new lover.

Max told Jacqueline that he had recently moved from a lower level of the Dark Horse to this penthouse on the twentieth floor for its balcony. She asked, "Did you have any trouble getting the penthouse?" He laughed and said, "No, I own the building. I wanted the balcony for you." He then told her, "Come see our balcony." It had a chaise lounge, much nicer than the one at the Hyatt. The lounge chair was covered in a beautiful print of roses; it had overstuffed pillows and a matching ottoman. It was just glorious. Next to it sat a marble table.

"I bought that chaise just for you Jacqueline," said Max. "No one has been allowed to sit on it, not that I have many visitors in my home. My tennis partner thought I was crazy when he started to sit on it and I told him no. I explained it was for you." Now she knew what Mike had meant when he said, "I almost sat in your chair!"

Max kissed her, as he sat her in her chaise. Then he lit an oil-filled candle, which sent a familiar fragrance into the air. Jacqueline enjoyed the scent. Max re-entered the apartment and returned with a bottle of champagne and poured her a glass. As soon as she finished one glass, he poured another, and more. Her head was spinning as she felt the effects of all of the wine. The weather was warm and sunny this spring day in Washington. Max told her, "You are so beautiful, and I am so pleased that you have chosen to share yourself with me." Then he asked her, "Are you comfortable?" She told him, "Completely."

Max asked "May I remove your robe and just look at you sitting naked in the sun?" She told him, "Yes." She had a feeling that there would very little she would ever want to deny Max. He was so kind and gentle, and she could not think of anything more pleasurable than sitting with Max naked in the sun, drinking champagne. Slowly he removed her robe, barely touching her body. Then he opened a small black box and removed an impressive diamond pendant on a platinum chain. He placed the necklace around her neck, kissing Jacqueline softly. The pendant was a star made of large diamonds, and it was the only thing she was wearing.

Next, he poured her another drink and said, "Rest, my dear, and I will be right back." Jacqueline sat in the heat of the sun wearing only a diamond necklace and sipping champagne. A few minutes later he returned with a tray of fruit, and placed it on the table next to her, kissing her and telling her to enjoy herself while he showered.

She lay naked on the balcony, sipping the champagne; eating the fresh fruit and watching the diamonds sparkle against the brown skin between her breasts. Her body was beginning to heat up from the beautiful surroundings and her anticipation of Max's return. She could feel the warmth between her legs beginning. Max returned naked and clean from his shower. He placed a beautiful, black lacquered oriental box on the marble table next to her. It was inlaid with ivory, jade, and mother-of-pearl in an intricate pattern. "Max, no more presents, this necklace is beautiful," she stated. "This is a present for both of us," Max answered.

His beautiful runner's long, lean body sat on the matching ottoman next to her. He began kissing her deeply, long slow wet kisses. Her lips were completely his. He sat up to refill their champagne glasses. Jacqueline's body was hot in anticipation of Max's touch. He opened the box, which contained a small bottle of oil, and he began rubbing the oil on her body. She recognized the fragrance, but she could not place it. Suddenly, she recognized the scent in the air! *Opium!*

She asked Max, "Is that opium?" He smiled, as he told her he had arranged for this to be delivered from the Orient especially for her. He asked, "Do you mind? You will be feeling its effect soon, if I continue." She asked, "Is this like the kind people smoke?" "Yes, darling, but this has a wondrous effect without the danger of addiction. There is a small amount in the candle, too. The oil is specially produced for use on the body. I would like to rub it on you. Do you mind?" "No, I want to feel the effect!"

He continued to rub the opium oil on her breasts. She could feel a sensation that she liked, but could not quite describe. Not hot, but warm, a kind of numb, yet tingling feeling. The sensation was wonderful, and her mind was reeling with pleasure. Max began to lick the oil from her nipples, never taking his eyes from hers. Max placed his hand between her legs, and she could feel the warmth of the oil immediately. It was the most euphoric feeling she had ever felt. He traced the oil on his lips and kissed her once again. He had found another sensation that she loved. Jacqueline could not believe what she was feeling, and Max had barely touched her body.

She was so very wet with pleasure, as Max continued to slowly place small amounts of the oil on different parts of her body. She had never felt anything like this before. Max rubbed her lips and tongue with this wonderful, sweet oil. Then he slid to the floor at the end of her chair, his hands softly placed on the inside of her thighs. He slowly touched his tongue to the oil he had so carefully placed. She thought, "My God, what is this I am feeling? My body is seeping! I feel sensations from my nipples and tongue that I have never felt before!" Max slid his tongue deep inside, and her body was snapping in multiple spasms within seconds.

She could not move, nor did she want to! It was as though she was floating on a cloud and dripping off of the edge. He continued to rejoice in her body, as her mind smelled the flowers of that long ago opium haze. Max placed pillows under her, as he lifted her body gently. She could see his eyes as he slowly moved his tongue about her. Softly, he rolled her body, slipping his hands upon her oiled nipples. She was wild with anticipation as he continued to moisten her body with his lips. Then he placed more oil on her body. Slowly, he kissed her neck, as his body began to enter hers.

She was feeling the massive seeping as he began to slide slowly inside her. Her head was spinning from the opium scent of the candle. His body was sliding deeper into her, as Jacqueline's body responded in the snapping wet orgasms of her opiate haze. Max moved in and out of her body, slowly picking up speed and depth. "There is so much of him!" she thought. He was holding her shoulders as he buried himself deep inside, seeking her wet response. She responded without hesitation, in complete trust as he moved the opium candle closer for her to smell. The opiate scent catapulted her into spasms of wet orgasms on Max's body.

She was screaming with each massive orgasm, as they discovered new pleasures together. The oil on Jacqueline's body had gone from warm to hot, and her juice was the only thing cooling her body. Max asked, "Are you okay Jacqueline?" She told him, "I am wonderful!" He began to lift her upper body slightly from the chaise as he pushed her deeply onto him. She screamed in pleasure as he thrust the last inch of his huge, oil soaked body inside her. Jacqueline's voice echoed as he entered. "Are you okay baby?" Max asked. "Yes, yes, Max." Then he began giving her the full power of Max.

When he had applied all of the physical strength he had to pleasing Jacqueline, he slowly laid her back onto the pillow. Then he reached for the candle and said, "Smell, baby." She inhaled deeply, and the opiate fragrance made her body float. Then Max placed the candle back on the table. "Are you very high, little one?" he asked. "Max," she said, "I am spinning in pleasure." "Not yet," he said, just as he placed his tongue on the very tip of her body and slowly moved it back and forth. He played on her lips with his tongue until she was wild with desire. His gentle licks became the suction of a vacuum. She flowed in a maelstrom of massive, hot, wet, orgasms; as Max received, she gave!

The next morning, she awoke with Max's arms holding her closely in the chaise. He kissed her and said, "Hello beautiful." "Maxwell, you are a powerful man. I have never felt anything like you in my life. I cannot believe the loving you gave me! Explain what that was Max?" she asked. His smile grew as he said, "It was about $5,000.00 worth of purely handled opium oil, my love!"

"I told you I would never waste money on some addicting drug like cocaine. But I will gladly spend $5,000 to take you on a trip to the Orient! This is a harmless way to play with the drug. Jacqueline, I have plenty of money. In my life I have been good at making and keeping it. I have had so much fun preparing while I was waiting for you to arrive. The box was delivered only yesterday. I am so glad we discovered a way for you to feel more pleasure. Later, I will show you another." "I can't wait Max," she said

Late that afternoon they had drinks in the city with Max's friends from the Washington war days. One friend of his, a government lawyer, came over to see Max in the bar. He asked, "Would you excuse us please? I need to talk to Max for a minute." So Jacqueline excused herself and went to the ladies room. Giving them plenty of time, she sat in the lounge area. Linda and two of her girlfriends came in. One lady whispered to the Judge. She replied "Don't worry, that is Max-A-Million's girlfriend!"

Out came the cocaine vials, and they snorted from the caps. One lady said she worked in the Energy Administration. The other was Linda's law clerk. She offered Jacqueline a line and this time Jacqueline took it, maybe because she didn't want to upset them, maybe because she wanted it. They asked how she had met Max. "We never see Max with a lady. Everyone in Washington knows he is a workaholic." Unexpectedly, the lady from the Energy Administration stroked Jacqueline's long hair and told her she was quite beautiful. Then she said to Linda, "Do you think Max would mind sharing?" Jacqueline made a graceful escape back to Max at the bar.

When she returned to the bar, she told Max about the encounter in the ladies room. Maxwell seemed upset as he asked, "Why did you take the cocaine?" Jacqueline said, "Max, I am not sure." "You can do what you like, but do not do their drugs to make me happy. That is what that asshole from the government just wanted, to borrow money for cocaine. When is the last time you did it before this?" She said "Nineteen seventy-five or so." He laughed and said, "Forget it baby, and let's go. By the way, did you catch the name of the other two women?" She said, "No, just job descriptions." "Even better" said Max with a laugh.

They returned home, and played with the oil and each other. Jacqueline enjoyed pleasing Max for all the pleasure he had given to her. She never remembered much conversation of importance, just laughter, meeting new friends, and wonderfully tender, *hot* sex. By the end of the each day, she would place the Opium Oil on her lips and mouth, beginning hours of returning the favor to Max's delicious body. You get what you give in this world!

One day, Max informed her that he was to attend a party in Alexandria, Virginia that night. He asked, "Would you care to go with me?" She told him "I would be delighted." He said, " Do not be surprised by what you see. I need to go, in case I need anyone's help later in business. This party brings out the powerful, and they put themselves in the most compromising positions. You will see men with their mistresses and plenty of drugs. Just keep saying that you just had a line. I wish this party were at another time, but one of the sex magazines and some of those publicly proper politicians put it on only once a year, so

I can't help but attend. They think they're safe from the prying eyes of the press, but they are not safe from me."

Max told her, "I really think Washington is made up of very foolish people, with strange desires. They let me see them in embarrassing positions, and later if I need something, they are more than willing to help me. Knowledge is power, and power bestows money on its holder." As they dressed for the party, Max told her that she would probably not recognize anyone unless she was familiar with Washington insiders. She said, "I am not." "Well, just enjoy yourself, and I will stay beside you all evening." Max said with a smirk.

When they left the Dark Horse for the party, Jacqueline expected a taxi, but a limousine was waiting for them instead. It was a beautiful black stretch limousine with a full bar and overstuffed leather seats. The lighting inside the limousine was as soft as candlelight. Slowly, they headed into the Washington night for Alexandria, and then they left the lights of the city behind. She could feel the excitement building inside of her, that wonderful feeling that comes from being with the powerful. Max turned to her and said, "Jacqueline, you look stunning. I will be the envy of every man at the party." She had chosen a white floor length dress of silk that buttoned completely down the front, with white heels and matching bag. She assumed most women would wear black evening dresses, so she had decided on evening white. The limousine began to slow as they approached a turn onto a very quiet road. They followed the road for a few miles, ending at a set of large iron gates with guards and dogs to greet them.

Max handed a gold invitation to the guard, who asked for picture identification. Max gave the guard his identification and Jacqueline's. He was told that he could proceed, but that the driver must stay in the vehicle at all times. Once they exited the limousine, the driver would be sent back outside the gate. When they were ready to leave, he would be allowed back in. Max said, "That will be fine." The guard handed Max back the invitation, and told him he would need it on two more occasions before they entered the party. The gates powered open soundlessly, and the limousine slowly entered the property.

The driver continued up a long, dark, winding road. There were only a few dim lights ahead. After about a quarter of a mile, the lights of a huge mansion with no cars in front appeared. It was the biggest house Jacqueline had ever seen! In the distance stood a number of men in dark suits scattered around the house. As they approached the beginning of the drive, guards again stopped them. Max was asked to produce the invitation. He again gave them the invitation and it was returned to him; the limousine was permitted to continue up the long, horseshoe drive. The limousine stopped at the mansion's steps and the doors were opened by yet more guards wearing dark business suits. The driver did not attempt to open his door. A gentleman assisted Jacqueline in exiting the limousine, and another assisted Max. The men told the driver to stay in the car. Max was asked to produce the invitation again, but this time it was not given back to him. One of the gentlemen asked if they had any cameras, and they said, "No." "Any weapons?" he asked. Maxwell's reply was the same.

They were told to proceed through an x-ray scan, and to enjoy the party. As they walked through the scanner at the bottom of the steps, the limousine left. They were invited to enter the doors of the beautiful mansion. From first appearances, this just seemed to be an upper class party of the rich. Jacqueline realized her instincts were right – all of the women she saw were wearing black formal dresses. But it was a party with an awful lot of security and secrecy! Max lifted two champagne glasses from a server's tray, and then he began introducing Jacqueline. He used first names only. They continued through the house, observing the social graces.

As they walked up the spiral staircase to the second floor, things became a little more interesting. The smell of hashish caught Jacqueline's attention. She asked Max, "Is that hashish I smell?" He laughed and said, "You are correct my dear. Would you like some?" Jacqueline quickly replied, "Max, I would love some." He laughed and said, "Sure, baby." He walked over to a mahogany coffee table with pipes laid out, and picked up a fresh one, already full. They both smoked a little as they walked and talked. "Are you stoned?" Max asked. "Definitely," she said. "Well come on, this will give you a laugh," Max whispered. "Just so you know, I am going to show you what assholes these politicians really are." The people around them just seemed to be stoned, drinking and laughing. Max was doing short introductions only when he felt the need; mostly he would just give a quick handshake.

They took an elevator to the third floor; while they were alone, Max kissed her and asked, "Are you having fun, baby?" "Yes Maxwell, I am." As the elevator doors opened, Jacqueline could hear music. Soft jazz filled the air. Max and Jacqueline walked down a long corridor and into a large library. "Maxwell obviously knows his way around this place," she thought.

Seated in the library were four men in suits, resting in leather high-backed chairs and smoking pipes; women sat next to them on the floor, with their faces resting in the men's laps. The women's lips were locked and their mouths were full! One man looked up and asked Max, "Would you and your beautiful lady like to join us for the orgy? It will be starting soon, especially if your little lady is staying." "We may be back later," Max said, "but there is someone I have to see. Enjoy yourselves, as I can see you are." Max slowly turned Jacqueline by her arm, and they left the library. She had a look of complete shock on her face. When they reached the corridor she said, "I didn't expect to see anyone I recognized, but the man who wanted us to stay was Senator...." Max shushed her, as he quietly chuckled.

Max asked, "Are you surprised at what you are seeing?" She said, "Yes, but I will tell you now, I am not interested in joining them." He said, "I would share you with no man! I just need to see who is here and what they are doing, and then we can leave." As they proceeded down the corridor, a server passed with more drinks. Max grabbed a couple more drinks and Jacqueline told him, "I need that drink!" Max laughed. They turned into a room filled with four men and five women on a big round rug in a full-blown orgy. Traces of cocaine lines were on the carved mahogany table. They did not even notice or care that Jacqueline and

Max were at the door. The couple walked away after only a few seconds, and made their way back to the lower floor of the house. After being in the upper floors, Jacqueline was glad to return to the normal party of the rich and famous.

Max did a little more hand shaking, and then using a house phone, he called to the guardhouse for their limousine. After they left the party and were back in their car, Jacqueline asked Max, "Have you been involved in some of that sex? He told her, "No Jacqueline, I go there for business. I would not allow those people to have power over me. It is important that I know who is doing what they should not. Washington is a place of power, and I hold a lot of power because of what I know." Max tapped on the driver's window. When the window slid down, Max said, "Jonathan, put up the privacy shield and drive around Washington for a while." Up came the original window, and then a solid black shield. Max turned up the music in the back. "Don't worry, the limousine is soundproof, Jacqueline. I had it specially constructed. Jonathan cannot hear us, and in any case, he is a trusted employee," Max offered.

"I will show you what I want, and it just requires the two of us," Max said with a smile. Then he began lighting a hashish pipe he had pulled from his pocket, and handed it to her. He popped the cork on a bottle of champagne. Max asked, "Is that an expensive dress?" Surprised, she said, "not too expensive, why?" "Well if I ruin it, you will get to go shopping tomorrow." She laughed. He told her he loved the button front, as he opened the first button. Chills of anticipation began going through Jacqueline's body.

"Have you ever made love in a limousine?" "No," she replied, "am I about to have the pleasure?" He kissed her deeply, as he laid her back onto the seat. His hands unbuttoning her silk dress slowly, button by button.

"Oh my beautiful lady, I love when I find you wearing nothing under your dress!" "I am here only for your pleasure Maxwell. You know that," she smiled. She was still smoking the hash, feeling blissfully stoned. Max handed her another glass of champagne, and set the pipe down. She asked, "Where is your champagne?" He smiled as he continued to unbutton the rest of her dress. His smile increased as he unveiled her naked body. Taking the champagne, he dribbled it on her nipples, and then he began to lick it off. "You are my champagne glass, my dear." The alcohol had a numbing effect and his lips were intoxicating. He poured more on her stomach, and started his descent. Then he poured the champagne lower on Jacqueline's body, and filled his mouth with champagne.

His lips proceeded to let the champagne flow from his mouth into her. Lifting her lower body and placing her legs around his neck, he proceeded to blow the champagne inside of her body. Jacqueline was thinking, "What will this man come up with next?" Then he unbuttoned his tuxedo pants. He was as large and hard as she had ever seen him. He continued to grow, as his lips were blowing her into massive orgasm. When she could no longer hold her body still to his lips, he lifted her and lowered her directly onto him. Slowly he placed his never-ending, massive organ deeper and deeper. Jacqueline screamed in pleasure, as he held her tightly. He kissed her wildly and deeply, as he continued his slow ascent into the depths of her body.

Slowly, he moved round and round. As she was screaming in abandon, he was pleasing her more than she thought was possible. Then in a gentle, swift move, he rolled Jacqueline unto her stomach without ever leaving her body, kissing her back as he reached the deepest possible point. He whispered in her ear, "I need no one else." He began stroking inside her faster and harder, as he commanded her, "Come for me, baby!" Jacqueline seeped in orgasm from the power of Max; as she felt his explosion, she was soaked with his warmth. They laid back in complete satisfaction for a while, as she felt him soften inside her. Then he slowly slipped her dress back on, and began to button it, as he pushed a switch and instructed the driver to take them home.

The morning was breaking over Washington. It was another day for them. The limousine driver slowed to a stop, the valet opened Jacqueline's door, and to the driver's surprise, Maxwell exited first. In a sweep, Max cradled Jacqueline in his arms, as he carried her from the limousine into the Dark Horse, and then into the elevator. With the push of his key button, he opened the penthouse door. Carrying her to his bed, he kissed her as he laid her down and told her, "I will run your bath." Jacqueline rested, stoned and satisfied, the evening playing like a movie in her head. Max returned to the bedroom to carry her into the bath.

Gently he placed her in the Jacuzzi tub. He began to kiss her as he reached for the soap. "Rest little one," he said, "You have had a busy evening!" Then he began to bathe Jacqueline, gently cradling her shoulders with one arm. He soaped his hand and he placed it upon her breast. He kissed her, as his gently lathered between her legs. He rolled Jacqueline over as he lathered every inch of her body. Gently rolling her back, he kissed her as he lifted her body from the water and wrapped her in an oversized towel. Reaching for another towel, he kissed her softly, as he dried her body. When he placed his lips on her breast, she felt her heat begin again.

He kneeled below her, and she was wet with anticipation of what was to come. So slowly, his tongue met her lips, just enough to cause her to soak. Then he carried her back to bed, and rested her head on a pillow. "This is how I will put you to sleep, little one." Removing his clothes and resting his head between her fresh warm thighs, he very softly licked her as she fell asleep from exhaustion in a quiet, wet, wonderful orgasm. When she woke the next morning he had begun again! She awoke with an orgasm, as Max was softly joining his body with hers. To wake from a sleep in such pleasure is truly a remarkable high. When it came to great sex, Jacqueline had always loved the morning best.

Jacqueline left on a trip to see Maxwell in Washington. She had never expected to visit the Orient. She pondered the relationship as she packed to return home. She thought, "Our best sex seems to be drug-related. Of course, we were straight that first time on the Hyatt balcony! I really do not believe Max is the one man for me. There is a lack of mental connection that will probably limit us to being no more than friends, but each of us fills a need in the other's life; and Maxwell fulfills my needs very well!" With Max at her body, she felt no fear of unlimited pleasure.

CHAPTER THREE

LIGHTING STRIKES

In the real world in which Jacqueline lived, except for her long weekend adventures now and then, business was great. She had settled in well on the little Gulf coast town of St. Augusta. She seemed to meet many kind and interesting people. In the sunshine state, people seem more relaxed. "Maybe," she thought, "it is because they do not have the wear, tear, and stress of fighting the elements." She had lived in warm weather for thirteen of the last fifteen years.

The power elite of this breezy little Florida town were referring her more business than she could ever have dreamed. One morning while she was at her office, she received a call from a gentleman by the name of Solomon Rosenberg, Esquire, as he introduced himself that day. Hereinafter, he will be referred to as "The Rose."

That day would change her life forever. Rose needed malpractice insurance, and his office was only about three blocks from Jacqueline's office. Being good at what she did, she knew it was a guaranteed sale, so she made a quick appointment for eleven o'clock that day. She figured that she would be in and out in fifteen minutes, and she would have a sale made for the day. It would be simple, but lucrative. As a matter of fact, she decided that he would be her only appointment that day.

She planned to close the sale and take the rest of the day off. Maybe she would take a trip to the beach for the afternoon. She liked to reward herself when she made a good sale. There is a lot of money to be made selling professional liability insurance. She did not need to sell a lot of polices to make a good living.

Rose had told Jacqueline that another attorney by the name of CJ Lock had recommended her. CJ Lock reminded her of Captain Ahab. He was tall, about six feet or better, was of slender build and had curly, soft gray hair. His smile could light up a room. CJ was always happy, even when he was sad. Had she known of CJ's interest in her before that day, her story probably would not have been the same. CJ was a man with whom any woman could have fallen in love. But Jacqueline did not know how he felt about her.

St. Augusta is on the Florida coast, just north of Tampa. Downtown St. Augusta has been passed over by growth. Just that week, the town council voted down another chance to develop. Jacqueline was kind of glad, since some of her most glorious memories were of downtown and of "lawyers' row." The area fronts the courthouse, and consists of five or six blocks of lawyer's offices. This was her stomping ground. Behind the courthouse rest the white sand beaches of the Gulf of Mexico. Lawyers' row was filled with the good, the bad, the rich and the poor – a small-town sampling of all that the legal profession had to offer. Since she wrote the malpractice insurance in the area, she knew many of them, and their applications told the story. Most were good. She found that a lot of them screamed poverty when it came time for them to pay their malpractice premiums, but overall she liked the lawyers, and she had great respect for their demanding profession.

The buildings of lawyers' row are of the old 1940's quaint, Florida style. The streets were lined with wind-blown palm trees; the flowers bloomed without season. The buildings had been divided into office space filled with young lawyers, with their dreams of righting wrongs; with old lawyers living off the Wills and Trusts businesses they had built after many years in practice; and with others between the two – those who had lost some of their idealism, but who had active practices. Even some bad lawyers without notable consciences passed through lawyers' row.

Jacqueline saw what most people don't realize. The professions are just like every other walk of life, filled with the good and the bad. CJ was one lawyer who loved to right a wrong, even after more than twenty years as a lawyer. He still had that spark that makes a lawyer great. In later years, Jacqueline recalled CJ's description of her as he first met her.

He told her that he would tell other lawyers, "Look for the lady in the black convertible, with a black suit, red shoes and long, dark-colored hair. You can't miss her!" Jacqueline never really thought much about it until then, although she did buy the black convertible to advertise in business. She thought she was just a good salesman; she knew her products and worked hard. She had never really considered the fact that her clothes matched the car.

Her suits were mostly dark in color, and she wore conservative white blouses beneath. Although she did own red shoes, the shoe colors did vary. "But," she thought, "CJ made his point." She had learned to wear always-appropriate business attire. She never wore anything to show cleavage as some women do, believing it will get them ahead. She was conservative in her business, with a flair all of her own. Jacqueline tried a simple concept in sales - knowledge. She studied every policy and flyer that came through her office. In the middle of her bed on Sunday morning, she worked. This is why she did not feel bad when she rewarded herself with an afternoon off.

Jacqueline was still a rebel from the 1960s, and she refused to cut her hair, even for the business world. Her hair always hung in one length of thick brown to just about the middle of her back. Her makeup was just a tube of lipstick and the sun on her skin. To Jacqueline, her hair was her last bit of freedom. It was a reminder that she was not just a mother and businesswoman. She lived by most of the rules the business world requires for her to be successful. Her hair reminded her that first and foremost, she was Jacqueline.

Jacqueline would be forty years old before she cut that hair. When she did, she donated it to the cancer society's wigs for kids program. Jacqueline never regretted cutting it; she smiled each time she saw a sick child in need of a wig, her heart feeling that she had helped. Her hair had since grown long again; apparently she was still not ready to give up that last bit of freedom.

The sidewalks connected the offices of lawyers' row. The sidewalk, along with lawyers' row, ended at the firm of Parker and Mack, were she was to meet the "Rose." Parking her convertible at CJ's office, she stopped by to say hello and thank him for the referral. Briefcase in tow, down the sidewalk she began her journey, on a Florida winter day in 1983.

Parker and Mack was a very old, well-respected law firm living on the Will and Trust business. When lawyers are young, they write a lot of wills for their clients, usually fairly inexpensively, while they are doing other work for them. By the time they get old, those people die, and the lawyers usually make better money doing the probate of their clients' estates. Secretaries watch the obituaries in the newspaper and track the wills. It was really very simple, and usually very profitable.

The firm was dark and very quiet as she entered. A beautifully dressed, lovely lady greeted her as she entered the firm. In later years, she would grow to have great respect for this lady. How could Jacqueline not admire her? The woman typed 110 words per minute with long fingernails, and took Gregg shorthand just as fast.

She escorted Jacqueline down the long hall, into the office Rose rented in the building. Seated at his desk, the wall behind him filled with diplomas and certificates of achievement, sat the Rose. His skin was naturally dark, intensified from the Florida sun. His hair was straight and black, and it receded a slight bit in the front. He was about six feet tall and was of slender build. That day, he wore an Oxford button down shirt and an Ivy League stripped tie. His eyes were so brown they appeared black, and his facial features were perfectly formed and slender, yet manly. His smile was more kindly than any she had ever seen.

Stunned at the beautiful appearance of this forty-three year old man, she tried not to show the lightning coursing through her body. Jacqueline thought, "Is this love at first sight?" As she came toward the desk, he came around it to shake her hand. She felt the warmth run through her body from his hand touching hers. "Jacqueline, it is a pleasure to meet you. You do not mind if I call you Jacqueline, do you? You seemed so friendly on the telephone. Please call me Solomon." "Thank you Solomon, Jacqueline will be fine." "Please, have a seat," as his hands touched the back of her chair as a gentle guide. Before Jacqueline stood one handsome, perfectly elegant gentlemen. Trying not to show her attraction to this handsome, obviously well educated man, she immediately got down to business. "Tell me about your professional history," she said.

Rose informed her that he had never been sued for malpractice in the twenty years he had been practicing law. He also said that he did not need the retroactive coverage, also known as tail coverage, for his previous years of practice. The United States Government covered him for those years, as he had been a government lawyer.

Rose jested, "Maybe I have not been sued for malpractice because I am a good lawyer, or maybe it is because I have had the United States Government behind me." They laughed, and she told him, "I don't care which it is," but she asked him if he knew which it was. He replied, "Yes, I am that good as a lawyer." Rose told her that for him, law had been the love of his life. From his childhood, the guests at his family dinner table were lawyers and judges. He said that the first real conversation he could remember was a legal argument. As usual, in about five minutes he was ready to sign the contact.

She pulled the application from her case. With a bad case of nerves from what she knew was her obvious attraction to this man, she suddenly realized that she could not even spell his last name, Rosenberg. She was so unnerved by his quiet, lion-like appearance, that she did not even think to look at the business cards, which sat on the edge of his business desk, or, for

God's sake, the twenty diplomas and certificates she had seen on his walls as she entered. Jacqueline was totally infatuated with this handsome, funny and most interesting man! So she did the only thing that occurred to her.

Jacqueline turned the application around to him and said, "Please fill it out. I am sure you know the information better than I do." He filled it out! Much to her amazement and relief, he had done what she asked, and saved her certain embarrassment! When he finished the form and wrote the check, Jacqueline started to leave. As she stood to go, he asked, "Have you had lunch?" She replied, "No, I have not eaten yet," as he walked her out of his office. He told the lovely lady who had greeted her earlier, "We are going to lunch." The smile on her face showed that the secretary was pleased. They went to a place called "Tio Pepe's" Restaurant; it was one of those places where professionals went to be seen.

For Jacqueline, it was fairly common for her to have lunch with business people more educated than herself. She had learned how to get by in conversation, and over the years she had gained a lot of knowledge at these luncheons. Her dress was always appropriate, and her manners came directly from the best etiquette book.

Jacqueline had realized in California that this Midwest girl needed to be polished, if she was to succeed. She watched each and every person who crossed her path. In the fine restaurants of San Francisco, she observed every move that people made. This was how she learned proper table manners. She looked carefully at the doctors' wives, and listened to the proper English that was spoken around the hospitals. In her spare time, while Marie was recovering from surgery, she read. Books on medicine, law, manners, English, style; she tired to learn everything that a young girl needed to know. After she was around the teaching hospital for a few months, people recognized her and thought she belonged there. She took advantage of that, by attending many of the college courses the hospital taught. This is what Jacqueline called, "college without tuition." So she always survived these silly little business luncheons. She never drank too much, and she was a good conversationalist. This would be just another one. Besides, she was hungry and had already given herself the afternoon off. And then, there was Rose....

"Tio Pepe's" was a happening place, a Spanish restaurant with a pleasant décor, wonderful smells, and attentive male waiters hustling about. The sounds of business chatter filled the rooms. This was a place she had never been, but they knew the "Rose!" The special table waiting for them in the back, and the fanfare, and greetings both from the owners and the patrons, told her that he was someone special.

They were seated at his quiet, reserved table in the back. Rose ordered two Tio Martinis. They were the largest martinis Jacqueline had ever seen. The dish of choice was Sea Bass à la Russe. They talked and talked as the afternoon passed. When she asked if he needed to get back to work, he said that he was done for the day. He asked if she needed to go, and she told him the same. Hours passed, as Rose told her of his life and asked of hers, while they sipped martinis. He was filled with questions about Marie and Jacqueline.

His story was of a life of privilege. He was the son of a New York City Judge; his mother was a news reporter. He was raised on Long Island. Rose read six books a week in school, he was a member of MENSA, he spoke seven languages, and he was schooled in New York City. He had enjoyed a fine upbringing in a wealthy Jewish family. He graduated Columbia University Law School in 1964. He specialized in International Double Tax Treaties!

"Hello! Boy, am I out of my league," Jacqueline thought. This was the story as she heard it that day. This man had practiced law for one of the largest law firms in Manhattan. He worked in the White House under Presidents Johnson, Ford, Nixon and Carter. Rose had worked in the Energy Administration, and he had served on the National Labor Relations Board. He helped put us in lines for gas during the Arab oil embargo fuel rationing in 1973. He had invented the odd/even system of enforcement that allowed all of us to have some fuel. Rose had argued before the Supreme Court of the United States. He had lived off the stock market in Jamaica, practicing pro bono law for the Jamaican people. Rose had even lived over a whorehouse in Paris one summer. After he left Washington, he practiced law in a small town on a mountain in Georgia, where his car was bombed for jailing a banker. Apparently, they did not like his high-tech city law in Georgia! Rose retired to Florida, only to realize that he was only forty-three. So he opened his solo practice.

They had finished lunch and each had drunk the last of a second Tio Martini. Rose casually asked her, "Do you smoke?" Since they had been chain-smoking cigarettes throughout lunch, she knew he did not mean tobacco. She responded with what she thought was a safe answer. "I lived in California in the 1970's!" He asked for the check, and they left the restaurant.

It was only a couple of miles to his home; he lived behind the walls of a gated community. When they arrived, the sheer number of books in his home shocked her. They covered most of the walls and half of the floor of his three-bedroom house. Signed pictures of Presidents and Senators with Rose were framed and hung on the walls, and more diplomas than he had in his office lined the other walls. On one of the shelves were thin, book-like jackets, containing the bound form of the many briefs he had written, argued, and won before the Supreme Court. He had written them on behalf of the United States while stoned on marijuana, she would later learn! There must have been twenty or so, including arguments on labor and energy issues.

She had never seen so many diplomas and certificates of achievement. They were from universities, Columbia Law School, the Federal Government, the Energy Administration, the National Labor Relations Board, the Arbitration Society, the United States Government RICO (Racketeer, Influenced and Corrupt Organizations Act) Bureau of Enforcement, and the Supreme Court of the United States of America. More history degrees, intellectual society awards and trial court certificates continued throughout the house. The number of certificates and awards for his achievements was at least in the fifties, but probably many more than that. Most of the unusual awards hung tucked away together in his upstairs book room.

Rose pulled out the marijuana and asked if she knew how to roll. Jacqueline said, "Sure!" She told him, "As Bogart said in Casablanca, 'I think this is the beginning of a beautiful friendship.' " Both of them were single - he wore no wedding ring, and he had told her so at lunch. That was a good thing, because she was interested in this man, and Jacqueline never dated married men. He was so smart and handsome, and he had a quality that Max did not seem to have. His education was very important to him. Rose had already taught her at least ten new things at lunch! She found his sense of humor hysterical.

This was not the first time Jacqueline had been around well-educated drug users. She was not completely shocked that Rose smoked marijuana. Over the years, Jacqueline had known accountants, doctors, lawyers, judges, and politicians who used cocaine and pot. Still, she was a little surprised because of his elite background. But he just smoked pot, as far as she knew.

He told her that he had begun smoking marijuana in his first year of law school in 1962. He found that he could really focus on his studies stoned. He continued smoking pot while at the Manhattan law firm, and throughout his career as a government lawyer in Washington. He wrote briefs stoned. Even when the FBI and CIA did their standard background checks, they never discovered his pot smoking. He said, "They were too busy looking to see if people owned any communist books to notice a little pot smoking." He also owned a copy of the <u>Little Red Book</u> by Mao Tse-Tung! He joked, "Those FBI and CIA agents were worthless! They couldn't even find that out about me!" He told Jacqueline that he felt the only way for him to fully understand whether communism was truly wrong was to read the book.

He told Jacqueline that he never, *ever* appeared in court stoned. He said that he almost always smoked a joint after court. Later, she would discover that in every inside pocket of every one of his blue blazers, he carried a little pink tranquilizer pill called Xanax. Those were for the courtroom. He said that no one else in town knew that he smoked pot.

They were comfortable smoking in his home. Jacqueline knew they were becoming fast friends. She did not expect that he would be interested in a serious relationship with her. After all, not many men are willing to take on a ready-made family. That day she knew they would only be the best of friends...maybe. Jacqueline could hope it might turn into something more. She knew that he was way out of her reach, but still, she would just be glad to have this man as her friend.

They smoked pot; neither of them had anyone controlling their schedule, so they could do as they pleased. Jacqueline's business was based on production and she was a good producer, so that gave her a lot of freedom. They laughed and smoked, as he showed her books and played operas for her. Rose had music from all over the world. He had a collection of recorded political speeches, and pictures from the marches on

Washington in the sixties. He even had a transcript of the Nixon White House tapes.

He showed her more in one day than she had learned in the last five years! He never made her feel inferior. Anyone who has smoked marijuana knows that time can just pass by unnoticed. And it did. Afternoon became evening in what seemed the blink of an eye, but it only took a telephone call to her parents for Jacqueline to know that Marie would be cared for. Having the help of her parents had given her freedom she had not known in California.

Rose was very curious about her life. He told her he was single and rarely dated. He asked if she was dating anyone, and she told him that she was dating a gentleman that lived far away. He asked, "How does it work?" She explained, "Well, since we are 'in like,' not in love, it works perfectly!" He laughed and asked, "Do you believe in love?" She told him, " With all my heart, and someday I will meet the man who also believes in it."

He changed the subject, and began to ask many questions about Marie and her years in the hospitals. "Just what did the doctors do? What were the end results? Who paid for the operations? How did she survive, being so young?" The questions came at her rapid fire, but she somehow knew they were born of interest and concern, and not of idle curiosity. His questions never seemed to be prying or judgmental. Rose had a way of making her feel comfortable and safe.

He seemed genuinely interested in Jacqueline, too. He asked, "What insurance licenses do you hold? Are you licensed through the state or the federal government?" She answered his questions one by one. At the time it seemed odd, but she had just written his malpractice insurance, so she just wrote it off as that. Mostly he wanted to know about her, not her work. "Were you scared in California alone? How did you hide your age? Is your documented age correct now? Are there any problems from that time that I could help you clear up?" She explained that she had hired a lawyer in California to clean up her falsified age. It was all taken care of. But she thanked him for the kind offer. They spent the remainder of the evening telling stories, listening to music and smoking pot. Like a child, he loved showing her his books.

He told her of the far-away places he had been. He had been skiing in the Swiss Alps, and had visited places like Ireland, China, Israel, Cairo and even Mongolia. He described, with vivid color and detail, places Jacqueline had never even heard about! He even told her how to smuggle enough pot aboard a plane to stay high while on vacation! His laugh was contagious. It was clear that Rose felt his life had been a combination of good fortune and hard work.

He was playing an album of a French singer from WWII in the background. The singer was Edith Piaf, and the music was beautiful. Rose played the songs in French for her as he explained the songs' meanings. Then, when one particular song came on the record, he did not want her to hear it. He stopped the music and moved to the next song. She asked him, "Could I hear that song?" He said, "No, Jacqueline

someday I will play that song for you, but not now."
He began showing her pictures of the Vietnam protest
marches on Washington. It was his way of changing
the subject about the song she understood that he did
not want her to hear.

He showed her surveillance photographs taken
from the White House. Then he asked her if she would
like to take a walk; they walked together in the Florida
night air. Still talking and laughing, Jacqueline was
hoping he would kiss her in the moonlight.

He told her that he wanted to change his life
from one of all-consuming work. He said, "I hope to
meet someone, marry and have children." Jacqueline's
heart fell, and she told him that Marie was the only
child she could ever have. He seemed sad as he said,
"You have a wonderful daughter; you don't need any
more. I have never had children. To be honest, I would
be happy to adopt. Does it really matter where a child
that blesses your life comes from?" "Rose is quite a
good man," Jacqueline thought.

She asked him, "A man like you does not want
to have a child of your own genes?" He said sincerely,
"Well, I guess every man wants that, but being this
smart is not always a blessing and it could be a curse
that passes on." They sat at the edge of the bay
enjoying the night air. He began talking about the law
firm he planned on building. Jacqueline asked, "How is
that going to keep you from working so much?" He
told her that he planned to wire the firm to his home by
computer. "You see Jacqueline, I have been around
computers for a very long time, and I understand their
ability to make man's life better. The technological

discoveries of the last twenty and the next twenty years will change the way men and women work. It will make life more comfortable. I see the future of technology."

They began a slow walk back to his home. She told him that she wanted to find someone who could love both Marie and her. Rose said, "I cannot imagine that it will be hard. Can I meet Marie some time?" Jacqueline told him she would like that. They continued their walk back in the beautiful Florida night air. He told her how happy he was to be living in warm weather; he had spent too many years in the north. She told him that she could not agree more. Rose told her he began coming to Florida as a young child. His parents bought apartments in Miami and Palm Beach.

The evening too soon came to an end. Jacqueline craved more, but knew she had to go. Everything in her wanted never to leave this man's side; he was a wellspring of knowledge, and she was highly aroused by him. His was a well from which she wanted to drink! Even if there was some spillage, she knew she would ingest a great amount of knowledge while trying to drink it all in. It was exercise for her mind just keeping up with him, but she loved the challenge and she wanted more.

Rose was a shining star, full of energy and knowledge, and sharing it all. Playing, laughing and smoking! Being with him was like watching a one-man play on a stage. As evening turned into night, he informed her that he had extra rooms if she wanted to spend the night, and that she would not be bothered. She knew this perfect gentleman was telling the truth, but she decided that she should go.   Without him offering even a kiss goodnight, she left.

CHAPTER FOUR

THE COURTSHIP

In her home, late that night, Jacqueline lay in bed with her head spinning. It was filled with wonderful thoughts and ideas. Rose had opened her mind again. It felt just like it did in the California years; it had tasted knowledge, and it longed for more. She could feel the sudden desire to learn again. Her brain was requiring food, and she knew that it was a craving that would not subside. Jacqueline first felt the hunger in California, and she felt it again tonight. As she drifted off to sleep, she recognized that while she was with Rose, she felt his brainpower bring her to life. Jacqueline wished the evening had never ended.

Her physical attraction to Rose was wonderful. He was a tall, dark and handsome man, but Jacqueline knew many of them. She was attracted to intellect – that was a man's real attraction. If a man had nothing to teach her, she would not stay around him for very long. She knew that she had made a friend when Rose trusted her with the secret of his pot smoking. Rose had judged her in only a few hours, and made the decision to trust her. He was right; she would never use his confidence to harm him.

The next day was Saturday, and Jacqueline had promised to take Marie shopping for school clothes. They always had a lot of fun. At breakfast with her dad and mom, Jacqueline was bursting with excitement as she told her family about this wonderful friend she had met yesterday. She explained they were only friends. Her father immediately replied, "Then he is a fool." Oh, how her father loved her! After his death, he became the chief star jumper in God's universe, according to Jacqueline. "He jumps from star to star making sure everyone is being good!" She was the product of a fortunate childhood, filled with love and attention. She had a good upbringing, and her early marriage was strictly a thing of the times.

Just as Jacqueline and Marie were about ready to walk out the door to go shopping, the telephone rang. Her dad handed the telephone to Jacqueline. It was Rose! She was shocked when he asked, "What are you doing today?" She replied, "Marie and I are going school shopping." He asked, "May I join you?" Jacqueline turned to Marie and asked her if she would mind. With a smile, Marie said "Sure, Mom." Marie loved to see her mom happy, and she knew this man had made her mother happy the day before. Besides, she was curious and wanted to meet him. She didn't get to meet many of Jacqueline's friends.

They agreed on a meeting place outside of the St. Augusta Mall. By the time they arrived, she had no expectations, as she was completely shocked that Rose would want to join them shopping for school clothes! "Anyway," Jacqueline decided, "we will just shop as we normally do." After introducing Marie to Rose, Jacqueline explained how they shopped for school clothes. Rose was excited. He had never done this before, since he had no children. Jacqueline explained, "It is simple, we all pick out outfits until we have ten complete ones, then we lay them all out, and Marie picks the five that she wants the most. Any questions?" He had only one. "What size does Marie wear?"

Like an overgrown kid, Rose was finding things on the racks, laughing and enjoying himself. They laid out all ten outfits, to the total dismay of the sales clerk, on her counter. They stood back and Jacqueline told Marie to pick her favorite five outfits. Rose and Jacqueline were watching as she picked her five outfits. When she had decided, Jacqueline told the clerk to give her the five she wanted. Out of the blue, Rose handed the clerk his credit card and said, "Give them all to her." Marie jumped for joy! What could Jacqueline say except, "Rose, you don't have to do that!" Rose smiled and said, "I became a lawyer so nobody could tell me what to do! Now hurry, I am buying lunch."

The sales clerk smiled as she bagged the clothes. Rose insisted on carrying all the bags, only to surrender some on the way to the car, when his arms were breaking. Rose said, "Let's go to Tio's." Marie liked him. "Oh, Mom, he is so nice." "Marie he is just a friend," Jacqueline warned. She had planned on spending about four hundred dollars; Rose had just spent eleven hundred without blinking.

He and Marie were talking about going to another store while they were sitting at the table in "Tio Pepe's," but Jacqueline had to put a stop to that. While Marie was in the rest room, she explained to Rose that he could not keep spoiling Marie. He declared, "No one could spoil that child! She is extremely nice. Just let me spend what I want. Nothing I do could undo the good raising you have done, Jacqueline. I am enjoying it, and I can afford it."

When Marie returned to the table, they agreed: no more clothing stores, as long as they could go to the bookstore after lunch! In the bookstore, Rose was just as excited as Marie, showing her all the maps of the world. He bought her five or six maps and a couple of books, and then he took them to dinner. They took all of their new books and maps into the restaurant. Rose asked for a large table, where they ate and played for hours. You could see the joy in his eyes as he was teaching Marie. The same joy was reflected in hers from learning. Rose said, "When I was a child I was never allowed to take a book to the table. Now I love going into a restaurant with books."

As the evening ended, Marie and Jacqueline went home. Jacqueline still could not believe how wonderful this man was. Her father, laughing at the mountain of Marie's new clothes said, "He must be nice." Marie says, "Oh Grandpa he's real nice." The telephone rang. When Jacqueline's father answered it, he said with a smile, "The gentleman would like to pick you up for cocktails." Jacqueline's father relayed Rose's message to her. "He could pick you up in an hour, if that is convenient." She said simply, "Yes," and her father gave him the directions. Her dad laughed, and said with love in his voice, "Just friends Jacqueline? He seems to be very interested in you!"

Within an hour, the doorbell rang. Rose greeted Jacqueline's father with a handshake, and handed him a business card. Rose told him not to worry. "If we are going to be late, I will call." Then he assured her father of Jacqueline's safety, spoke pleasantly with her mother, and admired Marie in one of her new outfits, never saying that he had bought them. Not a nicer gentleman had ever appeared at her door. She knew that she would always remember Rose the way he was that day. He was the kind of man every father dreams will someday come to the door for his daughter.

He took her to Caramels, a 1950s place. They spent the evening talking, dancing, laughing and drinking. He was a wonderful dancer, and Jacqueline liked it when he held her in his arms. He held her very close, and yet extremely tenderly. She felt like she was floating as he moved her across the floor. Rose told her that it had been ten years since he danced closely like this. Jacqueline hated for the song to end; she wanted to stay in his arms. His scent was natural and wonderful. He took her hand so gently to lead her to the dance floor, and then just as gently, he returned her to their table.

He seemed more and more curious about Marie. He told Jacqueline how wonderful Marie was. He said, "Maybe God will bless me with such a daughter someday, but first I will have to find a wife. Jacqueline, being the best at law has consumed my life. I really did not realize just how much I had missed, until I played with Marie today. You have done a wonderful job with your child. It is even more amazing, because you were so young. She is smart, kind, and polite; she is a most beautiful child. She is any father's dream."

This man seemed so gentle and caring, but she could see his mind working all the time. Jacqueline had noticed a trait in Rose that she really liked, and he did it so naturally. He always stood when she left the table or room and again when she returned. He lit her cigarette in public or private. He was wholly and completely a true gentleman. There was nothing fake about Rose; he really was that way.

Not missing a beat, he bought Jacqueline a white rose from the flower lady. Unexpectedly, another woman that Rose knew came up to the table. She asked him, "Do I get one too?" Rose complied, and as the flower girl handed the other lady the rose, it broke. She told the flower girl to give her another flower. Rose said, "No that's enough." She left, and Rose explained that the woman is a friend with bad manners. He continued to explain to Jacqueline, that she was only an acquaintance.

The white rose he gave Jacqueline that night would last for eight days on his dining room table. As she would later learn, that was the same amount of time the oil lasted for the Jewish people who had just recovered control of their temple. Rose would later tell her that this sign confirmed his original thoughts of her. "Only for a good woman would such a flower bloom," he said.

It was about three a.m. as they pulled up to her house. Rose informed her that he had made the appropriate call to her father at midnight, so that her father would not worry. She was twenty-seven years old, but she thanked him anyway. He told her, "I had a wonderful evening." She told him that she could not remember having such a good time. They agreed that they would do it again soon. He walked her to the door. Without even a kiss goodnight, their evening ended.

On Sunday morning, the call came at about eleven-thirty a.m. It was Rose. "Would you and Marie like to go to brunch and go swimming after?" Brunch at the restaurant came after another book-buying spree in St. Augusta Mall. He told Marie of college, and of all that she had to look forward to. The books he bought her that day were picture books on art. Rose named the artist, and showed her how she could recognize the artist's work. He so enjoyed teaching her.

To be honest, Jacqueline did not know much about art either, but she began learning that day. After lunch, they went to the pool for a swim. Marie, as always, made friends with the neighborhood kids at the pool. Rose asked Jacqueline, "Is Marie a good swimmer?" She told him, "Yes, I was a diver in school, she came by that one naturally." He then walked over to his neighbor, who was a physician, sitting at the pool. "Dr. John, would you keep an eye on Marie and her friends? We need to step away for a few minutes, and then we will be right back." "Sure Rose, I plan on being here for a while; I will not leave until you return."

Rose said, "Thank you, Doc." As they started to leave, Rose whispered, "Good. Jacqueline, lets go smoke a joint." They took a few hits from the joint, and then they returned to the pool. Marie played, while Rose and Jacqueline talked as they watched her having fun. From the look on his face you could see he was enjoying every minute of watching Marie at play.

He had begun to give Jacqueline some of his personal books. Over the course of that first weekend, he gave her three of them. They were books she had never heard of, such as The Ideas and Opinions of Albert Einstein. "Jacqueline," he said, "Einstein was a great thinker." It was always one of her very favorite books. With each book Rose gave Jacqueline, he told her the reason he was giving it to her, and what treasures laid between the covers of the book. Only once did he give her a book to read with a cryptic explanation. What he said was, "Read this. This is how I knew you before we even met. When I met you, I saw Gabriela." The title of the book was Gabriela, Cloves and Cinnamon. The story was of a sensual girl from the tropics, filled with love for life.

Jacqueline was reeling from the amount of knowledge coming out of this man, and all of it in an environment of fun. Learning from him was like eating candy. My God, could she be falling in love with a man that had never even kissed her! This was possibly the healthiest, yet most totally unhealthy relationship she had ever entered. But then, love is a great contradiction.

The weekend was over, and they both went back to their work lives. At eleven a.m., flowers arrived at Jacqueline's office with an invitation to lunch. This time it was to a place called the "Judge's Chambers." The "Judge's Chambers" was located downtown on lawyers' row. The entrance to the restaurant was on the second floor, at the end of a slow walk up a dark staircase. As they entered the room, Jacqueline could hear the chatter getting louder. There were fifty lawyers drinking, talking, chatting and arguing in one room. She knew that cases were being decided, and lives were being changed, all before her eyes. Jacqueline had never seen so many brains at work in one room. She could smell power in the air.

Everyone turned to say hello to Rose. Some wondered who the woman was – Jacqueline could see it written on their faces. Some knew that she was an insurance agent who specialized in malpractice coverage, and were joking, "Watch out, she knows everything about all of us." Over at a table near the bar, CJ sat, awaiting their arrival. "God," Jacqueline thought as they walked toward the table, "CJ has a glorious smile." As they sat down, CJ called Rose "paper man." It was a joke. Rose had a reputation for hitting the lawyers on the other side with enough legal papers to read, that no other work but reading could be done for a week.

CJ turned to Jacqueline and said, "Had I known that this was going to happen, I would have never given Rose your telephone number! Leave him! I'm the man for you." Jacqueline could see that CJ was ribbing Rose, his old friend. They all just laughed. Later, she sometimes wished that she had turned right instead of left (wing) that day, but most days she was glad that she turned left. CJ later married his soul mate, one of Jacqueline's girlfriends, a doctor, and they lived happily ever after. CJ and Jacqueline were meant to be the best of friends, but only friends.

She had never been to the "Judge's Chambers" before. The walls were covered with cartoon drawings of judges. Later she would learn these were Spy prints from Vanity Fair. As she looked around this dark room filled with power, she realized that this was the world she loved. It was the aura of privilege, of people who can usually control their own destiny, and who can have what they want and do what they want. She knew this was the world she wanted.

Rose excused himself, and went to the restroom. As he walked away, CJ told Jacqueline, "That man has forgotten more law than most of us will ever know. But do not forget, Jacqueline, that the law is an evil mistress." She responded with, "No CJ, she is a great companion." He smiled and replied, "You are beautiful, kid!" CJ loved to call her kid. In CJ's eyes, she would always remain that very young woman who came strolling into his office one sunny Florida day. About a year before, he was one of the first lawyers in St. Augusta to whom she had sold insurance. They had been close friends since that day. Jacqueline always felt blessed because of his friendship and his enduring love for Marie.

Day after day, the fun and excitement continued. The "Judge's Chambers" became their favorite lunch spot. Rose would hold her hand or take her arm, but never gave her a kiss. He always made sure she was on the inside as they walked down the street. He was truly a gentleman. After a few months, they began seeing each other less frequently, as their business lives returned to their hectic pace. They would still see each other two or three time every week, and they always had fun, yet still he never tried to kiss her. Jacqueline was sure that he was not gay; he had told her that, as if he felt it was important for her to know.

Just friends; she knew from that jerk of a lawyer Charles, "Jewish lawyers from New York don't marry WASP woman with children." That is a statement she never forgot. Hell, she did not even know that she was a WASP; she had to ask Rose what it meant. He laughed as he explained with tenderness in his eyes, "It means a girl who is not Jewish, a White Anglo Saxon Protestant, Jacqueline - you." He asked where she had heard the term. Although she did not tell him of the statement Charles had made, she explained that someone had mentioned that she was a WASP.

Max still popped in and out of town, and Jacqueline flew to Washington now and then, and there were always kisses. They spent the days in Washington drinking with other business people. A few lawyers and judges passed through, but most were political figures and businessmen. One government lawyer Max and Jacqueline ran into knew Rose. He asked Jacqueline if Rose was still the tough lawyer he was in the old days. He said, "I could tell you stories of that guy in court. Lawyers hated to have 'the Rose' on the other side. He was a lawyer's lawyer, a commanding force in a courtroom. I always liked him personally. He was a really funny, personable guy." The man who was talking could see that Maxwell was not enjoying the conversation, and changed the subject. Jacqueline really wanted him to continue. She wanted to know everything he knew about Rose, but it was clear that Max was not happy to hear about Rose's virtues.

Most of the time, Max and Jacqueline would take a taxi when they went out on the town. On more than one occasion, they would drive Max's Porsche. If they drank to excess, they would take a taxi home, and sometimes they would forget where they had left the car. The next morning, they would have fun looking for it. Max's drug of choice was alcohol, but fifty percent of the people she met in Washington offered them cocaine or pot. Max always said, "Not today." After a while Jacqueline realized, not today was really not any day for Max. Max liked to drink, but she never saw him extremely intoxicated. He seemed to almost appear sober even after drinking. Maybe it was because Max was a people watcher. He obtained his power and money by knowing people in Washington and watching their bad habits.

Washington is a town of excesses. Jacqueline could not go to the ladies room without seeing someone with their coke vial out, offering it to her as though it were candy. Judges, lawyers and businessmen - all were using the favorite drug of choice, alcohol, but many also chose the more dangerous drug, cocaine. In Jacqueline's California days, she had seen the damage of heavy drug use; this was a road she chose not to take. Pot smoking had pretty much always been her limit.

She knew life was best lived not in excess, but in moderation. This allowed her to sample all of life's fruits. Jacqueline savored nearly every new experience she could find. But she lived her life without too many bad habits. Her temperance allowed her to survive her sampling days in California and Washington unscathed.

Some people in Washington drank from morning to night, each one trying to make the right connection, all of them trying to climb the ladder to somewhere. This is the city of alcohol use before, during, and after business hours; the days began with a Bloody Mary for breakfast and continued on to the afternoon Scotch. The evenings were filled with drinks. Max and Jacqueline drank as much as most. Max encouraged her to drink Grand Marnier, a 12 year-old orange liqueur. Jacqueline's father used to call it pure jet fuel; he said it was the closest thing to good moonshine he had ever tasted.

Rose knew of Jacqueline's trips to Washington and only asked if she enjoyed herself, then he told her of places to be sure to see on her next trip! Maybe he thought it was business. He never asked her. Or maybe he just did not care. She was sure he knew she was going to Washington to see someone. Jacqueline realized that she must face the fact that he was not interested in her in the same way she was in him. She thought that he saw her only as a friend, but even so, she still felt quite lucky. She knew that she loved Rose very much, but she realized that, "Jewish lawyers from New York do not marry WASP woman with children."

This was her last trip to Washington; when she arrived at the airport with Max, they had to say their good-byes at the security station. The police had informed them that there was some trouble in the airport, and only passengers could continue from that point. With one last, sweet goodbye kiss, Max was gone.

As she continued to her plane, she felt a sudden jerk, and her purse was stolen. Police came from everywhere, and tried to comfort her, but the purse was gone. They took a report, and she boarded the plane in tears. A few minutes before takeoff, an officer arrived on the plane with her purse. Everything was inside, including six hundred dollars in cash. How lucky could a lady be? She thanked the officer, then settled in for her flight home; with fond memories of another long Washington weekend, she fell fast asleep.

Jacqueline returned to Florida and was working hard again. One summer evening, after dropping money from malpractice premiums in Tampa, she began her drive across the Crystal Cove Bridge. This is one of the most beautiful drives in Florida. A long bridge stretches miles between Tampa and St. Augusta, providing a tranquil view of the bay. From the bridge she could see the blue of the water, the reds and yellows of the setting sun, and the palm trees swaying in the warm Florida breeze. She stopped at the beginning of the bridge, and abruptly decided to turn the car around. Jacqueline was dead tired, and she was feeling the stress of her hectic life. She decided that she needed a visit with Betty Jean at the Hyatt. Sometimes, everyone just needs contact with that special friend; Betty Jean was a person who always made her feel better.

When she arrived at the bar where Betty Jean worked, she was surprised to see that the place was completely packed. There was a pre-Super Bowl party in progress! Tampa was hosting the Super Bowl, and the town was buzzing! Jacqueline had been so busy that she had forgotten it was Super bowl weekend. The week before, she had attended one party on Saturday night, and she ended up being the tour guide for ten New York Yankees baseball players. They followed her black convertible in minivans all over Tampa. They all drank and danced the night away. Jacqueline's coworkers were surprised two weeks later when a telephone call came from those New York Yankees! Mr. Strong, who owned the company, came into her office as she took the call. "They just called to thank me," she said. Mr. Strong's only comment was, "Only you Jacqueline," with a smile. With ten Yankees in tow, she had been the envy of every woman in Tampa. They were nice gentlemen, and they just wanted to have some fun.

As Jacqueline was speaking to Betty Jean at the bar, she noticed a lot of commotion in the back. "What is that all about?" she asked. Betty Jean said, "Those are a couple of businessmen from out of town. They have been trying to find a fish house for dinner. How long are you going to be here?" "Just until I finish this drink," Jacqueline replied. Betty Jean asked, "Would you mind showing those gentlemen the way to 'Crawdaddy's Restaurant' on your way home? They are really nice; they have been coming here for a couple of years." Jacqueline replied, "Sure, tell them they can follow the black convertible when I leave." Betty Jean walked over to the crowded area where they were seated. Jacqueline could see them nod, as Betty Jean returned to finish her drink.

It was about eight p.m. Jacqueline had not eaten, and she was ready to go home. When she was ready to leave the Hyatt, Betty Jean motioned to the gentlemen. They stood and followed Jacqueline out. Outside, Jacqueline told them, "Follow my car; this place is on my way home." As they arrived at the area of the restaurant, she decided to go into the parking lot with them; there were three restaurants back there, and she knew which one had the best seafood.

In front of the restaurant, one of the gentlemen came over to the car to thank her. He asked if she had eaten. She told him that she needed to get home. He said, "It is Friday night. Come have dinner with us, so two old businessmen do not have to eat alone." They were right. It was Friday. She had no plans, and it seemed to be safe. She gave her car keys to the valet, and joined them for dinner.

The gentlemen were delightful; one was an architect. Years later, she would see his Philadelphia bachelor apartment in Better Homes and Gardens magazine. They had wonderful conversation and a great dinner. Then Jacqueline asked, "Why were all the people flocking around you at the Hyatt?" Dan, the architect, responded with, "Are you going to the Super Bowl on Sunday?" "No, I don't have tickets," she said with a chuckle. He looked the other gentleman in the eye, then he reached into the inside pocket of his suit coat, and pulled out two tickets to Super Bowl 18 in Tampa on Sunday. "You are going now," he said, as he handed her the tickets.

He told her that everyone at the Hyatt was trying to buy them. He said, "Normally, there are four of us from college who meet at all the Super Bowl games; this year two could not come. There was no one at the Hyatt who we wanted sitting next to us. Bring a girlfriend. We don't want to sit next to a guy." Jacqueline thanked them, and they parted company. The tickets were a complete surprise. Betty Jean was working Super Bowl Sunday, so that ruled her out for the other ticket.

Jacqueline's secretary was from Washington, D.C., and she had been talking about how she would love to see that game. Susan was a big football fan. Jacqueline really was not, but she knew that she would enjoy a Super Bowl game. About midnight, she called Susan to tell her that they were going to the Super Bowl. Susan was beside herself! In later years, Jacqueline was glad she took Susan, of all people. Eight years later, Susan's crazed, estranged husband would murder Susan Mills. He climbed into the kitchen window of her home while she was at work. When she arrived home from work, he was hiding inside, waiting for her. He would tie her up and shoot her, leaving two children behind. Jacqueline was so glad it was Sue she decided to take to the game; Sue was so excited, and they had a wonderful time that day.

They attended the game and everything was wonderful. The day was exhilarating! The stadium was filled with people and fun. The place was packed, and security was tight. As they made their way to their seats, Jacqueline could see that the gentlemen who gave her the tickets were already seated. She introduced Sue to them, and they all enjoyed the game together; the gentlemen were wonderful.

It was the Washington Redskins against the Oakland Raiders. Since Jacqueline had lived in San Francisco, California, next to Oakland, she was rooting for Oakland. Although they were called the Los Angeles Raiders, they were still the Oakland Raiders to her. Her team was winning by a landslide. About five minutes before the game was over, they all decided to leave. The gentlemen had a private plane at the airport awaiting them. Sue and Jacqueline hoped that they would beat some of the traffic. So they said their goodbyes at the gate; the gentlemen went to the left, and the women turned right. About three minutes later, as the women were walking toward their car, a car came through the parking lot and hooked Jacqueline's arm on the mirror. She could see a man and a woman through the window. The next thing she knew, she was thrown over the back of the car, flying through the air. The world went black.

She regained consciousness in the ambulance, with Sue at her side. Jacqueline told Sue not to call Jacqueline's family, because Marie would be hysterical. The hospital treated Jacqueline, wrote her some prescriptions, and released her with her arm in a sling and wearing a neck brace. Finally, all the milk she had drunk over the years paid off. She had no broken bones. To say the least, her family was stunned when she arrived home, but at least they could see she was alive.

Jacqueline returned to work the next day, with some pretty good bruises. She was very sore, and her arm was still in the sling. She did not like the look of the sling, so she decided to make the silk scarves that matched her suits into slings. Everyone got a laugh about that. Taking a Demerol tablet, she went back to work. For the next few months, she worked just like that. The doctors kept her very stoned on Demerol so she would feel no pain, since they knew her arm, back, and nerves were involved. They put her on Demerol, hoping that she would heal.

That Monday, Rose called her for lunch. He had received the white roses she had sent him for all the kindness he had shown Marie. He said, "This is the first time a woman has sent me flowers. Now I know why women like it so much." She told him she had a surprise for him, and they agreed to meet for lunch. He was quite shocked when she walked into the restaurant for lunch. With her bruises and her arm in the sling, she entered the restaurant. Rose saw her and came straight up out of his chair, with a scream, "Jacqueline!" She told him, "Calm down Rose, I am fine."

Even after an explanation of what had happened to her, Rose still appeared very upset. He started asking her many questions. The first was, "With whom did you attend the Super Bowl?" "Now, this is a first," she thought. "I traveled to Washington, and he does not ask who I was with!" Next he asked, "Who knew that you were going to the game?" Finally, getting some kind of satisfaction from her answers, he told her he would pick a lawyer in the area that handled that kind of law. She asked Rose; "Can't you handle it?" He said, "I prefer not to handle it myself." He also apologized for asking so many questions. His explanation for all the questioning was, "I wanted to make sure that no one did this with malice." Jacqueline said, "Of course not!" Rose picked a lawyer in town and the months passed.

The injury to her arm was more severe than the doctors had initially thought. It required surgery, and the relocation of the nerves in her arm. By now, she had spent months on Demerol, and she was no longer able to work. The lawyers were getting nowhere with her claim. Insurance companies are less than nice, even to one of their own.

Finally, out of frustration Rose said, "Fire them! I will handle this case. I want it done! Since we are not sleeping together, there seems to be no real conflict of interest. Besides, only CJ knows what good friends we are. There are no ethical laws against representing a friend!" Rose decided to ask for CJ's help to either get the case settled or to take it to trial. Jacqueline's two best friends were protecting her. The insurance company could not lay a glove on her no matter how hard they tried. They even had a surveillance man with a camera hiding in her father's bushes, watching her. The sad truth is that Jacqueline was not exaggerating her injuries, and so the private investigators never had anything juicy to report to the insurance company.

When the insurance company wanted to take Jacqueline's deposition, Rose was very upset and told CJ, "They are not deposing her even if I have to make new law to stop it." CJ told Rose that he would handle the deposition, and that they would be unable to take advantage of her. He advised Rose not to go because he was getting too close to her, and CJ was afraid the other side would see something in Rose's face. CJ's statement made Jacqueline feel good. She thought, "Rose is getting too close to me!" CJ attended the deposition ~ith Jacqueline. He caused so much disruption ___ insurance company's lawyers could barely w___ ___eposition. They rushed through it, and ___ ___ to depose her again.

___had grown to eight ___ The walls were filled ___ave needed; that was the ___ going to win, he needed ___ps. Rose had rented over ___located directly across from the ___ ___eline had first met him. Rose had built ___ ___is dreams during the year and a half or so th___ known each other. He was the rainmaker of new business for the firm. Everyone wanted Rose to handle his or her case, because he was that good. He would sign up the clients, get the litigation started, and the young associate lawyers would run with the ball. If they hit any roadblocks, Rose was right there to pitch in.

After her surgery, Rose suggested that while she was convalescing, that Jacqueline should spend some time reading up on the law. "After all," he said, "maybe some day you will want to become a lawyer!" Jacqueline wondered if that was Rose's way of suggesting that something more serious than friendship might eventually happen between them. She decided that the drugs were clouding her mind! Rose had given her no reason to think that – after all, he had not even kissed her. But she took him up on his kind offer. It was a chance to learn, and Jacqueline would never pass up an opportunity to gain knowledge.

Overlay (sales receipt graphic):
Sales Receipt
Abacus Books, Inc.
$9.42 Book Cost
.58 Sales Tax
$10.00 Total Sale

Jacqueline spent her days stoned on Demerol and reading in Rose's private law library. She learned more about the law every day. Betty Jean used to call her a bookworm, because of her quest for knowledge. She was in, as Betty Jean called it, "Jacqueline's heaven," as she studied every kind of law. Day after day, she would read in the law library. Weekends would come and go. Marie would play with Rose and Jacqueline at lunch and dinner. She would hang around the law firm when she was not in school. What a way to go through litigation! With Rose and CJ, she felt as though she had two bodyguards, one on each side of her.

CHAPTER FIVE

THE SETTLEMENT

As the trial of her case grew near, Jacqueline could not help but think of the long, tortured course her case had taken. When she first approached Rose about taking her accident case, he would not, because their relationship was too close. He told her that, "there would be an appearance of impropriety," because they were good friends. She hoped at the time that the real reason he would not handle her case was that he thought that his feelings for her might cause him problems in remaining impartial. So, she accepted his refusal of the representation, with high hopes for love to blossom. But the relationship had not gone where she expected it to go.

Nor had the representation by the local personal injury firm she had retained when Rose told her that he would not handle her case. It was a high profile firm that did a lot of advertising, and the firm had a good reputation among local lawyers. So Jacqueline signed a representation contract with them. But after more than eighteen months, the firm seemed to be going nowhere with her case. One lawyer was so overly attentive and sloppily sweet to her, she hated to contact the firm about her case's lack of progress. If she got lucky and didn't come in contact with him, all of the other lawyers were condescending to her. She couldn't stand that, either!

She was aware of what was needed to work up a case. Her dealings with all of the local lawyers in her insurance business had taught her much about the practice of law. She knew that the firm was not doing everything it could to effectively represent her. She also knew that unless the firm aggressively pursued her case, that she would not recover as much as possible for her injuries. There were two potential defendants, and Jacqueline had been seriously injured. If the firm played it correctly, the defendants would end up fighting each other, and make her case easier. After a year and a half, a lawsuit still had not been filed, even though negotiations with the insurance carriers had broken down months before. Jacqueline knew that the firm had been ignoring her case. That was when she went back to Rose, to ask him again to help her, this time by taking over the ongoing case.

Rose had been livid about how the other firm had mishandled Jacqueline's case when he agreed to assume control of it. Rose had immediately associated

CJ to help, and Jacqueline had fired the other firm. Rose had quickly filed suit, and in about six months, the case was set for trial.

Shortly before trial, Jacqueline overheard Rose tell CJ, "I want this case settled!" Only a week before trial, the first negotiations began. After six hours of negotiations, it was over. The lawsuit finally settled, and Jacqueline was just waiting for the check to clear Rose's trust account. Was Rose anxious to settle the case because it had interfered with his plans for romance with her? She had been waiting forever! Would her relationship with Rose be about to go to a new level? She had thought so in the past, and was wrong. She could no longer be sure.

The next day, while the check was clearing and Rose was in court on another case, Maxwell came to town. When Jacqueline arrived at her home, she found a dozen red roses and the key to his room at the Hyatt where he was waiting for her. There was also a note that said, "Can you meet me for lunch? Room 1200. Max." By now, she realized that she had to stop seeing him. There was at least a chance with Rose, and she wanted that chance. Jacqueline was completely in love with a man who had never even kissed her. She might be a fool, but Jacqueline felt she could see love in his eyes for her.

He had been her lawyer for the last six months, and because of his ethics nothing could have developed between them during that period. She still felt there was something looming on the horizon. Maybe it was just wishful thinking, but she had to find out. She still could not get that statement out of her mind: "Jewish lawyers from New York do not marry WASP woman with children."

She decided to accept Max's invitation for lunch and break off their relationship. As she pulled into the Hyatt, she knew that this would be hard, but she also knew that Max would understand. They were good friends and wonderful lovers, but they had never made any commitment to each other. That was always how they both wanted it. As Jacqueline arrived at his room, she realized that it was the same room where they had first touched one another, so long ago. She knocked on the door as she placed the key in the lock. The door opened, and as Max dropped his towel to the floor, his wet arms swept her up. He kissed her as he carried her to the balcony. His lips were so warm and tender. She did not want him to stop. She wanted to be touched; that was the one thing missing with Rose. She still knew that this was goodbye, but what a goodbye it would be!

Max laid Jacqueline down on the very same chaise of so long ago. His deep, wet, and wonderful kisses had not stopped since the door opened. He lifted her summer dress; her panties fell to the floor. His succulent lips were between her legs. She lost track of time as she had orgasm after orgasm. Finally, he slid his perfectly erect manhood inside of her. No woman could be expected to ask him to stop. God had blessed him with at least eight thick, wonderful inches of pure ability to satisfy a woman.

Hours passed, alternating between his strong, powerful body and warm soft tongue inside of her. He licked her nipples until they stood rock hard and erect.

Back and forth he went, attending to each part of her body. His only desire was to please her. Oh, how he pleased Jacqueline! Saying goodbye had never been so hard, or the prelude so pleasurable.

He rolled her over and began rubbing her body down with a wonderful cream. The scent of lemons was everywhere. How did he know that she loved lemons? After he had rubbed her with the cream from head to toe, he began licking every inch of her body again. He started at her feet. Then up her legs his tongue flowed. This was edible lemon cream! Across her stomach, up to her breasts, around and around her nipples went his tongue, then up to Jacqueline's neck and on to her lips, kissing her gently for a long time.

Then he slowly rolled her body over and began his decent down, first to the back of her neck, then down her spine to the outer part of her legs. Slowly, very slowly, his tongue licked his way up the insides of her legs. He finally returned to her back as though it were a world tour, with kisses. The shining sun intensified the heat from the cream. Jacqueline's body was on fire, cooled only by the wetness between her legs. Very slowly, his tongue slid deeply into her body as she began to snap again in multiple orgasms.

Max loved to hear her cry out in orgasm. Lying on her stomach, she began to feel his entry into her body. She was seeping as he slowly moved in and out of her, telling her how beautiful she was. He was kissing the back of her neck, while pushing himself deeper and deeper inside. His hands were free to hold her breasts as his fingers played with her nipples. The heat of the sun was baking the cream on her back, and then suddenly came the explosion of a man who had been waiting only for her. She could hear his cry echoing from the balcony as he filled her body. Finally, some six or eight hours after her arrival, they collapsed.

Max looked over and said, "Baby, it looks like lunch has become dinner. Where would you like to eat?" Simply numb, she told him to pick. "I need to go home and change clothes, then I will meet you." She kissed him and left, knowing that she would never return. She went home, showered, and left a message at the hotel. "Max, something has come up, so I will call you in Washington." Somehow, she knew he would understand the day had come for them to part.

Although Max had an unbelievable ability to satisfy her body more than she had ever known it could be pleased, there was no mental attraction between them. That mental connection lasts a lifetime. Jacqueline wanted her chance with Rose; after all, she was a single woman. Even if it did not work, she wanted to be completely available. If she was right, *a love like this comes around only once in a lifetime.*

Jacqueline returned back to the law firm, to discover court had run late. Rose had just returned to the office, and he was so busy that she had hardly been missed. "Where should we have dinner?" he said. Rose was busy with the case, and he asked if she would keep him company and give him a little help. They spent the evening together. His mind was occupied by the case of a paranoid schizophrenic who claimed discrimination. This was no time to mention the lunch she had today! Besides, Rose had never even kissed her. Maybe she was wrong about this man. Maybe he did see her as just a friend. Could she be so foolish? The human mind could attempt to justify anything. Jacqueline parted from Rose early that evening. Actually, she was glad to be alone. She felt that she had made the right choice about Max, but she needed time to herself.

Rose called her about nine a.m. the next day. He said simply, "Come to the firm." When she arrived, he asked, "Would you like your check?" The money was clear! The lawyers on lawyers' row had all been talking about this day. They were surprised about the Jewish lawyer and CJ, the Catholic, working together. Rose had become very successful, and his reputation was growing. Because of that, he was pulling a lot of business away from the other attorneys on lawyers' row, and there was some envy. Jacqueline had heard from one lawyer employed by Rose that some were taking bets in town about whether that "Jew" would pay CJ. Well, she was there that day when Rose wrote three checks. The first was to her, the second was to CJ, and the third was to Rose! Not only had Rose paid CJ his share, Rose paid him before Rose took his fee. They were all happy; the three musketeers had won.

Jacqueline went off to the bank, and turned the $50,000.00 all to cash. She placed it in a safety deposit box, taking out $10,000.00. She put $2,000.00 in her purse, and asked the man at the bank if he had a paper bag. Placing $8,000.00 in the bag, she informed him it was for her father. He said, "I wish you were my daughter."

At home, her dad was having coffee at the kitchen counter and looking out at the pool. She placed the bag on the counter and poured herself a cup of coffee. Her dad said, "What's in the bag?" With a mischievous smile, he peered over the top of his glasses at her. She knew he was hoping that she had brought doughnuts. She said, "It's for you." As he opened the bag, a look of complete and total shock came over his face. He said, "Jacqueline, I can't take this." She replied, "Take it, or I will burn it!" He just smiled and called her mother over to the counter. Finally, Jacqueline had been able to pay back the original two thousand dollars that her father had lent her so many years ago, along with a little interest. But she knew that she could never pay back all that she owed her parents; they had always supported her in every way.

That day, the family went to lunch and celebrated the long overdue victory. That evening, Rose called at about 7:30 and asked Jacqueline to come by his home. They talked about winning, drank Asian liquor that he called sake, and smoked pot. The music that was playing was that 1940's WWII love song by singer, Edith Piaf. Rose turned and took her hand as she was seated in the chair; he brought himself toward her as he drew her to her feet, and slowly kissed her for the first time.

It was the kiss she had longed for; the face she wanted to see when she opened her eyes was his. He took her breath away with his gentle warmth. Jacqueline knew at that very moment, Rose loved her. Piaf began singing *La Vie En Rose*. It was the song he had waited to play for her. Slowly but steadily, he dropped to one knee. With the next breath he took, his eyes looking deeply into hers, he asked Jacqueline, *"Will you be my wife?"* She said, *"Yes!"* He kissed her the kiss of love. There is no other feeling, even drug-induced, that can compare. Jacqueline knew at that moment that she would be happy for the rest of her life. Jacqueline had found the man who would love both Marie and her forever, until death do they part.

Rose kissed her deeply, and told her that there was something she needed to know. He asked that she please let him speak and not interrupt. He seemed very nervous; he was wringing his hands and pacing the floor. Jacqueline had no idea what he was about to say. He began by telling her that his involvement in the government was more than he had previously told her. He said, "Jacqueline, I hold a Top Secret, Q Clearance in the Intelligence Division of United States Government." His voice was completely calm, but he was still wringing his hands. "I am retired from the CIA."

She was completely stunned by what she had just heard. He asked, "Are you ready for me to continue?" She said, "Yes." Then he asked if she would be his wife, no matter what he said next. She told him yes without hesitation. Jacqueline knew this was the man she would love for the rest of her life. She had no doubt about it - she wanted to be his wife. He began by telling her that he knew all about her trips to Washington! That he was well aware of Maxwell O. Lanna!

Horror was the only look that could have been on her face. He said, "The windows in Max's building are one way, but Jacqueline, you have been under random surveillance by the CIA since shortly after our first meeting. That is when I first thought I wanted to marry you. Forgive me for this action. I don't mean that I was peeking in the windows, but I had to be sure about who you were. Everything was reported only to me, and all has been destroyed. There was nothing that changed my mind about marrying you! He looked at her with concern in his eyes. "Jacqueline, are you all right?" She said, "Yes" with a smile. But she could feel her heart racing, her mind filled with visions of that cherry wood desk in Max's office.

He continued to explain that the CIA had stolen her purse at the Washington Airport. "This was to assure me that Max was not having you carry, knowingly or unknowingly, anything that was illegal. I had to be sure that you were not a courier." Rose then told her that he could take no chances that she might have a criminal investigation begun on her. Her lack of any criminal record made it possible for this day, the day of his proposal. "The long courtship was a necessity, Jacqueline." Then he asked, "Do you love Maxwell?"

She told him, "If I loved Max, I would not have said yes to marrying you!" "I know that, Jacqueline, but I had to ask." She began to tell Rose about Max. He stopped her by saying, "I am sure that Max is a nice man. I know all I need to know. Do you love me?" "More than you know," she answered. Then Rose stated, "If you decide to marry me, Max is going to be offered a very lucrative business contact in Brazil, which will keep him there for years. Can you live with that?" She told him that she could live with anything, as long as she was with him.

Again, Rose asked if she was okay. How could anyone be okay? Her mind was racing, but she said, "yes," and asked him to please continue. He told her that he was retired, and he would rarely, if ever, be called to active operations status. But during their life together, it was possible he would be called to Washington. Rose went on, "I do not expect to ever be called to duty again. But you must know it is possible." He explained this part of their lives would always be secret. He said, "You will not be allowed to ask questions about my past operative work. You will live that part of our lives on a need-to-know basis. There are things I have done for the American government that I am not proud of, but I did everything for America."

He paused, and then continued, "If I have to go somewhere, you will travel with me as my legal assistant, if possible. Rosenberg will never be on your passport. Can you live with this?" She nodded, feeling quite overwhelmed by his secret life, and his knowledge of hers. Rose again asked her, "Will you be my wife?" She said, "Yes," even more sure than before. Tears came to her eyes, and almost heart-broken, she asked if she could carry his name at all. He said, "Yes, just not on your passport." He told her how pleased he was that she wanted his name. She knew she wanted to be Mrs. Solomon Rosenberg before the entire world. Never had she loved anyone except Marie so deeply.

Rose continued, "After we have been married a year, if Marie would like, I would be honored to adopt her." Jacqueline told him that they would need her father's consent. He said, "I will call him at the appropriate time. I believe that I can provide better medical coverage for her than he can. Even if I have to just pay any bills she might have, I don't care. I would never stop her from seeing her natural father. Jacqueline, this would make her my direct heir; it is in her best interest. Since we won't be having any children, she will be ours."

They decided to wait until they were married to make love. Rose wanted Jacqueline to think about all that he had told her. He lifted her from the chair and kissed her the kiss of unending love. Holding her tightly, he looked into her eyes and said, "I want you more than you know Jacqueline. I want to make love to you for the first time on our wedding night, not on the night I had to tell you that I had you followed. I am sorry for the need to have done that, but I needed to make sure. I have waited over forty years for you."

She told him there was one thing that he should know about her that the CIA could not tell him. She said it straight out without hesitation, "When I was seventeen, I was in an orgy in an opium den." He laughed and said, "I knew my lady had a zest for life! We all tried it in the sixties." "Which did you try?" she asked. He told her, "Both." He asked her, "Which did you like best, the sex or the drug?" "The drug," she answered. "Me too!" Rose replied. She confided, "Rose, that's why I only did it once. I knew immediately that I liked smoking opium too much." He responded, "I had the same feeling, Jacqueline. I am not concerned about that, and I really do not care what you have done in the past. From today on, I want you and you alone as my wife. Now, if you decide you would like an orgy, let me know. I want you happy at all times. After all, I seem to remember that I did not hate my orgy experience!" "Rose, you will be all I ever want," she stated without doubt.

Jacqueline was all for the idea of waiting to make love. She was exhausted from her final visit with Max. The idea of going from Max's bed to Rose's did not appeal to her. She wanted some time to put Max behind her; she was marrying the man she loved. Jacqueline wanted the first time they made love to be free of any baggage. She thought Rose sensed that. They had waited all this time for each other. She suddenly realized that he had thought of marrying her from the first day they met, some two years earlier! She had been right, after all! Rose placed his hands on her face and pulled her to his lips again. Then his hands slid down her throat, nearing her breast. He stopped and said, "My God, how I want you forever as my wife."

Next came the call to Marie and her parents. Marie was so excited; she knew her Mom had hoped that this day would come. Her parents gave them their love and blessing. The news he relayed in his call to his parents seemed to be no surprise to them. His mother asked, "Rose will she be converting to Judaism?" Rose told her, "Absolutely not. She is a Baptist girl."

His parents told him that they would be coming up to see them in a couple of days. Rose told Jacqueline that he was not looking forward to their visit. Jacqueline told him she was excited to meet them. He replied, "That is because you do not know them." She told him, "It cannot be that bad, unless you think they will not like me." He replied, "Oh they will like you, but it does not matter if they do or not. They are a bit overbearing. You will see. They love me; they are just classic parents, and I am their only son."

After they made all the calls, Rose said, "Write down all the people you have slept with, and I will do the same. This is so that if we ever run into one of them, the other will know. It will keep us from ever being in an embarrassing situation." Jacqueline replied, "Should we put approximate dates?" He said, "No, I do not care what you have done before today, Jacqueline." Rose's list was longer, but she did not think it was more recent! As they finished their lists and traded, they both read them and tore them up. "Rose," she said, "Max was in town a couple of days ago." He replied, "Jacqueline, I know and I do not care. I knew that this time with Max would be the last time; you are mine alone from this day forward." She felt his warm embrace and deep kiss, as her whole body relaxed in his arms. At that very moment, Jacqueline felt herself truly relax for the first time in her life. Jacqueline knew she would never be safer than in Rose's arms.

The next day his parents came to meet her! They paid a surprise visit to the law firm and they could not believe how large it was. After meeting everyone, they all returned to Rose's home. Jacqueline served coffee as they all talked. Rose's mother seemed concerned over the size of the firm Rose had built. Instead of congratulating her son, she began to interrogate him. His mother asked, "How much is the overhead? How much work do you have? How much money are you making? Do you plan on sending us any money for your college?" Rose asked, "Do you need any money, Mom?" His mother replied, "No, but we did pay for your education, and some of your money should go into the family estate." Rose said, "Could we discuss this later?"

Jacqueline could see an argument coming. Quickly changing the subject, she told his mother, "I think Rose's home is lovely, but I do not like the wallpaper on the kitchen ceiling. What do you think?" Rose's mother replied, "I think you have never been in any fine homes. It is quite proper." Rose was shocked at the mean-spirited remark. His father quickly jumped to the rescue, saying, "I have been in a lot of fine homes and I am with Jacqueline. I don't like that ceiling paper, either."

The evening was already tense, as they went out for dinner. Jacqueline would soon learn that the tension was just beginning. Rose's mother thought that "Tio Pepe's" was too expensive. Rose was starting to get angry. "This is where I want to eat, Mother," he said. As dinner proceeded, she was again discussing the law firm. She again asked how much money he was making. Rose told her that he did not know; he was waiting for the accountant.

Finally, his mother asked the big one. "Have you signed a prenuptial agreement?" Rose hit the ceiling! "Mother I love you, but that is between Jacqueline and me." In a split second, Rose decided to answer her question. "No, we are not going to have a prenuptial agreement. Also, how much money I am making is my business. I don't ever remember asking Father how much money he made. I know that you sold the Long Island house for five hundred and fifty thousand dollars. Based on your lifestyle, and the fact that you bought little sister Alice a home in Manhattan, I don't think you need any of my money. I will not be contributing to your support of poor, poor Alice. If you want to keep filling her hand with money whenever she puts it out, that's fine. I will not. I will be taking care of my wife and child. By the way, I am adopting Marie, so start getting used to that now. Also, I agree with Jacqueline. I think the paper on the kitchen ceiling is ugly, too."

They finished dinner with his mother silent, looking as though she was a wounded dove, instead of the tiger that she was. His parents left for their home right after dinner. Rose said, "Now you know why I was dreading their trip here. I bet you cannot wait to meet Alice, my sister." She told him they seemed nice, just concerned. Rose replied, "Jacqueline, do not kid yourself. You met them. It does not matter, we will be married shortly."

Rose told Jacqueline, "Come to work at the firm. I will set up the office next to mine for you. I really need someone I can trust to manage the firm. I need you! Let the insurance company know you are never coming back. Together, we can build one of the largest litigation firms in the area. Knowing that you are watching my back will give me the peace of mind I need to concentrate on my work. Besides, I promise to take you to lunch every day possible. I know how much you enjoy the law. We can buy a home in North Carolina, and with dual residency, you will meet the requirements to take the North Carolina bar exam. They still have an apprenticeship, they call it 'reading law,' for studying to take the bar. You would not need to go to law school. In five years, you can take the North Carolina bar. Then, Florida will agree to waive you to sit for the Florida bar exam, because you will already be a member of another state's bar. You would not have to practice, unless you want. It will be a whirlwind of learning for you, Jacqueline!"

Talk about whirlwinds! Jacqueline's head was spinning, and she could not seem to catch her breath! Rose looked at her and said, "Well, what do you think? Will you come work with me?" Jacqueline did not know what to think! She didn't know if she really wanted to give up her lucrative insurance business, and with it, her independence. Still, she heard her voice saying, "Oh, Rose! I would love to work for the firm!"

His mother called Jacqueline a few days later, explaining very nicely to her that she should convince Rose to get a prenuptial agreement, "Unless you are only marrying him for his money!" Jacqueline just wanted to scream. Instead, she calmly informed the woman that Jacqueline had her own money. She also told Rose's mother that she would not ask him to draw up anything. She said, "It is his decision to make, and I will not try to influence him. Whatever he decides is fine with me." Next, Rose's mother was asking how much money she had! Jacqueline was still trying to be nice, but she avoided answering. She told his mother that she must talk with her son about their finances, not Jacqueline. They ended the call pleasantly.

His mother called back about a half-hour later, and suggested it would be best if Jacqueline did not mention her call to Rose. She said, "He is already angry with me. Jacqueline, I just love my son."

Jacqueline told her that she understood and did not feel the need to relay their conversation to Rose. His mother told Jacqueline that she was happy about the engagement, and asked if they had set the date. Jacqueline told her that they had not yet decided; they were thinking about it. Jacqueline was not about to say that they were going to be married at the courthouse in a few weeks. Or that Rose wanted to tie up a few loose ends and free his mind...*for her.*

CHAPTER SIX

TRUE EVIL BEGINS TO SHOW HIS FACE

The following week was exciting, as they began to plan their life together. CJ was not at all surprised about the upcoming marriage, and he congratulated them. They also asked him to be a witness, and, of course, he said he would. Jacqueline savored the look of total disbelief on the young Charles's face. He was the lawyer who had told Jacqueline, "Jewish lawyers from New York do not marry WASP woman with children."

Charles worked for Rose, but there was something in his eyes that told her that he was not to be trusted. Later, she would find out that her feeling about him was right. On more than one occasion, she felt Charles had invaded her space by entering closed areas where she was alone. He never touched her, but his presence always made her very unconformable.

CJ did not appear comfortable with Charles either, although he never really said anything. Jacqueline could see it when they were all at CJ's office visiting, and Charles would come by. CJ's attitude would change as soon as Charles appeared. She had always considered CJ a good judge of people. Months later, CJ would say something to Rose, and Rose would acknowledge Charles's days were limited. When CJ and Charles were in the same room, Jacqueline could almost feel the tension between good and evil. It was at those times that she became the most uncomfortable with Charles. It is funny how evil begins to have a scent all of its own.

It seemed after a while that everything Charles did was prompted by negativity and ill will. When it came to women, he was always lying to this girl or that girl. He would run to Rose, tattling as Rose called it, about the other young attorneys. If Charles did not like a secretary, he would complain she had made mistakes, in an attempt to get her fired, or at least in trouble. It seemed that Rose tuned this kind of thing out. He knew his employees were all good people, except for the complaining Charles.

Charles was a local man who had come to work for Rose. He was from a wealthy Palm Beach family.

He was the son of an architect, and he had graduated from an excellent law school, although it was not an Ivy League school. In the beginning, Rose thought he was a good hire. Over time, Rose had become very discontent with Charles. Rose had recognized that Charles was manipulative and backstabbing to the other lawyers who worked for Rose. It was as though Charles did not want anyone but himself to have a relationship with Rose. Clearly, Charles did not like Jacqueline.

Rose had told Jacqueline that he liked all the lawyers except Charles. He said Charles had done a lot of work on the Molly case, the case where the paranoid schizophrenic was suing because of discrimination. As soon as that case was over, Rose wanted to get rid of Charles. Charles did strange things. He would lock his office door. He always wanted to take files home with him, and then he would stop at Rose's house on the way home, and start working on a case. It would be so late by the time they finished work, that he would end up sleeping on Rose's sofa.

Charles would check with a secretary over and over when he was waiting for a call. Then, if the call did not come in, he would accuse the secretary of missing it. The staffers would ask him, "What call are you waiting for?" Charles would just reply, "Put all my calls through!" He appeared very nervous. He seemed to want to be with Rose all of the time.

Rose remarked that Charles bought five hundred-dollar suits every week. He said, "It is a good thing he is from a rich family, because I do not pay him enough to wear them." Sometimes, Charles would get a call at the office and bolt out. Jacqueline just did not like or trust him; she was glad that his days were limited. The end of the Molly case could not come soon enough for her. Rose did not want to endanger the case by putting another lawyer on it, because a replacement lawyer would need to learn all of the thousands of documents in the file to help Rose during trial.

Rose was busy at the law firm over the next few days. The Molly case was ready for trial. Rose had drafted a pleading that had to be filed that day, and told Charles to file it. Charles was busy preparing another facet of the case, and the time slipped away. That afternoon, Charles asked Rose if Jacqueline could ride to Tampa and run in to the federal court building while he circled, because it was so close to five o'clock. He said he was afraid that the courthouse would close by the time he found a parking place and walked to the building. Rose asked Jacqueline if she minded going with Charles, and she said, "Of course I will go."

After they dropped off the documents at court, Charles said he needed to go by his parents' Tampa second home. Jacqueline did not even know they had a Tampa home. She was not happy, but what could she say? After all, he was fairly close to their home. They pulled up to a large gated home that looked to be well in excess of 6,000 square feet. Charles did not ask her in. Jacqueline noticed that it should have been a grand house, but it had an aura of sadness and foreboding that made it seem dreary. She waited in the car for about twenty minutes while he was inside. Finally, as it was getting dark, he came out. Jacqueline was getting angry; she just wanted to go home.

Next, Charles said he had to make one more five-minute stop. Jacqueline was frustrated, but stuck. By that point, there was no more dusk; it was completely dark. Charles drove to a darkened building with hardly any lights; Jacqueline could not see the name on the sign in the front. There was a parking lot, but Charles did not park in a parking space; he pulled right up to the front door. As he opened his door, Charles said, "This is the bad side of town; you had better come in with me. I will only be here for a minute." As she followed him into the building, it became very well lit by comparison to the utterly dark exterior.

She was standing in the "Tangerine Lounge." The place was full of loud, pounding music. Naked women were standing around; two were on a stage, gyrating to the throb of the music. Men were putting dollar bills in the only things the girls were wearing - garter belts or boots. Girls were sitting on men's laps, rubbing their bodies all over the reclining men. This was a strip bar; Charles had walked her into this shady place and suddenly disappeared! She had no idea where he had gone. The room was dirty and the smell was awful, but when she started to go back outside, someone at the front desk told her that the area was too dangerous, and that she should wait just inside the front door. The women just looked at her in her navy blue suit and loafers, and tried to make Jacqueline feel even more embarrassed. They stared at Jacqueline, and the women on stage started "dancing" at her, licking their lips, flicking their tongues at her, and making sure that she could not help but see every part of their anatomy. Then they began toying with each other, all the while smirking at Jacqueline.

A naked woman came up and draped herself on Jacqueline. She said, "Hey, baby, you're beautiful! I know you want to dance – I'll give you a really *special* dance!" Jacqueline shrugged her off, and told her, "Leave me alone – I don't even want to be here!" The girl was not taking no for an answer! She kept up her banter, trying to coax Jacqueline to go with her, until a bouncer at the desk told her, "Leave her alone, Destiny, she's here with Charles." The woman looked startled, and sauntered off. Jacqueline thanked the bouncer. He joked, "Even with Destiny in here, it is still safer here than out there," and gestured to the door. Jacqueline, although completely disgusted, felt that at least she could count on the bouncer to protect her, so she stood in the same spot by the door. About five minutes passed until Charles came back, but it seemed like five hours.

They left, and Jacqueline was furious. She called Charles every name in the book. He told her, "Just do not tell Rose we stopped for a drink." "Stopped for a drink!" she exclaimed. "I wouldn't have a drink with you, if you were the last man on earth!" Charles said, "You had better not tell him anything, or he will never marry you." She threw his earlier words back at him as he pulled the car into Rose's driveway. "Jewish lawyers from New York do not marry WASP women with children!" She jumped out before the car could even stop, and slammed the car door. She stormed into the house.

As soon as she walked inside, Rose spoke to her, and said, "Are you all right? I was worried because it took you so long; I was afraid you were in a wreck!" Jacqueline, still seething, said, "I am fine, but you will not believe what just happened!" She immediately told him about her adventures with Charles. Rose was angry with her at first. "What in Hades were you doing?" She responded, " I was not doing anything! I just went along to file the pleadings, as you asked. After that, I was trapped – he was driving, and he went where he wanted! I sure did not want to be along for the ride!" Then Rose pulled her into his arms and said, "It is not your fault; I should have never let you go with him." He held her and said, "My God, what did he walk you into? I will get him for this if it is the last thing I do." He hugged her closer and kissed her, as he told her, "I need Charles until I finish the Molly case, and then I will fire him, Jacqueline. I promise you, he will pay for this stunt." The next day Charles told Rose that Charles and Jacqueline had stopped at the "Tangerine Lounge" for a drink, and that it was Jacqueline's idea! Rose later told Jacqueline that his only reply was that he had already heard the story from her, and that he *never* wanted to hear about it again.

Over the next few months, she would see more unusual behavior from Charles. She would find him watching his car out of the law firm window, or whispering on the telephone. She told Rose about what she saw, and Rose said that he was aware of Charles's behavior. Charles was always following Rose as though he was afraid to leave Rose. Charles often stayed late at work, and he would end up sleeping at Rose's home. Jacqueline typically stopped by Rose's house in the mornings, on her way to work. On one occasion, Jacqueline found Charles on the staircase of Rose's house. He had some things from his car with him, including a shaving kit. The shaving kit was open, and Jacqueline could see a number of syringes in open view. When she asked Charles what the syringes contained, he told her they were vitamin B shots. He said that they kept him from getting tired. She told him, "Get them out of Rose's home now!" He left with them, saying he would meet Rose at the office.

Jacqueline told Rose when he came out of the shower, and he told her that she had done the right thing and that he would handle it. She knew Charles did not want Rose to marry her. She knew that Rose was just putting up with him because of his active involvement in the Molly case. It had gotten to the point where neither Rose nor Jacqueline could stand the sight of Charles.

Of course, Rose's parents thought he was a nice young man. Even if they did not, they still tried to use him to influence Rose. They called Charles at the law firm, and they asked him to talk to Rose about getting a prenuptial agreement. Charles approached Rose, and told him about the call he had received. He said he thought it would be smart to get a prenuptial. Rose told him to mind his own business. "If something happens to me, Jacqueline will own the firm! Since you are an employee, you had better get along with my wife." Charles told Rose how much he liked Jacqueline and that he knew Rose was making a good decision marrying her. Rose knew better. He recognized how manipulative Charles was, and in an effort to keep Charles from trying to further manipulate Rose by using Jacqueline, Rose told him, "I am glad you feel that way because there would be no choice between you and my wife."

Rose came into Jacqueline's office, which was next to his. He told her about his conversation with Charles. Rose said, "I know that Charles will spread the word that you are more important to me than any of my employees. They might as well get used to it now. After all, Charles thinks he is the most important person in this firm!" Then he said, "The next call will be from my uncle. I'm sure that my mother will enlist her brother to try to sway me!" He was right; about two days later Rose's uncle called. He had not talked to Rose in two years. He did not congratulate Rose on his up-coming wedding; he just said that Rose was upsetting his parents. Rose rejected any advice from his maternal uncle on the matter of their marriage. Then he asked his uncle to keep the rest of the family out of his personal life, or he would not be so tolerant.

Jacqueline asked Rose if he regretted not asking her for a prenuptial agreement. He said, "Absolutely not. In the two years we have known each other, I studied everything about you. I know that marriage includes sharing assets. I would sign all I have over to you, so having the law give you fifty percent does not bother me. I want you and Marie to have everything I can give you. I never want you to struggle again. If you want anything, just ask. You will have my credit cards. If you see something you want, do not ask me about it, just buy it. If you really like it, buy two!"

Rose continued, "When we marry and Marie comes to live with us, I want you to tell her to ask me for money, not you. You have been able to give to her all her life. I would be most grateful if you would allow me the opportunity to do that for her remaining years at home. I plan to send her to the best schools and colleges. She will have the finest clothes, and her first car will be everything she could ever dream of. This will be the greatest pleasure my money has ever brought me. I also want Marie to understand, that if she needs me, that my office door is open to her. I will make sure that my legal staff understands that Marie is my first priority. All telephone calls from her will be put through immediately; I don't care if I am in a meeting with God himself. The same is true for you, Jacqueline. I will never have you take second place to my work or have to wait to talk to me. I know you both have good judgment, and Marie should never feel she is interrupting me. I want to be a husband and father first and always." Everything Rose did in his life, he did with complete and total passion.

Jacqueline was so pleased that she was marrying a man who would love Marie so deeply. Rose insisted on taking Marie somewhere at least four or five times each week. He was very concerned that Marie would accept his love. Jacqueline watched as they fell in love as father and daughter. His face would light up at the sight of Marie. He loved to help her write her school reports, he enjoyed taking her anywhere, and he could listen to her talk for hours. They discussed her natural father openly. Rose always assured her that people show love differently, and he was sure that her father loved her very much. As much as he wanted Marie to be his, Rose realized the importance of making her understand that both he and her father loved her very much. Rose was one smart man.

He kept Charles away from Marie as much as possible; when she was around, Rose would tell Charles that it was family time. Rose once told Jacqueline,

"Charles is stupid; he has trampled sacred ground. He has no idea, Jacqueline, how much I love you. Our lives will be as perfect as I can make them. No one will ever be allowed to interfere with our happiness. God help the man who tries, and let his fate be a warning for any other fool who tries to undermine our love."

When Rose spoke those words, the look on his face and the tone of his voice scared her! She told him, "No one could ever come between us." He told her, "I know that Jacqueline, but I will remove any fool who attempts it. The clock is ticking on Charles, and he can't even hear it! He has messed with Caesar. Remember, Jacqueline, keep your friends close and your enemies closer! Charles never leaves my peripheral vision."

Rose continued, "I have made all the appropriate calls; we are watching him closely. He has no idea who he is tangling with, but I know who he is. When Günter, my old friend, came by the other day, it was to discuss the matter. I told him what I knew about Charles, and what my suspicions are. I told him that what I enjoy most is the fact that Charles thinks I am stupid. Günter found that absolutely hysterical; he laughed so hard in my office that he fell off his chair! When Günter was finally able to compose himself, I called Charles into my office. Günter wanted his fingerprints. I asked Charles to bring me his microcassette recorder, telling him that mine had quit working. Günter took the recorder with him – it had a good set of Charles's prints on it. Believe me, I have this under control, Jacqueline. Do not worry about it, just stand quietly by my side and watch the fallout. Charles thinks Günter is just a weird Vietnam Vet!"

Jacqueline decided not to ask Rose any more questions. She was going to take his advice. She would stay close to Rose, and watch the fallout.

One Friday morning, Rose sent Charles to the Federal Court to copy a number of large case files. Rose knew it would take Charles hours to do the work. Some time in the early afternoon, Charles called the firm and said his car was gone. Rose took his call, and immediately asked him if he parked on the street with a meter as he usually did. Charles replied, "Yes, but I had money in the meter. I checked it less than two hours before, and I put enough money in to last another two hours." Rose said, "I bet you are wrong. It has probably been towed. I will send one of the paralegals to pick you up, and I will call to see it was towed. What number are you calling from?" When Charles had told him, Rose said, "Just wait there, and I will call you back in ten minutes."

Rose hung up the telephone and waited about ten minutes. Then he called Charles back and said, "Your car was towed all right. I think that they said that it was an expired parking meter." Charles immediately went into a screaming rage. "I will sue them! My car was legally parked!" Rose told Charles to calm down. Rose said that he would locate the car. Rose told Charles that he had already sent someone to pick Charles up. Jacqueline asked Rose how he knew that the car was towed, and Rose told her, "This is one of those, 'need to know basis' times. Jacqueline, he is a problem and I am handling it. Just say nothing." Jacqueline told Rose, "I understand. I will not ask any more questions."

By the time Charles was brought back to the office, Rose told him what garage had the car, and they went together to retrieve it. When they arrived at the garage, Rose went with Charles into the lot where the car had been towed. Charles was on a rampage. He was swearing at the garage employees. Rose told him to calm down. "After all, the garage employees had nothing to do with the car being towed. Just get your car and we will go." Charles looked into his car and said. "Well, at least it looks like everything is still here." Charles paid the tow charge, and told Rose that he was going to come and work on the files at Rose's house. Rose told Charles, "Not tonight. Jacqueline and I have plans tonight." Charles and Rose went their separate ways for the day.

Rose returned home, and told Jacqueline that Charles was really upset about his car. Rose said, " If only he knew." Just then Günter arrived at the house. Rose asked Jacqueline to give them some time alone, and she went upstairs to relax. Rose told Günter, " Boy, you really pissed off Charles with this stunt!" Günter replied, "Well, we got what we wanted! The car now has a tracking device on it, and you would not believe the information we found inside." Rose told Günter, "You did a great job. Charles thought the car had not been touched and everything was there!" Günter replied, "Well, we left it all in the car for now, but we have copies of everything. You would not believe what was there. You are right about him. He is into drugs and there were some other very strange documents. My men are processing the documents, researching, and following up to find out what all the other documents mean. We want to stay on him for a while before we pick him up. We want to gather as much information as possible. How much longer until that case will be over?" Rose told him, "I really do not know. It will probably be another six to eight months. I am ready to fire him now. I am so sick of this guy. But I do need him for the Molly case, and I know we need time to see just how much he is involved in. I will wait." Rose called to Jacqueline, who was still upstairs, and asked her to come on down. The three of them had a cocktail and chatted pleasantly for a while, and Günter left.

The next morning at the office, Charles came in very agitated. He went straight into Roses office. Charles told Rose that someone had ransacked his car. He could tell that some things were moved. Rose asked, "Was there anything missing?" Charles told him that nothing was stolen. Rose told him, "Well, things always get thrown about when a car is on the back of a tow truck. I would not be concerned." Rose then asked, "Did you find a ticket on the car?" Charles said, "Yes. It is for eighty-five dollars on top of the tow charge of one hundred and fifty! I am fighting this ticket! I had money in the meter, and at best they should have just given me a parking ticket. They never should have towed my car!"

Rose said, "Let me see the ticket." He looked carefully at the ticket and read aloud a hand-written note on the bottom. "It says, 'Parked outside of marked parking line.' That's why they could tow you! Just live with it. It will cost you more in time to fight this silly thing than you will spend on the ticket." Charles replied, "I cannot believe this! I really want to fight it just for the principle of the thing, but if you think that I should not..." Rose interjected, "I need you to work on the Molly case. Your time is better spent here than wasting it on that lousy ticket!" Charles, heartened by the praise from Rose, said, "I know that you are right. It just does not seem fair. But, I will take your advice. I will just pay the damned thing!"

Rose told him, "After you write the check, get to work. I need all of the files you copied reviewed, and a memo to me on the status of each. So, you have a lot of work this week. All of these cases have a bearing on some aspect of the Molly case, so I need this done as soon as you can." Rose normally would pay a ticket that a lawyer received in the course of office business. Maybe that is what Charles was hopping to hear. But Rose had no intention of paying this one for Charles. Charles went to his office, but left about an hour later. He told the receptionist that he had forgotten to copy some things the day before, and he would need to be gone most of the day to finish. Rose called Günter as soon as he realized that Charles had left the office.

Jacqueline and Marie were going shopping, and Rose was meeting with CJ for lunch. Rose and CJ met at the "Lombardy's Restaurant" near the beach. After a little small talk, CJ said to Rose, "I really need to talk to you about something." Rose responded, "Sure, CJ what can I do for you?" CJ said, "Well it is not exactly what you can do for me. I think we have a problem." Rose was surprised. "What is it, CJ?" he asked. CJ began, "Well, I received my telephone bill today and there was a strange call on it." Rose raised his eyebrows, but said nothing.

CJ continued, "Yes, it was to Amsterdam, and I do not mind paying it but the call concerns me. Last month while you were out of town, Charles came to my office and said that your lawn maintenance people had cut the telephone line. He said that they told him that it would be fixed within the hour, but that he need to make a long distance call right away, and he asked to use my telephone. Of course, I agreed to let him use the telephone. When he was done, he said it was a personal call. He told me that he had left enough money to cover the call. When I went into my office, there was a twenty-dollar bill on the desk next to the telephone. I knew how long he had been on the telephone, and I could not imagine that the call would be more than a few dollars. I was not concerned about the cost. I was going to return the money to him. I put the twenty in my desk and forgot all about it. I never did give the money back to Charles. I guess I am getting absent-minded in my dotage!"

CJ went on, "Today, when I was going over the telephone bill, I noticed that there was a twenty-six dollar long distance call. I looked at the call's destination – it was Amsterdam. I was confused for a moment, and then I remembered Charles's call. He had called Amsterdam! I remembered the twenty that I had put in my desk and took it out. I was talking on the telephone as I was getting some cash a client had brought in ready for deposit into my trust account. I suddenly noticed that the twenty did not look right next to the other bills. I looked a little closer, and well, you take a look." CJ handed the bill to Rose. Rose took one look and laid his napkin over the bill. Looking at CJ, Rose quietly said, "It is counterfeit." CJ said, "That is what I thought. Rose, this guy is big trouble." Rose told him, "CJ, lets get out of here and talk at my home. This is a discussion I do not want to have in public.

Waitress, could you bring the check please?" Then returning his attention to CJ, Rose said, "CJ, I know we need to talk, so meet me at the house."

As Rose arrived at the house, CJ pulled up right behind. Getting out of the car he said, "What is going on with Charles? What is he up to?" Rose said, "Come on in, and I will explain." They sat down in the living room of the empty house. Rose said as he reached in his pocket and handed out a dollar to CJ, "Now you are my counsel, we have the protection of attorney and client." CJ laughed and replied, "Well you could have given me a thousand, but this is fine. What is going on?"

Rose told him, "CJ, in the last months we have all realized that Charles is not a good person. Recently, and I cannot tell you how I know this, an investigation has begun on him. It is in its preliminary stages, but we do know that he is involved in trafficking hard drugs and more." CJ's response was, "Are you sure?" Rose replied, "Yes, I am positive. It is much worse than anyone could have imagined. My problem is the Molly case. I cannot let them get him before I get this case settled or to trial. Charles has imbedded himself in this case, and he alone knows every one of the documents needed for trial. Firing him would put the case in great jeopardy. I have to hang on to him for a few more months. We have gotten a good offer from the defense, but it is not good enough. I think I can get $250,000.00 as a pretrial settlement."

CJ told Rose, "Well Rose, that explains the other thing that just happened. Last week, Charles was in the office. We were laughing and clowning around.

Charles said that he should give me a few thousand bucks just in case he ever got in trouble. That way, I would be on retainer, and I could come get him out. I thought he was joking, and I told him I do not defend lawyers stupid enough to get into criminal trouble. Of course, criminal defense is all I do. And you know that I have defended lawyers in the past. I really thought he was kidding. But, as you know, I do not like him. I just blew him off. Even if he was testing the water with his toe, I wanted it to be clear that I would not have any business dealings with him. I have been putting up with him only because he works for you. Now I am concerned that the telephone call is going to be traced back to me, because it came from my office." Rose replied, "You have nothing to fear."

"What makes you say that? *You* have nothing to fear, but I do! It was not your telephone or law office that the call was made from, it was mine!" CJ said. Rose replied, "CJ, I cannot tell you all I know, but I give you my word that Charles's call will never cause you harm. You are not involved with this mess. I wish I could tell you more, but I really feel it is best I do not. But you have my word I will protect you from any harm in this."

"Rose, we have been friends a long while. Based on your word to me, I will hold off reporting this for a while. But hurry up and get rid of this guy." Rose replied, "You do not need to report it. I will, when the time is right, and I will keep you out of it. Trust me, I am trying to figure out the fastest way to dispose of Charles without compromising the Molly case. CJ, I have another favor to ask of you. I need that twenty dollar bill he left on your desk." CJ still seemed worried, but he also seemed relieved to be rid of the counterfeit bill "Ok, I sure do not want it." CJ gave Rose the bill and said goodbye. Rose immediately called Günter and told him what had just happened. Günter said, "I want that telephone number as well, Rose." Rose told Günter that he could easily get the number. Rose said, "I can get it today. I will meet you at the house about ten o'clock tonight." Then Rose called CJ's office, but CJ had not made it back. So Rose drove to CJ's office. CJ had just returned to his office.

"CJ, I need to talk to you," Rose said. "I need that telephone number. I will need the number when I report Charles's call to the authorities." CJ was nervous. "Rose, I want to know what is going on." Rose told him, "CJ, I really do not want to tell you anymore." CJ said, "Then I am not giving you the telephone number! Not until I get more information." Rose looked around the office and asked, "CJ, is anyone else was in the office? Is there anything or anyone monitoring our conversation?" CJ said, "No everyone has left for the day. What kind of friend do you think that I am? Do you really think that I would bug my own office?" Rose asked, "Are you sure that no one can hear us?" CJ replied, "Yes Rose, I am sure."

"CJ, Günter is with the FBI," were Roses only words. CJ was stunned. He just looked for a few seconds at the sincere look on Roses face. CJ walked to his desk and got the telephone bill and handed it to Rose. Then CJ asked, "How long?" Rose was honest with him. "Most of his life, CJ." Finally, CJ seemed relieved. He said, "Well, that answers a lot of questions and takes a lot of worry off me. You did not even have need to give me the dollar, your secret is safe with me." CJ laughed, and said, "This may be the first time in my life that I am glad that the FBI is on the case! Normally, when the FBI shows up in one of my cases, I hate it. They always make cases much more difficult to defend!" They shook hands, and as Rose started out the door CJ said, "How are the benefits for FBI agents?" Rose responded, "Excellent. At least it appears so, from Günter's lifestyle."

Rose drove back to the house. When Jacqueline and Marie stopped by to show Rose their purchases, Rose seemed upset. She asked him if he and CJ had a problem. Rose told her, "Nothing I can not handle." Jacqueline knew something was upsetting him but she also knew not to ask about it. Rose told her that Günter would be stopping by around ten o'clock that night. He said, "This is one of those need-to-know moments. When Günter arrives, I will need to spend a few minutes alone with him." Jacqueline asked no further questions. She just nodded.

When Günter arrived, Jacqueline and Marie went into the kitchen. The men went into the library. Rose closed the door. Only then did Rose give Günter the twenty-dollar bill and the telephone bill. Günter told Rose that he could stay only a couple of minutes. He explained, saying that his men were at his office, waiting for him to return with these items. He did tell Rose, "We are analyzing all the information we have, so when the time comes, we have a contingency plan if Charles does not choose to cooperate. We need to be able to go forward without him, if necessary." Günter asked, "How much longer on this case Rose?" Rose said, "A few more months if we do not have any delays. It can't be soon enough for me. If I could do it without damaging that case, he would be out of my office and out of my life tomorrow." Gunter replied, "Well I know you want to get rid of him, but the months will help us build a good case. We will be ready as soon as you are." Gunter then took his leave, after exchanging pleasantries with Jacqueline and Marie. He was at the house far less than ten minutes.

Over the next months, Rose kept a very close eye on Charles. He doubled-checked all of the assignments Charles was working on. Rose seemed to give Charles very little new work, and no new cases were assigned to him. When Charles asked why, Rose told him "The Molly case is about to come to a head. I need you to concentrate completely on it. I do not want you to be distracted by other assignments. Just make sure you know where every document is in the Molly case, in case this thing goes to trial." Charles was satisfied with the explanation. In fact, he seemed pleased.

Rose watched Charles, and would call Günter to follow Charles's car when he appeared to be leaving in a hurry. Günter would let Rose know what he was doing. Sometimes the report would shock even Rose. He tried to keep Jacqueline out of the loop. On the occasions when she asked why he was letting Charles get away with so much, Rose told Jacqueline that there were things happening that she did not want to know. But Rose hung in, keeping Charles as an employee. The whole thing made Jacqueline very nervous. But Charles did seem to accomplish what work he was given, and he did it well. Almost all assignments involved the Molly case, and Charles was intimately familiar with every document in the file.

Charles was involved with a number of women. They all seemed to accept the fact that he would wait days to call them back. If the women called more than he liked or questioned where he was going, he would be very rude to them, and the spineless women would take it from him! He still reported to Rose every move the others lawyers made, and Rose pretended that he valued Charles reports. Charles also seemed to be able to deal with Mr. Molly. Most of the time, at least on the smaller issues, Rose did not have to talk to Molly at all. Rose liked that, because he hated to deal with that client. His case was interesting, and it would be lucrative, but the client was a pain.

Günter told Rose that they were building a number of cases against Charles. "Before it is over, he will have only two choices. His choices will be prison for the rest of his life, or cooperate with the government and then enter the witness protection program. Rose, you know what his cooperation could mean to us. Most recently, he was in a well-known arms dealer's house. I wish he had been wearing a wire on him then. But when we do arrest him, he will wear a wire for us or he will go to prison."

Rose tried to keep Charles so busy, that Charles would not be around Rose and Jacqueline too much. But Charles always seemed to find them. They had to be civil to Charles to make this work, and although Rose had not told Jacqueline nearly everything, she knew enough that it made her sick to see Charles come into a restaurant if she and Rose were there. When CJ was with them, he would just make an excuse and leave as soon as Charles came in. CJ never asked Rose any questions about Günter's work. He seemed to accept that Charles would be going down, and that CJ would be kept off any witness lists. CJ clearly did not want to know all of the details. CJ never asked Rose about Günter, and even when CJ, Rose, and Günter were together, he never would ask about the investigation or say anything to Günter about what he knew.

One Monday morning a beautiful young woman about 26 years old, tall with natural blonde hair and blue eyes came to the firm. She had the face of a beautiful model, and a knockout physique. She asked for Charles. Jacqueline explained that he was not in, and asked if she could take a message. The women asked, "Are you Jacqueline?" Jacqueline replied that she was. The young woman said, "Oh, it is such a pleasure to meet you! I am Stacey, Charles's fiancée." Jacqueline was stunned. She asked how long they had been engaged and Stacey said, "It has been only a few weeks, but we have known each other since childhood." Jacqueline said, "Would you mind waiting a minute? I would like to introduce you to my husband, if he is free." Stacey said, "No, not at all. I would love to meet him."

Jacqueline went immediately into Rose's office with the news. She said, "You are not going to believe this one! Charles has a fiancé and she is in the waiting room! I thought you might want to take a look. She is beautiful." Rose said, "This is too good! I have to see her." He came straight out of his office, introduced himself, and invited her into the conference room. As they all entered the conference room, he asked, "Would you care for coffee or a soda?" She replied, "Please, I would like a soda."

Jacqueline started to get the soda for Stacey, but Rose insisted on getting her drink himself. "Jacqueline, please sit down. You have had a long day. I will get it. Jacqueline thought, "How strange," but took the cue, and continued in conversation with Stacey. She watched as Rose reached up into the top back of the glass shelf and took out a clear crystal glass and filled it with soda. Then he made some small talk with Stacey as she drank the soda. He asked her, "What do you do?" She said, "I am an accountant." Rose said, "Really? Where did you go to school?" She replied, "I got my MBA from the Wharton School." Rose said, "Very impressive. The University of Pennsylvania is a fine school. Charles continues to surprise me!"

"So, have you and Charles been going out long?" Rose asked. "Well, as I told you wife, we have been friends since grade school. Everyone knew we would eventually get married. We come from the same kind of family background, and have lived next door to each other most of our lives. I still live in Palm Beach, and I hate that Charles is all the way up here. But I know how much he loves working with you." They continued to chat. As she was ready to leave, she asked to leave a message for Charles that she was in town. Rose asked, "Is there a number where he can reach you?" She replied, "Oh he has it." As soon as she left, Rose told Jacqueline, "Do not touch that glass! I want it for finger prints." He went to a drawer, pulled out a napkin and a baggie, and using the napkin, put the glass carefully inside the baggie. Then he looked at Jacqueline and said, "This is a little gift for Günter."

Rose could not believe this one. He made a call immediately to Günter. Rose told Jacqueline that Günter was most interested in Stacey.

Charles came in the office about two hours later. Rose was the first to see him. He said, "Charles, your fiancée was here today. She would like you to give her a call. She is in from Palm Beach. She said that you would know her telephone number." Charles was stunned. He said, "I was going to tell you, but we have been so busy on the Molly case that I had not gotten around to it." Rose just smiled, and went back into his office. Charles left the office for the day and did not return. That evening, after business hours, Günter came by the office to visit with Rose. He and Rose talked for about thirty minutes, and when he left the office, the glass with Stacey's fingerprints was in his briefcase.

Over the next few weeks, Stacey stayed in town a lot. Charles was still taking calls from other woman at the firm, and on one occasion Jacqueline and Rose ran into him with a redhead at a local bar. He did not introduce her, nor did he ask Jacqueline and Rose to join them. Jacqueline quickly said, "I am Jacqueline and this is my husband, Solomon Rosenberg," as she offered her hand to shake. As Jacqueline expected, the woman met her shake and said, "I am Charlene. It is a pleasure to meet you." Charles jumped in and said, "Charlene and I are friends from college." Charlene seemed a little put off at Charles's explanation of their relationship to Rose and Jacqueline. Jacqueline could see it in the woman's face. Rose and Jacqueline took a seat at another table. After they were seated, they could not help but notice that the woman seemed a little upset with Charles. Then a few minutes later, she seemed to have calmed down. She was more than friendly with Charles. In fact, she could not keep her hands off of him! Charles seen to be very nervous, and they left as soon as Charles could get the bill.

Stacey seemed to be clueless about this guy, and Rose and Jacqueline realized that she was as deceptive as he was. They could never get a straight answer out of her, and she would agree with whatever Charles said. She seemed like a puppy dog with no mind of her own. She was no longer the friendly, out-going woman they had met the first day. She had changed during those weeks. Jacqueline remembered thinking, "What a beautiful waste this woman is. Whatever personality she had, Charles has stolen." Then nearly as fast as she came into their lives, she was gone. Charles said that they had broken up, and that she had moved to Chicago. He did not seem upset by this at all. Jacqueline thought Stacey had probably come to her senses and ended her engagement with Charles. For Stacey's sake, Jacqueline hoped that the relationship was over.

Günter and Rose had a meeting in private at least once each week, and after every meeting Rose seemed to be in very good spirits. Jacqueline wondered what these two had found out, and what they were going to do. But she never asked any questions. After all, she lived on a need to know basis. One afternoon while Günter was at Rose's office, Rose told Jacqueline that he and Günter had a meeting to attend in Tampa. She assumed, as always, that she would go along. But Rose told her that it was best for her not to accompany them on this trip. So they left for their meeting, and Jacqueline went to Rose's home to wait for his return.

Shortly after she arrived at the house, she received a telephone call from Charles. He wanted to know where Rose was. She told Charles that Rose had a meeting that evening. Charles questioned her relentlessly, and he seemed very agitated. He told Jacqueline that he was going to come by and do some work while he waited for Rose to return. "I need to talk to him," said Charles. "Well, he will not be in until late and I do not feel like having company. Besides, I am not sure how long I will stay. I may not even wait here for him to arrive home," she replied. Charles accepted her reply, but his behavior made Jacqueline very nervous. She immediately got up and rechecked all the locks on the doors. Eventually, she fell asleep on Rose's sofa.

Charles called on two more occasions, and Jacqueline just let the recorder answer. About ten o'clock, Rose returned from the meeting. Jacqueline told him about the calls from Charles. He immediately called Charles, and told Charles that he had been with old friends that evening. When he asked Charles if there was a crisis, and what was so important, Charles stated, "Oh, nothing. I just wanted to get with you on the Molly case." Rose hung up the telephone, and told Jacqueline, "He is such a liar." Jacqueline left for the evening and returned to her home for a good night's rest. At least until she was married, she could get out of this mess with Charles, and return home to a peaceful night sleep. As much as she was looking forward to her new life, this Charles creature was really upsetting, and not knowing exactly what was going on was even worse.

One of the other lawyers at the firm had noticed Charles acting strangely. Most were so busy with their own work that they did not even notice it. Kim was always the brightest of the young lawyers. He came to Jacqueline one afternoon, and wanted to talk with Jacqueline about Charles looking out the window at his car all the time. Kim felt it was strange. Jacqueline told him to discuss it with Rose. Later that afternoon, Rose and Kim had a meeting on the subject. Rose told Jacqueline after the meeting that he had told Kim, "Charles is not looking at his car. He is thinking while he is looking out the window. That is how he rolls ideas around in his head when he is trying to write a memorandum or something. I saw the same thing and it took me a little while to figure out what he was doing." Rose said he was not sure, but he thought Kim accepted his explanation. "I guess Kim does not have enough work if he has time to think about Charles, so I will load him with work. That way, he will not have time to think about this. I always knew Kim was bright, but I think that I can throw him off for now," Rose said.

Jacqueline decided that since she was not to be involved in what was going on with Charles, that all she could do was just put up with him being around. When the time came, she was sure Rose would fire him. Then he would be out of their lives of for good. Besides, she had a new life to plan. She would not let Charles and his evil ways stop her. Rose promised to get rid of him after the Molly case, and until then, she would just stay away from him as much as possible.

CHAPTER SEVEN

GLORY TO GOD

They decided to marry at the courthouse on December 30th. Jacqueline would later refer to it as, "Before taxes." That day Rose was in court in the morning, and they had decided to meet for lunch. Rose and CJ arrived as expected, and then Charles found them; this was not as expected. As usual, he was sticking as close to Rose as he could. Jacqueline wished that Charles had not been able to locate them. But it was clear that they were stuck with him today, and every other day until the Molly case was over. Jacqueline wished that day had already come and gone; she wanted Charles out of their lives.

But today was not a day to think about Charles. Today was a day for celebration! Around two o'clock, Rose said, "Jacqueline, let's go get our marriage license. I will grab one of the judges to marry us." Charles tried to look happy, but they both knew he was not. They just did not care. Today was their day, and even Charles could not put a damper on the joy they each felt.

Jacqueline wore her black skirt and white silk blouse. Rose had asked her to wear that outfit. All of them drank a few too many cocktails with lunch, but they headed to the courthouse, just the same. Charles said, "Do you really think that we should seek out a judge with liquor on our breath? I think that we are a bit tipsy – maybe you should wait for a little while." Rose told him, "Don't be silly, Charles! I'm sure that every judge in this courthouse can easily understand that Jacqueline and I have much to celebrate! After all, this is the day our lives become one."

CJ just shook his head and smiled, but when neither Jacqueline nor Rose was looking, CJ shot a warning glance at Charles. That look said, "You are here, and here you will stay, unless you keep it up. If you even think another negative thought, I will personally see that you are gone forever." Charles saw the look, and by his expression, CJ knew that he had understood the message. CJ tried never to let Jacqueline or Rose see just how much he disliked Charles. CJ was a friend to both Rose and Jacqueline, and Charles was Rose's associate. CJ was aware that Rose had developed distaste for Charles. CJ felt that whether or not Rose continued to employ Charles was none of CJ's business. But one thing was crystal clear in CJ's mind. He would not allow Charles to spoil this day, the most important day in the lives of his two best friends. He would not allow it!

After they had gotten the marriage license at the clerk's office, Rose saw a judge he knew, and spoke briefly with him. They all trooped into the judge's chambers. The judge performed the marriage ceremony, with CJ and Charles standing as witnesses. Jacqueline was now before God with the man she loved. They were man and wife! After the ceremony, the judge jokingly said, "Mrs. Rosenberg, I will hold this license until Monday, in case you change your mind. Mr. Rosenberg, you cannot change your mind. This is the best thing you have ever done, and I will not permit you to have any second thoughts!" They all laughed, and Rose and Jacqueline thanked the judge for his kindness.

They skipped out of the courthouse door like children, laughing all the way back to Rose's office. When they arrived, Rose immediately called Marie, and told her to start packing her clothes; they would pick her up in the morning. Jacqueline told him, "We should call your parents." Rose said, "Not today, I am too happy, and I do not want to spoil my mood." They stayed at the office only long enough for Rose to make the call to Marie, and to accept the sincere congratulations of everyone there. This was no day for work! On the other hand, just because Jacqueline and Rose were not working did not mean that Charles should have the rest of the day off! Rose called to Charles, and gave him a complicated assignment on the Molly case.

After Charles walked away, Rose said to Jacqueline and CJ, "That should keep him busy for the rest of the day, and out of our hair!" Jacqueline, Rose, and CJ left the office, and had more cocktails around town with clients and friends. Jacqueline could think of no better way to celebrate their joy than to share it with CJ and their other friends. Well, she could think of *one* better way, but she knew that the moment she had been awaiting forever was soon to come – at last she would be one with her husband!

At last, they returned to their home. Jacqueline could finally call it their home. She had wondered for so long if this day would ever come! Rose tenderly lifted Jacqueline into his arms, and carried her over the threshold of the house and into the beginning of their life together. She could see the full moon over his shoulder as they entered the house. He did not put her down until they were in their bedroom at the top of the stairs. "Our bedroom!" Jacqueline thought. "How strange that seems, and yet how right!" There, he laid her gently on their bed. Her thoughts were only of Rose. His eyes looked deeply into hers. His kiss was soft and gentle, as he stroked her hair. He began to undress her for the very first time. His hands were shaking wildly while he was unbuttoning the white silk blouse he had asked her to wear. "Jacqueline, I have dreamed for nearly two years of seeing your brown skin as these buttons opened."

He told her that he would love her for the rest of his life and even after the last breath had left his body. His hands slowly touched every inch of her skin, feeling her body for the first time. His hands were so soft! They felt as though they were softer than satin, touching her breast. He laid his head upon her breast, holding her so very close, his eyes gazing up at her as they laid there in silence for a few minutes.

Then he began to speak, with his head upon her naked breast and his eyes looking directly into hers. He told her, "I have never loved anyone with such depth. If I loved you any more, my heart would surely burst." Slowly, he continued to explore her body, as he told her, "You are softer and more beautiful than I had ever dreamed." Jacqueline watched as his body grew from the mere touch of hers. He kissed her deeply, as he stroked her hair and gazed into her eyes.

They made love, never closing their eyes. Each saw only the beauty of the other's gaze. The intensity of their lovemaking was beyond this universe. It was the kind of love where one body joins another body, and two souls become a single, living, breathing entity *until death you do part*. They had been in love since the first day they met; now they were one on this, their wedding night. They made the kind of love that cannot be described to anyone. Anyone who is fortunate enough to experience it will forever know its deep, irreplaceable feeling within.

Rose made love to her over and over. Then he rolled over next to her, and she gently rested in his strong arms. Jacqueline was overwhelmed. She had never before felt this way. It was the power of total love. She asked him, "Why me? Why was I so blessed with your love?" Rose responded, "Jacqueline, you are the most complex, complete woman I have ever known. I loved you before I ever heard you speak. When you walked into my office that very first day, as you took the ten steps to my desk, I fell in love with you. You were wearing a black dress with a white collar and red buttons. I remember it as though it were yesterday. I could not help but realize how beautiful you were, but the only thought that went through my head was not that. The words that kept playing over and over in my mind were, '*this woman will be my wife.*' I had waited all of my life for you to walk through that door."

"Never in my life had such a thought entered this very analytical brain of mine. My brain is not emotional, but rational. I am not the sort of man who makes leaps of faith. I cannot see the future. But before you sat in the chair across from me, I heard those words. I knew somehow, even before you spoke, that you would be my wife. I never kissed you, because I knew that once I did, I could never stop. You were 'La Vie En Rose.' That is why you could not hear that song the day we met. I could not play it for you then. I already knew it would be playing for us when I asked you to be my wife. You see, the music was playing in my head as you began the walk to my desk that very first day."

He paused and then he said, "I don't know why, with all the things I have done in my life Jacqueline, that God has blessed me with you. I am forever in his debt." He softly sang some of the lyrics:

Claudette Walker

FROM "LA VIE EN ROSE" BY EDITH PIAF

Life in Pink

"I thought that love was just a word they sang about in
songs that I heard,
It took your kisses to reveal that I was wrong and love
was real."

She could not believe his love was hers. He was wrong; God had blessed her, that little girl from the other side of town. Jacqueline knew that her heart had not led her astray. This was the perfect love that she had yearned so long to find. She thought with wonder at the twists and turns in her life that had brought her to this moment, and she realized that her fate was a life filled with only joy from that day forward. Her life was complete. Then he held her tightly, as she drifted off to sleep in those strong, wonderful arms – the arms of the man she loved.

When she awoke in the morning, it was to the sound of Rose calling her name. "Mrs. Rosenberg, Mrs. Rosenberg, hurry we have to go get my daughter!" How excited he was. An unending smile came across her face as she realized this was not a dream, but her life forever after. His acceptance of Marie only made her love him more. She had found the man who would love her and Marie for the rest of their lives. Her search was over.

Marie was so excited! Her biological father and Jacqueline had been separated since she was only a few months old. They divorced during the surgery years, and she saw little of him, because they lived so far apart. Now she had a full time dad, and the dad had a daughter. Rose seemed so happy with her. Perhaps it was because he knew Jacqueline could not have more children, or perhaps it was Marie's magical power over Rose. Whatever it was, all of his love was for Marie. This would be their family.

He was ready to be a father at 45. He attacked fatherhood like everything he had done in his life. He wanted to be the best. Every spare moment he had was spent spoiling Marie. Teaching her was his new hobby. His subjects ranged from the great operas of the world to plays, history, and even French. On Sunday mornings, she would bring the newspaper to him in bed, and he would reach for his wallet and give her a one hundred dollar bill! After a few weeks, he still got the paper, but Jacqueline stopped the hundreds! He really did have great intentions, but like any new father, he was not always sure how to carry them out. Jacqueline had the advantage of her experience raising Marie, and Rose took instruction from her well, and her suggestions to him to heart. Rose gave them anything they wanted. Jacqueline never wanted for anything, but she never wanted much; as long as she had Rose's love, she felt that she had it all. Everything she had dreamed of for Marie and herself had come true in Rose. Jacqueline was so in love with him.

By that time, Rose had the law firm connected to the house by computer. That way, he could work at home a lot. He would dictate by telephone into a machine at the office. The secretaries would transcribe it the next morning, and a messenger would deliver the draft to Rose at home. During the first months, he gave Jacqueline numbers to put in a spreadsheet on the home computer. He told her that she was helping him prepare his tax return, and that he would give the spreadsheet to his accountant.

Finally, about the middle of March, they were finished, and Jacqueline's work was ready to be given to the accountant. She was shocked at his income. "Rose, this spreadsheet says you made $950,000.00 last year! I did not know that." He said, "I know; that's why I married you, you never ask. I also knew how much I made last year when my mother asked." They laughed. He said, "I am sorry - you married a poor man. I was trying for a cool million; I am a failure." "Maybe next year," she said with a laugh. Rose told her he hoped so, because their new home could cost that much. Jacqueline said, "I do not think so." He said, "I do."

They spent a lot of time on the beach playing with Marie, taking her to open-air cafés for lunch. Sometimes, they would just stay at the beach all day, and listen to musicians playing metal drums at sunset. Marie could bring her friends, and Jacqueline and Rose would watch them play as the couple planned their life together. In a few months, they would start looking for a new home. Rose wanted at least five bedrooms; the house had to have plenty of light, and a swimming pool for Marie was a must! They worked hard and played hard. Sometimes, Jacqueline wondered how he could keep up the pace; he wore her out. But Marie loved it. He took Marie to every art exhibit he could find; he taught her to play chess. Rose always introduced her as his daughter, and she reveled in all the attention he gave her. Their home was filled with her friends, and Jacqueline and Rose loved it that way.

The preparations for their first Christmas together started early. They began shopping in for Marie October. Rose and Jacqueline would spend all afternoon shopping, and then Rose would come home and give Marie all of the presents they had bought within an hour! They would buy her a dress for school, then he would say, "Doesn't she need a purse and shoes that match that outfit?" Jacqueline told him, "Next year we will start shopping on Christmas Eve!" They were always having fun with Marie; Rose enjoyed Marie as much as Jacqueline always had.

The next year was filled with business, and of course, filled with Marie, who was growing up beautifully. Prom dresses and pictures seemed to be their world in her ninth grade year. When Jacqueline asked Rose how much money she should spend on a prom dress, he said, "Whatever it takes." Rose seem to love to interrogate the young men who came calling on Marie. He would make Marie photocopy their driver's licenses upstairs in the office, while Jacqueline wrote down the license plate number of the car. If everything met with his approval, Marie and the boy could go out. He did not make it easy for the boys. Marie loved it; she just warned the boys to be ready to present a driver's license when they picked her up.

Rose asked one young man, who had two brothers in MIT and whose father was a doctor, "What do you plan on doing with your life?" The young man responded, "I'm going to be an evangelist; three years in, three years out, and I'll be rich." They all laughed at his words. The boy went on to MIT. Jacqueline always smiled when she thought of the young boy's quick-witted answer to Rose.

The boy who Jacqueline and Rose liked the best was just a friend of Marie's named Peter. Although they were the best of friends, Jacqueline saw no signs of a budding, youthful romance. Peter had such a good heart and he had a great intellectual capacity. He was enjoyable to be with. Jacqueline realized that her child was growing into a young woman. She and Rose were having so much fun together watching Marie grow up.

Rose always had time for them. On Marie's birthday, she asked for a cat from the SPCA as her present. Rose was in a very important meeting that day, and the meeting was running long. Jacqueline sent a note into him to let him know that the SPCA closed in an hour, and she would let Marie know that they would go tomorrow. When he got the note, Rose jumped up from his seat at the head of the conference table and announced, "Gentlemen, this meeting is over for today. It is my daughter's birthday, and I must leave now to get her a cat." There were a few snickers, followed by shocked silence when Rose said, "Reschedule with my secretary. We will continue our discussions later," as he strode out of the conference room.

As they drove to the SPCA, Jacqueline told him that he did not have to cancel the meeting. He said, "It is my daughter's birthday! And besides, I didn't like the way the meeting was going anyway." They laughed, as they continued on their way to get Marie's new cat.

One afternoon, Rose and Jacqueline stopped by the Bombay Bicycle Club for lunch and drinks. It was a local bar with a tropical theme in St. Augusta, and it was on their way home from the office. As they were seated at a table enjoying their drinks, Jacqueline saw Max across the room at the bar. She looked for a moment to make sure she was right. Then she told Rose, "Max is here." "Where?" he said. "Over at the bar in the suit with the black glasses," she told him. Rose suggested, "Invite him over for a drink; I would like to meet him." Jacqueline, thinking it was better for her to go to Max before he saw her, headed across the room.

She was thinking, "Oh, this is great! Why did we have to stop here tonight, of all nights? Well, hopefully, Max will not be able to join us." But she knew that this meeting between Rose and Max was destined to occur eventually, so perhaps it was best to have it behind her.

Max was standing at the bar. As always, he was laughing with a group of people, buying drinks for the house and telling stories. As she approached him, he saw her. Suddenly, he picked her up in the air above his head! Jacqueline said quietly, "Max, put me down, I am here with my husband." Slowly, her feet were placed back on the floor. "Max," she said, "Rose would like you to join us for a drink." Max said, "Sure" with a twinkle in his eyes. Jacqueline was not looking forward to the next few minutes. Max told the barmaid to send a round of drinks over to the table.

Rose tried to engage Max in conversation, but Max focused his comments on Jacqueline. He told Rose that his wife was the most beautiful girl in the world, and that Rose was a very lucky man. Eventually, Max asked Rose, "What do you do for a living?" Rose replied, "I am just another lawyer, like you." Max told them that he had a new contract in Brazil, and he had just gotten back to the United States. He said he would only be in the states for a week, and then he would be returning to Brazil.

Max wished them well in their marriage. Then he told Rose, "I know she will make you happy. Take very good care of her, or someone like me will be around the corner to take her." Rose assured Max that he would take good care of Jacqueline. Then with a wink, Rose told him, "I hope this contract in Brazil is a very lucrative, long-term one. I like the idea of you being in that far-away corner of the hemisphere." The men shook hands, and Max kissed Jacqueline's hand. In a few more seconds, Max left their table, and the bar. That was the last time she ever saw Max.

After he left Rose said, "I could see the pain in his eyes over you, Jacqueline. But I guess if he had been smart enough or lucky enough to take you from me, the pain would have been in my eyes, instead." She told Rose, "I married the man I want." Rose asked, "Didn't he go to Harvard?" She told him, "Max has a law degree from Harvard, and a business degree from Yale." Rose's reply was simple. "Well, well. All that education, and he still is not as brilliant as I am! I married you."

Rose turned Jacqueline to him, held her face so gently with his hand and said, "Jacqueline, I do not know how it is possible to love you more each day, but I do. You are the greatest gift God has ever given to me. I will love you for all eternity." She told him, "I am the blessed one. You are my best friend, my husband, and the most perfect lover a wife could ever have. My body heats at the thought of making love to you. I will be with you for all my life."

"Let's go," Rose said. As they left the Bicycle Club, he asked if she would like to take a ride. She said, "That is a great idea! It is such a beautiful afternoon." He asked, "Is Marie staying with her grandparents tonight?" She said, "Yes." They lowered the convertible top and headed south. Rose drove with his arm around her. They rode with the wind in their hair, listening to music and laughing until they arrived at Marco Island at about eight p.m.

As they entered a resort, Rose asked the desk clerk if she had a very private beach house. She informed him that she had three on one beach and none had been rented, but she could not guarantee that the other two would not rent for the night. Rose confirmed that they were the only three houses on the private beach. She told him that they were in a gated area, and no one but the people staying in the three homes had any access to the beach. Rose told the young lady he would take all three houses for two nights. Looking surprised she said, "The cost would be two thousand, seven hundred dollars, for all three!" He said, "That will be fine."

Jacqueline was stunned. What was he up to? Rose asked, "Can you tell me where I will find food and liquor stores?" The clerk said, "They are on the way to your houses," with a laugh. They got back in the car and headed to the beach homes. Jacqueline asked Rose, "Why did you rent all three?" He answered, "I wanted us to have the beach to ourselves. Besides, maybe tomorrow your parents will drive down with Marie. But not tonight; I have plans," he said with a grin. They stopped at the convenience store for food and drinks. Jacqueline saw an apparel shop next door. She went in to find some lingerie, while Rose shopped for food.

They arrived at the gated beach homes, let themselves in, and re-locked the gate behind them. The girl was telling the truth; no one could enter the beach area except through the gate. As they entered the largest house, Rose pulled a candle from the bags of groceries he was carrying. Then he took out a couple of glasses, and put a bottle of champagne into the freezer. Jacqueline started to place the groceries in the refrigerator, but Rose told her he would do that while she took a bath and relaxed. Then he tapped her on the bottom as he sent her off to the bathroom. After her bath, Jacqueline put on the white nightgown and lace robe that she had just purchased. When she returned to the living room, Rose had showered and was wearing only a towel. He told her that he had used the shower in one of the other houses, while checking out the area. "See, I told you we need all three houses," he chuckled. Jacqueline said, "Well, that's two houses we have used."

"Jacqueline, you look so beautiful in white," he said. Then he handed her the champagne and grabbed a candle. "Let's go to our beach," he suggested. As they walked toward the beach, she could see that he had placed a blanket and two pillows on the sand. Flower petals adorned the blanket. "Rose, how beautiful!" she told him. He said, "Not as beautiful as you are. I realized tonight that I wanted more than anything to make love to my wife on the beach." He fired up a joint and passed it to her.

They lay on the blanket, watching the waves and drinking champagne. Rose slowly reached over and unbuttoned the thin lace robe, kissing her softly and telling her he loved her. As he opened her gown, he told her that he wanted to look at his beautiful wife. His kisses slid slowly down to her breast. His lips echoed the warmth of the night air, while he removed her robe. "I love you Jacqueline, and this is the life you deserve." He began kissing her lips with more passion than she had ever known. She could feel the desire in his kiss.

His hands were searching, touching every part of her, while her hands touched every inch of his beautiful, dark, lean body. She could feel the rising heat as his body locked inside of her. Warmth beyond compare began to fill her, his lips still tasting her breast. Quietly he said, "This is my love for you Jacqueline," as his lips reach the organs of her body. She began a silent scream, as he slid his lips more deeply inside her. "My beautiful wife," he said, "I am before God with the love I feel for you." Her body was in rapture for the Rose. They made love over and over, unable to stop touching one another, until nearly daybreak. They explored every inch of each other.

Just as the sun was rising, Rose stood at the water's edge. Raising his hands to the rising sun, he screamed, "Thank you God, for Jacqueline." Then he came to her on the blanket, and began kissing her as he carried her into the water. Holding her, kissing her, as his body was once again one with hers. They began making love as he held her in the water, spinning, turning, laughing and kissing. He was far stronger than she had known. Then they returned to the blanket, Rose carrying her in his arms, naked through the sand. He laid her back and began drawing juice from her body one more time. She thought, "How could I still be so moist?" She did not know, but she was, more than ever.

From between her legs, his gaze caught hers as he told her, "You are my wife and the most delicious woman on earth." Then he returned to pleasing her. Rose made love to her for a very long time, and then he brought his lips up to her breast and rested his head, then to her lips and their bodies became one again. Picking her up and holding her tightly, he moved Jacqueline slowly upon his body. Her screams were no longer silent; he asked for more and she gave generously.

He slowly placed her feet on the sand. Naked, she dropped to her knees before him, filled with complete desire for him. With only her lips, she placed him inside her mouth and she began to return the pleasure he had given her. She could feel him swell, her eyes watching his face express ultimate glory. Jacqueline slowly increased the tempo on his body. His face appeared lost in a place he had never truly found before; it was marked with pure pleasure. With the power of her mouth, she sought his explosion, and she received her husband with the purest of pleasure.

They gathered their things, and returned to the beach house for the first time since their arrival. Once they were inside, he immediately laid her across the kitchen table and said, "You take me higher than I have ever known Jacqueline." He began kissing her, touching her and feasting upon her body again! She could not have stopped the warmth of her body's response for him, even if she had wanted to do so. And she did not want to stop. They were truly blessed by

God in their love. After a few minutes, he picked her up and placed her on the bed. Then he stroked her face with his hand and said, "I am not done with you yet." As his body joined with hers, he swore his never-ending love. Then he slowly removed his joy from her, only to replace it with his tender lips of happiness. She pulled his body to her lips as they dined upon each other's sweetness.

After only a moment of rest, he reached for the telephone and placed a call to Marie. Rose told her where they were, and then he asked if she and her grandparents would like to join them. After hanging up the telephone, Rose looked her and said, "We have five hours before they can possibly be here. Come here!" as he lifted her into his arms. He carried her to the sunlit veranda. He stood behind her at the railing, as they looked out onto the ocean. Rose told her how much he loved her, as his hands fondled her breast. Then he turned her around, and kissed her for a long time.

Slowly, he dropped to his knees; his face and tongue separated her legs. She began to come immediately, still standing on the balcony and looking at his beautiful face between her legs. My God, how she loved her husband and wanted him unendingly. Rose lifted her up in his arms and carried her to bed in the loft. Then, with all of his energy, he slid deep inside of her. Holding her tightly, they became one in orgasm. Just as he exploded inside of her she heard, " I love you, my wife."

When Marie and her grandparents arrived, they could not believe Rose had rented the entire beach. They all had a glorious time, but most of all, Rose and

Jacqueline made the hottest love she had ever felt. He was hers, only hers until death do they part. There was so much love between them. This deep love they shared made their lovemaking beyond this world. It was the most *natural* high she had ever found.

Dinners out, bookstores, cocktails and the law filled their life. Since Rose was completely connected by computer to the law firm, they could spend more and more time at home with Marie. Jacqueline was so grateful because she had to work so much when Marie was young. Now, they could be with her in her teenage years. When Rose was working at home, he would ask Jacqueline to get him some coffee, while he sat in his chair billing thousands of dollars in legal work. She would call him her lean, mean, moneymaking machine.

He once told her his biggest problem in billing was that he rarely needed to look anything up anymore, because he knew the answers. He could write most complaints in just a few minutes. That, he said, was not good for billing purposes. When he first retired to Florida, he had read a great deal of Florida law. With his photographic memory and vast understanding of the law, he completed things too quickly for billing purposes. They never argued; the three of them just lived as happily as any family had ever been.

About every two or three hours while he was working at home, Jacqueline would hear him call her name. She would always come immediately. Sometimes he would need her to locate a law book for him. Sometimes he would just be calling her to tell her how much he loved her; other times he would just want her to sit next to him. He loved talking to her about legal theories. She loved learning the law. He dealt with conspiracy law, corporate law, civil racketeering, corruption, discrimination, and even wrote appellate briefs for the Supreme Court of the United States. His knowledge of the law was unending, and he never stopped learning.

Jacqueline attended depositions and court with Rose most of the time. Sometimes when he was bored, he would pass her a note as though it was important. On it would be the three little words, "I love you." She would tuck it in her pocket and write something on a legal pad as though the note had been important to the court case at hand. This was their life. Rose did not have to think about the law. He knew the law. He began to learn it as a child sitting at the dinner table, and practiced it at all levels, including the Supreme Court.

One fall day, their mail contained an invitation to a costume party. It was from another lawyer in town and his wife. Rose knew the man, but not his wife. Jacqueline wanted to go, and so Rose agreed. The theme was from WWII: The Last Train to Paris. He was to be dressed as a General; she would wear the costume of a high dollar prostitute. The invitation specified their costumes! Rose was a historian of WWII, and he owned a German General's hat that his friend Günter had given him, along with some other memorabilia. Jacqueline wore a black crape dress with a pillbox hat and veil.

As they arrived at the party, the lawyer's wife greeted them, speaking in French to Rose. Rose immediately said, " Please speak English; my wife does not understand French." The woman changed from French to English, "I am sorry, Rose. Do you remember me? I was at Barnard College when you were at Columbia University. I am Candy Gold-Thorn!" Rose said, "I am sorry, but it has been a long time. You say you went to Barnard?" She began speaking in French again. Rose was shocked and said, "Please speak English." Candy immediately replied, "You have not forgotten your French have you?" Rose was starting to get a little irritated and said, "No. I remember that and six other languages, but my wife does not speak French! I am sure you remember etiquette. One should not speak a foreign language when in the company of people who cannot, and another language such as English is available."

Candy made two or three attempts to speak French to Rose during the evening and Rose was going from firm to angry. To say the least, she was snooty all night. But her husband and the other gentleman were quite taken with Jacqueline. Rose got a real laugh watching all the men so smitten with his wife. They went home early, since they really were not party people.

After they arrived home that night, Rose asked Jacqueline to wait before going into the house. He stood behind her with his arms on her shoulders, and both of them looking at the moon. "Jacqueline," he said, "You are the most beautiful woman I have ever seen. Your scent is of spice, and your skin is like smooth silk. Your eyes twinkle with green lights in the moon. You are my wife, and I love the very being of you."

They walked slowly into the house arm in arm. Marie was staying at her grandparents, since they did not know when the party would end. They were dressed in their WWII costumes. Rose pulled Jacqueline to him and kissed her deeply. He told her, "No woman in that room tonight compared with you. No woman in the world ever could. Each and every man envied me tonight, knowing you are mine."

Then he kissed her again, as he lifted her in his arms. Carrying her up the staircase to their bed, he laid her gently down. Then, lifting the large silk skirt of her dress and removing his General's hat, he climbed under the skirt, sliding her silk panties from below the garter belt, which was moist with juices of love that had seeped onto its black silk from his touch. Rose sent her mind on a euphoric journey of satisfaction. She awoke with his head still resting on the black silk of her dress.

She reached down and stroked his head as she called softly, "My General, please wake for me. I want you." His eyes were slowly opening, as she rolled him onto his back, placing him in her warm lips, to start his growth. Her body was still dressed in black silk, as she slipped him into her and began moving him deeper inside her until she was completely upright upon him. Then she slowly made love to him, only stopping when she was ready to place her lips upon him. The heat from his body was intense, and he filled her with all the joy of love he had. When she had greedily sought every drop he had to give, she collapsed, smiling.

The telephone rang, and Rose answered. "Hello, Günter. How are you? It is so nice to hear your voice! What? Okay." Rose put the telephone back on the receiver. Jacqueline asked "Is everything okay?" "Yes honey, just business. We will talk about it later. May I have a cup of coffee, please?" As Jacqueline was going downstairs for his coffee, she thought, "That was a strange call." Then she remembered, "I live on a 'need-to-know basis!' " If she needed to know, Rose would tell her. She smiled when she saw the sunlight peeking through the kitchen window. Morning had broken.

CHAPTER EIGHT

GÜNTERS STOLEN BRIEFCASE

The next day was their first anniversary; they had planned dinner out at "Tio Pepe's" and then a quiet evening at home with Marie. Shortly before dinner, an express courier arrived at the door with a package for Rose. Jacqueline told the gentleman, "I will sign for the package." The gentleman replied, "I am sorry, but this package requires Mr. Rosenberg's signature." "Okay," she said, and she called to Rose, who was resting in the living room. Then she suddenly noticed how proud and erect the man stood as he was waiting for Rose.

Rose entered the doorway. "Come in," he said to the messenger, and then he closed the door. Rose told the messenger, "Continue." The man raised his arm in a salute to Rose. Jacqueline was shocked by this sudden sharp cracking salute. Then the courier opened the box he was carrying with the same precision. Inside was an unusual clipboard, with a wooden cover on the front and a red seal on the bottom. Rose looked closely at the seal while the man was still holding the clipboard. Then Rose asked Jacqueline to please stand next to the gentleman's right. Jacqueline moved from Rose's side to the right of the messenger holding the clipboard.

After Jacqueline moved, Rose told the gentleman to proceed. With precision movement, the man turned the clipboard to face only Rose. With a gold tool, he broke the seal on the cover of the clipboard that was facing Rose. The man holding the clipboard could not see what it said, nor could Jacqueline. He held it as Rose read the document. When he was finished reading the document, Rose signaled the man to close the clipboard. The man closed and resealed the wooden clipboard. Rose placed his fingerprint in the new seal, and the man saluted and left.

Rose turned to Jacqueline and said, "Call your parents to come take Marie. Tell them we have decided to go to Jekyll Island for our anniversary. We will need them to pick her up within the hour! Pack enough clothes for one night, and give me your purse." Jacqueline did so immediately without asking a single question. Rose removed all of her identification except for the passport that he had insisted stay in her maiden name.

Rose sat deep in thought for a few minutes, and then he said, " I have been called to Washington. You will be traveling as my legal secretary. You need to call me Mr. Rosenberg and give no indication of us being married. "What about my wedding rings," she said. Rose replied in a firm voice, "Leave them on; you will be called Mrs. Walters. Do you understand me, darling? I love you more than life itself. This is for your protection, so just be careful. I know you are smart; you can do this. It will just be a fun trip and you are in no danger. I have just been called in for an assignment; we will be home in a day or two. I am sorry dear, this is not how I wanted to spend our first anniversary." "Rose, as long as I am with you, I am happy," Jacqueline said as she smiled softly.

Jacqueline's parents arrived at the house to take care of Marie within the hour. Rose immediately told them they had decided to go away for a night or two for their anniversary. Jacqueline had never seen Rose lie before; he did it without hesitation. They accepted his explanation without question. Marie thought it was a good idea, too. Rose told them that they would be back in a day or two. Marie had the emergency number to reach them, behind the kitchen telephone. He made sure Marie had a copy with her. They were all happy that Rose and Jacqueline had decided to go away for their anniversary.

A limousine driver by the name of Harry picked up Jacqueline and Rose about an hour after Marie and her grandparents left. Rose seemed to know the driver by name and gave him no instructions. As they arrived at the Tampa airport, Jacqueline saw a beautiful needle nosed, white plane with only numbers on its tail for identification. Günter, Rose's college friend, was there to greet them. "The plane is ready, Rose. Good to see you and Mrs. Walters!" The game had begun, and Günter seemed to know the rules.

Marie and Jacqueline had known Günter as Rose's crazy college friend. Gunter was a Marine Vietnam vet. Rose had told her to trust Günter completely, and that some day he would tell her about him. Günter made her laugh and he was always so nice to Marie. He was happy that Rose and Jacqueline had married. Günter loved to take Marie places she needed to go. Whenever he came to visit, Günter would volunteer to take Marie and her friends anywhere they wanted to go. He had the patience of a saint with her.

Marie said he was even more protective than Rose, and he was good for a twenty-dollar bill when he dropped her at school! She told Jacqueline that he would never pull away from the curb until she had gone inside the school. "Mom, that is a little much," Marie said. Jacqueline told her, "That is just Günter. Like Rose, he has never had any children, and he is overly protective. Besides, you are nailing him for a twenty every time, so put up with it." Jacqueline could see that Marie understood and really did not mind. Jacqueline could not have been happier about them being protective of her.

Günter could be annoying, and he could eat you out of house and home. He stood just about six feet, an inch shorter than Rose, and he was always on a diet!

He wore black-framed glasses, and his mode of dress had always been a little sloppy, except when he wore a suit, or when he left for military duty. Then he was always in full uniform. He had the ability to anger Rose more than anyone she had ever seen, but their friendship was deep, and she knew it. How deep their friendship was she was only beginning to understand.

As they boarded the plane, Jacqueline was stunned by how nice it was. It had eight seats and a center area with couches and a television. Over to the side was a table with four more seats. The interior of the plane was a beautiful blue and red. There were no stewardesses on the plane that she could see, and it was Günter who opened a globe bar and poured champagne for her. Dinner was under glass in the center of the table. Wonderful white and gold china was set deep into grooves of the mahogany table as permanent tableware. They all had begun dinner on the private jet as she barely felt the plane take off.

While Günter and Rose talked quietly, they did not drink. Both seemed to be very serious about what was going on. Jacqueline did not listen too closely; she was in complete awe just looking around the plane, but she heard Günter tell Rose that the meeting was set and that they would talk in Washington. Suddenly out of the cockpit appeared Harry, the man who had driven the limousine to the airport. She had not even seen him board the plane. "Who else is on this flight?" she thought. They arrived in Washington late at night, and Günter announced, "We will be deplaning in a few minutes."

Another limousine was waiting for them. As they entered the limousine Harry was again driving. "Man," she thought, "this guy does get around." They were taken to a luxurious apartment in Washington. Rose and Günter did not give Harry any directions; he knew where he was going. When they arrived, it was as though Harry knew he was to wait. The apartment had all the signs of being Rose's apartment. Jacqueline did not ask any questions.

Rose told Günter, "Excuse us for a moment." Rose walked Jacqueline into the bedroom. Rose asked quietly, "Are you okay? Remember that you are Mrs. Walters, okay?" Jacqueline told him, "I am fine. I have it." He kissed her as he told her, "I knew you could handle this. Get some rest; you are completely safe. I will be back shortly." She heard the door close and lock. As she began walking around the apartment, she was convinced that it was Rose's apartment. Books he had at home were there in duplicate, but there was no Little Red Book of China! The reading glasses that were lying on the table were the same as Rose's glasses. The choice of art on the walls was the same style as the art at home. The chessboard was set up, and the same chess clock Rose had at home was on the table.

But there was nothing with his name on it! The clothes in the closet were blue blazers, white oxford button down shirts and the style of loafers he wore, all in sizes that Rose wore. All were the same kind of clothes he wore, except for a tuxedo. It was Rose's size, but she had never seen one at home. She thought, "Who is my husband?" Her next thought was that she did not care; Jacqueline had agreed to live this part of their lives on a need-to-know basis, and her life with Rose had been wonderful. She decided to stop looking around and get some rest.

About five a.m., Rose and Günter returned to the apartment. She did not get out of bed, in case they need to talk privately. She heard Günter apologize for keeping Rose so long and then he left. Rose came into the bedroom and kissed her softly. Then he looked so sweetly at her and said, "I want to be inside my wife." They made love as the sun came up over Washington, and then drifted off to sleep. About two p.m., a call came from Günter. Rose told Jacqueline, "We will be leaving at six o'clock this evening." "Are we going home?" she asked. Rose said, "No, we are attending a New Years Eve party at the State Department. Your clothes are in the living room," he told her with a smile. Jacqueline dashed into the living room to find boxes with red bows on the sofa. "Oh, Rose!" she said as she began to open them.

The veil of secrecy was wide and she knew her place. She asked no questions. Rose told her," We will be attending a New Years Eve dinner party and you will be introduced as my wife." That made Jacqueline happy! The thought of not being able to tell the world that she was Mrs. Rosenberg was devastating to her. Rose told her, "Just enjoy yourself at the party. You have nothing to fear. I will be next to you at all times except for about ten minutes. Do not worry in those ten minutes; I just have a quick meeting. When we return to the plane you will be Mrs. Walters again, understand?" "Yes, dear."

Rose continued to say, "by the way, Marie is fine. I checked on her from the Pentagon." Jacqueline thought to herself, "My husband has spent the last few hours at the Pentagon!" Then she began dressing for the party. Someone had purchased a strapless dress of solid black, with a floor-length full skirt in a size four. The material was made of fine silk with tapestry trim. A diamond necklace and earrings were in a separate box. Black heels, clutch bag and a fur coat were there to adorn the dress! Everything she could need was in the bathroom; the packaging never opened: hair dryer, makeup, creams, nylons, and perfumes from France. She looked wonderful; everything was a perfect fit.

Rose came into the living room wearing the tuxedo from the closet. She said, "It is your tuxedo!" He smiled and said, "Remember, ask no questions, my beautiful wife!" In his tuxedo, with his thin, long body and coal black eyes, he was the most handsome man she had ever seen. She wanted him inside her mouth; at that moment he looked delicious. She asked, "How long until we leave?" Rose replied, "Günter should be here any minute." "Well, forget that idea," she thought.

Rose asked, "Do you have everything you need?" She smiled as she told him, "Yes, I can't believe all these beautiful clothes are for me." Rose said, "They are yours, precious. I hope you like them." He kissed her and told her beautiful she looked. Jacqueline had put her hair on top of her head to go with the low back of the dress. Rose gently started removing the hairpins from her hair. He asked, "Do you mind?" She told him, "Not if it pleases you, Rose."

"My pleasure is to see your long hair flow as you walk. I am going to be so proud to introduce my wife to Washington," he said. Günter arrived just then at the apartment. "Well" he said, "Jacqueline you look beautiful; you even make Rose look handsome! I am just kidding. Both of you look wonderful tonight." They all left for the State Department with Harry again driving. Jacqueline knew that she would have to wait for what she really wanted for her anniversary!

The limousine was different from the one Harry had driven from the airport. This one was even more amazing. It was much longer, a beautiful black on black. Gold adorned the champagne glass that Rose filled for her. Neither he nor Günter had anything to drink. The lights of Washington were on in full force as the limousine headed downtown. Dressed more beautifully than she had ever been, she felt like Cinderella on her way to the ball, but she already had her prince charming with her. As the limousine came to a stop in front of the State Department, Günter told them to have a good time, and then he thanked Rose. Günter watched from the car as Jacqueline and Rose walked to the building. As they walked through the door, the car slowly drove off.

As they entered the State Department, Rose took Jacqueline's arm. They were stopped at the main entrance to the reception area. Rose said, "They are going to announce our arrival, so just enjoy it." "Mr. and Mrs. Solomon Rosenberg, Esquire," a strong voice said. Rose was holding Jacqueline's arm, then he placed his other hand on top of her arm for a little extra assurance.

They glided down the steps together with all eyes on them. She could see the people watching as they whispered to one another. The State Department was filled with red and gold adornments everywhere. There were never-ending, mile-high ceilings, and fine tapestry furniture filled the room. Huge paintings and marble statues, like she had seen in the books Rose bought for Marie, were on the walls. Military men were all around the building, beautifully dressed in white uniforms. They wore shining brass Marine Eagle Globe and Anchor insignias and every one had a chest full of ribbons and medals. Many had Mameluke swords at their sides.

Rose told her as they finished their entrance walk, "It has been a long time since I made that walk, Jacqueline. Never have I been more proud than I am tonight." Rose stopped and kissed her as he told her, "Happy Anniversary." She told Rose, "Happy Anniversary darling, but you did not have to go to all this trouble for me." With a smile and his beautiful laugh he told her, "I love you, baby."

Everyone seemed to know Rose, and they all seemed delighted to see him again. They were given glasses of champagne as they mingled with what appeared to be old friends of Rose's. Musicians playing violins roamed the rooms, filling the air with beautiful music. Rose never took a drink from his champagne, and placed it back on a server's tray a few minutes later. The room was summoned to dinner by a man in black tie, standing tall and proud.

As they entered the dining room, tables arranged to seat at least one hundred guests appeared before her eyes. Flowers of red and white filled the room; and red roses had been placed so carefully in the center of each table. Subtle sparkles of gold were in the weave of the massive tablecloths. Wonderfully comfortable tapestry chairs of gold and red with blue piping surrounded the tables. As they took their seats, Jacqueline had a sudden fear of making a mistake and embarrassing Rose.

Then he pulled out Jacqueline's chair and helped her to be seated, as he had done so many times before in their life. He kissed her as he took his seat. It was as though he had known she was having that moment of nerves and calmed her. At that moment she realized she could do nothing to embarrass this man who loved her so. Jacqueline's body relaxed as though she were in Rose's arms.

Dinner was wonderful, with an array of seafood. The beginning was lobster bisque with a surprising Presidential Seal engraved at the bottom of the bowl. It was followed by a delightful shrimp cocktail served in bite-sized pieces, and a main course of Lobster Oscar with fine white asparagus. The meal concluded with fresh berries and red raspberry sauce adorning the finest of white chocolate mousse, served on gold-laced plates. Jacqueline's glass was constantly being refilled with a wonderful white wine.

Dinner was followed by cocktails and dancing; music from an orchestra filled the room. Suddenly the song "La Vie En Rose" began to play. Rose smiled as he took her hand to lead her to the dance floor. He took her in his arms and they began to float across the floor. Rose whispered, "Happy Anniversary," in her ear and said, "I love you. This song was all I had time to arrange for you on this our anniversary, Jacqueline." "*All*" she said. She could see the room full of people watching them, seeing their love, and enjoying the sight.

Every little while Rose would look over at her during the evening, and say quietly, but not secretly, "I love you, Jacqueline." He did not care who heard him. He was a happy man and wanted the whole world to know it. Rose introduced her to people she could have never imagined meeting in her life: ambassadors, senators, and all sorts of powerful people. Everyone was excited to meet the lady who captured the Rose, and they all seemed to know Rose well. She recognized many names and faces from the news, and here she was, seeing them and meeting them in the flesh! She thought to herself, "who is the man on my arm, the man I love so dearly?" Not that it really mattered to her – all that really mattered was their love for each other.

Rose and Jacqueline danced away the New Years Eve of 1987 at the State Department in Washington. The entire time he was whispering his love in her ear. She had the time of her life. She saw how much he adored her that evening and how proud he was that she was his wife. Each and every time that he said, "This is my wife," his eyes would light up. They were so happy that night, as though they did not have a care in the world.

Rose walked Jacqueline down a long corridor and pulled her to him in a passionate, wet kiss. A few seconds later, a picture-perfect Marine guard came up to Rose. "Mr. Rosenberg, sir, would you please come this way? The Ambassador from Hungary is waiting." Rose looked at Jacqueline and said, "Ten minutes, and then I will be back," as he followed the Marine guard. She sat quietly on a tapestry sofa not five feet from where Rose had left her.

In military white and gold, his sword flickering in the light, the most handsome Marine came down the corridor. His hair was black and curly; his eyes of emerald green almost appeared outlined by an artist's brush. His skin was of an olive tone and revealed facial features that were perfectly formed. The muscled mass of a body builder was before her, reminding her for a fleeting moment of that young intern so long ago. She watched as he walked steadily toward her. Stopping near her, he introduced himself as Lance Corporal Kelly, and said, "I will be with you until you husband returns." Then he asked, "Are you having a good time madam?" She said, "Thank you, yes I am." "Would you like to dance, ma'am?" was his next question. She said, "No, thank you."

"Your husband would like me to stay with you," the Corporal said. "Thank you," she replied. Jacqueline was starting to become uncomfortable with this very handsome Marine standing next to her; she just wanted her husband back at her side. Within a few minutes, Rose returned with a briefcase in his hand. Rose thanked the Marine for keeping his wife company. Her eyes left the beautiful Marine at that moment and focused only on her handsome husband. The Marine said, " I am sorry, sir, but your wife did not care to dance." Rose said, "thank you," again. The Marine saluted Rose and walked in front, leading the way, as

Rose and Jacqueline followed him down the corridor, returning to the reception hall they had first entered at the party. Their host was there, and saying their goodnights, they left.

Günter and Harry were waiting outside the State Department in the limousine. As the couple climbed into the limousine, Günter said "Thank you Rose!" Günter's eyes were focused on the latches of the briefcase that Rose was carrying. "I see you had no problem disarming my case. I do not know how I let that damn Budapest woman get her hands on it!" Günter continued, "Thank God, no one took lightly the warning light by the latch of the case, and tried to open it. The compounds mix upon illegal entry and there was enough Astrolite A-W-1 in the lock to blow up the case and the person who opened it."

Günter was excited and babbling as he said, "If they had tried to bypass the failsafe on that case it would have exploded. When that damn girl from Budapest decided to sell it unopened to the Hungarian Embassy she saved her own life. Rose, your old friendship with Ambassador Kelman is the only reason it was returned quietly. But most of all thank you for going to that party. I know how you hate these parties." Rose replied to Günter, "Don't get any more of these ideas, just because they keep sending me these party invitations. I am retired remember. By the way," Rose said, "Günter, *please date women from countries far away from communist zones! We can't afford for this to happen again!*"

The limousine pulled into the hazy lights of a rain soaked Washington night as they returned to the airport in silence. They boarded the plane for home. Rose asked that he and Jacqueline not be disturbed and Günter said, "I have intruded enough on your anniversary. You have my assurance, you will not be disturbed and I will announce our arrival at home from the cockpit." Günter and the briefcase joined Harry in the cockpit of the plane. Jacqueline laid her head on Rose's shoulder as the plane took off. They just sat quietly for a little while, the entire evening replaying in her mind.

Then Rose pulled her face gently to his and said, "Even Shakespeare could not have written of a love greater than ours. Happy Anniversary, Jacqueline." He softly kissed her as he laid her chair back. She felt his hand go under her dress. Quietly but intensely he asked, "Jacqueline have you ever heard of the mile high club?" "No Rose, what is that?" she asked. Rose replied, "Well baby, it has to do with altitude and cabin pressure. You like science don't you?" With a smirk all his own he said, "I will show you!" Then slowly she felt his hand sliding into her panties. She began to feel the sudden warmth so familiar when Rose was near her. He slid to the floor of the plane. His hand slowly retracted as he slid her panties down. "My wife," he said, " I want to show you just how much I love you."

His head slid under the long skirt of her evening gown. His lips began their journey. Slowly, softly and with great passion he applied his tongue to her. Wanting to scream, but knowing she could not, was a high all its own. Rose knew this, as he pushed her evening gown down so he could see her face aglow from the pleasure he was providing her. The entire evening was playing in her head as her love flowed into his lips. Then in total silence, the sounds exploding inside of her, again and again, Rose sought to give her more pleasure. He stopped only to ask, " Are you happy being my wife!" "Yes, yes!" were the first words she could say.

Then she told him, " I love you more than you could ever know. Being your wife is a blessing." His lips began seeking joy from her again. Unable to scream, she came in his mouth relentlessly. His eyes were locked onto hers. She began to snap wildly in his mouth with multiple orgasms, without the use of drugs! Never before had anyone made her snap like her husband did, initiating Jacqueline into the mile high club. She had married the man of her dreams. When she was a little girl, she dreamed of a knight on a white horse. She was told to quit looking for her knight by someone who did not have the ability to reach for the stars. Jacqueline refused to stop looking for him. Now, here she was today with her knight from the *White House!*

His eyes adored her as he continued to marvel in her pleasure, knowing she could not scream, feeling the only pure release her body could offer, over and over upon his lips. Lifting her from her airplane seat to one of the couches on the plane, looking most passionately at her as he said, "This is your *initiation into the mile high club!"* Rose placed his lips more deeply inside her and his tongue moved more wildly. Then he blew gentle streams of air inside her body, two or three times.

As his mouth began its wild feast, Jacqueline's snapping was relentless; she was blessed in her freedom

of orgasm for her husband. Rose was right, as always;
altitude, cabin pressure and her husband's lips caused
Jacqueline to have the deepest orgasms she had ever
felt. "Jacqueline," Rose said, "*You, my wife, have just
become a member of the mile high club!*" Rose did
everything with great intensity, including loving her.

As the plane landed, Jacqueline's head was still
spinning from the enormous pleasure her husband had
bestowed upon her. Her mind was racing at the
excitement of attending a New Years Eve party at the
State Department, along with the realization that Rose
had retrieved Günter's stolen briefcase, and her
admission into the mile high club all in one evening.
Not that she would be able to tell anyone, but she would
always remember New Years Eve of 1987.

In later years, she would find out the reason for
her having to travel under the name Mrs. Walters. Rose
was afraid of hijackers and air pirates. He knew that
they kill the CIA agents, the FBI agents and the Jews
they can identify, even if all of the other captives
survive.

Her thoughts were of complete pleasure as
Günter's voice came over the loud speaker, "Rose, we
are about home. Happy anniversary!" As when they
left, a limousine was there, waiting for their arrival.
Once again, Harry magically appeared, and drove them
home. This time, they were alone. Günter was not in
the car. The divider window was closed and the
privacy shield was up. They returned home as though
they had been on a holiday. Rose told her how
beautiful she had looked in that black dress in the
Washington moonlight. He spoke of how much he

enjoyed the party just because he could show his wife off to the world. He asked, "Did you enjoy our plane ride and our first anniversary?" She told him, "I had the time of my life. Most of all Rose, I enjoyed my initiation into the mile high club."

Jacqueline could barely wait to be home. As soon as Rose closed the front door of their house, Jacqueline kissed him softly as she unleashed the desire she had been holding in. Lowering herself to her knees, still dressed in silk and diamonds, she slipped her husband into her waiting, wet, wanting mouth. Feeling his growth inside her lips, slowly she showed him how much joy he had given to her, as he filled her body with a screeching roar of pleasure....

He raised Jacqueline from her knees and held her closely to him, as he unzipped the back of her dress and let it fall to the floor. He lifted her in his arms and placed her on the sofa. Rose told her, "I have never felt so free to provide and receive pleasure as with you, my wife." His hands unsnapped her strapless bra. His lips kissed hers deeply, as his hands touched her breasts. Then he began drinking from her nipples. The heat was so intense. He told her, "Since my baby enjoyed her indoctrination to the mile high club, now we will see how you like it on the ground."

He slowly slipped her panties off, as he told her, "I love you Jacqueline. I want you to be the most satisfied woman on earth." Then his lips sucked intensely on her, as she began injecting her juice into his mouth, filling it. She screamed, in full of passion, as he slid so deeply inside her. Holding her face with his hands and kissing her wildly, he confessed his love for her. She was soaked in pleasure. The power he used to please her was beyond description. Then her lion roared one more time and they fell fast asleep, still joined as one. He was proud to be the man he was. She was proud to be his wife.

Their lives returned to normal, and Rose went back to his law practice. It was almost as though it had all been a dream. But she still had the dress, the memories of her initiation into the mile high club, and of course, the diamonds!

CHAPTER NINE

THE CASES

THE MOLLY CASE

The Molly case was the case from hell. Mr. Molly sought out Rose to handle a discrimination suit between Molly and his ex-employer, a very large corporation that was owned by an even larger corporation. He sought out Rose after hiring and firing a host of other lawyers who could not get the case to trial. Mr. Molly was an obese, red haired, red faced, angry man. Some clients are good, some are just bad; this one was awful. After Rose had signed on to take the case, he would find out that his client was a paranoid schizophrenic with congestive heart failure. He was running around town with a gold detective's shield stolen from the sheriff's department, and he was subject to tantrums and fits. Mr. Molly was known for eavesdropping and spying on people. To make matters worse, it was his habit to fail to show up for depositions.

Rose said, "If the other side knew all we know about this case, it would be dismissed." That did not matter to him; Rose was an advocate, and it was his job to win. Some kind of mild discrimination might have happened to Mr. Molly. Jacqueline believed that this case was the only reason they had to keep the lawyer Charles, who worked for Rose as an employee at the law firm, long after Rose wanted to fire him. Charles had managed to make himself indispensable by mastering all of the intricacies of the Molly file. Rose could not devote all of his time to only to one case, but Charles had done exactly that.

She also believed that by the time the case was over, Rose hated Mr. Molly. Rose would have liked to drop the case, but the judge made him stay on the case because he knew Rose could handle the mess. So much for Rose's idea of becoming a lawyer *so no one could tell him what to do*. Mr. Molly had put two or three of his children through private Catholic school, telling the nuns he would pay their tuition when his case settled. Rose had known about this for a long time.

All of Jacqueline's worst fears about Charles would come true during this case. Charles called one day and upset Rose terribly; Jacqueline did not know why he was so irate after the call. She later found out that Charles had slept with a paralegal who was working on the Molly case for the opposing law firm, and he did it only two weeks before trial. The other law firm claimed Rose knew the settlement amount they were ready to offer. Charles had supposedly been told the settlement number while have sex with the paralegal. Then the other law firm filed a motion to have Rose involuntarily dismissed as counsel for Mr. Molly on charges of *pillow talk*. The other side wanted the judge to take Rose's firm off the case.

This was after two years of work on a case that Rose believed he would win at trial, and not only because Mr. Molly was discriminated against. Rose was a very good lawyer, and a lot of hard work had been put into the case. Rose had managed to make new law during this case. He had to take an interlocutory appeal to win on the issue. The appellate court stated that, "a wholly owned subsidiary and its mother company can conspire." This meant that neither of the two very large companies that were being sued by Rose could be dismissed as a defendant from the case. This also meant that if Rose was correct, and he was able to convince a jury to award a large verdict on damages, Rose knew that he could collect! "There are three elements a plaintiff's lawyer looks for in a lawsuit: liability, damages and a deep pocket to pay the money," according to Rose.

One night a few months before, a group of people had gone out for drinks. Rose, Jacqueline, CJ, and Charles were among the group. CJ and Rose were deep in conversation over the law, as always. Charles was distracted as usual. He was pacing, going back and forth to the bar. Every now and then, he would act like he was paying attention to what they were saying. When the check came, Charles insisted on paying. The lawyers were all engrossed in conversation, except for Charles. When the bill arrived, Charles handed Jacqueline a credit card and said "Just sign it for me." She did not like or trust Charles, and she told him to sign it himself.

It was three months later that the call came to Rose at home. It was Charles; the FBI had just searched his home. He needed to see Rose right away. Rose agreed to see Charles. Jacqueline tried to dissuade Rose, but he told Jacqueline that he had to keep Charles's criminal activity from hurting the law firm. Rose wanted to fire Charles when he heard that the FBI had searched Charles's home. But Charles was so involved in the Molly case that Rose had to keep him in the firm until the case was over, Rose told

Jacqueline. She never questioned what Rose told her about his work. He was a pro at the law.

Rose learned that the FBI was going to arrest Charles, so Rose contacted the FBI, and offered to bring Charles to the FBI office to talk with them. When Rose went to the FBI with Charles, they were escorted into a conference room. The FBI agents had placed large posters all over the walls. Each was a driver's license, blown up to an enormous size. Every one had Charles's picture, but each one had a different name, and none of the licenses had Charles's name. The lead FBI agent told Rose that Charles had used various identities to illegally get credit, and that the driver's licenses that they saw were just a few of the names Charles had used to fraudulently obtain credit cards. Rose realized that Charles was one bad boy.

The FBI agents were not really interested in giving Charles a break, but Rose was able to strike a deal with the FBI and the United States Attorney. The U.S. Attorney agreed that Charles would not be prosecuted on credit card fraud charges, but that other charges were still being investigated. There was no agreement as to any other charges. In exchange, Charles agreed to become an informant for the FBI. He did not have to go to jail on the credit card charges. It was the best that Rose could do for him.

By the end of the week, Jacqueline would know that Charles was being investigated for the credit card fraud and also for transportation of drugs from Amsterdam, at the very least. He had taken the names of his classmates from law school, and used their credit. Now Jacqueline knew where those five hundred-dollar suits came from. This was not just a young man from a very wealthy family. Who knew what else he had done? But as smart as Charles thought he was, he had walked right in to the arms of the CIA and the FBI.

It turned out that Charles's criminal involvement was the reason he had been staying so close to Rose. Charles must have known that the FBI was catching up to him, and Rose had one of the best legal minds in the country. If they busted Charles, Rose would have to step in just to protect the law firm, or so Charles thought. And Charles, master manipulator that he was, had correctly assessed Rose's reaction.

Charles's assignment was to shoot pictures of drug deals at the Gasparilla parade in Tampa, and at various other events. In the town of Gulf Shore, he was required to photograph arms dealers and drug dealers, using their reflections in the mirrors of taverns or through windows. It seemed to Jacqueline that the FBI had him committed to working for five or ten years as an informant. Charles came over to their home one Saturday afternoon, after one of his covert photography sessions, to sort the film. Rose became very angry and told Charles, "Get that stuff out of this house! I don't want this around Jacqueline and Marie. You got yourself into this mess, and you are damned lucky that you are not rotting away in jail! Do not involve my family in your sordid affairs! Now, just go home. I will see you at work on Monday."

Rose had not fired Charles, and Jacqueline could not believe it was just because of the Molly case. She asked Rose again, and he said "Jacqueline, just trust me." She did, as she always had, for she believed that Rose would handle it. One Monday, Charles came into her office while Rose was in court. He said he needed to talk to her and closed the door. Then he tried to come around to the back of her desk, telling Jacqueline that he was so attracted to her. She told him, "Get out, or I will scream rape." He said, "Oh, you misunderstood me, Jacqueline," and left. She told Rose about it that night. He said, "Charles is desperate, and he is trying to get any hook in us any way he can. Desperate men do desperate acts. Say nothing; I will not leave you alone with him until this is over. Trust me."

Rose told her at that point, "Do not open the door to him if I am not home. Do not get in a car with him." He told Marie the same. Marie said "That's okay with me; I do not like him anyway." Rose said, "Don't worry, child; he will be out of our lives very soon." Anyway, Rose had to keep him on for the Molly hearing; that is what Rose told Jacqueline and she did not ask him any more questions.

Two days later Rose and Jacqueline, with Charles following in his car, drove across the Crystal Cove Bridge, to the federal courthouse in Tampa. The hearing to disqualify Rose and his firm from the Molly case for "pillow talk" was at 10 a.m. The other side had brought in a New York law firm, which included a Jewish lady lawyer who was an expert in the field of legal ethics.

Jacqueline was surprised to see that Rose seemed extremely calm on the drive to court that day. He was laughing, and talking about the vacation that he was planning. All the arrangements had been a secret and Jacqueline was trying to guess. All Rose would tell her was that they would be leaving in a few days. He told her, "Pack light for a warm climate and you can buy whatever else we need when we arrive." Her mother, father and Marie were all in on the surprise, but Jacqueline could not get them to even give her a hint of their destination. Rose was chipper and laughing all the way to court, dressed as always to perfection in his Ivy League attire. His briefcase had been prepared the night before, as usual.

When they arrived at the courthouse, Rose insisted on waiting until the last minute to get on the elevator to go to the hearing room. Rose sent Charles ahead of them to the courtroom. They entered the elevator alone to go up to the hearing. Rose immediately removed his blazer and tossed it over his shoulder and messed his hair up a bit. He opened his briefcase and re-closed it with a few papers hanging out. As they got off the elevator, he kissed her and said, "Sit in the courtroom and watch the show."

Rose entered the courtroom just prior to the judge, racing in as though he were late. The four lawyers from the other side were already neatly seated at their table. Rose, with his jacket half on, his briefcase disarrayed, walked straight to his table and put down his brief case with a bang. Suddenly he turned to the other side and focused directly on the lady lawyer. Rose stuck his hand out to shake the hand of the ethics expert. Just as their hands gripped to shake, Rose said, "Hello, I hear you are the *Ethics Maven.*" Jacqueline knew that maven is a Yiddish word for "the self-proclaimed one." She recognized that it was a terribly derogatory term to use, and it was quite shocking for Rose to say it to her face. The lady ethics expert and the other attorneys seated with her were absolutely stunned. At that very moment, the bailiff called the court to session, and the Judge entered the room.

As the hearing began, the defense lawyers told how Charles, who was an employee of Rose, had slept with their paralegal and alleged that it was Rose's fault! They even implied that Rose had put Charles up to sleeping with their paralegal, in order to get information on the amount that the defense was willing to pay to settle the Molly case. Rose and his firm had to be taken off the case because the settlement amount was revealed and he must know that settlement number!

The Ethics Maven began her argument, but she was so flustered from Rose's remark that she could not even look at Rose. Jacqueline knew that the Ethics Maven's argument made almost no sense; the woman was so agitated by Rose's remark that she could not think clearly. After only a few minutes, she had one of the other lawyers complete most of the argument before the court. The "Ethics Maven" remark had hit home. She stayed in useless shock throughout that entire hearing. So much for the *Ethics Expert* from New York! It was the best Colombo routine Jacqueline had ever seen from *The Rose*.

Then it was Rose's turn. He quietly explained that he knew nothing about a settlement number. He had no idea his young lawyer had slept with their paralegal. If his young lawyer knew the settlement number, which Rose believed he did not, Rose had instructed the young lawyer not to tell him. Rose also had suggested that if the lawyers in his firm would like to keep their jobs from now on, "They had better not sleep with a paralegal on the other side of a case."

The Judge thought for a moment, then he asked Rose, "Would you have done that?" Rose responded, without hesitation *"Your Honor, I am a married man!"* The Judge dismissed the Motion for Disqualification and set the case for trial. The Judge saw that this had been a last ditch effort to prevent the case from going to trial the following week. He was a very wise judge, and he was not going to allow that particular abuse of the legal system.

Rose's curve ball knocked the Ethics Maven completely off balance. Rose argued like the master of appellate law that he was. He was so fast on his feet! Rose passed the Judge's integrity test in one statement, with seven little words! Those words were, "Your Honor, I am a married man!"

After the hearing, back at the office, Jacqueline could not believe how angry Rose was. He had, for the first time in his life, been called up on an *ethics violation*. For a young lawyer to cause him to be involved in an ethics hearing! Rose was all over every young attorney in the firm. He decided they needed an office conference on *ethics*. He explained in a very angry voice, "In my entire career I had never been brought up on any ethical violations. Lawyers in this firm *will* live up to the appearance of propriety, *or their fate will be swift*. Do I make myself clear, or shall I be more specific? If anyone ever again causes the ethics of this firm to be questioned, that person will *never be permitted through the front door of this office!"*

Jacqueline knew that Rose never knew any settlement number. After he calmed down, they went to dinner alone. Over dinner, she commented on his Colombo routine in court. He said, "Don't tell the other lawyers, but it was the most fun I have had in court in years! I did my homework on that New York firm they brought in. I knew that she was Jewish and I was telling her just what I thought of their entire hearing and her. To sick an Ethics Maven on me - I am an ethical man, if I am nothing else in this life, Jacqueline!"

They returned home in a most glorious mood; the day had been so much fun for Rose. He came into the kitchen as Jacqueline was making the coffee. "Jacqueline," he said as he kissed her cheek, "I want one more thing to make it a perfect day." She could feel her smile grow as Rose began lifting her dress from behind. She felt his warm, wet entry into her body, his hands upon her breasts. He was still filled with energy! Slowly, he turned her body unto the dining table. Gently laying her forward, she was rewarded for his victory in court!

Two days later, the case settled for $250,000.00. It was time to settle up with the lawyers who had worked on the case before Rose. A Catholic school also needed to be paid. After the settlement, Mr. Molly decided that he did not want to pay any attorneys but Rose. Mr. Molly also refused to pay his debt to the Catholic school. Molly owed $10,000.00 to the school. His children were educated in the school, based upon his promise to pay for their education when the case was resolved. The lawyers had agreed to a hearing before the Judge to decide on the fees for each attorney, but Rose didn't know what to do about Molly's refusal to pay the Catholic school.

Finally, Rose decided. He asked Jacqueline, "Will you call the nuns at the school? Tell them of the attorney's fee hearing, then suggest they attend the hearing themselves and advise the Judge during the hearing of the monies they are owed. Make it clear that they are on their own." The nuns arrived at the hearing to *almost* everyone's surprise. At the appropriate time, a nun dressed in full habit addressed the court. It was ordered and adjudged that the Catholic school was to be paid immediately. Rose grinned at Jacqueline when the Judge made that order! Think about that, the "Jew" who protected the Catholic school! Jacqueline has always found a strange truth in that. A good man is a good man, no matter what his religion.

Rose and everyone else got their money. Mr. Molly got about $163,000.00, and the Molly case had finally ended. Rose had taken Charles and Jacqueline to the federal courthouse for the signing of the settlement documents and the filing of the case dismissal the next day. After the settlement signing was over, the courtroom emptied except for Rose, Charles, the judge, and Jacqueline. Rose had told Charles and Jacqueline to wait while he filed the dismissal paperwork.

About two minutes later, six men in suits entered the courtroom from all doors. One said, "Charles Pardon, you are under arrest for Arms Dealing under the Racketeering Influence and Corrupt Organizations Act of the United States of America. You have the right to remain silent. If you give up the

right to remain silent, anything you say can and will be used against you in a court of law. You have the right to an *attorney*. If you desire an attorney and cannot afford one, one will be appointed for you before any questioning, if you wish." Charles was aghast! Five FBI agents cuffed him and started to remove Charles. He was calling to Rose for help. Rose asked the agents to wait a moment, and he whispered something in Charles's ear. Charles looked shocked, and hung his head. The FBI agents then took him away. The judge, who immediately realized that Rose was somehow behind the arrest, said, "Good work, Mr. Rosenberg." The sixth man was Günter; he just laughed and said, "Another one for the good guys, Rose."

As they left the courthouse, Rose turned to Jacqueline and said, "Would you like to know what I whispered in Charles's ear?" "Yes!" she replied. Rose said, "I told him, 'When I helped write the RICO statute, I wrote it to take care of an evil man like you. I might have found some sympathy for what you had gotten mixed up in, if you had not walked my wife into the '*Tangerine Lounge*.' For that act, you lost any compassion I might have had for you!" Rose then said, "Revenge is best served cold my dear; I waited a long time for this day."

When they arrived back at Rose's law office, everyone was gone for the day. Rose asked, "Honey, come into the library and lock the door." Kissing her, he sat her on the huge conference table that they had custom-built for the library. He looked into her eyes and said, " I have removed all of the evil from our lives today. Now Jacqueline, only good is ahead for us." He began removing her suit coat, and then slowly unbuttoned her silk blouse. Lifting a nipple from inside her bra cup, he placed his soothing lips upon her breast, as she reached out to feel her husbands swell. His warm hands slowly removed her bra.

Laying her back, he removed the other articles of clothing – they were obstacles to the good that Rose was intent on doing. Then he slid her to the end of the twelve-foot table, smiling as he lowered his lips to hers. Moisture began to flow from Jacqueline. Rose separated her legs more, seeking complete passage into her body. Still fully dressed in his courtroom attire, Rose's lips searched and found every pleasure point inside of her. She lay in stunned satisfaction, enjoying the unending pleasure of her husband's love.

After providing her with full and complete pleasure, Rose insisted on dressing her himself; lastly he brushed her hair. They returned home, never to speak much of Charles again. When people asked Rose about Charles he would always say he went on to bigger things. Jacqueline loved Rose's victories in court!

DEAR SARA

Life at the law firm was filled with fun. One day a nice young girl, who was an old client of Rose's named Sara, came to see him. Sara was a simple looking girl, attractive, but not a stunning beauty. She was extremely intelligent. Sara owned a medical business and had become very successful doing outside laboratory work for dentists.

A Romeo in gold chains had ripped off Sara by promising her love. She gave him permission to take $15,000.00 of her money to buy them a boat. Then he titled the boat to himself, hooked the new boat and trailer to his car, and packed the car and boat with all of his belongings. He informed Sara he was leaving for California with the boat, and without her! She was so embarrassed; she had trusted him and she had acted out of love, abandoning her good business sense.

Sara said, "How could I have been taken like that?" She was more upset with herself for being so foolish than she was with the Romeo. Rose said, "Are you telling me that everything he has is in that car and trailer?" Sara said, "Yes." Next Rose asked, "Does he have a Florida driver's license or is there a local telephone in his name?" "No," replied Sara. "Well," said Rose, "he has no permanent address in Florida." So Rose seized the boat and car within an hour, pending the outcome of litigation.

The next day, the man called the firm and wanted to pay Rose for the boat. He came to the firm with no shirt on, and sat down in one of the very expensive chairs Jacqueline had bought for the firm. Jacqueline told Rose, "That guy who took Sara is here, with no shirt on, to pay you!" When Rose saw him, his sweaty back against Jacqueline's beautiful cloth chairs, Rose immediately ordered him out of the firm until he put a shirt on. The man said, "I don't have one! Everything I own is in my car and my boat! I need to pay you so I can get into my car where my clothes are." Rose quickly pointed out that the boat was purchased with *Sara's* money, not Romeo's, and so the boat was Sara's, not his, at least until Romeo satisfied his monetary debt to Sara. Rose pointedly told him, "Only after you pay all of the money that you owe to my client, may you call that boat yours. I will not permit you to enter my office dressed inappropriately. Return only when you are properly dressed!" Rose made him go buy a shirt and come back in proper attire to pay the $15,000.00. Rose said, "I wanted him to suffer at least a little of the humiliation he inflicted on Sara."

TAX DAY

Rose had obtained a judgment for one of his clients. The person that he had obtained the judgment against kept so little money in the bank that Rose couldn't collect on it. Every attempt Rose made in collecting this judgment was of no avail. Rose knew the man had the money to pay the $25,000.00 judgment. The man owned a large company and he had told Rose, "Good luck finding my money!" Rose knew if he seized the account with less money than the amount of the judgment that he would be not be able to collect the balance of the debt for his client.

Finally, Rose prepared to seize the account after months of unsuccessfully attempting to find assets of the judgment debtor. He filed a Motion for a Writ of Garnishment and found a judge to enter an order. Rose and Jacqueline then went to the clerk's office and had a Writ of Garnishment issued. Then they proceeded to contact the sheriff's office and had a deputy meet them at the bank. Rose and Jacqueline entered the bank along with the deputy. They walked up to a teller, and asked for the bank manager. A small man of about fifty came over and introduced himself as the branch manager. Rose introduced himself to the bank manager and said, "Could you tell me what time it is?" The bank manager answered, "It is 9:15." The deputy handed the bank manager the judgment, as Rose told the manager, "It is 9:15 a.m., on April 15, 1988, and there is enough money in the bank account of the debtor to satisfy the judgment. I am seizing it for the full amount!"

The bank manager said that he would check to see if the funds were there. They all went into his office, where he pulled the account up on the screen of the bank's computer. Then he called the customer to notify him. After he called the customer, the bank manager informed Rose that he was right; there was enough money to cover the judgment. The bank manager said he would like to call the bank's attorney. Rose told him to go ahead. The bank's attorney asked what lawyer was seizing the account. The bank manager told him it was Solomon Rosenberg. The bank manager hung up and cut the cashiers check for the $25,000.00. As Rose and Jacqueline were leaving the bank, the man whose account had just been seized came screaming into the bank. Rose already had a cashier's check for the full amount; he and Jacqueline just kept walking.

Later that day, Rose and Jacqueline had lunch with the clients, and delivered the cashier's check to them. Rose's clients had finally gotten their money. They asked Rose, "How did you know the money would be there?" He said, "What is today's date?" "April 15th" was the reply. He said, "I seized the money today, because I believed that he would have made a deposit to his account to pay taxes. Based upon my estimate of his income, I figured that his taxes would be considerably more than $25,000.00. It was a guess, and I was right. I guess we made the check that he wrote to the IRS bounce! What a shame!"

A LITTLE GIRL'S SAFETY

In another case, one of Rose's young male lawyers named Kim called Rose in Ft. Lauderdale, while he and Jacqueline were on vacation. A policeman who was divorcing a woman of most questionable character had come into the office. She was planning to leave for California the next week with the policeman's daughter. The woman had been named as the primary custodial parent, and the policeman was granted visitation rights while the divorce was pending in court. The policeman wanted to get custody of the girl, because he thought that his child would be lost to him forever if the woman took her out of Florida. Kim told Rose that he could handle the custody dispute. Rose became a little nervous about letting his young associate handle the case alone. He decided that he and Jacqueline would drive back to the St. Augusta the next morning, so that Rose would be available in the office, if Kim had a problem.

About 11:00 a.m., Kim came back to the office from court during a recess. He told Rose that it looked like he could lose the case. Rose said, "We cannot lose, we are right. That woman is not removing the child from this state. Do you have the list of men floating through her home?" Rose had just arrived from Ft. Lauderdale, and he was dressed in a sport shirt and slacks. The week before, he had been caught in the rain and he had used his spare court clothes he kept at the office. He had no courtroom attire, and he had only ten minutes until court resumed!

First Rose asked the young lawyer, who was a small man of about 5'6', to remove his coat. Rose attempted to put Kim's jacket on, but it was to small to even get across Rose's shoulders. He gave Kim his jacket back, and told the young lawyer to come to court with him. Rose, who had never appeared in court without his Ivy League attire, took the young lawyer into the courtroom. When the Judge entered the room, he was shocked by Rose's sudden and unusually casual appearance. Rose raised himself to his feet, and dressed in a sport shirt, he addressed the court. "Your Honor, I beg the tolerance of the court on my lack of appropriate attire, but I was on vacation when I heard I was needed to stop a terrible wrong that my associate felt was about to occur in this court.

He reached for Kim, who was seated next to him at the lawyer's table dressed in court attire. Bringing Kim to his feet he stated, "Your Honor here is my suit and tie; now let us argue this case." Stunned, almost laughing, the judge permitted Rose to finish arguing the case. Rose recited a list of eighteen men's names, and said that they had all slept in the woman's home while her daughter was present and her husband was not. All before her daughters fifth birthday! To say the least, the child did not leave the State of Florida. The mother was removed as primary custodial parent, and the judge specifically ordered that the child was not to be transported from the State of Florida by either party. The policeman father was ordered to be the temporary, primary custodial parent, pending a full custody hearing.

The policeman was quite grateful to Rose, but told him that Kim had been about to lose. Rose disagreed, saying, "You owe Kim a debt of gratitude. That young lawyer is the only reason you now have custody of your daughter. Had I been in town, I might not have accepted your case, but Kim lobbied me until he wore me down, and I agreed. He also had the wonderful foresight to ask you to compile that list of paramours. Without it, you surely would have lost!" After Rose's comments to him, the policeman asked to speak to Kim. The client thanked Kim for winning the case, and insuring the safety of the client's daughter.

THE MIAMI MEN

The son of a political figure in the Tampa Bay area was arrested for selling cocaine. His father was a friend of Rose's, and came to him for help. The police have the young man, who had never been in trouble before, dead to rights. There was no hope of a victory at trial. The young man had sold the drugs to an undercover agent, and the whole drug deal was on videotape. Either he had just begun dealing drugs, or he had been very lucky and had avoided the attention of the police for a while. Rose advised the young man to "drop a dime" (a term used for squealing) on his drug suppliers. Rose believed he could negotiate probation if the young man cooperated with law enforcement. The boy could then take probation and go off to college. Since the young man had never been in trouble, and could provide the police with a major ring of drug dealers, Rose knew he could get the kid a second chance in life. Rose negotiated the deal with prosecutors before the boy informed. He dropped a dime on the men from Miami who had sold him the drugs for resale, and he was given a sentence of probation.

The Miami Men were mad that they could not find this kid who had, "dimed them out." So they came after Rose. First came the threatening telephone calls. Then as Rose and Jacqueline opened the office one morning, she saw Rose trying to hide the dead fish he had found at the door of the office. Finally late one evening, after running over to the law firm for some documents, Jacqueline noticed a car behind her that seemed to be making the same turns as she was. Feeling a bit uncomfortable, she began to make sharp turns with no blinker, but the car stayed on her tail.

Rose and Marie were at home, and Jacqueline did not want the car to follow her there. Turning in the opposite direction from home, she began going north on a quiet stretch of road. The car was still with her, riding on her tail, coming up very close and forcing her to speed up faster and faster. Then the car would drop back; she sped up one final time to get back to the main road. The car was still there, as she headed for the police station.

Still coming up on her from behind, it followed her in pursuit. Nervous, she made a wrong turn. Jacqueline was grateful to see that she had turned right into an area where two police cars were parked. The other car continued on straight past the police cars. She jumped out and told the police to call it in, but the car was long gone. They escorted her home and told Rose of the incident. He thanked them and said he would handle it. A telephone call came within minutes of the police leaving. Who Jacqueline's pursuers were and why they were following her became clear to Rose in that call. Rose kept Marie and Jacqueline in one room of the house. He sat with them, holding a loaded gun in his lap.

Then Rose made a call to Günter at the Tampa FBI office. Within an hour, Günter arrived at their home. Several hours later, an air-conditioning repair vehicle pulled into the driveway. Three more men entered the house over the next thirty minutes. Günter let them in. One was Harry the limousine driver! The other two, Jacqueline had never seen before.

Harry was a tall, strikingly handsome man of about forty. Jacqueline did not know Harry as well as she knew Günter, but he seemed to know Rose well. Harry had all kinds of high tech computer equipment, and he was giving orders to the two other men on the installation of his equipment. An hour later, two men left in the air conditioning repair vehicle, but Günter and Harry stayed.

Günter was a Special Agent for the FBI and somehow, he was also on active duty in the intelligence division of the Marine Corps. Günter usually looked like an unmade bed in civilian clothes. Jacqueline knew that Günter could dress well if he chose to do so; he had certainly looked sharp on the day of Charles's arrest! Günter never wore a uniform unless he was returning to a base. Marie was surprised to see him with all this computer equipment. Rose told her, "Günter is an old military man, and he is just going to help us get this problem resolved." Marie was happy to see Günter; although she did not know the other men there, she understood that they were at the house to help.

Günter's job since their marriage was to stay next to Marie when trouble was on the horizon. She liked him and knew him only as Rose's friend; she knew that he was one person she should contact if anything went wrong and she could not reach her parents. Rose and Günter had done well developing

Marie's relationship with Günter; she accepted and adored him.

The wiretaps were in place, and they all waited for the next call. Harry's eyes brightened up as he looked intently at his computer screen. The call came shortly after midnight. Rose answered the telephone. As the one half of computer screen began showing every word said by both parties, the other half showed some kind of map with numbers racing in the corner.

The voice said, "Did our message sink in? We almost had your wife tonight! We are going to kill your family, you mother-f...er! We will rape them first! Who do you think you are? Tell us where that punk is." Rose tried to strike a deal, pleading for his family's safety. They said, "We want to know where the stool pigeon is." Rose kept begging, to no avail. Then the voice began describing what they would do to his family. Rose kept begging, saying he did not know where the young man had gone. The voice said, "You know, and you will tell us or wish that you had, you dumb f...ing lawyer." Finally, with another threat the caller hung up. The call seemed to last for hours to Jacqueline, but she knew that it had only been two or three minutes. Rose was mad.

Harry nodded to Günter. Günter said, "We have the location." Günter began speaking into a microphone hooked up to Harry's computer. "Location pinpoint Golf, Uniform, November, Tango, Echo, Romeo, 1525 Lake View Drive, Miami Florida, 999930555219949999. Pick up authorized, Golf, Uniform, November, Tango, Echo, Romeo and out.

Harry packed up and left; Günter stayed the night with them.

About eight a.m., a call came in for Günter. As he hung up he said, "It is over." Rose told Günter, "Kill the SOBs; they threatened my family!" Günter said, "I will do my best to deliver them safely into custody, if possible. You know, sometimes they resist!" And then he winked at Rose. Jacqueline never heard of the Miami Men again.

A LAWYER'S PAINFUL SECRET

When a young man with no criminal record is arrested for simple, misdemeanor possession of marijuana, even a bad lawyer should be able to keep him from getting convicted. A father, prominent in the community, came to see Rose. His son had been arrested for possession of pot. The father said, "I want you to get him off. Even a hint of any sort of impropriety would destroy my reputation. I will pay your fee for my son." Rose agreed to represent the boy, and in doing so, told the father, "You do understand that my client will be your son, and not you. He will be the person who must make the decisions regarding his case. If he chooses to consult you, that is fine, but I will not tell you anything regarding the case that your son will not authorize." The father responded, "Sure, sure – whatever. Just get him off." Rose ordered the police report. To his surprise there was a little more to the story, so he called in the son.

When asked about the strange position that he and another man were found in when they were arrested in the car, the son replied, "My father must never know I am gay." Rose tried to convince the young client to come out of the closet to his father, so Rose could effectively defend the possession of pot. Rose told the client, "I am sure that I can win the Possession charge for you, but the police are threatening to charge you with committing a lewd and lascivious sexual act if we fight the pot charge. I believe that we could prevail on that charge, as well. The problem is that your father would find out about your sexual activity. If you tell him now, you can pick the time and place for your father to learn your sexual orientation."

The boy's response was immediate. He would not tell his father, and he would not allow Rose to tell him, either. Despite several conversations with Rose, the client's position was still clear. If the boy's father found out that he was gay, the boy would commit suicide. Nothing Rose said to him would change his mind. After careful consideration, they decided to plead guilty to the possession of pot charge if Rose could convince the police to brush the oral sex charges under the carpet. Rose still hoped that he could convince the police not to proceed on either charge, but the cops were adamant. They would not drop the marijuana charge, and they were still thinking about filing the oral sex charge. The cops gave Rose a very hard time, but finally, he was able to get the officers to agree not to file the sex charge, and the boy pled guilty to marijuana possession. Rose convinced the judge to withhold adjudication of guilt, so at least the boy would not have a formal drug conviction.

The father came roaring into Rose's office, steaming mad, after the plea. He was furious that Rose had not made the drug charge disappear entirely. "I paid you perfectly good money to make that marijuana charge disappear! I told you what this would do to my reputation! Now, I am ruined! No one will be willing to do business with a man whose son is a convicted drug addict!" Rose tried to calm the man down. He pointed out that the man's son was not convicted, and that many teens experimented with pot. He and the father, who were about the same age, "could hardly avoid smoking a joint when we were teens!" The father acknowledged that he had smoked pot when he was a teenager in the 1960's. He said, "That's completely different; I wasn't ruining my family's reputation in the community! Because you ruined my name, I will do everything in my power to ruin yours. You are worthless as a lawyer, and I will make sure that all of my friends know it!" Rose never even hinted that there was some other reason for the boy's decision to plead guilty.

When the father came in to Rose's office, he caused such a commotion that the whole office could hear his every word. Kim, Rose's young associate, had been involved in the case, and he knew why the boy insisted on the plea arrangement. Kim came into Rose's office after the father left. Kim asked, "Why didn't you tell that man the truth – that it was his son's decision to enter the plea, and why? You could have at least have told the father that there was more to the story, and that his son entered the plea to keep from getting worse charges!"

Rose told Kim, "The client in this case was the son, not the father. Even though the father paid the bill, I have to follow the client's instructions. That boy was adamant that his father could never find out about his sexual orientation. I am ethically bound to maintain the confidences and secrets of my client, and that is what I have done and will continue to do, unless the boy tells me otherwise." Kim pondered for a moment, and asked, "So you have to maintain silence, even if it causes you personal harm? After all, that man all but promised to destroy your business!" Rose told him,

"Even if it causes me harm, I cannot reveal my client's confidences. I must follow my client's instructions if those instructions do not require me to commit an illegal act. It does not matter that my personal or professional interests are not the same as my client's. It does not matter that keeping the boy's secret may harm me – I cannot reveal what he will not permit, nor can anyone else who works for me."

Rose never breathed a word of the boy's real reason for pleading guilty, even though the father bad-mouthed Rose every chance he got. Rose weathered the storm, but the father did cause some harm to Rose's business. Rose suffered in silence, as he was ethically bound to do.

CHAPTER TEN

DOOMSDAY AND THE DAYS BEFORE

After the Molly case, Rose and Jacqueline took off on his secret vacation; it was to *Jamaica*! He was so excited to take her there. He wanted to show Jacqueline where he had spent that year or so of his life. The number of people who remembered Rose surprised Jacqueline. They arrived at a beautiful beach resort, but they left for the countryside in a new convertible almost as soon as they checked in and had lunch. Jacqueline was disappointed to leave the white beaches with their coconut palms, and the amazing shades of azure blue water. She wanted to go dive into that clear water, but Rose told her there would be time for that later.

Rose told her that he was going to take her into the villages to visit families from that time more than twenty years ago, when he had lived in Jamaica and made his living from the stock market. And Jacqueline, always eager to learn more about her husband's past, was ready to go! There were so many things that she knew she could never know about Rose. Here he was inviting her into his past! She thought to herself, "The beach and the water can wait!"

The people were so nice, and they loved to tell of Rose's kindness to them. Rose had stopped and filled the trunk with food on the way through town. He gave the food to the families, and fruit and candy to the children. The children crowded and clamored around Rose and Jacqueline. Some of them even called him by name! Since he had not been there since any of them were born, Jacqueline thought that the parents and grandparents must have remembered Rose in their stories to the children. Jacqueline was amazed to see the vibrant colors of the children's clothes. They wore bright orange, purple, blue, yellow, and green. The children were laughing, and they were happy to see the man of whom they had heard so much.

Rose passed out books to the children. He had purchased the books in America, and he had carefully packed them for the trip. She could not believe how Rose had prepared for this trip.

It was amazing to see Rose being treated so fondly in another country; they remembered and adored him. Rose's acquaintances told the couple that they had told their children of his kindness so long ago. They remembered Rose for his kindness and generosity, and the stories of him had grown into fables over the years – his good deeds were larger with each telling of the stories! Rose and Jacqueline spent the night dancing, drinking, and smoking Jamaican pot with his old friends.

Then, as it was getting light over the water, they drove toward the beautiful ocean side, with the convertible top down in the already baking hot Jamaican sun. Rose stopped the car on a narrow road near the water's edge. The temperature had not cooled below eighty degrees that night. When he had parked the car near the back of a waterfall, Rose grabbed a basket and a blanket that one of the men in the village had given him.

Walking hand and hand, Jacqueline and Rose entered a field of beautiful flowers, rocks, and trees, surrounding the blue-hole of the waterfall. Jacqueline was thunderstruck at the beauty of the waterfall! It began high in the cliffs above, and tumbled hundreds of feet to the lagoon below. The mist from the fall reflected every color of the rainbow in the morning sun. It was breathtaking. And the sounds! Jacqueline could hear the chirping and caws of birds over the roar of the waterfall, and the rustle of underbrush moving in the gentle salt breeze. She saw brilliantly colored birds flying and perched in the trees around the fall. These were the birds that were making the beautiful clamor, she realized.

Rose laid the blanket out and set the basket down. Opening the basket, he pulled out a bag of rolled joints of marijuana. "Now, you are going to smoke some really good Jamaican Gold! I wanted to save this pot for when we were alone," he said. It tasted wonderful, and Jacqueline became completely stoned. He said, "Let's swim," as he began to strip off his clothes. She quickly followed suit. Naked, they played in the warm water under the hot Jamaican sun. Jacqueline had never seen Rose so free of spirit.

"Follow me!" Rose cried out to Jacqueline, as he swam under the waterfall. He lifted her from the water and sat her on the hidden rocky bank. Then they began kissing and exploring one another's bodies. "Jacqueline, I want you to move over to this rock," he said. She did and suddenly a hot spring of water came pushing up between her legs. Rose separated her legs and realigned her body as he held her still; he placed his lips on her breast. Every five or ten seconds the water would gush as Rose held her firmly on the rock. First the water would gush inside her body and then her body's juice would flow out, following the receding water. It was too pleasurable to move.

"That, my wife, is a small spring, doing pleasure for you." Rose held her tightly while his tongue licked her nipples and his hands played with her in the water. As the pleasure increased, he dipped his head under the water and came up between her legs. His face was so beautifully water soaked, as she felt his mouth touch her warm, wet lips. His lips joined together in harmony with the spring for her pleasure. She could not believe the effect of both at once. She watched the water splash his face as her husband dined on her warmth.

As the sun was beginning to set, he lifted her onto his body. They made love in the water behind the fall. Rose gently placed her body onto the bank, and she came to rest on the green grass. They watched the sun set over the ocean in the distance. The colors of the sunset, reflected in the water, were unbelievable. Rose was stroking her hair and face as he began pleasing her again.

Their love continued until the sun was gone. Rose put a small lantern from his basket on the edge of the blanket. The lantern cast a dim glow on the waterfall. The mist from the fall changed from yellow nearest the lamp, to deep blues and purples farther away.

They lay on the blanket near the water's edge, and she folded her body down upon his, as he pulled her to him. There were no sounds. They shared their love for each other for hours. As they lay cuddled in each other arms, smoking the Jamaican Gold, Rose asked her, "Is there any pleasure you want, that I have not given to you?" She told him that he had given her every pleasure a woman could dream of, as the sun began to rise from behind the waterfall, magically turning the mist from white to shimmering colors.

"Well," Rose said, "I just want to make sure that my wife is always, completely satisfied." Then he lifted her to her feet and walked her into the waterfall, again. Kissing her the endless kiss of love, he put her back against the warm wet rock wall behind the fall. "Stand there, pretty," Rose said. She stood with the warm water dripping from the rocks down onto her breasts, and rivulets of water running down between her thighs.

Then Rose stepped below her into the water. Standing below her, just waist high in the water, Rose slowly separated her legs with his water-soaked face. Placing his tongue so gently on her and looking directly up at her, he said. "Tell me you love me Jacqueline." She told him, "I do love you, Rose." She was anticipating what was about to come next. Then she began to flow with warm juice. "Tell me again," he said. "I love you Rose!" Then her body seeped again. She stood baking in the sun, against the rocks, screaming her love for Rose as she repeatedly had orgasms for her husband below. With the warm water running down on her, her body flowing continuously into her husband's mouth, she confessed all of the love she had for him.

In the early afternoon, on the second day since they had left their hotel, they began their drive back. The drive to the waterfall had consisted of about thirty miles of secluded road. Jacqueline told Rose, "I am the most satisfied, pampered woman I know!" As they began the long drive back down the quiet dirt road, Jacqueline told Rose to drive slowly, as she unbuckled his pants and lowered his zipper. Then she placed her wet lips onto his seated body. She raised her head only to tell him he must keep driving or she would stop! There was no one on the dirt road and he swerved quite a few times, but it was fun. The harder he got, the more he swerved. Eventually he stopped the car and opened the door.

Leading Jacqueline onto the grass at the side of the road he said, "Don't tell me that I have to keep driving with your lips on me!" He lifted her gently and placed her quickly on the soft grass. Tossing her dress completely over her head, Rose stated, "I will show you who is boss!" He climbed inside her; deeper and deeper he went. Fast and hard as the rocks, he showed her who was the boss, with his detonation inside Jacqueline. Lifting her into his arms and carrying her back to the car, he said, "Come on, boss." They were both laughing hysterically.

They had the time of their lives in Jamaica. They thought about never returning to the states at all. Rose wondered how long their money could last. If it were not for Marie, they never would have come home. Rose made love to her in more ways and places than she could have ever dreamed. They stayed stoned the entire trip. When their final night in Jamaica came, they spent the night on the beach in Jamaica, promising to return again soon. They professed their love for each other, showing it in wild, wet sex anywhere and everywhere they could be alone, and in Jamaica there were many places to be alone.

They walked to a local bar, and had a few drinks with friends they had promised to see before they left. Rose had no racial prejudice of any kind; Jacqueline loved him so for that kind of goodness. They danced and laughed the night away at the bar full of Jamaican locals. They had Jacqueline up in the air over their heads, and Rose too! Saying goodbye the Jamaican way was fun; they were such nice people.

As they started walking back to the hotel, two of the Jamaican women they had been dancing with said something to Rose. Jacqueline was unable to understand due to their Jamaican dialect. On their way back to the hotel, Rose told her, "If you want any pleasure that I am not able to give you, man or woman, I can get it for you in Jamaica." "Rose, do you want to sleep with one of those Jamaican ladies?" she asked. "No. Jacqueline, don't be silly! When I was here a long time ago, I tried everything. I just want you to have anything you desire. That is what those two ladies were offering. They wanted to know if there were any sexual pleasures that they or their mates could provide for us. I told them that I would let them know, and that if it were a Jamaican man or woman or both that you wanted, I would see you had it." "No, Rose, just you!"

Rose pulled her into a field under the moonlight and placed her on the ground, kissing her as he told her he loved her more than she could ever know. He said, "I would have gotten you anything you wanted, and you chose me." He removed her swimsuit and sarong, and slid deep inside her. "I will always love you for that choice," he said. I love you were the words she heard, as she came with her husband one last time under the Jamaican moon.

They returned from the island completely rested and satisfied. Rose had more energy than anyone she had ever known before. She asked him, "How did you wait for over a year to make love to me after we met? I wanted you the whole time!" "I knew that you loved me," he said. "I knew you would be my wife. I planned your pleasure for the rest of our lives during that time, in my mind." That was the Rose.

CHAPTER ELEVEN

BACK IN THE USA

Rose was ready to go back to work. The date was May 25, 1988. He had a simple hearing scheduled to last 15 minutes. It was nothing much; Jacqueline knew that they would be in and out in no time. The judge entered the courtroom, and the hearing began. Suddenly, without any warning, Rose told the judge, "Your Honor, something is wrong. I am not feeling well. We need to continue this hearing." The lawyer on the other side objected. The judge said, "If Mr. Rosenberg says he is not well, he is not well! Case continued. Mrs. Rosenberg, have your secretary call to reschedule." Rose walked back to Jacqueline and said, "Take me to Dr. Green, now."

271

Dr. Green was his physician in Florida, as well as his friend. After a few minutes in his office, Dr. Green sent Rose and Jacqueline over to the hospital for some tests. About an hour and a few tests later, the hospital sent them back to Dr. Green's office. Rose and Jacqueline entered the office around five o'clock in the evening with the famous question, "What is going on?" As they sat down in the chairs, Dr. Green started by saying, "I am not going to pull any punches, Rose. You have terminal, inoperable lung cancer!"

There is a sound of silence when your mind hears something so terrible. The sun was shining that day, then the rain came, and cancer blew in with the wind. Time seemed to last forever, as Jacqueline's brain began telling her she had heard it wrong. Just as she completed that thought, she realized Rose heard the diagnosis clearly! His only question was "How long do I have to live?" Dr. Green told him six weeks. "Go to Tahiti; we will give you enough medicine so you will not be in pain!"

Jacqueline was numb; she listened to them, but talked little, other than trying to comfort Rose. The six miles home took forever. They drove in silence. As she was getting Rose a cup of coffee, she turned to him and said, "Isn't you uncle a doctor in New York City?" Rose replied, "Yes, but what good is that? You heard the diagnosis!" "Well, Rose," she said, "we just got back from Jamaica, and I do not want to go to Tahiti! You may have resigned yourself to dying, but I will not give you up without a fight! At least, get a second opinion. Maybe there is some treatment, some hope! Dr. Green is certainly not going to do anything to fight this! Get your uncle on the telephone for me." As she waited, all the memories of the years that she had spent in hospitals with Marie came racing back through her mind. Those were memories so far buried in her subconscious that she had felt they were never to return.

Rose called his uncle, Dr. Samuel Rosenblatt, and got his answering service. Rose's uncle called him back immediately from Vermont. Jacqueline began to tell him the story; Sam became very angry that Dr. Green had just written Rose off like that. He informed her that he would be back in New York after the Memorial Day weekend. "In four days, Jacqueline, on Tuesday, get Rose to New York then. Just have me paged from the emergency room when you arrive."

Jacqueline telephoned Dr. Green for Rose's medical records and medications. She also wanted to let him know that they had decided to go to New York. He informed her that if Rose was going to fly, he must fly tonight! All of the test results had come back, and one of Rose's lungs had collapsed. Dr. Green did not seem happy that they were going to get a second opinion. Jacqueline called the airport for reservations.

Thinking back on her experiences with Marie and with Rose, Jacqueline realized that each time was the same. She thought, "The way that a serious illness like cancer, and whatever treatment that follows, comes into your life is similar to a hurricane. You look up and suddenly it is there, coming in for a landing from over the water, toward your back door. From that point on you react, not act. Your only instinct is the survival of you and your loved ones. That is how it really is; treatment comes from the sheer need to survive. Picking the best course of treatment during this time is partially luck, and partially good instincts. A diagnosis like this takes on a life all of its own."

Rose had a sister in New York City; surely they could stay there. He made a call to tell her what was happening, and that they were on the way to her home in Manhattan. He told her that they would take a cab from the airport. His parents were in West Palm Beach, in shock. A quick call to Jacqueline's parents, and they came to stay with Marie until her school was out in a couple of weeks. Then she would join Rose and Jacqueline in New York.

The banks were closed. They had plenty of credit cards, but Rose wanted some cash. He told Jacqueline to call all of the Greek restaurant owners he represented. "Tell them what has happened. Ask them to bring any cash on hand, and I will give them a check." Without hesitation, they all did. Some did not even want to take the check, they just wanted to give him the money, but he gave them all checks. By then, Marie had been told and was devastated; she found the courage to tell Rose not to worry: "You are in great hands; after all, Mom saved my life."

After Jacqueline did the packing, she put on two pairs of panty hose, and stuffed about $25,000.00 in cash inside her nylons. Her parents arrive, devastated; she could see the look in her father's face. He felt pain for Rose, but he also knew that his baby daughter was about to live her déjà vu! Off they went to the airport for an eleven p.m. flight to New York City.

In the six hours since Rose saw Dr. Green, he was getting worse. He had begun to wheeze and he was getting weaker fast; he needed the inhaler that Dr. Green had given him more and more on the plane. Jacqueline wished that there was something she could do that would help her husband, but she knew that there was nothing that she could do for him except to keep him as comfortable as possible until he could get into the hospital on Tuesday. Thinking back on that trip later, she could not remember flying on the plane, or much of anything about the flight, except how badly her husband was doing, and how worried she was for him.

The plane arrived at New York's Kennedy airport at about 3:30 a.m. Rose had to be removed from the plane in a wheel chair; he was barely able to walk. A porter was not to be found. Rose watched in total dismay; Jacqueline pulled the luggage from the carousel. This is not how he wanted life for his wife! Finally a thin man in a porter's hat comes close enough for Rose to get his attention. Rose called to him, "Please help my wife." The kind man could see the distress on Rose's face as he watched Jacqueline. "I will get those, madam," the gentleman said.

He took the bags, and Jacqueline pushed Rose's wheel chair to the taxi stand, where a taxi was waiting. Accepting a tip, the porter said, "God Bless," and she knew he meant it! Rose gave the driver the address on 72nd Street where his sister Alice's lived. Once there, they felt that they would be safe until Tuesday, when Dr. Rosenblatt will return to New York. He told Jacqueline not to take Rose to the hospital over the holiday weekend because Rose would just lie there, and they would do nothing until Tuesday, anyway.

The taxi arrived at Alice's home in Manhattan at about 5:30 a.m. Jacqueline noticed that there appeared to be a lack of affection between Rose and Alice. She and her brother talked, then they all fell asleep. Then, later in the morning, when they woke up, Alice was sitting at her kitchen table. She informed Rose that she had a list of hotels for him to check to find a room!

Rose said, "It is Saturday and we were just planning to stay here until Tuesday. Once I am admitted to the hospital, Jacqueline will stay elsewhere. We will not bother you for long." Alice said, "That will not be possible, because I have a girlfriend coming in from California tomorrow for a visit." Rose told her to, "Cancel it!" Alice refused. Rose's response was angry. "Fine! If your girlfriend is more important than your family, then so be it! I don't know why I am surprised. You have always been a spoiled brat. I guess I had hoped that you would have grown up a bit by now!"

As his temper began flaring, he told Jacqueline to get their suitcases. Jacqueline could hear his tirade from the bedroom, where she was repacking their suitcases with the few items they had removed when they arrived. They left as soon as she was done. Neither Rose nor Alice uttered another word as Rose and Jacqueline left. Rose was growing weaker, minute-by-minute, as they got into a taxi. His burst of anger had exhausted him.

Rose remembered some hotels from his days living there; the taxi stopped at five or six. Every one was booked full for the Memorial Day weekend. Finally, they found a not-so-nice hotel that had a room.

Rose was so weak that he could not make the single step from the entry into the lobby of the hotel. He sat on the step of the hotel lobby, hardly able to breathe, as Jacqueline checked them in. There was one person in line to register in front of Jacqueline, so she told Rose, "This should not take long. Rose, just rest and catch your breath." Rose was using his inhaler, and just nodded.

The man ahead of Jacqueline checked in. Because she was right behind him, she could hear the room rate that the clerk quoted to him. When he was done, the clerk quoted her a rate that was almost double the rate he had charged the man in front of her! Under any other circumstances, Jacqueline would have argued with the clerk about the rate, or just walked away. But Rose was so weak that he could go no farther. They were stuck!

She handed the man at the desk a credit card. He made an impression of the card, and handed a slip to her to sign. Looking at the receipt, she realized that the clerk had not filled in an amount. When she inquired, he told her she must sign in blank, or they could not have the room! Quickly, she ripped the receipt in two, placing it in her purse. Then she told him, "We will pay cash." Jacqueline thought, "Welcome to New York, the town where room rates vary from person to person, and where the sky is the limit if a credit card is used!"

The room had a musty smell. It was extremely small, with only one three-quarter-size bed. The bedspread looked as if it had been there for years. Quickly taking everything off but the sheets, Jacqueline put Rose in bed and used one of her T-shirts as a fresh pillowcase. In bed they rested, holding each other and trying not to cry. Rose suggested that she go to the market they saw next door. "Get us some coffee and sweets and bring them back, while I rest," he said.

She really did not want to leave him, but they needed to eat and there was definitely no room service at this hotel! She decided to go, and she returned in just a few minutes; it was no more than fifty feet down the sidewalk. By the time Jacqueline returned, Rose was feeling better, and he enjoyed the coffee and sweet rolls. After a couple of hours, Rose suddenly said, "We are going out on the town! I will not bring my wife to New York City, have her sleep in a fleabag hotel and not see the city. Besides, if I die in the street, we will be together!" Then with a laugh he said, "and not in this miserable hotel."

She tried to talk him out of it. He insisted that was what he wanted to do. "If I get weak, just sit me down," he said. Off they went, Rose with terminal cancer, using an inhaler, and with one collapsed lung, and Jacqueline on his arm, hoping that he would live to reach the hospital! They toured New York City. They ate lunch at a sidewalk café, and then went to his favorite bookstore, "Shakespeare and Company." There, Rose sat on the floor for hours; he would point to books, and Jacqueline would bring them to him. They had been on their own in New York for about seven hours, and Jacqueline was scared. Rose was sitting down a lot; he could walk no more than twenty or so steps at a time. Why did he insist on leaving the hotel? It was a terrible room, but she knew that at least they were safe there. What if something happened on the street? She knew no one in New York but Alice, and she had made it clear she was not willing to help at all.

Rose seemed happy and not at all concerned. As Jacqueline was bringing him another book off the shelf, he asked her, "What time is it?" She told him, "It is five o'clock, and it is time to go back to our room. You, my friend, need some rest." Rose smiled as he arose with her help from the floor of Shakespeare & Company. He placed his arm around her as they walked to the door for a taxi. Rose said, "Jacqueline, while we were out our luggage has been moved to a new hotel. I saw your interaction with that desk clerk and knew I had to make a call."

Just then, as Jacqueline looked out the front door of the bookstore for a taxi, a limousine turned the corner. Suddenly, it stopped and the door opened. Jacqueline saw a man climbing out of the limousine; looking at her with concerned eyes stood Günter. Kissing her on the cheek, he said, "You should have called before you left Florida!" In an apologetic voice she said, "Günter, I was in a panic." "I understand," he said. "Rose called me this morning. All of your bags have been moved to your new hotel. Rose, get in."

Looking over at his old friend, Günter said sternly, "You know you are not to be back in New York without us knowing about it!" Rose told Günter with a smile, "Anyone who wants to kill me only has six weeks to get me, then I will be dead!" Günter rolled his eyes at Rose. Jacqueline saw by the look on Günter's face that he did not find the statement as funny as Rose did.

Günter told Rose, "I had Tampa put an agent on Marie, before I left Washington this morning. Also, I made sure Marie's emergency number for me would come through here. I will be staying with you and Jacqueline in New York." As Jacqueline entered the limousine, she recognized the driver. It was Harry. As the limousine proceeded through the streets of New York, Jacqueline and Rose could both feel a sense of peace coming over them. The limousine slowed to a stop at the Ritz Carlton. She knew they were safe; Günter had taken care of everything.

The suite at the Ritz was a long way from the fleabag hotel they had started out in that morning. It was oversized, with a full living room. The bar was completely stocked. The furniture was made of white leather, and modern art adorned the walls; the view of the city was spectacular. Their luggage had been unpacked for them. Fresh flowers and fruit bowls were carefully placed about the suite. Günter's room was behind a connecting door, and Harry's computers were in the second bedroom off Günter's adjoining suite. It seemed as if they had the entire floor!

Günter told Rose, "If you need anything, just pick up the hotel phone. Guards will be around the hotel, and they will go with you while you visit the city. I will never be far from either of you." This would be their home until Tuesday. As they settled into their suite, holding each other like the young lovers they were, they played with their new books and laughed at what could only be life's turns.

Günter came in with the dinner cart their first night at the Ritz; they ate and laughed together.

Jacqueline listened to the two of them talking of their life and times together, the exciting times they had, and the places they had been. They talked about having to lift Günter off a mountain in Mongolia because he had broken his leg. They reminisced about the fun they had when Günter came to visit Rose in Jamaica, and about their college days in New York. Every now and then, when the conversation became too deep, they would say to each to other, "Stop. We don't want her knowing about anything that can hurt her." Then they would laugh and Jacqueline would tell them, "I understand my limits: I am on a need-to-know basis."

All telephone calls came to Rose as though he were still staying at the fleabag hotel, instead of the Presidential suite at the Ritz. "If any strangers call, give no information," instructed Günter. "Harry has the telephones monitored; we will pick up the call. Other than that, enjoy yourselves as best you can, considering the circumstances. Rose, I am so sorry this is happening to you, but I know you will be fine."

Each day, they would tour the city by limousine and return in the evening by the same black limousine. Any time they were out of the limousine, it followed them. Harry drove, and Günter was always inside the car. He was, as always, an entertaining companion for the couple; of course, Jacqueline understood that the primary reason that Günter was there was in case he was needed.

Rose insisted on taking Jacqueline out to see Manhattan. He took her to Columbia University. Located at about 116th Street in Manhattan, this fine old architectural dream, hidden behind iron gates, was

Rose's alma mater. They walked the grounds together, resting every ten or fifteen steps. He was adamant that he must climb the stairs one more time; it took him three attempts to make it to the top. He looked up and pointed to the engraving above the pillars. It read "Athletes of the Mind."

Rose had to buy Marie a Columbia University backpack for school. Jacqueline told him, " It is one hundred dollars!" He responded, "It has a lifetime guarantee." Rose would not be dissuaded. He continued, "I know it will carry her throughout life Jacqueline, even after I am gone. By the way, do you know that Marie can go to college here if she likes? Make sure when she comes to New York that you bring her here. Promise me." "I will Rose," she told him as she kissed him softly and he kissed her back so deeply. Rose said, "When I was in school here, it was all business and I have never before kissed a woman on these steps. Jacqueline, it was never before an appropriate place, nor was there ever an appropriate time before now. But now, it is the best place I can imagine to kiss my wife." Then they began their journey back down the marble steps, arm-in-arm.

They went back to the limousine and on to the New York Library. Rose told Jacqueline that as a young boy, he would take the train from Long Island to his father's office across the street from the library. Then he would spend the entire day in the library, until his father came looking for him. He felt that he was really lucky to be raised in New York in the fifties, when it was safe.

By that time, Günter truly realized how weak Rose had become. He followed Rose and Jacqueline into the library, instead of waiting in the limousine. Rose asked, "Günter why are you coming in?" Günter's reply was, "I just want to share a few of our memories, if you do not mind, Jacqueline." Jacqueline thought that Günter was coming for another reason entirely. "No Günter not at all," she said. Rose smiled. He did not believe a word Günter had just said, but he did not object.

As they began to go down the steps of the library, Rose collapsed and Günter caught him. Then two other men came from out of nowhere to assist him. One, a very large man, picked Rose up in his arms and carried him back to the limousine. Rose submitted to the man's arms and said, "Philip I guess you are going to loan me your muscles again." Günter said, "Thank you, Philip. I could see it coming." Rose told Günter, "I did not know you had Philip here." Günter said, "That means he must have been doing his job well!" They all returned to the Ritz, and that was their last outing in New York.

On Monday night, Dr. Rosenblatt returned to town; he had received Jacqueline's message from his answering service. He called, and told them to come to the emergency room that night. Günter came into the room from his adjoining suite. He told Jacqueline and Rose, "Harry is waiting. I will take care of everything here." They spent many hours in the emergency room; Dr. Rosenblatt told Rose he was waiting for a private room to be prepared. Dr. Rosenblatt said that he did not want to put Rose in the regular ward at the hospital; his treatment was going to be too dangerous.

They could see the madness of the city from the emergency room. It was as though everyone in the entire city had overdosed or had bullet holes in them. The emergency room was overflowing with the city's casualties; people lay bleeding on gurneys in the halls, with blood pooling below them on the floor. The staff seemed to never stop moving, and it seemed that they never moved at anything less than a run.

After several long hours, they were taken to the Laura Pavilion of Saints Physician's Hospital. When they arrived on the floor where Rose was to stay, they noticed guards posted outside the first room they saw. Then, at the second room, there were two more guards. There were no guards at the other end of the hall. As Rose and Jacqueline walked down the corridor, he asked the nurse who accompanied them, "What are the guards for?" The nurse explained, "The guards are here for some special patients we have on the floor. They just brought in a new crew a couple of hours ago. We have some very important people here. The first room is Sunny von Bülow's room. She is still existing in the coma that began eight years ago."

Rose seem a little concerned. "No guards down at this end of the hall?" he said to the nurse. "You have to be very important to have guards," she said. Rose replied, "Well, I certainly do not qualify, then." Jacqueline could see the concern on his face. He did not recognize any of the guards, and they were just brought in a couple of hours ago. She could see Rose's mind working, and she could tell that he did not like the feel of this.

They entered the room at the end of the corridor. To Rose's surprise, Günter was sitting in a chair! Rose's concerned look vanished at that moment. The nurse who walked in with Rose and Jacqueline asked, "Who are you, and what are you doing here?" Rose explained, "He is my college friend, and he will be spending a lot of time with me." The nurse began to explain that Günter would not be allowed to visit Rose.

But just then Dr. Rosenblatt entered the room with another nurse. Günter and Dr. Rosenblatt told the nurse that Rose would be having private nursing care, and a sign was being posted on floor, "CONTAGIOUS.... NO ONE TO ENTER THIS HALL WITHOUT CLEARANCE." Another sign would be posted on this door, "CONTAGIOUS.... NO ENTRY." Günter showed the nurse his FBI identification, so she would know what to look for. "Anyone who does not have this must not come down the corridor." Günter spoke with more authority than Jacqueline had ever heard from him.

Günter went on to say, "If someone presents this ID, you must call this room before they proceed." The nurse looked at Rose and said, "You cannot be that important!" Günter immediately responded to the nurse, "Would you like a transfer to another floor? You are on your way there right now!" She apologized for her remark. She said, "I assure you that I will keep quiet and handle it appropriately." She left the room. The private nurse left with her, saying she wanted an update on Rose's medical condition.

These were the private rooms of the rich and famous, and that is where they wanted to put Rose!

Jacqueline believed it was because they knew how experimental the treatment was going to be. Later, Günter informed Jacqueline that he needed time to secure the hospital and put his men in place. The new guards near Sunny von Bülow's room were Günter's men; Rose just did not know them.

She could sleep in the room with Rose on a folding bed. "Perfect," she thought, "because I have no intentions of leaving my husband's side." The other patient on the floor at that time was a Sheik from Saudi Arabia. Each patient was in a private room, with a large bath. The halls had red carpet, and there was a solarium at the end of the hall overlooking New York City. Rose's room was the room at the hall's end, next door to the solarium.

Dinners consisted of lobster tails and filet mignon, with silver salt-and-pepper shakers adorning the trays. Günter loved the food part, and he spent a great deal of time eating in Rose's room with him. Fine food was the standard menu on this floor, unlike the menus during the university hospital days of Marie; there were advantages to being rich when you were sick.

Except for the chipping paint, you would not know you were in a university hospital. Jacqueline had always said that, "In a university hospital, you cannot get twenty dollars for a gallon of paint into the budget, but you can have a million dollar medical machine delivered in fifteen minutes." It is the way things should always be.

A team of the best doctors in the country was being assembled. From the beginning, they told Jacqueline and Rose that the treatment was experimental and could kill Rose. Since Rose had less than six weeks to live anyway, they all felt that they had nothing to lose. The day after Rose arrived, a schedule of radiation in the morning and chemotherapy in the evening began. It was the regimen every day. Rose began losing weight almost immediately, but the doctors were able to make it fairly painless, or as Rose would say, "It depends on which side of the knife you are on." All of the doctors seemed to be smart, handsome and very kind, but most of all they were the finest of physicians.

Rose refused to ever allow his sister to visit him at the hospital. Jacqueline really couldn't remember if he ever changed his mind about that, but she did not think he did. The wounds must have been deep between the two of them; she never knew the why. After a few days, Jacqueline told Dr. Rosenblatt that she needed to get to a bank. He told her there was a credit union in the hospital; he would take her down.

As they arrived, he told the teller that she wanted to open an account. The teller asked, "How much would you like to deposit to open the account?" Jacqueline told her, "$25,000.00," then she opened her purse and pulled out the money in cash. Dr. Rosenblatt was stunned. He asked, "What are you doing with all that money?" She told him Rose insisted she bring it. He said, "Is that Rose's money?" She said, "No; Rose has all of the liabilities and I own all the assets. That is the way he wanted it from the day we married. This account is to be in my name only." Dr. Rosenblatt asked if that was fair. Jacqueline said, "It is the way Rose wants it."

When Rose's parents came to New York, his father and mother decided to have a talk with Jacqueline. After exchanging pleasantries they asked, "How are you fixed financially?" She assured them, "We are fine." Then they asked about the bank account! She told them the same thing she told Dr. Rosenblatt, just what Rose told her to say. Then they asked, "Does Rose have any life insurance on him?"

Jacqueline explained about the life insurance policies they had bought for each other. This was a big mistake; the tiger businesswoman came out. His mother did not miss a beat in explaining that they wanted her to turn over some of the insurance polices to them. Rose's mother said, "You two have not been married long, and Marie is not his daughter." Jacqueline was shocked! Roses' father sat quietly until the end and then he said, "I agree." His parents were old, and Jacqueline did not want to upset them. She also believed that the policy benefits were for Marie and herself. If his parents needed the money, it would have been different. She did not believe they did, from what she had seen and heard.

Jacqueline explained, "Rose and I would have to discuss this, and now is not the time." His mother said, "Now is a perfect time." She marched back to Rose's room, where he was playing chess against a machine. His mother began by saying, "Rose, we were just talking with Jacqueline outside and realized you have quite a bit of life insurance."

Rose looked up from his computer chess game as though he knew what was coming next. "Yes," he replied to his mother. "Well," she said, "we think Jacqueline should sign some over to us." Rose replied, "You have plenty of money. That is for Jacqueline and Marie. Besides, I have told you before, I have no intentions of fatting up your estate for Alice." Rose turned to Jacqueline and said, "It is money for you and Marie, after I am gone. Do not give it up, even to me." His mother and father left the room.

Rose thought for a minute and said, "As a matter of fact Jacqueline, I want to write a dual family power of attorney. Get me a legal pad." Rose wrote a document that basically gave her power over everything, including his medical treatment. It could not be rescinded until he was considered by three doctors to be cured. Then, Rose told her to go find a notary and have the notary come to the room. She did so. When the notary came, Rose had two doctors, one being a psychiatrist who was unrelated to him, to witness him sign the power of attorney. He carefully explained that he was giving full control of everything to Jacqueline, and had each doctor question him and write a statement that he was of sound mind. Rose knew what was about to come. Jacqueline could not see the storm brewing on the horizon.

As they began to settle into the hospital, Jacqueline realized that Uncle Sam Rosenblatt was a research scientist in the cell division at Saints Physicians. She had often wondered what he was working on in his lab so very late at night. She guessed she knew that his uncle, Dr. Rosenblatt, was trying to save Rose's life. By putting a team of the greatest medical minds in the country together for Rose and, she discovered, by working non-stop in his research lab, he was doing everything he could do for his nephew. Dr. Rosenblatt seemed to have a heart that was pure.

Jacqueline later discovered that the doctors had worked for forty-eight hours straight after the doctors had all arrived at the hospital. Since Rose's cancer was terminal, there was no predetermined course of treatment. Inoperable lung cancer had not been successfully treated. The doctors felt that the treatment course had to be a team decision. They had decided on an experimental formula of drugs that they had been working on, to be given to Rose. They decided that the chemotherapy needed to be given at the same time as radiation.

Normally, cancer treatment involved a sequence of radiation and chemotherapy, but not both at the same time. The experimental plan was going to get its first human test - on Rose. Dr. Rhineman, the chemotherapy doctor, explained the sequence of drugs. He told Jacqueline to watch to make sure they were given in the proper order.

During the first weeks of treatment Rose did not lose his hair, as was expected. He only appeared mildly sick, thanks to the anti-nausea drugs that the doctors used to counteract the side effects of chemotherapy. Jacqueline also realized that she was not the one getting the treatments, so it was hard to judge how sick he was feeling from the drugs. He had become irritable, yelling at everyone, sometimes even at her if she could not find something he wanted. He would just yell at the doctors and nurses over anything. The only people he seemed to like were the maids from Jamaica. He would talk in one of the Jamaican dialects with them. He played chess against Günter and sometimes against the computer. He read his books, always wanting whichever book he did not have.

One day, flowers arrived for Rose. It was an arrangement of six-dozen pink carnations. They were from one of the former lawyers on the Molly case. The note read, "Only you could have won this case! Thank you for seeing we were all paid. God's speed in your recovery." This made Rose smile for a while. This note came from the attorney who originally wrote the Molly complaint. He realized only after he had filed the case that it was far too complicated for an attorney as inexperienced as he was. He was right. Jacqueline believed that there were few attorneys who had enough experience in the many fields that the Molly case required. Without all of that experience, it could not have been won.

The chemotherapy formula had to be given exactly. "These drugs are all toxic," Dr. Rhineman told her, "so Jacqueline, watch everything the nurses do. They have many patients." One day as a nurse began to administer the formula, Jacqueline realized she had missed a drug in the sequence, the Leucovorin 5FU. Jacqueline told her, and the nurse promptly administered the drug. The doctor had known the danger of the nurses making mistakes, and he was right to warn Jacqueline. That was why Jacqueline had always believed in having a family member stay with a patient. They can double-check the care, and they only have one patient to worry about. She knew this from the days of Marie's illness; Dr. Rhineman had just confirmed it for her. Even the best can make mistakes. That was especially true of the nurses, since the nurses were over-loaded with patients.

The hospital added a psychiatrist and a Rabbi to the team. The Rabbi was a very large, strong man, towering at six feet five inches, wearing his yarmulke. He came in to visit Rose one day. Rose told him, "Rabbi, I haven't been a good Jew. What is it we believe in? Is there life after death?" The Rabbi responded, *"I don't know, but you are going to probably get there before me, so send me a message back."*

Jacqueline has never really been able to decide if he was kidding. Something in the Rabbi's eyes looked at Rose as though if anyone might be able to send a message back, it would be someone like Rose. Because the doctors knew how smart Rose was, every time he needed a brain scan, all the doctors wanted to see his brain activity. Interestingly, they said his brain was very small. The doctors said that is quite common in geniuses. Rose never believed that he only used three percent of his brain like the scientists say; he believed he used one hundred percent. The doctor's agreed that he used more than most, and it showed in his brain scans

In another conversation between Rose and the Rabbi, Rose was very depressed and told the Rabbi he wanted to die. He did not want to live with no quality to his life. The Rabbi told him, "It is God who chooses the quantity and quality of life, not you." The Rabbi was a wise man.

The doctors would poke their heads in the room and say to Rose, "Are you still alive? Amazing!" Rose would verbally joust with the doctors. It was all in fun. These men were all of equal education. If the tables had been turned, Jacqueline could hear Rose asking one of doctors over lunch, "Did you mind giving up the two million dollars to your ex-wife?" So this humor was completely acceptable.

The doctors also kept Rose's mind busy with the law. One of his doctors came into Roses room, and told him that the doctor's maid was being deported. He went on to say, "If she gets deported, my wife will divorce me. Our maid has raised the children." Rose asked if she was an illegal alien. The doctor said, "I guess so." Rose told him he would look into it. Rose told Günter and he said, "It will be handled." Jacqueline never heard about the maid again. She was sure that Günter made certain that the maid was not deported.

Another doctor was getting a divorce, and Rose was helping him keep his assets. Rose needed anything to keep his mind off the reality of what was happening. Rose and the doctors were on the same intellectual level, and they had the same kind of elite backgrounds. The physicians were some of the finest men Jacqueline had ever had the privilege to become acquainted with. The level of medicine being practiced at Laura Pavilion of Saints Physician's Hospital was of the most superior quality. This had been her experience in all university hospitals.

Dr. David Fieldman, the psychiatrist, was the son of a great Philadelphia physician. He was no more than forty years of age. He was a thin man with dark hair, and he had a kind face. In some other time, Jacqueline was sure she would have found him attractive. He was a very nice man. He seemed to be able to talk with Rose. He had a wonderfully calm way of speaking, and he was extremely smart. Rose liked that about Dr. Fieldman. Rose's attitude was, "The smarter they are, the better I like them."

The days passed; Rose was still alive, a little irritable, a lot thinner, but he still had not lost his hair. His throat and chest were sore from the radiation. The chemotherapy was not making him sick, per se, but it was making him weak. He stayed pretty stoned on morphine, and he liked that part. Mostly, he was having trouble eating, because they were radiating a tumor located in his esophagus. He could not swallow food, and that problem was getting worse. He was taking all of his nutrients through an IV.

On the Fourth of July, Jacqueline gave him a party between radiation and chemotherapy; after all, this was the day he was supposed to *die!* It was six weeks from the date of diagnosis. While he was in radiation therapy, she hung crepe paper from the ceiling with a big ball in the middle. She had streamers all over the room. Rose seemed to enjoy all the fuss when he returned.

Günter, while talking with Rose after chemotherapy, asked him an unusual question. "Rose, do you think the carcinogens from the Astrolite A-W-1 or other explosives we used over the years caused your cancer?" Rose said, "No, I think the three packs of Marlboros a day from the stress of using the explosives caused my cancer!" They laughed, and then a sudden silence came over them. They realized Jacqueline should not have heard that. Rose said, "Jacqueline, delete that from your memory." "Delete what?" she said, as they all laughed.

When Marie arrived in New York, Dr. Rosenblatt gave Marie and Jacqueline his fiancée's small Manhattan apartment to use. He was getting married anyway, so he just sped up his fiancée's move into his home. The apartment was a three-floor walk-up on Manhattan's upper West Side. It had a wonderful view of Central Park, and a pizza parlor next door. Günter was not happy about the two of them staying in the city instead of the hospital. He had to place another team on the Manhattan apartment. Günter was so protective of Jacqueline and Marie.

When Rose knew Marie was coming to New York, he gave Jacqueline a list of things he wanted from home. It included 75 or more books from his personal library at the house in St. Augusta. Jacqueline told Marie to locate as many of the books as she could. After all, their home had in excess of 10,000 books, and they were not in alphabetical order. When Marie arrived, Rose was so glad to see her. Even though they had the apartment in Manhattan to use, most nights they just stayed in the room with him. He rarely wanted them to leave, and they did not want to leave him either.

He had become more and more irritable over time. He threatened to leave the hospital during the middle of treatment. When he felt he had waited too long on a gurney after treatment, he would just get up and walk away. He was driving the hospital staff crazy! Finally, he asked the doctors to prescribe some marijuana for him. Dr. Rhineman laughed and said, "Your room is private, so do what you want, but we can't prescribe marijuana; the state will be after our licenses! There are probably only five prescriptions for marijuana in the United States."

Funny, the doctor didn't realize he was talking to a federal agent; or maybe he did, and that is why he said no. Jacqueline believed that he had no idea Rose was a CIA agent. The doctors and staff knew he was important, but she did not think they realized that Rose was CIA. She was not sure how much any of the doctors knew about Rose. She was not even sure that his Uncle Sam Rosenblatt knew about Rose's past.

Later that day, Rose told Jacqueline, "I wish I had some pot. I am sure I would feel better if I could just smoke a joint once in a while." Jacqueline told him that if he had a connection, that she would get the marijuana for him. Rose told her, "No, I do not want you to buy me pot." Jacqueline let the subject drop, but she was willing to do anything at all, if it would make Rose feel better.

The next day, Rose mentioned pot again. Jacqueline responded, "Honey, this is ridiculous! There is no reason in the world for me not to get you some weed! I will do anything to make you feel better. So just find it, and I will buy it! In fact, I'll find you some pot. I am sure that it is not hard to locate!" She was so adamant that, despite his reluctance, Rose agreed to let Jacqueline buy marijuana for him. He wanted to be sure that it was safe for her – he did not want her to buy from a street dealer.

So Rose called an old buddy in New York, and Jacqueline went to Long Island to buy pot. Dressed as a college kid to keep from being mugged, she headed out to the Island to pick up a small baggie of pot, sporting the Columbia backpack that Rose bought for Marie. Jacqueline was sure that Marie would not object, but of course, she would never know. The backpack contained five hundred dollars in cash. Boy, was pot expensive in New York!

Günter and Marie stayed with Rose while Jacqueline went to Long Island. Marie was disappointed that her mother was going out without her, but Rose told her that Jacqueline needed a little time completely alone. Besides, Rose and Marie needed to play chess, and they didn't want to bore Jacqueline to tears! Marie seemed to accept Rose's explanation.

Jacqueline left the hospital at about noon for Grand Central Station, and purchased her ticket. Just as she started to place her foot on the train, she heard a message come over the loudspeaker, "Grand Central Station will be closed for 24 hours due to an electrical problem. Please take an alternate route of transportation."

Well, she was not a New Yorker, but the loudspeaker told her that there was, "an alternate means of transportation!" Somehow, she found the subway to Queens, and made it to Long Island from there. She knew Rose was worried about her making this trip. If she went back to the hospital because Grand Central

Station had closed, she knew that he would not let her out again – not even to buy him pot. Besides, she knew that she had not been alone since they arrived at the hospital. By now she knew Günter's men, and he had them babysitting her. She ran Günter's men all over New York City that day. Rose wanted the pot, and she was going to get it for him. Can you imagine going to get pot under a federal guard? They had to know what she was doing. She arrived back at the hospital with the pot, only to find out that it hurt Rose when he smoked it.

Dr. Fieldman had been spending more time with Rose, as Rose's anger was mounting. He had yelled at everyone, including Marie. His tirade at her was because of a single book she had missed, when she was collecting all of those books to bring to him. He had taken on a very angry personality. Jacqueline apologized to the nurses after he berated them, and she was able to keep them calm. They were some of the best private nurses in New York. These ladies were highly educated and worked hard, while showing enormous concern for their patients. The nurses and Jacqueline had become very friendly. They seemed to accept her apology for Rose's temper and to understand that he was not the same man who had walked into the hospital. Some nights, Jacqueline would order pizza for them as a way of saying thank you.

One night, the nurse from the first day in the hospital joined in the pizza party. She was a floor nurse. Finally she asked, "Who *is* your husband?" Jacqueline's reply was, "Remember Günter? He is twice as mean as he acted that first day. You seem like a real nice woman; if he hears you asking any questions or speaking of this, your next nursing job will be in Alaska, if you are lucky. Please don't ask again." The nurse apologized and said, "I will not mention it again." Jacqueline remembered thinking to herself, "Good question, who *is* my husband?"

Each day, Rose became angry at some point. As she saw it starting to happen, Jacqueline would take Marie and go for walks around the city. She would tell Rose exactly when she would return, each time she left. Each day as she returned, she prayed that he had missed them, and she hoped that he would be calm again by the time they returned. Jacqueline took Marie to Columbia University, as Rose had asked. Marie loved it, and she could barely wait to return to the hospital to tell Rose that she wanted to go to college at his alma mater. Jacqueline took Marie shopping in all the back-alley stores the nurses had told them about. These stores housed the merchandise that "falls off the backs of the trucks."

Saints Physicians Hospital is located at the north end of Manhattan, on what is the border of Harlem. While Marie and Jacqueline were out shopping one day, they took a wrong turn and landed in Harlem. It was two o'clock in the afternoon, and the streets were filled with people. Jacqueline did not seem to be able to find the way out, and she could not find a taxi. The people were very nice, and she eventually got out safely with help from the local people. They told her that not everyone was nice and that Jacqueline and Marie had better hurry, so they would be out of Harlem before dark.

Things began to get even worse at the hospital. Rose's weight had dropped to as low as one hundred and eleven pounds. That was a far cry from the one hundred and seventy five pounds Rose weighed when he was admitted to the hospital less than three months before. Rose was getting wrathful for longer periods each day; no one was immune from his fits. Rose had refused to continue speaking with the psychiatrist, Dr. Fieldman. Dr. Fieldman was upset, and he decided to speak with Marie and Jacqueline.

He began with this statement. "You know the treatments are only magnifying Rose's *mental illness*." Jacqueline said, "What mental illness?" He said, "Bipolar, Manic Depressive Disorder." Bingo! The light went off in her head. That was why he had prescriptions for Lithium and Prozac! Now she knew why Dr. Green would put him to sleep on Thorazine. She thought it was just when he worked too hard; no one had ever explained this to her. Whenever she asked, she was told it was for stress.

Dr. Fieldman continued to say that Rose was hiding something. "Jacqueline, do you have any idea what it is?" She responded with "No." Although she knew it probably had something to do with his CIA work, she knew that she could say nothing. Günter walked in as they were speaking. "Günter" she said, "Dr. Fieldman feels Rose is hiding something. I have no idea what it could be. You have known him a long time; do you have any idea?" Günter said, "No, I think he has just decided not to talk. You know Rose." Dr. Fieldman said, "If he changes his mind, just call me. Good luck."

Throughout their marriage, Rose was happy. All Jacqueline really saw was the manic side; he was always full of energy. He needed little sleep, and would work till four in the morning. He would tire her out in bookstores. And he had a wild sex drive, which she had no complaints about! She saw very little of the depressive side, although he had been known to pull the covers over his head and refuse to get out of bed on rare occasions. Mostly, what she had seen was his marathon working habits and sex drive. He would sometimes work on a brief for seventy-two hours straight, and then Dr. Green would put him to sleep for thirty-six hours on Thorazine.

That was where all the energy and his need for little sleep came from. Now she understood. She felt a little foolish, but she had no way of knowing. Dr. Green had never used those words. Dr. Green did not like Jacqueline much; Rose said it was because she was not Jewish. Rose said, "There is a segment of the Jewish population who believe that WASP woman are wiping out the Jewish people by marrying the Jewish men. Dr. Green is one of those people."

Rose and Jacqueline never had a religious problem. She was born Baptist. He was born Jewish. She had a great respect for the Jewish people; she felt that most had good family values and were honorable people. Rose thought the same of the Baptist people. They shared all holidays and Sabbaths, and Marie was exposed to both. Jacqueline still searches for peace in her soul on Yom Kippur. It was all right with her that Dr. Green did not like her, for over time she would think less and less of him.

Dr. Fieldman had put a name to what was going on. Rose had come to the table with this mental illness that he had been able to manage for all his life. With the massive cancer treatments, the illness had shown its demon face. Rose had taken a very elitist attitude toward everyone. No one around the university was very smart; they were, just as Rose's favorite word had become, "stupid."

There was a Sheik from Saudi Arabia in the room across the hall. The Sheik had been seriously injured in Paris when a car hit him, and he had been brought to New York for treatment. He was hospitalized with his family and bodyguards at his side. Interestingly, the bodyguards all had PhD's; they were very nice, well-educated multi-lingual people.

One afternoon the Sheik's family members, who were Moslem, were beginning their daily prayers. Moslems pray in the direction of Mecca six times a day. Rose realized that they did not have the correct direction to Mecca. Being a native New Yorker, he explained to them the direction for their prayers amidst the high rises of New York City. He then assisted in blocking off an area of the solarium for their prayers. The families all became friends; the Sheik's relatives were very kind people. They had special foods brought in for Rose, hoping he would be able to eat them. If he mentioned he liked a certain type of their food, they would have the servants prepare it, and the bodyguards would deliver it.

A few days later, the Prince sent his mother, who spoke French, to ask Rose if they could take Marie for an outing in New York. They assured him that she would be under the protection of their bodyguards at all times. Jacqueline and Rose agreed to let Marie go; she needed a break from the hospital. Günter sent his team from the apartment to follow the Saudi Prince and Marie.

They took Marie on a tour of Manhattan. The tour included dinner at their Manhattan home, filled with servants serving from golden trays. She traveled the city in an armored caravan of Mercedes. She had the time of her life; they showed her such kindness. Jacqueline asked Rose, "Don't those people have political immunity if they take Marie out of the country?" "Yes, dear, but we have their father across the hall! I had already taken that into consideration. She is fine, plus our men are right there with her; relax, she will have a great time."

While Marie was out touring the city, Rose felt that he had enough energy to make love. Jacqueline's lips were locked on to her husband's body, at the point of nearing complete satisfaction; Rose's arms were reaching down, stroking her face and hair. Suddenly, Dr. Rhineman, the chemotherapy doctor, walked into the room. He smiled and said, "I could not even get my wife to roll over this morning!" He left, and Rose laughed. It was so nice to hear Rose laugh again. The doctor came back later; this time he knocked. Rose told the doctor, *"Not bad for a dead man."*

When Marie left for Florida to start the new school year, it was the Sheik's family who offered their cars and bodyguards to take her to the airport. At the airport, Jacqueline gave the ticket agent her credit card. The clerk looked at the name Rosenberg, then at the people dressed in Saudi attire. The clerk said, "I thought you two didn't get along." The Sheik's family understood the clerk only too well, but they did not react at all; they just stood silently with Jacqueline and Marie. Jacqueline was devastated, and she wanted to tell the clerk exactly what she thought of him, in the most derogatory terms she could summon. His Italian heritage was clear from his nametag and his accent. But she realized that lashing out at his prejudice would only lower her to his level, and would do no good in the long run. Feeling totally embarrassed for these extremely kind people, she told him, "Just process the ticket and mind your own business."

When Jacqueline told the clerk she wanted to walk her daughter to the plane he told her no. Then he yelled down the line, "Don't anyone give her a pass." Marie boarded the plane with Jacqueline unable to walk her all the way to the plane. Jacqueline came back to the hospital crying; Rose was in the solarium with a lady named Mary Richard-Field.

Mary was a woman of about sixty. She was five foot ten inches in height and of slender build. Her blonde hair was styled in a pageboy. The advantages of money had allowed her to age well. Like Rose, she spoke many languages. Upon hearing Jacqueline's airport story and seeing how upset she was, Mary told Jacqueline to come with her.

They returned to Mary's room at the hospital, next door to Rose's. She picked up the telephone, and told Jacqueline's story to a man on the other end of the call. Then she uttered only two more words into the telephone: "Fire him!" After she hung up she said,

Claudette Walker

"Don't worry, that man will never treat anyone that badly again at my airline." Mary had a seat on the New York Stock Exchange, and was on the Board of Directors of that airline and many other companies.

Mary, Jacqueline believed, had some sort of alliance with Günter. Jacqueline did not quite understand it, but she was convinced that Mary and Günter were working together to protect Rose. Mary seemed to spend three months at Saints Physicians for tennis elbow. She had befriended Rose and Jacqueline, and Rose seemed to really enjoy her company. Like Rose, she had been all over the world. Rose asked Jacqueline after a while if she would mind them speaking in other languages. She told him, "Of course not." On one occasion, she found Mary and Günter in another part of the hospital, talking very seriously.

The weeks turned into months; Rose was still alive! He had gone from 175 pounds to 111 pounds and he was mean, but alive. They had read books, played games, made love in his hospital bed, and watched the Olympic games of 1988 on the television set in Rose's room.

Jacqueline had walked the streets of New York; Rose had insisted that she have an outing a couple of times a week. He would pick a museum for her to see or a place for her to lunch, like the Russian Tea Room. She would go and then come back to tell him of her adventures. Günter offered to go along, but Rose said, "No just have someone follow her. I don't want to sit here thinking of you enjoying my wife's company." Rose's mind seemed clear as a bell sometimes, and sometimes he would seem to be as crazy as anyone she

305

had ever seen. The switch seemed to flip without warning, and it was worsening with every chemotherapy session.

Rose sent her to visit the old apartment he rented during his college years, to visit his old professors at Columbia University, and to his old office in Manhattan. She would come back and tell him the story of her outing. He would call old friends and arrange lunch dates for her, but he always asked them not to come to the hospital. He told them he would visit when he was better. All of his friends were nice, and they had wonderful stories to tell. Like the one about the time someone marching in New York called Rose a f...ing Jew. Rose's friend told her, "Rose punched the guy so hard, the anti-Semitic slob fell into the horse of a New York City policeman and he was arrested for assault on an officer."

Finally after ninety-one consecutive days of radiation in the morning and chemotherapy at night Rose said, "Enough! We are going home." There were no longer any signs of cancer in Rose, but the doctors seemed convinced that it could still be lurking somewhere in his body. Against medical advice, they left the hospital for the airport. It was 4 a.m.

He had been practicing his walking for weeks, preparing for this day. As they left the city, the sound of silence filled the Manhattan streets. The only thing they saw on the limousine ride was a stripped car in the middle of the street. That was Jacqueline's last memory of this trip to New York City.

They had spent the last ninety-two days of their lives in Saints Physicians Hospital. They were at last on their way home. They had no idea if this was remission or cure. Only time would tell.

CHAPTER TWELVE

THE DAYS TO COME

They had to close the law firm when they went to New York. Some of the young lawyers had taken cases and gone out on their own. Rose seemed to get his old personality back upon his arrival at home. As soon as they were settled in he said, "Jacqueline I need to talk to you. I am so very sorry for what I have put you through. I could not stand the thought of never being with you at home again. It was driving me out of my mind. All I could think was that we would never be alone here in our home as a family again. The days in this house with you and Marie have been the happiest days of my life!" "Rose" she said, "we are home now, alone, just the three of us." Rose replied quietly, "Inside these walls, I feel safe with you and Marie."

Now it was time to put some weight back on him. He had a catheter in his chest that he was being fed through. It would have to stay until he could eat and gain weight. When Jacqueline would close the catheter after using it to feed him, she would inject it with a flush. She would always stand over him and say, "How much do you love me?" They called the feeding machine Beethoven; it played the Fifth Symphony when it was out of liquid.

Jacqueline alone took care of Rose now. She called the insurance company, and told them she needed a feeding machine for the upstairs. They told her no. She explained that if she fell down the steps while moving the machine from floor to floor, the carrier would be responsible. Since she was also insured on that policy, they would have to pay her bills, too. Another machine was delivered the next day. When Rose was released from the hospital, he had a prescription for morphine. The New York doctors made it very clear that when the prescription for morphine was used up, they did not want him to have more. They felt that he should not be in pain, unless the cancer came back. And Rose had no sign of cancer in him.

Jacqueline continued to feed him by the tube and he began to eat by mouth, too. Jacqueline fed him; she gave him anything fattening she could find. Rose's mother informed Jacqueline that they were going to raise his cholesterol with the foods he was eating. Jacqueline told her that if he lived, she could worry about his cholesterol. But he needed to put on weight. They outfitted their living room with a complete gym to help him regain his strength. In six months, he had gained back 61 pounds and he was even practicing a little law.

Rose still refused to speak to his sister. He said, "We were never really close, so it is no loss." Jacqueline tried to get him to forgive Alice. "Rose, maybe if you just speak to her, you can mend your fences. It is not right for you to be estranged from your only sister," she said. He was not interested. Dealing with his parents was very stressful for him, as well. Jacqueline believed he was just so full of anger that he was lashing out randomly at people.

She had always liked his parents, but she could understand how Rose felt. His mother felt Jacqueline was getting too much money if Rose died. Did she not realize that Jacqueline did not care about the money; it was Jacqueline who was fighting to keep Rose alive? She would rather have him healthy that ten thousand times all of his money. His mother felt that he should give their money to his parents. Rose did not want to talk to his parents about it, and his mother always wanted to talk about the money. This was a large part of the tension between them.

Rose and Jacqueline had bought equal life policies for each other. Besides, it wasn't that much money. They had spent a great deal on his care. She mostly would have the insurance that Rose had bought for her. She took Rose's earlier advice, and refused to discuss with anyone but Rose the insurance on his life. He wanted only Marie and Jacqueline to have the insurance proceeds whenever something did happen to him.

As if things weren't tough enough, Rose had now discovered a new habit from a dentist friend of his: cocaine! Jacqueline discovered what they were doing after Rose had used it only a couple of times. She told Rose he must stop. Rose refused, and said for her not to tell him what to do. She spoke to the "friend." The doctor and Jacqueline discussed his wanting to keep his license. He denied that he had given the cocaine to Rose, but it was Rose who told her where he had gotten it. Her conversation with the doctor stopped that! Rose and Jacqueline argued, but he finally agreed not to use cocaine. He said, "I have plenty of other legal drugs to play with!"

A few weeks later, Rose informed Jacqueline that he wanted to see a psychiatrist again! She was shocked, but glad. He told her he had contacted a gentleman he knew from his law practice. His name is Dr. Pillar. "I really didn't like him much, but I think he is a good psychiatrist," Rose said. Rose told her not to tell anyone, not even Marie.

She agreed, and he began seeing Dr. Pillar. At first it was twice a week. After a few sessions, Rose said, "I think he is helping me Jacqueline. He is the first person I have ever talked to about my work." This really surprised her. She asked Rose, "Is that such a good idea?" Rose said, "I do not care." Then he proceeded for the first time to tell Jacqueline about his work as an operative. He started by saying, "When I told Dr. Pillar about my use of explosives, he understood my stress."

"Jacqueline, I have caused many explosions for the benefit of the United States Government. Whether I

carried the bomb or gave the order, I am responsible."
She just could not believe what she was hearing. This
man whom she loved so deeply, who had shown
nothing but kindness and compassion for Marie and
her, was an explosives expert! Although Rose knew
chemistry as well as he knew other subjects, he had
never even appeared interested in chemical compounds
such as explosives. Now he wanted to tell Jacqueline
about it!

He explained he had worked undercover after
graduating law school in Manhattan. His stay in
Jamaica was at a CIA training center. He used the
stock market and pro bono work as a cover for the time
he spent training for the CIA. He said, "I mostly
worked with getting explosives transported to different
locations around the world." He explained that the
American government was heavily involved in getting
explosive materials into the hands of people who could
serve American interests, without directly involving the
United States.

Rose told her that he also spent a great deal of
time in counter-intelligence. He had formed
relationships with professionals from different
countries. "This is why I speak so many languages. I
worked as an undercover agent within the IRA. After
some highly placed people were arrested, it was no
longer safe for me in New York, so I returned to
Washington. After a couple of other stops, I finally
retired to Florida. That was why Günter was concerned
about my safety in New York. There are people who
would like to see me dead. I figured I only had six
weeks to live, and decided to play Russian roulette.
Besides, I knew I had to bring Günter in sooner or later.

Things had been so hectic since the diagnosis, that I had forgotten to call him until I needed him."

He continued to tell her, "Günter and I had worked for different branches of intelligence for the United States Government, but the branches were all interrelated when we began. We worked together so frequently, that you would have thought that we worked in the same department, instead of in different agencies. Günter worked for the FBI and I had been in the CIA since shortly before my graduation from Columbia. Both of our positions were so high in our agencies that we worked together for most of the first fifteen years. We always thought that was great, since we were roommates in our first year of law school. We felt we could trust each other no matter what; although during the last few months, I have had my doubts. He does have a job to do. But I guess if anyone is watching, I am glad its Günter. We have a great history. So Jacqueline, I guess what I am saying is that when it comes to Günter, trust him, but be aware that he has a job to do."

Jacqueline did not want to hear any more; she had become comfortable living on a need-to-know basis. She again questioned if telling her these things was a good idea. Rose said, "I am not going to tell you anything else about it, but I am going to keep seeing Dr. Pillar. As long as no one else knows, it will be safe. I have warned that guy to keep it confidential. I know that after all these years I have a need to talk about it."

Rose decided that he would drive himself to his appointments. "This way," he said, "you are not involved." He had now increased his visits to three one-hour sessions per week. Günter had come by twice when Rose wasn't home. She told him, "Rose just went for a drive." Günter seemed surprised, because he knew Rose liked to have Jacqueline go everywhere with him. She told Rose, "Maybe I should start driving you to the appointments so Günter does not suspect anything." He told her "No, I do not want you involved. If the CIA found out what I was telling Dr. Pillar, none of us would be safe. That is why I decided to refuse to cooperate with the psychiatrist in New York; I knew he would be in danger if I let him treat me."

Rose was still showing no signs of cancer. They spent a great deal of time on the beach; he had always loved playing in the sun and water. His drug abuse was growing, and he would not even discuss stopping. Dr. Green was sure he would be dead any day, and continued giving him massive doses of prescription medications. Jacqueline believed that the drug abuse would kill him before the cancer ever returned. Well, at least he was seeing a psychiatrist. She realized it was risky, but she knew he needed to talk about his government work with someone.

One Saturday morning, a call came from some gentlemen with the National Democratic Party. They asked Rose if they could come by to talk. Rose had been heavily involved in the Democratic Party in Washington for many years. He welcomed the visit from his old friends, although he had no idea what they wanted. Jacqueline put on Rose's favorite white hostess dress, and prepared refreshments for them.

The two gentlemen arrived at their home a short time later. Rose introduced Jacqueline. The gentlemen talked with Rose about their Washington days together, the current state of America, and where they thought the country was headed. Jacqueline served coffee as the three discussed current politics. Then they dropped the bomb. One gentleman told Rose that the Democratic Party believed that they could elect a Jewish President. One of the gentlemen suddenly stated, " Solomon, we believe you are the man who can be elected to the Presidency. Think of it, you could be the first Jewish President of the United States!"

Then they proceeded to discuss the political climate for the possibility of electing a "Jew" to the office of the Presidency by the year 2000. This was December 1989, so they were planning eleven years into the future. The conversation continued for quite a while, when Jacqueline suddenly realized that Rose had not told them he was recovering from cancer. She said nothing as the conversation continued.

After about fifteen minutes of the gentlemen trying to persuade Rose that he was their man, they told him he even came with a lovely wife. That's when Jacqueline knew they were politicians! Rose told them "On that point we do agree. But, gentlemen I could not even consider doing what you ask. I have cancer!" Finally, he had told them. The men were shocked and after a few well-chosen social graces, they said goodbye. Jacqueline asked Rose why he had not told the men sooner about his cancer? He replied, *"You, my dear, were almost the First Lady of the United States of America!* I could not resist."

The love that Rose had and showed to Jacqueline is the greatest gift one human being can give to another. During their years together, Rose would not even have lunch with a female client unless Jacqueline was available to join them. It was not a mater of trust; Jacqueline trusted Rose implicitly. It was simply one of his ways of showing his love for her. He was always an honorable man. Rose always made her feel secure and loved. This kind of love spoils you for the rest of your life.

After the gentleman left, Jacqueline sat on the floor with her head in Roses lap. She began to cry, "You must get better Rose! I do not want to lose you, ever." As he stroked her hair he said, "My darling wife, I will stay with you as long as God allows. I will fight leaving you with every breath I have. I do not want to ever be apart from you. I chose the only woman in the world for me. I want to keep you with me for all eternity."

During the early days of his recovery, he insisted on talking about what she would do after he was gone. Rose and the doctors in New York had told her to keep a journal. She had always kept a journal anyway, so she continued it during the hospital stay and at home. Rose said, "When I am gone, live off the money I am leaving you, and write a book. Once I am gone you can tell everything, just change everyone's name except mine, that one I know you can use. Take a little writer's liberty and turn it into a novel. Get a good lawyer to advise you about what you can get away with. To hell with them all, *just print the truth within the story.*"

He also made it clear he did not want her to remarry. He said, "I will be looking for Mrs. Rosenberg, calling your name in heaven when the time comes for you to meet me." He said he wanted to be sure he could find her. Jacqueline was his wife and he wanted to keep it that way, even after his death.

Rose was not ashamed of his pot smoking or the life he had lived. He had to keep his pot smoking quiet because it was illegal, and they would have taken away his license to practice law, thrown him out of the government, and probably jailed him. It was one of the few crimes he ever committed in his life. He had not had a parking ticket in 20 years. Günter knew Rose smoked marijuana. Günter did not smoke pot, but he was the king of speed and tranquilizers. He was always getting prescriptions.

When Günter came for a visit, Rose told him of the "job offer" from the Democratic Party. They laughed saying, "Those fools don't know we run the government already." "Well," Rose said, "I let them go on for a while, before I told them of my cancer. You know, I just wanted to make Jacqueline First Lady for fifteen minutes."

Günter knew how much Rose loved Jacqueline. Günter was one of the lawyers who Rose recruited, early in their marriage, to sing his college song outside Jacqueline's bedroom window while Rose pinned her with his college pin of pearls and emeralds. This came about after she mentioned she had never been "pinned" in college. He wanted her to have everything. What a great love and a wonderful sense of humor he had.

As his recovery continued, his weight rapidly returned to his pre-cancer weight of 175 pounds, and his physical stamina was getting better. Still he was getting more and more drugs from the doctor in Florida. He was taking, in any given day, morphine, Prozac, chloral hydrate, Xanex, Percocet, and more. He was self-medicating in doses that would kill anyone, and he was getting even meaner. Jacqueline spoke to Dr. Green, who was convinced that Rose was still dying, and he refused to stop prescribing. She was begging Dr. Green for help. Rose would not listen to her and she could not stop his drug excesses. She cringed as he popped four or five pills at a time, swallowing them down with his coffee. She feared that someday she would be blamed for his death, due to the amount of drugs in his system. It would be difficult for anyone to believe that he was not poisoned, if he died of an overdose.

Early one Sunday morning, as they were watching the news, a special report said that there had been a pedestrian traffic accident. The person was a victim of a hit and run driver. The news said, "Dr. Edward Pillar, a local psychiatrist, was struck by a vehicle in the parking lot of his office. There were no witnesses." Rose screamed, "That was no accident! Those sons of bitches found out that I was seeing him!" Jacqueline, trying to calm him said, "Rose, that is impossible." He said, "Jacqueline you just do not know."

She sat silently as Rose telephoned Günter. Then he just said, "I do not want to talk about it, Jacqueline." A few hours later Günter came by and Rose said he would like to speak to Günter alone.

Jacqueline went out to the swimming pool while they talked. After Günter left, she asked, "Rose, how did it go?" Rose said, "I was wrong, it was just my overactive brain." For the next few months Rose's drug abuse continued to increase, and he remained extremely depressed. He also refused to attend the funeral of Dr. Pillar, or to allow Jacqueline to send flowers.

She knew from the look in his eyes that his original feeling was correct. The CIA had ordered the hit on Dr. Pillar. Rose could avoid telling things to her, but he could not lie once he had told her. Jacqueline knew that she could never say anything about what Rose had been telling her about his work. Even to Günter, or especially not to Günter. Rose was now going from silence and depression to bouts of anger at a moment's notice.

She remembered the day Rose heard that Mr. Molly had died. He said, "At least I outlived that SOB." His anger was getting completely out of control. Mr. Molly was not a nice man, but Rose's statement surprised her. He began saying things like "God gave me two hands to take." Her father heard Rose make that statement, and it stayed with her father until the day he died. Jacqueline's father liked Rose until the day he heard Rose speak those words. Her father knew Rose well, and he knew that Rose's words that day were not spoken by the left-wing humanitarian he knew. Her father worried for Jacqueline from that day forward.

Rose had begun saying other things that were just not normal. Rose told Jacqueline he wanted to convert to Christianity! She explained, "Remember,

Claudette Walker

you were born a Jewish boy and I a Christian girl. That is who we were meant to be, and it is not subject to change. God already decided that on the day we were born." He agreed that statement was pretty foolish. He had also begun calling a psychic. Now, that was out of character for Rose! Fortunately, it only lasted for a couple of weeks.

Jacqueline knew that it was his massive drug use that was affecting Rose. He told an old client that Jacqueline was pregnant, when he knew she could not have any more children. She was stunned, and when she asked him about it, he did not remember saying it. He told a neighbor he would shoot her. He had begun waking Jacqueline in the middle of the night. He would complain about her not staying awake with him, and if she did not wake up to be with him, he would start getting angry. No one could keep up with him; he was sleeping only a couple of hours each night, even though he was taking potentially lethal doses of the sleeping medication chloral hydrate. He was constantly calling people stupid and ignorant, and he often forgot where he had put things.

He had started telling Jacqueline of terrorist activity he investigated, and what the United States Government was capable of doing if they wanted someone gone. During one of these soliloquies, he slipped and said, "You saw what they did to Dr. Pillar!" He had never really spoken of his operative work; now Rose had begun to babble about tales of his operative work. They were the stories that he had never wanted her to know. He spoke of a bombing in Ireland; he talked of government meetings deciding what people had to be resolved. Jacqueline knew what he meant;

"resolved," was his way of saying assassinated! Rose had been telling her about the government's participation in allowing the importation of drugs to America from Vietnam during the Vietnam War. She just tried to change the subject as fast as she could. Rose was scaring the hell out of her.

Sometimes he insisted on telling her things, and she could not change the subject. He told her about the undercover agents that the government had in place during the Vietnam marches on Washington. How he would watch the operatives out of his White House office window, laughing at the hippies who had no idea their every move was being watched from within. He talked constantly about this high-powered explosive called Astrolite A-W-1. How little it would take to blow their house up; he said that it would take no more than a small amount. She was absolutely petrified; she was so scared that she sent Marie to visit her grandparents as much as possible.

Rose had never wanted to talk about his government work before; now she could not stop him. Jacqueline said nothing to Günter about Rose's stories. When Günter visited them, Rose seemed to say nothing about their work to Jacqueline. It was as though he still had that much control left. He was also cutting Günter's visits short by saying that he was not feeling well. Things were worse than bad, and Dr. Green refused to hospitalize Rose for detoxification from all the drugs. Dr. Green still could not admit that although his diagnosis was right, his treatment plan and his assessment of Rose's life expectancy were wrong. Still, there were no signs of cancer.

Jacqueline asked Rose, "Does Dr. Green know of your government work?" He said, "No, he is just a pill supplier to me. Let's walk to the swimming pool." Outside he told her, "Dr. Green is not even in the league of someone I would tell. Remember when he would sedate me on Thorazine? I always insisted that he come to our house to give me the shot, or that you go with me to his office and then take me home immediately. I never wanted to take the chance that I would start talking around him. Jacqueline, there are so few people who even knew of my work. I am only alive because I began insuring my continued existence a long time ago with recordings that will be destroyed only if I die of natural causes."

Rose continued, "If I die any other way, they will be turned over by a lawyer to the New York Times. I no longer know if Günter is my friend or just assigned to make sure I do not tell anyone anything. I do not want to discuss these things in the house. If I start to talk about my past, just put your hand over my mouth and point to the door."

In a very scary voice Rose said, "Günter may bug our home. That is why I am keeping his visits short, and I watch him closely when he is in the house. I do not have the equipment to sweep for bugs. I do not believe we are bugged yet; I have watched him whenever he was around and I have searched the living area completely. Also, whenever we leave, I rig the door so I will know if anyone has entered the house while we are out. I am pretty sure that we are not bugged, yet. Just help me if I start to say anything. I know I am out of control, Jacqueline. I need to talk about those years, but I know how dangerous it is. I also know that this information could help you after I am gone. Just get me outside of the house if I start to talk about anything with the government." They returned to the house and just sat quietly

Jacqueline's mind was reeling; she did not know if Rose was getting paranoid, or if they are truly in danger. Her head was full of questions, and she suspected that she might never really know the answers. Her brain would not stop. "Who is my husband? He has always told the truth. Why would he lie about the possibility of our home being bugged? After all, look at the equipment they brought over to catch the Miami Men." She had a feeling that her years of living on a need-to-know basis might not have been a good idea. Jacqueline suddenly lost all doubt. Rose was telling her the truth, and Günter could bug their home!

That was a big dose of reality for Jacqueline. Her first thought was she could never let Günter catch on that Rose was telling her anything about his work. As far as Günter knew, she did not know anything more than the evening at the State Department and the few slips they made, talking while she was in the room. That is all she would ever admit to Günter that she knew.

Rose and Jacqueline were sitting in their chairs with the coffee table between them; this was how they usually sat in the living room. The only windows are two sets of double glass doors with the blinds closed. Rose had his clipboard in his hands and passed it to her.

On the legal pad Rose had written, "I want to tell you things by writing them down. After I am gone, knowing these things could keep you and Marie safe. It can also make you a lot of money. Read them and respond. When the paper is full, go into the kitchen and burn it in the garbage deposal, then run the ashes down the drain. This will keep me from talking, okay?" She wrote back, "OK."

Rose began by telling her the name of the lawyer and the number of micro-cassette tapes he held. "Mark Steinberg, Esq. NYC, 35 tapes. He was a lawyer in the Manhattan law firm that I went to work for immediately after law school. Remember, I sent you to see the office in New York? That firm was my first CIA assignment. Commit this to memory." She looked at the paper for a long time, memorizing it. Then she wrote back, "OK, I have it." He responded, "There will be a test later. This could be very important to you. Now, burn this paper." Jacqueline walked into the kitchen, set the paper on fire in the sink, and ran the ashes down the garbage disposal.

From time to time over the next month or two, he would hand her a note. She would read it, respond to it in writing, and then burn it. One of the notes he passed her was about Dr. Pillar. He said, "Pillar was no accident." Jacqueline wrote back, "I know. Your eyes cannot lie to me." Then she burned the paper.

Another note was about drugs from Vietnam: "Do you know how many pounds of grass can be transported in a C130 cargo plane?" She responded, "No." He wrote, "They say that the maximum load capacity is thirty-five to forty-two thousand pounds. I know that they can carry fifty thousand pounds, but you need a road that can handle that much weight for the landing! Americans can build a road that can handle it. The desert is perfect because the ground is hard. We watched them transport hundreds of thousands of pounds of pot. Vietnam can grow an unlimited amount of drugs in its climate. Remember the code name VEGAS BY SEA AND OCEAN. It means that they were running over the South China Sea and the Pacific Ocean. We watched for a long time to find the Russian involvement." Jacqueline burned the paper.

There was a story on the TV about a statue that had been bombed in Ireland in the sixties or seventies. He passed Jacqueline a note that said, "I authorized the Astrolite for that bombing. That was the only time I regretted giving my go-ahead." She burned the paper without a response.

He sent her another note saying, "Whatever I did, I always believed it was right for America." Jacqueline wrote, "I know, you are a good man, Rose and I will always love you." He responded, "I can't imagine living without you. I love you so, Jacqueline." She burned the note with tears in her eyes. They continued to write notes; this seemed to keep him from speaking of these matters, because of his concern that the house had been bugged. Jacqueline continued to learn more than she ever wanted to know about his work.

Each night while Rose was reading, Jacqueline would enter the notes, from her memory, into a small black journal. She kept her journal in her purse at all times. Since Rose told her these things might be important to her someday, she wanted to make sure she had them written down. Unlike Rose, Jacqueline did not have a photographic memory. When she filled a journal, or became nervous about having it around, she would seal it in an envelope and take it to her father's home for safekeeping.

Jacqueline was learning what the man she loved so deeply was capable of. She was shocked, even though she knew everything he had done was for America. His belief in his country was as deep as his love for her. She still found it hard to imagine Rose's involvement. He had never said it, but people must have died in those explosions. And then there were his words about having people "resolved." He had a part in the deaths of other human beings.

Rose seemed lost in his thoughts again one day, but at least he was not angry. He was watching the World War II tapes he had collected. Jacqueline believed he had every newsreel from both the American and German sides of the war. They were just finishing dinner when he began to write on his legal pad. Rose wrote, "Test time: where are the tapes and how many are there?" "Mark Steinberg, Esq., on Third Avenue in Manhattan, 35 tapes," she wrote in reply. He responded, "Very good! That could keep you alive." She burned the note. The next note said, "Where is his office located?" "It is the law firm in New York you had me go visit," she wrote back. "Very good, " he replied. Then she burned the note.

In the next note, he told her that during the Vietnam War, he and Günter flew to Vietnam, then took a helicopter to Quang Tri, landed and stayed on the DMZ for about three minutes, just so Rose could see the war in action. Günter had finished his tour of duty there, and had returned to Washington. He thought that Rose should go to Vietnam, so Rose could get a CIA war-zone commendation.

Jacqueline remembered thinking how the soldiers must have felt when they saw two men from Washington D.C., in clean white shirts, land in a helicopter on the DMZ just to look around. And how the soldiers felt when they saw that the pair were free to just fly back out of the war, unlike the fighting men on the ground. She burned the note.

Everything about Rose's past life now came to her in notes that she burned. It was a way for Rose to vent what he was recalling from his life without being overheard. Günter had made three or for more trips to "visit." Rose wrote, "I am sure we have been bugged by now." He thought that only the downstairs was bugged, because Günter had no reason to go upstairs. "Besides, they are not interested in our bedroom." Günter knew they spent most of their waking hours in the lower level.

One afternoon in late March, Rose began writing Jacqueline a note. He started off by saying "Forgive me for what I am about to tell you." She wrote back not knowing what it was, that she forgave him.

The next note read, "I met a woman in Northern Ireland in 1973. I must tell you about her. Claire was beautiful, kind, and good - like you. Her eyes were as green as yours, her hair was flowing red curls, and her skin was the purist of white. She was a native of Ireland. We were both young, and my career was just about at full swing. I had been spending a lot of time in Ireland, as I was working undercover for America in the IRA. Claire had nothing to do with the IRA. She was just a college student. We met by chance while I was eating lunch. I was watching a location that the United States had wanted to bomb. Jacqueline, can I continue?" She wrote back, "Yes." Then she took that paper and burned it.

Rose began writing on another sheet of paper, "She slipped on the floor of the outdoor café where I was eating. I was also watching the possible target, across the street. I caught her, and she sat down alone at the table next to me. Finally, she joined me and we talked for an hour or so. I just remember her beauty and her simple innocence. If I had not been on assignment, I would have pursued her. But I was, and so I left her at the table."

Rose continued, "About two weeks later I left Ireland when my assignment was complete. Two days after I arrived back home, there was an explosion in Northern Ireland. It happened when we had planned. But something went wrong and it destroyed a half of block, including some of the outside tables of the cafe. Claire was seated at the café that day, and she died."

"I was in Washington when the list of victims came in. As I was skimming the list, I saw her name; praying my wonderful memory had failed me, I requested a college picture of her from CIA Info Stack. It was Claire, and I had ordered the bombing that killed that innocent girl."

Rose passed Jacqueline the paper. She cried as she wrote back, "You could not have known she would be there that day, or that something would go wrong." Rose wrote back, "It was my work and the very early days of Astrolite. We were unsure how much to use. I am still responsible." She wrote back, "You were serving your country; you are no more to blame than the solider on the battle field." Then she took the paper and burned it.

Rose wrote, "I have been responsible in one way or the other for many deaths, including Dr. Pillar." Jacqueline wrote back, "How many lives have you saved through your work?" He wrote back, "Thousands, but does the end justify the means?" Her last message to Rose was, "You have been a true American. I love you." Then she burned the paper.

Over the next couple of days, Rose seemed deep in thought. He talked little and he did not write any more notes. Jacqueline just left him alone, bringing him his coffee and meals to the coffee table. She understood what kind of pain he felt, and why he was so desperate to talk about his work. Jacqueline wished she could help him more, but he seemed to need quiet and solitude. His eyes were glazed over; he seemed to be just staring into a book.

CHAPTER THIRTEEN

APRIL FOOLS DAY

Rose begins to dictate into his microcassette recorder. Jacqueline goes into the living room and asks him one more time if he would like to eat dinner. He abruptly tells her, "No I told you, I am not hungry." He begins his dictation again. Rose appears to be making a list of people; some of the names she recognizes. They are people he does not like. She hears Rose again; this time it is the explosive Astrolite A-W-1 that he is talking about on the recorder. She continues quietly cleaning up the dinner dishes. Rose calls to her in the kitchen, "Jacqueline will you copy the libretto to the 'Three Penny Opera?' " That was a fast change - from explosives to opera! Jacqueline just had no idea what Rose was thinking these days.

331

She calls back to him, "As soon as I finish washing the dishes, honey." She can still hear him dictating into the machine and he is *snickering* while he is doing it! A couple of minutes later the same request, "Will you copy the libretto, Jacqueline?" She responds, "Honey, I am almost finished with the dishes, and I will copy it in just a minute." The next voice she heard was angry. "Can't you do anything I ask?" Marie was doing her homework at the kitchen table. Jacqueline and Marie just look into each other eyes as Jacqueline goes immediately to copy the libretto, so Rose will not upset Marie. While upstairs in the office, she hears an argument brewing downstairs. Rose is yelling at Marie about something. Quickly, she returns to the living room, and sends Marie upstairs to do her homework.

When Jacqueline inquires about what was going on, Rose angrily says, "Marie left the light on in the kitchen!" Jacqueline explains, "Marie must have thought I was coming right back." Knowing that his anger will continue to flare, she tells him, "I am going upstairs to read a book and let you just relax for awhile." His outbursts have been a daily occurrence since New York; the only questions each day are when something will trigger him, and what it will be. With a gentle kiss to his head, she leaves the room. Stopping by Marie's room, Jacqueline tells her, "Take it easy. He is just upset again."

Jacqueline enters the bedroom she and Rose share, at the top of the hallway stairs. Laying herself on the bed, she begins to read a novel. She had been looking forward to starting the book, and finally, she is able to start reading it. Despite her anticipation of the novel, she can't help but think about life with Rose.

By now she is completely exhausted; the day-to-day care of Rose has not been easy. Dealing with his bipolar mania, anger, and depression is wearing her out. His mood swings are now only intensified by his extreme drug use. She spends every hour of every day worrying about his pill popping. She has looked at the many drug reference books Rose keeps at the house. She knows that some of the doses he is taking exceed a lethal dose. She cannot stop him! He cannot die of an overdose after all the work that was done to save his life in New York.

Dr. Green is of absolutely no help to her. Green is encouraging Rose to use the medication. He writes Rose prescriptions just as fast as Rose asks, and Jacqueline knows that Green doesn't care that Rose is addicted. After they returned from the hospital in New York, Dr. Green told Rose and Jacqueline that he would give Rose the drugs for a while. If he saw that Rose was going to live, he would put him in St. Adele Hospital and quietly withdraw him. Jacqueline had made a calendar to follow Rose's medications. Dr. Green had been at their home recently and she showed him the calendar and how long this over-medicating had gone on.

Dr. Green told her that he cannot put Rose in St. Adele Hospital because, *"they do not do drug withdrawal!"* "But you said you would!" she told him. He told her, "Mind your own business, I will deal with Rose." She asked if he was going to cut down on the prescriptions. Green said "No," and left. This most recent clash over his prescribing drugs to Rose was just two days earlier, when Green increased the dosage of Prozac that Rose was taking. Jacqueline knows that the

Prozac dosage increase, combined with all the other pain and sleeping medications Rose is taking, is going to result in disaster

Jacqueline gives up trying to read. She decides to rest on the bed; at least it is a retreat from the turmoil in her life. But her mind won't let her rest. She thinks again about the conversation with Dr. Green a few days ago. Questions racing through her mind will not let her relax. "Why is Dr. Green doing this? Why is he prescribing for Rose like this? Does Rose have something on him? Does Green really believe he is doing the right thing? Is he afraid to attempt to take Rose off these drugs? Does Green truly believe Rose is a walking dead man? Is Green afraid that without the drugs Rose will die in pain?" Finally, her thoughts drift off this terrible mess, as she begins to relax. It is so rare for her mind to allow her to rest since Rose's *cancer blew in with the wind.*

After only a few minutes of resting on the bed, Jacqueline hears Rose coming up the stairs. She knows that he is sorry. Rose is always sorry; after all, he does love them. Rose enters the room, smiling at Jacqueline as he walks toward the end of their bed and places his hand gently on her ankle. She smiles, as his fingers touch her skin. She is ready to accept his apology. His touch has become so rare since the cancer, that even the smallest touch to her ankle pleases her.

Suddenly his soft touch is hard and violent, as though at that moment he has forgotten what he is doing. Rose's hand latches in full grip, his hand to her ankle. She can see his fingers, as they go from a soft touch to a cruel, vise-like clamp. Then she feels the sudden tug as he pulls on her ankle. Jacqueline's body is being violently pulled from the bed! The door is getting closer; he is dragging her toward the hallway! She falls to the floor with a *thump!* In complete shock, Jacqueline is struggling with him every inch of the way. As her adrenaline begins to pump, she is fighting her way back toward the bed, reaching for anything to hold onto!

But she cannot overcome his strength. He has pulled her the ten feet from the bed to the door. He is now dragging her by the ankle out of the room. Now, she is entirely in the hall. Suddenly, he releases Jacqueline's ankle in the hallway. For a split second, she breathes a sigh of relief, only to feel pain as her head is being smashed into the hallway wall. She can hear Marie screaming through the sharp pain each time her head connects with the wall. Just as suddenly as he pulled her from the bed, Rose releases her head and he flees down the staircase. She can hear his feet connect on every third step with a thud, until he hits the lower level.

Gathering her wits, she staggers to her feet and heads to Marie's door at the other end of the hall. Marie has it blocked! Jacqueline quietly calls her name. "Marie can you hear me?" Jacqueline hears Marie tearfully say, "Yes Mom." "Marie, listen to me! When you hear me downstairs in the kitchen, take flight down the staircase and out the front door." Jacqueline whispers, "Don't stop for me or anything, *Rose has lost it.* Do not open this door until you hear me down in the kitchen. Do you hear me?" Marie's voice is shaking, "Yes Mom, but I am scared!" Jacqueline replies in a firm voice, "Just listen for me to get to the kitchen. Get ready!"

As Jacqueline turns to walk toward the top of the stairs, she sees Rose out of the corner of her eye. "My God! He is coming back up the staircase, with a 10-inch knife held high over his head! He looks like a madman!" Jacqueline swings into their bedroom, barricading the door closed with her small body. Rose is pushing on the door and it opens about six inches. Suddenly, his arm and the knife come through the six-inch space in the door. Rose is stabbing wildly at her from the other side with the knife!

She is pushing with all her strength. Five, six times the knife misses her by an inch. She is looking directly at the blade. That is the only way she can avoid his wild swings, while still keeping her weight on the door. The door opens wider, as the knife abruptly retreats from the open space. Then just as suddenly, the door slams closed with a bang! She hears Rose heading down the stairs again. Quickly, without a thought, she goes to Marie's door again and tells her "Get ready!" Then she heads down the staircase, not knowing where he and the knife are. Jacqueline is simply thinking, "I have to get Marie out of this house!" Jacqueline knows she must flee or fight, and when it comes to getting Marie out, she will fight!

Entering the kitchen from the hall stairs, she can see Rose is at the west side of the oblong dining table. His eyes are wild, but he is not holding the knife! Jacqueline heads toward the east side of the table, to draw him away from the front door, Marie's only exit. Suddenly, he grabs her; the buttons pop from her blouse as he swings her into a chokehold and begins to squeeze. She cannot breathe! Her lungs are on fire, and her heart is pounding! She knows she is losing consciousness. Rose is screaming, **"I will not die and leave you,"** then over and over again, **"You are going with me, Jacqueline! I cannot leave you behind!"**

Finally, Jacqueline heard the sound that she had been straining to hear, the noise of Marie fleeing out the front door. With the last of her breath and strength, Jacqueline swung her body around and slapped his face with her open hand. The slap was not hard, as she was hardly able to move her body with his arms around her neck. But it was enough, and stunned, he released her. She fled out of the front door into the arms of a neighbor who had heard all of the commotion.

The neighbor was an architect from Boston by the name of Matthew. He was a large man of six feet two or three, probably weighing some 225 pounds. He was about sixty years old, and he had gray hair. He lived part time in Florida, and part time in Boston. Matthew said, "I have been afraid something like this would happen. Jacqueline, Rose has been acting strange, and I figured it was from the cancer and drugs. I have often prayed that I would be here the day it happened, to help you." God answered both of their prayers; he was there that day

Rose ran out of the door after her, only to see Matthew. He then retreated into the house. Marie was standing in the background with Matthew's wife. Suddenly, the police arrived. As Jacqueline began to tell the policeman what had been going on, the officer cut her off by saying, "I will go in, I have known Rose for years, he was the president of the FOP." She told him, "Rose has a German Luger in the house." The officer headed toward the door. There was another man dressed in street clothes, and he stayed in the police car. The uniformed officer called to Rose from the door. Rose responded, "Is that you Mike? Come on in. My wife is just acting crazy!"

Outside, Jacqueline sent Marie to her grandparents; thankfully Marie thought ahead, and tossed her purse out of her bedroom window. She had her car keys inside. Marie had her driver's license, so she could drive herself. She did not want to leave her mother, but Jacqueline insisted. She wanted to be sure that at least her daughter was safe. She told Marie, "Let your grandpa and grandma know what has happened, and that I am all right. Tell grandpa to stay with you. I will call." Then she kissed her daughter goodbye. Both of them were in tears as Marie drove away, headed for her grandparent's home. Jacqueline knew her father's instincts would be to immediately come to her aid. She did not want him in this. She knew that he would kill Rose on the spot. In their family, under no circumstances did anyone lay a hand on a woman. Her father had two daughters that he loved more than life itself. She did not want him to become involved because she knew what he would do!

After Marie left, Jacqueline asked to use Matthew's telephone, to call her parents and Rose's doctor. Her father answered the telephone on the second ring. It took too long for Jacqueline; she had time to figure out what to say, but she couldn't think! What she said was, "Dad, I am fine, Marie is fine, but Rose has lost it. I sent Marie to you. She is pretty upset. I would have come, too but I need to stay to make sure that Rose doesn't harm himself." When her father tried to question her about what happened, and whether she needed his help, she said, "Marie needs you much more than I do. Be there for her! I will be all right here. As soon as I am sure that Rose is safe, I will call you, and explain all of this, but I do not have time to talk right now."

Then she called Dr. Green. She was only able to talk to his answering service; the operator would not patch her through to him, even though she told him it was a life-and-death emergency. The operator told her that the doctor would be paged to call her. It was the best she could do for the moment. She hung up the phone, thanked Matthew and his wife for the use of the telephone, and left the safety of their home.

When she got outside, she walked over to the police car, in an attempt to talk with the man in the car. He asked her what happened and she thought, finally someone will listen to me! She told him, expecting some help from this plain-clothes officer. He informed her, "I am just an observer. You will need to speak to the uniformed officer."

A few minutes later, the uniformed policeman came out and said, "Rose is perfectly calm; he said you were just screaming, and that it was you who had lost control." She could not believe what she just heard! The officer told her to leave, and let things cool down. Jacqueline tried to tell him that Rose had a loaded gun and enough drugs to kill himself, all in that house. She was sure that if, while he was still manic, Rose realized that he had attacked her, he would commit suicide. He would kill himself out of remorse.

The officers informed her that they were not going to hospitalize him, or do anything else. She insisted on going back in the house. She told the officers, "I have not brought him through terminal cancer, only to have him commit suicide!" The uniformed officer went back into the house with her.

Rose talked to the officer like it was a lodge meeting, and the stupid officer fell for everything Rose said. While the officer was in the living room talking, Jacqueline put two pans of water on the stove to boil. She ran upstairs, located the gun, unloaded it, and hid the bullets. Then she returned downstairs to the kitchen, just as the officer was leaving.

"Mrs. Rosenberg," the officer said, "I am leaving now." The officer spoke to Jacqueline, and said, "I have known Mr. Rosenberg for some time, and he seems perfectly calm to me." As the officer exited their home, Jacqueline took a seat at the table closest to the stove. After the officer was gone, Rose stood at the kitchen door, and informed her, "I could kill you and get away with it." Jacqueline told him, "Not tonight! I am waiting for Dr. Green to call. I have two pans of boiling water sitting on the stove, just six inches from me. If you come near me, I will throw them on you! Then they *will* have to hospitalize you!"

Rose stood in the living room, looking into the kitchen. Then he said, "That cop is so stupid! He believed everything I said! I guess you have to pass a stupid test to become an officer! That's why I like having them in court. They can be controlled completely; weak minds, I think." On and on he went. For nearly an hour he paced, talking about how stupid cops were.

The telephone rang. Rose answered in the living room, and Jacqueline answered in the kitchen. He hung up when he realized it was Dr. Green, returning her call. She told the doctor what had happened, and begged him to involuntarily commit Rose for psychiatric treatment, and get him off all of the drugs at the same time. Dr. Green asked to speak to Rose. Jacqueline told Rose that Dr. Green wanted to talk to him. She heard Rose admit to Dr. Green, "Yes, I did it!" Rose told Dr. Green to keep his nose out of it. Jacqueline got back on the line, and Rose hung up. Dr. Green informed her that he would not make Rose do anything he was unwilling to do voluntarily.

Rose finally sat down while he was talking to Dr. Green. After Jacqueline, disgusted, hung up the telephone, Rose told her, "He will not do anything; no one can make me do anything!" Rose returned to his reverie for a while and then he moved to the sofa and lay down. Finally, after another half-hour of staring into space, Rose passed out on the sofa. When she was sure he was asleep, she breathed a sigh of relief, because she was sure that Rose's bout of mania was over, at least for the night, and that he would sleep for several hours. She made another call to her parents and Marie. She let them know that she was safe; Rose was out cold. Jacqueline again told her father, "Stay with Marie. I will be there as soon as I speak to the psychiatrist in New York. That will be first thing in the morning."

Her father begged her to leave. She was adamant. She had to stay, to make sure that Rose was safe. Compromising with her, Jacqueline's father told her to leave the telephone lines open between the houses. He said, "Go upstairs and place Marie's telephone at the top of the stairs, and call me back from that phone. Leave Marie's line open, so I can hear what is going on in that house. Since her telephone is on a second line, I can listen to make sure that you are safe, and you will be able to use the other line to call for help, if something goes wrong. I will stay on the telephone all night. Jacqueline, I wish you would just come home now." "Dad I am afraid he will kill himself." Her dad said, "Better him than you!" He knew she could not leave. Jacqueline sat all night at the kitchen table to make sure that Rose did not kill himself; she was scared that he would wake up, and realize what he had done.

She was sitting at the kitchen table with her arm a foot away from the boiling water. She may have been courageous, but she was not foolhardy; she made sure that the pots stayed full and the water stayed at a low boil throughout the night. While she was seated there, she began to wonder how the police came so fast. The neighbors told her that they had not had time to call the police. No one else was close enough to the house to hear anything. Suddenly, she realized that Rose was right! The house *was* bugged!

Jacqueline sat quietly in shock as she realized that Günter's men were listening, and that they must have called the police. No one else could have done it. She remembered the other man in the police car who was in plain clothes. That was who he was!

He must have been one of Günter's men. "Thank God they bugged the house," she thought. Gunter's security men must like her; they had intervened. She realized what was more likely - they did not want Rose arrested on murder charges. Jacqueline had wondered when Rose had told the officer that she was the problem, why the cop had not arrested her. If he really thought she was the one acting crazy, she would have expected him to do so. Finally, she understood. She was pretty sharp with him when he refused to help or take a report on the spot. He had reluctantly told her that he would write a report.

When morning arrived, Rose was still unconscious on the sofa. Jacqueline thought, "Thank God! I don't know what I will do if he wakes, and he is still acting crazy. He is changing as fast as Dr. Jekyll does!" She went upstairs. She picked up the telephone that she had placed at the head of the stairs, and took it back to Marie's bedroom. Her father had spent the whole night listening in on that telephone line. After she closed the bedroom door, she asked her dad to hang up. She told him that she needed to use that telephone to call New York, because Rose was still sleeping, and she did not want to risk waking him. She assured her father that as soon as she talked to the psychiatrist, she would leave the house.

Jacqueline wanted to use that telephone to call Dr. Fieldman, the psychiatrist in New York. It was only partly because she did not want to awaken Rose; she figured that Günter probably did not know about that upstairs telephone. If he did know, he would have realized that only Marie used it, and only to talk to her friends. It would be a waste of manpower to monitor it. Marie's telephone was probably safe. She had to risk it.

She got through to Dr. Fieldman on the very first try. Jacqueline told Dr. Fieldman exactly what had happened. She also told him the things that Rose had been saying, and what Rose had been hiding from him. She told the psychiatrist that Rose was with the CIA, and that his work had been with explosives. Jacqueline told everything that she knew. The only way that the doctor could help Rose was if he knew it all.

Dr. Fieldman was in a complete panic! He told Jacqueline to get out of that house, "Now! If he wants to kill himself you can't stop him. *He is trying to take you out with him!* Now I understand what Rose is capable of, Jacqueline. He is in an acute psychotic state. Because of his psychosis, he may have no idea that it is you he is killing. In his mind, you could be just another government target." His words shocked Jacqueline. Even though Rose had tried to kill her, she thought that he would next turn the violence inward. "Is Marie in the house?" he asked. She told him, "I sent her to my parents when everything happened last night."

"Good. You need to join her, *right now!* Jacqueline, I want you to hang up this telephone and walk directly out of the house. Call me back when you are in a safe place. I will wait right here. Go now!" She did as Dr. Fieldman ordered; she hung up the telephone, walked down the staircase, picked her purse up off the kitchen table, and walked out the front door to her car. She started the engine and left without even looking back.

Jacqueline drove toward her parent's home, but she knew that they must be crazy with worry, so she stopped at the first pay phone to call them. Her father answered. She told him that she was safely out of the house, and that she was on her way. She continued on to their home; the thirty-mile ride seemed like seconds.

Her mind was racing. Did she do something to cause this? Then it all became clear. Of course it was not her fault! It was Rose's psychosis, and all of the drugs that Dr. Green insisted on giving Rose to feed it. It was the cancer treatment that saved his life, while it sent his mind tumbling into the abyss. It was his horrible, secret history. It was all of those things, and so many more. But it was not her fault. She was lucky to be alive! "And Marie," she thought, "my God, the danger Marie was in!"

Jacqueline could see her father watching out of the window as she arrived at her parents' home. Her father was the kindest man she had ever known. She heard him scream to Marie, "Your Mom is here!" The look on all of their faces was one of pure relief. Her father looked tired and stressed, but as soon as she entered the house she could see his face begin to return to normal. His first words were, "Are you all right, baby?" " I am okay, Dad. I am just a little worse for the wear." "That SOB, I will kill him." "Please don't do that!" "Jacqueline, I am sixty-five years old – what can they do to me?" "Dad, he is already dying and crazy, and we all need you!" "Are you sure you are not hurt?" "Yes, Dad, I am sure."

After Jacqueline sat down, he poured her a cup of coffee. Her mother, who had been busy comforting

Marie and had her hands full keeping Jacqueline's father from rushing to his daughter's aid, sat with them. Jacqueline explained that Dr. Fieldman had told her to leave the house immediately. Her father said, "I owe him! He is probably the only person who could have gotten you out of that house."

Jacqueline finally began to relax, and she started to dial Dr. Fieldman's office in New York. She stopped, and she asked her mother to take Marie out of earshot. Marie did not need to know any more than she already knew, either about the incident last night or Rose's background. After they left, she started dialing again. She did not ask her father to leave; she knew that she could speak freely in front of him, and besides, she needed his support. She suspected that this would not be an easy call.

"Dr. Fieldman, this is Jacqueline, and I am with my parents and Marie." "Are you all out of the house?" "Yes," she told him. "Jacqueline, I wish you had told me all about Rose in New York. I might have seen this coming." She explained that she could not have done that, because it was not safe to tell him what she knew. He said he understood. "Is that what you were trying to get Günter to tell me at the hospital? Did he know everything?" She told him, "Yes, Günter knows everything about Rose's history with the CIA and his work with explosives; they worked side-by-side for Rose's entire career."

"The doctors thought something more was going on up here with Rose, but no one could or would give us all the information. A few of the doctors knew he was a lawyer who had been in the government and we were pretty sure it had something to do with covert operations. Rose threw me out when I questioned him about his government work. He became so angry! I knew he would never talk with me again. The rest of the doctors were afraid he would walk out in the middle of treatment if they pursued it."

"Jacqueline, did Dr. Rosenblatt know what Rose did for the CIA?" "Absolutely not; Rose's Uncle Sam might have known that Rose had worked for them, I think he knew that. He definitely did not know he worked with explosives. I didn't even know that until after we returned from New York." Dr. Fieldman said, "I didn't think so. We were not sure what you knew about Rose. I want you to move Jacqueline. Take Marie with you, and change your address. Do not give it to him; you have done all you can. Rose is absolutely dangerous to you and Marie. We will keep up with him." "Dr. Fieldman, whatever you do, don't tell Rose or Günter you know. I think we are already into this deeper than we can imagine."

She explained to him what she *thought* had happened to the psychiatrist that Rose had seen in Florida, and she told him that Rose was convinced that the psychiatrist was murdered. Jacqueline told him she did not know for sure, but at all cost not to tell anyone else what he knew – it was too dangerous for all of them. There was a long silence on the other end of the line. After a few seconds, Dr. Fieldman said, "Jacqueline stay away...never go back! I will not breathe a word of what I know, of what you have told me. We have all done everything we can for Rose."

"Jacqueline, where did you first call me from?" Dr. Fieldman asked. "I called from home, but I used Marie's private line. When Rose became sure that he was going to be bugged by Günter, he told me to use Marie's line, because the upstairs would probably be safe. Günter had no excuse to go up there, and if they knew about Marie's line, they would not bother with it, thinking it was just a child's telephone."

"Jacqueline, promise me you will do as I ask. Do not let him around you, even if he appears normal. He can, and probably will, snap again. I am going to stay out of touch with him. I notified Dr. Rosenblatt of the recent developments. I think we have both done everything we can do to help Rose, and now we must all protect ourselves. If you need me for anything, call the hospital and have me paged. Do not call my office. You have to look out for yourself and Marie. I will look out for myself. But if I can help in any way, or if you just need to talk, call me. By the way, is that quack still prescribing for Rose?" She told Dr. Fieldman, "Yes, he has morphine, Percocet, and so on. All the things you guys did not want him on. He has large amounts, he has a box full of pills." Dr. Fieldman's voice was sad as he told her, "We have done all we can, Jacqueline. Goodbye."

As she hung up the telephone, Jacqueline glanced at her father. The look on her father's face was one of pure shock. He had heard everything she had just said. They sat quietly for a minute, sipping coffee. After a time her father said, "Only God knows what could have happened to you and Marie. How long have you known that your husband was in the CIA?" She told him, "Since before we were married, Dad. I am sorry, but I could not tell anyone. Up until the cancer and drug use, it was not important."

"Dad, Rose was retired, except for the one assignment on our first anniversary." "Do you mean that you didn't just go away for a couple of nights, like you said?" "Yes Dad, we did. I danced that New Years Eve at the State Department. Rose retrieved a briefcase at the party from the Ambassador to Budapest, for the American Government. He had to disarm the case because it was sealed with some kind of high explosive."

"My God, what did this man have you involved in? You two are staying right here." He walked slowly to his gun cabinet. Sitting at the table, he loaded four guns, placing one near the front door and one near the back door. The third gun he laid next to him on the table. The forth was a derringer; he stuck that one in his boot. He told his daughter, "I will do everything in my power to make sure that my family is safe."

About two days later, Jacqueline decided she would like to see the police report. She went to the police department, and asked for a copy of the police report from the night of the incident. She was informed that there was no report! She realized that this had to be Günter's work. Jacqueline left quietly, before anyone started to question her. She felt like she was living in the twilight zone.

Over the next weeks, Rose and Jacqueline spoke by telephone. Rose refused to admit what had happened. He told her, "I can't believe this! Jacqueline, you are talking about attempted murder. I am a lawyer! I would be disbarred." She tried to file for divorce, to force him into drug treatment but he just turned that into a war. The only way that she could win the war carried a high price – it would cause him to be disbarred! That price was too high. Rose had been a lawyer all his life, and disbarment would have killed him. She dropped the divorce. Jacqueline could not stop his drug abuse, and she also knew that she could never live with him safely again.

Jacqueline called Günter and asked him to meet her. They met in Tampa. She told him the story of what had happened that night, and what she had to do. Pretending that she did not know the house was bugged, and that his men had called the police then quashed the report, Jacqueline told him, "I told no one about Rose's operative work. Besides, I don't know much anyway. Günter, you know that." Günter said, "It is best that you know so little. Have you told anyone that Rose is in the CIA?"

She said, "Absolutely not, Günter," praying to herself that Dr. Fieldman would keep his word and would say nothing. Günter agreed that Rose was dangerous to her, and that the CIA had been concerned about Rose ever since his diagnosis. "Jacqueline, the CIA has dealt with agents who have become ill or drug addicted before. We expected problems as soon as we heard his diagnosis." He told her that she was right to take Marie and go. She and Marie would be safe. He also made it clear that her silence would buy their safety. He told her that if she needed anything, to call him. Rose would never know her location.

He also said that until Rose's death, the CIA would always know her location. They would be keeping an eye on her, to make sure that she was safe from Rose, and from anyone else who might do her harm. That was another hint about keeping silent. Jacqueline thought, "They have no idea how much Rose told me about his work. The notes that Rose had us write back and forth probably saved my life. Even the bugs in the house must have been planted too late. They must not have heard anything he said before he insisted that we begin writing." She was convinced that they believed that she knew very little.

Günter told her he would never contact her again unless she contacted him. He said he would be near Rose until the day Rose died. "He has been a valuable operative and valued friend."

The only other thing that Jacqueline ever knew about Rose's operative work was about Rose's and Günter's early history with the CIA and FBI. Günter was already in covert operations at Columbia University, and he went straight to Vietnam after he graduated. He continued his FBI service after Vietnam. Rose joined the CIA in his senior year at Columbia University. That was 1964. The two men worked together for many years.

Over the next year Jacqueline and Rose talked on the telephone, and tried to put their lives back together. God, how they loved each other! Rose even went to her father and told him the whole truth about April First. Marie and Jacqueline met him outside her parents home that day. He knew if there were any hope of getting them back, he would have to make peace with Jacqueline's father. Outside of the house, he put his arms around Marie and Jacqueline, and as they walked in the door with his trademark wit he asked, "What is a ten inch knife among friends?"

Her father listened to Rose. Her dad still had the gun in his boot. As far as Jacqueline knew, her father was one of the few people to whom Rose ever told the complete truth about that night. Her dad attempted to comprehend what could drive anyone to hurt his family. Jacqueline knew that he gave it everything that he had. He just could not understand. Her father made it clear to Rose that her father did not want Rose near his daughter or anyone else in the family. Rose said to her father, "I though Christians were forgiving!" Her father replied, "Yes, and I do forgive you. But stay the hell away from my daughter, or I will kill you. Now leave. I listened to you, as I told Jacqueline I would." Rose turned and asked Jacqueline to come with him. She told him "No. Leave now!"

On the night of April First, her father had said, "I will go shoot him. Jacqueline, I am 65 years old; what threat is prison at my age." She knew her Dad would kill Rose. And she knew that her father had reached his limit; Rose's death was imminent, if he stayed in the house a moment longer. Rose heard it in her voice, or he sensed it in her father's demeanor. He turned without another word, and he walked out the door.

CHAPTER FOURTEEN

TILL DEATH DO WE PART

Jacqueline stayed with her parents for a few more days after Rose talked with her father, while she looked for a home. Jacqueline moved with Marie to a home about sixty miles away from Rose. This was a quite area in the north of Florida. Taking Dr. Feldman's advice, she did not give Rose her address. Rose was still on the drugs, and whenever she was near him she feared for herself, and even more, for Marie's safety. Jacqueline and Marie settled into their new home, and

Jacqueline immediately took a position as a corporate trainer in the diamond industry.

They had been living in their new home for only three weeks when Rose somehow got the address. He showed up at the door one weekend day, saying that he wanted to try putting this behind them. Rose wanted Jacqueline to return to his home, just like it had never happened. Jacqueline was sure that Rose was still unstable, and he might even be dangerous again.

Jacqueline realized that she could not put Marie in that kind of danger, so she sent her daughter to a friend's home to spend the night. Both Jacqueline and Marie pretended that Marie was going to her friend's for only a short time, to avoid angering Rose. Rose was still addicted to the drugs, and Jacqueline knew it. She was unsure how he would react to Marie leaving them for the night.

Rose and Jacqueline talked. They spent several hours of Saturday afternoon and evening, together at her house. He was still popping pills and showing fits of anger. His eyes were no longer the warm, beautiful, coal black she remembered. They were now hollow and empty. He paced around the patio in the caged pool area of her home, and talked about his CIA work. Holding his head, he started talking about the bombing he had done.

Jacqueline was sure that Rose was still not of sound mind. He had begun listing the different household ingredients he could use to make a bomb. "Jacqueline, even the chlorine for your swimming pool could be used," he said. Then he insisted that she come out in the pool area with him. She was more scared that she had ever been in her life. She told him no, that she wanted to take a bath. With that, she went into the bathroom and ran a tub of water. She could still hear him taking to himself. But he stayed in the chair on the patio.

She closed the bathroom door and started to lock it, but she was afraid that Rose would get angry over a locked door. She climbed into the bath, hoping it would clear her mind. She needed to think of a way to get him out of her house. About five minutes after she got into the bathtub, Rose walked in. He sat down on the toilet seat, and continued talking about explosives. Rose seemed to keep coming back to Dr. Pillar, who had been killed. Suddenly, Jacqueline thought, "He could drown me a split second in this bathtub!" Quickly gathering her thoughts, she calmly said to Rose "Yes it was a shame about Dr. Pillar."

She slowly reached for a towel; she got out of the bathtub and wrapped the towel around her. Jacqueline was careful to make no sudden movements. Then, as Rose followed her out of the bathroom; she slipped into some clothes that she had placed on the dining room chair. She had dropped them there when Rose had asked her for coffee, just as she was going into the bathroom.

The entire time, it was as though Rose had not seen anything she was doing. He just continued to talk. His eyes were looking straight through her. Jacqueline's heart rate was just beginning to return to normal, as normal as it would be this day, as she walked to the kitchen. She asked, "Rose, can I fix you something to eat?" He just continued his talking without answering her. Jacqueline went ahead preparing food, as she was trying to think how to get him out of her home. He was staying within fifteen feet of her, and she was plenty scared. She knew that she had to try to appear calm.

She made an excuse, telling Rose she had to leave for few minutes to pick up Marie. Rose said he would ride along. Jacqueline told him that she had to pick up the neighbors kids and, they had four. Rose became agitated and said, "I wish that you had not let Marie go over there!" Jacqueline told him not to worry. It was only five minutes away, and that she would be right back with Marie. "You can eat the sandwich I made, while I am gone." She had placed a spare set of keys that had been hanging in the kitchen into her pocket. Then she put the sandwich down in front of him, and walked straight out the door. He followed her out, still talking about bombing a car in the past. She quickly got into her car and drove away.

Jacqueline stopped at a store on the main road, and called her home from a pay telephone. Rose answered the telephone on the second ring. She told him to leave her home, and that it was over. She told Rose that it was not going to work, ever again, between them.

He insisted that Jacqueline come back and talk to him. Even though he did nothing to harm her that afternoon and evening, she refused. She knew that she still feared him when he was on drugs. And she knew that he would forever be on drugs. He left her home quietly.

Jacqueline was parked where she could see him leave the area. He never saw her car as he sped away from her home. She drove her car back near her home and parked for about twenty minutes. He did not return. She called and told her father what had happened. Jacqueline and her father made the decision that both Marie and Jacqueline would immediately move far away, to a place her father was sure that Rose could not find. Jacqueline and Marie left for the mountain by themselves in Jacqueline's car.

Her mother and father packed her home and ordered the movers, as soon as Jacqueline had found a home in the mountains. Only her family knew where she was headed. She found a home 14.8 miles up a mountain in North Carolina. It was a red brick ranch that sat on an acre. The home faced the forest, and from her living room window she could look up and see the tops of the trees. Looking down, she could see the road at the end of her land. The house was positioned at the top of the ridge of the mountain. There was only one road accessing the land. Behind the home was a 400-foot drop into a cattle-grazing ranch. The beauty of the mountains was all around her.

The airport was one hour and ten minutes away, and she could fly to the diamond shows. The following year, Marie went off to college. She did not go to Columbia. No one in the family spoke of what college she attended. Jacqueline traveled for her work, training groups around the country. She often flew in to see Marie at school. Jacqueline began her life-long dream of becoming a writer during the long plane flights around the country, and in the quiet solitude of her mountain home.

After another year of separation from Rose, Jacqueline divorced him, using her parent's address. She took only the life insurance she owned on his life as her settlement. He had bought the policy for her after they were married. She was the owner and beneficiary, and no one could take it away. She paid the premiums, and she would continue to do so.

The last time Jacqueline saw Rose was at the courthouse, on the day their divorce became final. Her father sat in his car, parked three rows over from her car. Although she had done the only thing she could, her feelings for this man were even deeper than the day they married. She had her named changed back to her maiden name. After the hearing was over, he walked her to the car. She knew it in her heart - a part of her would always be Mrs. Rosenberg. She also knew that changing her name would signal the end of any connection between them. It would be clear to Rose. Rose told her as he opened her car door, one last time, "Jacqueline, I know why you changed your name. But I will still be calling for Mrs. Rosenberg in heaven. There, God will have removed all the evil from my brain, and you will feel safe in my arms once more."

The last time Jacqueline spoke to Rose was around the time of the O.J. Simpson trial, while she was visiting her parents. They spoke on the telephone, and he asked her what she thought about Simpson's innocence or guilt. She told him that she did not know enough about the evidence. Rose said, "You of all people, should know he is guilty. The guy snapped."

He ended the call to her with, "I am glad I am just a bookworm, and not an athlete. I love you, Jacqueline. Don't forget when I am gone to write the book. Good-bye, Mrs. Rosenberg."

While living quietly on the mountain, far away from everyone, Jacqueline felt very safe over the next couple of years. She had begun dating a Marine she called GI Joe, and he knew of the possible danger from Rose. She always felt safe with him. She often cried, wondering what she could have done differently. One day, she was sitting at her kitchen table, writing on her laptop and looking out of a window. She noticed a car driving past her mountain home. It was July 2, 1999. She saw the car three times that day. It was too far from her house to the end of her land for Jacqueline to be sure who was driving. The license plate was white. She loaded her gun and sat in the window, watching. The car came by again, and this time, the man saw her in the window and waved to her slowly and steadily as the car drove past. Her look was of sheer terror as she realized it was Günter. They did know where she was!

She told no one but GI Joe. She was not running, and there was only one way on to her property. GI Joe kept her with him at all times for the next two weeks. The car never passed again. After a few weeks, she convinced herself it could not have been Günter. But she never unloaded her gun. If the government wanted her, she couldn't stop them. She continued her life on the mountain, but she looked over her shoulder a little more often.

Marie had grown up. She married in April of 1999, at the age of 26. She wed the neighbor boy she had grown up with. Peter was always Jacqueline's choice for her. Her wedding was on the sponge docks of Mexico Springs, Florida. She was married by candlelight. The ceremony was followed by a white linen reception, in the grand fashion Marie so deserved. CJ and his wife attended, and Marie's biological father walked her down the aisle.

Rose was not informed about the wedding. Jacqueline attended with GI Joe. Yes, he was that very same United States Marine who stood before her, so devastatingly handsome, at the State Department some years ago. Jacqueline had met him again when she went skiing in Boone, North Carolina a couple of years after she and Rose had parted for good. While Jacqueline was resting at the lodge after a full morning of skiing, a man walked up and said, "Hello, Mrs. Rosenberg!" Stunned and more than a little scared, she turned to see the Marine she had met at the State Department so many years before. He was the Marine she had turned down when he asked her to dance. At first, she was afraid that Günter or Rose had sent him. After talking with him for a while, she realized that the last thing this gentleman knew of Rose was that night at the State Department. He was now out of the Marines. He asked about Rose and she said he was fine, just not with her this trip.

They continued to talk at the ski lodge for a while. He told her he had finished his tour of duty a few weeks after they met at the State Department. He had owned a couple of restaurants in New York and that he had eventually sold them. He was now living in Florida. He had come up to the mountains looking for another restaurant to purchase. Jacqueline looked closely into his eyes, as she listened to him talk for about an hour. She realized that this man had no idea about what had happened to her while she was married to Rose. Finally, she told him the truth, as the sun set behind a mountain. He was completely shocked, and sad for her. The sun rose. They had talked all night! They had already begun falling for each other.

GI Joe decided to stay in North Carolina. He made arrangements to have his belongings sent to the mountain. He never left her side. He opened a restaurant. They lived peacefully, tucked away on Jacqueline's mountaintop in North Carolina. Her home overlooked the Cherokee National Forest, far up the mountain. How they had found each other again, she would never know. Jacqueline was unsure if her attraction to him was out of her great need for safety, or if it was something more. Only time would tell where this friendship would lead.

Although Marie's wedding was held in Florida, Jacqueline knew they were safe. GI Joe knew *almost* everything about the Rose. He spent the entire evening watching for Rose to enter the door. Marie's husband knew Rose from his childhood, and would have recognized him immediately.

On September 1, 1999, Marie received an unexpected telephone call from the social security office, asking her if she was making a claim for Mr. Rosenberg's $225.00 death benefit. She said, "Are you telling me that my Dad is dead?" They apologized for being the ones to inform her. He had died June 30, 1999, of heart failure.

That was why Günter had come to the top of her mountain! He was letting her know it was over. If the CIA had wanted her, they could have had her at any time they wanted. Jacqueline thought, "I must be safe, now that Rose is dead. That is what Günter was telling me, when he drove by my home on the mountain." Günter had remained Rose's friend, and hers, to the end.

When Marie called her mother on the telephone about Rose's death, Jacqueline and her daughter cried together. Jacqueline stood on the ridge of the mountain, looking up into the sky and sobbing. After the call from Marie was over, Jacqueline said her final good-bye to the man she had loved so very much. She thanked him for all of the knowledge and tender kindness he had shown to her and to Marie. She asked God to forgive him, as they had.

GI Joe was there when the call came. He understood her tears; he knew she had *loved the Rose*. He had seen the love in her eyes, first hand, at the State Department that night so long ago. GI Joe said, "I only met him once, but I know that you two were in love. After all, it was me he sent to dance with his wife, so she would not be alone for even a few minutes. I am sorry for your loss."

Jacqueline knew she had found a friend in GI Joe. She flew to Florida the next morning to be with Marie. She discovered that Rose had only a simple obituary, and that the Florida Bar had not been notified of his death. She wrote a proper obituary for this great man, never mentioning the CIA, and sent it with his death certificate to the Florida Bar. She filed a claim for the insurance a few days later.

Marie, her husband Peter, and Jacqueline spent the next few days together. They talked of the good times with Rose; Peter had been the boy down the street, and knew Rose well. Peter had played chess with Rose on his computer during Peter's childhood years. Peter became a computer software developer and Marie a Public Relations Specialist for a charitable organization. The children decided to make their life in a small beach community in Florida and planned to adopt children. Although it took Peter longer to completely forgive Rose for his terrible acts of April First, Jacqueline believed Peter found forgiveness in his heart, too.

Marie and Jacqueline had long ago found peace with the man they loved. Even as an adult, Marie blamed her overly analytical mind and love of art on the Rose. She was always able to retrieve the wonderful memories of her time with Rose before cancer *blew in with the wind.*

Rose had lived eleven years, one month and 27 days from his original diagnosis of *six weeks to live.* It was Rose himself who told her, "Become the writer you have dreamed of and publish this story after my death. Because you know Jacqueline, **you can't slander a dead man.**"

EPILOGUE

Jacqueline awoke this morning, nearly twelve years after she almost lost her life to a 10-inch knife. She rarely ever thinks about that day anymore; she is far too busy enjoying each day as much as she can. She has traveled during this time from the North Carolina mountaintop to the Caribbean Sea, finally settling on the Gulf of Mexico. Some women are just naturally single for major parts of their lives, and she is one of those women.

A NOTE FROM THE AUTHOR

A writer of fiction holds the key to a vehicle that can take the reader away on a little hiatus from life's trials and tribulations. The passages of this book have given this author the opportunity to create an escape from our busy worlds. An author of fiction wants the reader to have a great getaway in the pages of a book, and from that getaway, to come back to reality refreshed and ready for the heady taste of life.

This author hopes that she has succeeded in her mission. It is left for you, the reader, to judge.

COMING NEXT

"Where is my translation book?" Jacqueline frantically asked herself, as the taxi started to pull away from the airport arrivals building. She was still asking herself the same question that she had been contemplating on the plane. "What in the hell am I doing here?" Jacqueline loved being an American living in America. She had never really wanted to leave American soil. She was wondering what ever possessed her to take this trip.

"Take me to the Coast Sea Hotel," she said in pathetic Spanish. Hell, she knew he did not understand a word of her Spanish. He kept nodding his head and saying, "Yes lady." She assumed she would find out soon enough if he really understood. Maybe if she tried to write it down and gave him the note, he would understand her. Jacqueline sat back in the taxi, trying to translate English into Spanish, and get it on paper for the taxi driver. Suddenly, the spectacular mountains in front of her caught her attention. This is why she had come, to see the rain forest and the Caribbean Sea. Besides, she wanted a break from her everyday life. She needed some excitement!

The trip came up on short notice. When she first heard about it, she knew she wanted to go. Fifteen business people in the New York Diamond Market, where Jacqueline had been working for years, had all planned to stay at the same hotel. But this would not be as a tour group; each would visit this paradise as an individual. They would join together only now and then, purely by chance, for lunches and dinners during the ten-day stay.

A man, who had recently met Jacqueline at work, found himself unable to go on the trip shortly before the departure date. He contacted Jacqueline at one of the diamond shows, and told her that he was willing to sell Jacqueline his ticket and prepaid hotel reservation for practically nothing. His offer was too good to pass up. But she had just realized on the flight that the other members of the group were shady criminals from the sub-culture of the retail market. When she decided to take the trip, she had no idea who the other Americans were. If she had known, she would not have come at all. Jacqueline had heard them talking on the plane and thought, "I think they are here to launder money! What have I gotten myself into?"

The men on her plane were not the kind anyone in their right mind would want to be alone with for very long. Now, Jacqueline found herself thousands of miles from American soil. The American men who came on this trip had a seedy nature, and no one seemed to speak much English in this country!

She had climbed into the taxi at the airport, thinking she would be safer alone than with any of those men. Jacqueline thought, "This taxi is headed for who knows where, at seventy-five miles per hour!" The taxi's brakes were squealing as the driver took the mountain curves. Jacqueline struggled to find the words for "slow down" in Spanish! *SLOW DOWN! STOP! STOP….*

I would like to give my great thanks and express my appreciation to my friends and family, who have given of their time to assist me in this endeavor. *I am a fortunate woman to be surrounded by persons of great character and knowledge.*

Claudette Walker, Author

Technical, Cover Art
& Web Design: Christopher P. Egan

Marketing: N. M. Egan

Technical Editing By: Margaret L. LaMarca, NY
D. E. Siar, FL
Christopher P. Egan, FL

375

ABOUT THE AUTHOR

Claudette Walker is an author living on Florida's scenic coast. Her travels have carried her from the small Midwest town she left as a young woman to San Francisco. Relinquishing the shores of San Francisco to spend time in Washington, D.C., and on to New York's upper West Side, Claudette even found time to discover the beauty of the white-collar criminal haven of Costa Rica. Her life among the powerful and her observations that the radicals of the 1960s and 1970s became the people in power in the 1980s and 1990s, and that their drug use continued, although their drugs of choice changed. The realization that those same people entered the new millennium in power became her inspiration for this novel.

Claudette Walker lives a quiet life on the Florida coast with her husband, an attorney.